Praise for Aviva Vaughn

"This book...this series...this author. A must read - every single freaking time. I cannot say enough good things about my love of everything Vaughn writes. Real, raw, emotional, and relatable, this series has taken her readers on quite the emotional journey. This latest installment further solidified my esteem for the author and these characters. One thousand percent recommended!!" –Heather, 5-star review

"I'm not just writing on this book but the entire series. So thoroughly enjoyed this series. You are a gifted writer." –Linda, 5-star review

"Ms. Vaughn is an amazing writer. She has built Soren up through five books so this one was like coming home to an old friend. The writing is both lyrical and poetic. Overall, this book is a fantastic addition to this series. 5 stars and highly recommended" –Krystal, 5-star review

I cannot believe that the final book in this series is finally here! I almost didn't want to read because I have been on such an amazing journey with these characters that I didn't want it to end but the author absolutely did an amazing job with this final book and it is probably my favourite form the series! It was everything I expected and more! –Katie, 5-star review

Love on the Ropes

A Novel

Aviva Vaughn

Legal Stuff

AvivaVaughn.com

This is a work of fiction. Names, characters, businesses, places, events and incidents are either the products of the author's imagination or used in a fictitious manner. Any resemblance to actual persons, living or dead, or actual events is purely coincidental.

ISBN: 978-1-947420-21-2

About the Author

Aviva Vaughn (ah-VEE-vah VON) loves reading, traveling, and eating…preferably all at once. She isn't afraid to try new things, which has made for an interesting—although not always straight forward—life.

She is an avid reader and especially likes books with multifaceted characters who reveal something about that most compelling of all subjects: human nature; no matter what species they are or what planet they are from.

Other Titles from Aviva Vaughn

Novels (all books available at tinyurl.com/AmazonAviva)
    BECKONED
    -Part 1: From London with Love
    -Part 2: From Bath with Love
    -Part 3: From Los Angeles with Love
    -Part 4: From Barcelona with Love
    -Part 5: Adrift in Costa Rica
    -Part 6: Adrift in New Zealand

    Love in Action Series (standalone romcom)
    -Book 1: Love on the Ropes
    -Book 2: Love on the Slopes **COMING SOON**

Short Stories
    -PRESSURE (available in Beckoned, Part 4)
    -Her Haven (available to newsletter subscribers)
    -BECKONED, Part 1, Chapter 2, Angela's POV (available to newsletter subscribers)
    -Knotty Naughty Bits Volume 1: a collection of tangled romantic shorts

Links

Subscribe to Aviva's list **at TinyURL.com/followAviva** to be notified of new releases and special offers—and get her favorite
FOOD | BOOK | TRAVEL tips.

Table of Contents

<u>Dedication</u>

July 2020

For Mommy and Daddy,
Popo and Gung-Gung,
Abuela y Abuelo.

There was no me before you.

Becoming

> We can not become
> what we want
> by remaining
> what we are.
> ~Max DePree

Prologue: The Night Everything Changed

San Marino, CA

It's not every day you get run over by a T-Rex while stalking the love of your life.

"*Abraham Lincoln*," I cursed under my breath as a group of costume-clad children ran by, one of them bouncing off me like a pinball.

"Sorry, mister," said a kid in a blow-up dinosaur costume after he oriented himself so that his Jurassic face was level with mine.

Looking back, it was pretty funny, but I was too focused on the couple thirty-feet away to appreciate it. After a few moments, the kid waddled away yelling for his friends to "wait up".

It was a good thing I was standing on a sidewalk. I was so distracted by my quarry, if I'd been in the middle of the street I might have been run over.

"Stupid Halloween," I muttered.

The funny thing was, I usually loved this time of year: the cooler temperature, the faint smell of Fall in the air, the trick-or-treating kiddos. But on that night, Halloween officially became my least favorite holiday.

He said they were just friends, I thought, massaging my heart.

They laughed as they finished straightening their matching costumes, just another sign of the connection they shared; a connection that felt like a betrayal.

Maybe it's too late. I sagged beneath the realization. Maybe too much had passed between us to move forward. But I couldn't stop thinking about her; her bright laugh and sparkling eyes haunted me.

Then again, I'd spent years avoiding emotional connection. Maybe love just wasn't in the cards for me.

I sighed, feeling like a creeper half-hidden behind a tree, watching them enjoy each other's company.

How can I make things right with her?

I rubbed my hand over the rough bark of the tree that hid me from view, hoping for inspiration.

I *needed* to be dramatic.

I *needed* a grand gesture.

I needed to tell her the *truth*.

Taking a deep breath, I set my jaw.

"No more secrets," I said, before squaring my shoulders and stepping out of the shadows.

Chapter 1: Badass

~Erin~

Two months earlier

"Hey, Erin, breakfast is ending soon. Do you want me to wait for you?" My cabin-mate Margarit's voice seeped into my consciousness.

I stretched and blinked against the bright sun filtering in through the screened-in windows. "How much longer is breakfast?"

"Fifteen minutes before they close the cafeteria."

I groaned and waved. "Go without me. I'll never make it."

"Okay. See you at the next exercise. It starts in forty-five minutes," she said as she banged out the screen door of our diminutive wood cabin, the omnipresent scent of pine entering our one-room space.

My eyes flew open. *Our next challenge!*

We would be climbing telephone poles and I couldn't wait.

My bladder reminded me of its presence and I sighed, throwing off the heavy sleeping bag, the cool air sending a shiver through me, reminding me that I hadn't packed appropriately for this trip.

Sliding open the closet door, I removed my cotton nightgown—printed with the words "Miso Cute" and a picture of a bowl of miso soup—and hung it up. We were in the mountains for only five days, so I'd packed light; maybe too light.

September was still a hot month in Los Angeles, and after two days in Big Bear, it was clear that I hadn't accounted for the change in elevation. My wardrobe of shorts and floaty muumuus meant that the one sweatshirt I'd brought had been in constant rotation.

I threw on a neon-pink sports bra, a white tank top, and a pair of khaki shorts. When I went to grab my sweatshirt—a black hoodie with a rainbow cartoon of singer Israel "Iz" Kamakawiwoʻole—my hand touched something sticky and crusty. "Ewwww." I pulled my hand back and sniffed. *Marshmallow.*

With my clean hand I took out the hanger and eyed my hoodie. A huge gob of roasted marshmallow was slathered over the back of one sleeve.

"Gross."

I checked my watch—a Garmin that had been a gift from my favorite cousin and my most prized possession—noting that I had just enough time to wash my sweatshirt and get ready before I needed to leave for the ropes course.

Throwing on my slippers—or flip flops as the Mainlanders like to call them—I ran to the communal bathroom.

When I got back, I hung up my sweatshirt on the primitive window frame, stood in front of the full-length mirror, and started brushing out my hair for my habitual braiding. Ten minutes later I spiraled the final hairpin into place and tugged the thick, crown-like plaits encircling my scalp. *Secure.*

Not for the first time, I was grateful that I'd upped my braiding game when I'd moved to Los Angeles four years earlier from my native Hawai'i. Despite the popularity of long hair in the islands, my knowledge of braiding had been limited to the traditional three-strand which was not nearly as secure or decorative as I'd come to prefer. Not only did my double crown French braids make me feel like a warrior princess, they kept me cool and ensured my long hair didn't get in the way when I climbed.

Ready, I thought, giving the mirror a final glance, surprisingly happy with how my legs looked in my mid-thigh shorts. The hours I'd spent at my climbing gym had not only made me mentally stronger, but had sculpted my body into a litheness I hadn't thought possible. I did a little spin, whipping my head around as I spotted the mirror. *I am rocking these shorts!*

This confidence would have been unthinkable a few years earlier. But I'd grown a lot since moving. I was a different person—well, *mostly* a different person.

I grabbed my tennis shoes and sat on my cot, lacing them up, thinking about how far I'd come.

Four-years-ago me? Twenty-eight and still living at home with my parents, in the coral-pink bedroom of my childhood, working as an assistant for an ophthalmologist after graduating from college. And not just any ophthalmologist, but my mom's ophthalmologist. Dr. Lau couldn't go a month without reminiscing about my childhood and my braces with neon pink rubber bands, or the time I gave myself asymmetrical bangs, or the Coke-bottle glasses I wore before contact lenses saved me.

It was grand.

My days used to stretch in front of me like the ocean on a flat day, monotonous and unending. In my mind, coral-pink was the color of failure and stagnation. I could pretty much guarantee you that I would never, *ever* own anything that particular shade again.

New-and-improved me? Marketing Coordinator for America's number-one-rated morning-drive-time radio show. Paying my own mortgage on a small—but adorable—condo in Old-Town Pasadena, with the love of a great man…okay, great *male*, my adorable Shiba Inu, Atticus.

While I hadn't achieved everything I'd hoped to by thirty-two, I was a lot closer. Operation "Brand New Me" was almost complete. The final step was getting my career to the level of a manager—

Or director. As I sometimes allowed myself to imagine. Although, Director Erin Hung still didn't sound believable to my ears.

Me? A director? Better to stay "grounded" and "realistic" and stick with manager.

I winced, knowing that my cousin, Angela—who was really more like a big sister—would not approve of my self-defeating thoughts. "Don't limit yourself, Erin, you can do anything, be anything, have anything you want, as long as you are willing to put in the effort," was one of her favorite pep talks. And she was an excellent poster child for her mantra. Seeing Angela's life—master's degree, successful business, happy marriage—had inspired me to leave Honolulu in pursuit of my own happiness.

"Hey, Erin. You coming?" The booming voice of my office spouse, Fern, brought me back to the present as he called through the screen door of my cabin.

"Yup. Just a sec." I finished tying my laces and tested the sleeve of my sweatshirt but it was way too wet to wear out which meant I was going to be a tit bit nipply today.

A few years ago that might have bothered me, but no longer. I could just imagine how upset my grandmother would be if she knew. "Nice girls don't show their nipples, Erin," she'd cluck. When puberty hit, she "gifted" me adhesive flower petals to "protect my modesty". I tried them once, horrified by how sweaty and sticky they made my boobs. Needless to say, I never wore them again.

Oh well. Nipply it is.

Grabbing my copper aviators, I banged out the screen door.

"Hi." I smiled at Fern and then inhaled the fresh, pine-scented air that was so new to me. It surprised me every time its sharp, almost medicinal flavor hit my lungs.

Fern and I were part of a work retreat designed to increase teamwork and creativity at Universal Public Radio or UPR. The almost three-hour bus trip to the alpine village was the first time I'd left L.A. since moving.

Fern glanced at my hands. "You forgot your water bottle."

"Right!" I pivoted and retrieved my huge, stainless-steel water bottle.

Fern joked that the roughly forearm-sized bottle was my fifth appendage because it was omnipresent. I chalked it up to the lack of humidity in SoCal. I swear, I drank three times more water.

After I grabbed my bottle, we started walking to the site of our next training exercise. Despite our vast height difference, we fell quickly into a comfortable rhythm; Fern slowing, me speeding up.

Fern Haddad was easily the largest person I'd ever known. At six-foot-seven he wasn't just tall, he was also broad and had shoes that looked impossibly big. However, in the months we had worked together—I'd hired him as our in-house graphic designer almost a year earlier—I'd learned that the heart of a unicorn was housed in this body of a giant, for he was the gentlest person I'd ever met.

"Do you know what the next challenge is going to be?" he asked.

Nodding, I smiled. "We're climbing telephone poles." A thrill zipped up my spine.

He humphed. "No wonder you're excited. You're going to scamper up that pole like a squirrel, aren't you?" His shoulders slumped, making him look even more solid than usual.

"Yup!" I was practically skipping with excitement.

I was itching to climb. My five-days-a-week habit needed an outlet.

The retreat was a combination of outdoorsy activities, creativity exercises, and personal development. I'd considered myself lucky to be included in the group of roughly seventy and had lobbied to get Fern invited. As a graphic designer, he was the most junior person present. I'd argued that getting to know the reporters and producers would help him to better represent our brand visually.

UPR had made quite an investment in this event; transporting about a third of its L.A. office to the small resort town about one hundred miles northeast of the city. We were staying at a retreat center that operated as a sleepaway camp for kids during the summer months and reminded me of the movie *The Parent Trap* (the Hayley Mills version). The property was filled with tiny cabins, each structure just large enough for two twin cots, two bedside tables, and two closets. The cabins were so close together that a snoring coworker a few cottages away sounded like a baby buffalo being strangled. Needless to say, I hadn't been sleeping well.

Just like in other parts of life, the sleeping arrangements had been hierarchical, with more senior employees situated closer to the main buildings where we ate and did all of our exercises. Given our lack of seniority, Fern and I were located in a couple of the cabins furthest away. I didn't mind though; quiet walks through an evergreen forest were hardly a punishment.

As we walked, dried pine needles filled the air with their snapping sound and sharp scent. Although there were a lot of trees, they were spread out, allowing ample amounts of filtered sunlight to cascade down. The sun's rays illuminated the collection of small cabins with a dappled light that made them seem as though they'd sprouted out of the forest floor like mushrooms.

"Did you get a chance to look at the layouts I designed for Clint's new press kit?" Fern asked.

I nodded. "The picture of him in the fighter jet is a winner. We should play up his TOPGUN past. The listeners think it's sexy."

Fern humphed. "Not like there's a lot of competition," he said, referring to the—not entirely unfair—reputation of public radio hosts as highly educated, trustworthy, and perhaps a little bit boring.

We exchanged guilty looks and giggled…well, I giggled, even Fern's giggle sounded more like a chuckle with his deep voice.

Together, Fern and I were the dedicated marketing team for UPR's biggest show, *Wake Up America*—referred to as *WUA* or "woo-ah"—and we'd won high marks the last two weeks overseeing the unexpected change in main hosts. After a decade as one of the most beloved voices on American radio, *WUA* host Devon Lopez had unexpectedly quit the show to take over a television anchor position that paid five times more and was sure to launch her into mainstream fame.

Clint Davenport had slid into the top spot easily after eight years as the show's West Coast correspondent and substitute host. His irreverent humor and lazy self-confidence had earned him legions of fans even before he took Devon's place. His past as a fighter pilot hadn't hurt, either.

So far, Fern and I had managed the transition gracefully, quickly updating the website and issuing press releases, although there was still a lot of work to be done.

"Has he told you his callsign yet?" Fern asked.

I scowled. "No. He's being obnoxiously obstinate about that. We might have to issue the press kit without that fun little factoid."

I wondered how long it would take to win over the famously private former-lieutenant. While gregarious on the air, in person he guarded his personal life jealously, making it hard for me to do my job. And it wasn't like I could interview any of the other staff members, because Clint wasn't the type of person who fostered work friendships. Whereas many of the reporters grabbed coffee or lunch together, or even drinks after work, Clint never did any of that. He ate his lunch alone in his office every day and he left promptly at two p.m. like he might turn into a pumpkin if he stayed a minute later.

So how could I update the man's bio if he refused to answer my questions?

I'd thought it would be easy to get him to open up. People usually loved telling me their secrets. I'm not sure what it was about me; maybe my short stature or my innocent-looking face, the combination of which made me very approachable. Add that to the fact that Clint and I had known each other for a while should've made him more forthcoming. While we hadn't worked together closely, in my two years as WUA's marketing coordinator, we'd had our share of professional interactions. We'd even shared the occasional laugh in the office kitchen.

"Are you cold?" Fern said, cutting into my consternation.

His words made me realize I'd been rubbing my bare arms.

"I didn't think it would be so cool up here."

"Yeah, we're a lot higher up. In a few more months, this town will turn into a ski resort."

I shivered.

He gripped his windbreaker tighter as though thinking about the snow had made him cold. "Do you ski or snowboard?"

I shivered again. "No way. I don't like the cold. I'm an island girl, remember?"

He shrugged. "It's fun. It feels like flying. Besides, it's not cold once you have all the gear on."

I arched a brow, but reserved judgment.

He glanced at his hands clutching his jacket. "Do you want my windbreaker?"

I shook my head. "I'll warm up as soon as we start moving. Thanks, though."

As we approached the designated forest clearing, we found the other UPR employees huddling at the bases of a dozen telephone-pole-like apparatuses. Many were staring up at the top of the poles, mouths agape.

"Looks like we found the right place." Fern's voice held a hint of trepidation.

The looks of dismay didn't surprise me. Most of the group were ten to twenty years older than me and not particularly athletic. The few who exercised regularly limited it to hiking and yoga. There were a handful of notable exceptions: Clint was a long-distance runner and still very fit at thirty-nine, and Jacinda Hill, one of the show's youngest senior editors at forty-four, was a triathlete. And Fern, who'd played basketball his entire life, although he didn't seem to enjoy it that much. I suspected he played just because it was expected of his height.

Off to the side of the pole nearest to me, Clint was talking to the show's senior producer, Yolanda Sousa, an intimidating sixtyish blonde who reminded me of Glenn Close; cool, calculating, and intimidating AF. In contrast to her rigidly upright posture, Clint's slender six-foot-one frame hunched in lazy self-assuredness—as though his spine were trying to form an "s"—while he listened.

Inwardly, I rolled my eyes. I don't know why, but Clint's inches-thick layer of self-confidence always riled me up. His lazy smiled seemed to imply that he was the smartest person in the room—as if his status as host wasn't enough to make people pay attention to him. The fact that he was a Rhodes Scholar, had the cheekbones of a runway model, and the ass of a Greek statue were further cause for annoyance. My brain seemed to short circuit whenever he entered the room. which infuriated me now that I was spending so much time in his presence.

Clint turned my way, his eyes widening just the tiniest bit as they took notice of me.

I attempted to rearrange my face into a neutral expression. His smug chin-lift told me I failed.

My face heated.

I scowled and glanced away quickly, the hair on the back of my neck prickling self-consciously.

I needed to learn to immunize myself against Clint's swagger, worthy of a TOPGUN fighter pilot—which, of course, on top of everything else, he'd actually been.

Jiminy Cricket, I cursed mentally.

I tried to reserve swear words for serious use only. They were behind a glass panel labeled "Break in Case of Emergency" in my brain. I guess it was a holdover of living with my parents for so long. My Colorado-born mother had serious issues with swearing. So, Jiminy Cricket was my go-to curse of choice.

"Don't let Top Gun get to you," Fern said under his breath, using the code name we'd made up…although it wasn't much of a code name.

I tried to shrug it off. Looking back, the fact that Fern could so easily read the situation should have given me pause. "He's just so cocky," I exhaled.

Although *WUA* was the only radio show I'd ever worked on, I imagined that most hosts with millions of listeners were a bit self-important. Big egos were an occupational hazard, although I had the feeling that Clint probably had one even before becoming a host. Of course, all the listeners emailing marriage proposals probably didn't help. Going through the listener email was part of my job, and there had been a sharp uptick in proposals since *WUA*'s host had gone from a fifty-something, married woman with two grown children to a not-yet-forty-year-old bachelor.

"Okay everyone, listen up because this is one of the more physically challenging activities we'll be doing during the retreat," said the commanding voice of Sonja Gutierrez, a petite but muscular woman who was one of the lead team members. She'd served as a Marine.

Clint's posture tensed up, perhaps in respect of Sonja's military service.

"If any of you don't want to participate, you are welcome to pass, however," Sonja raised her eyebrows, "The *reason* you are here is to challenge yourself. The goal is to *try* the activity, not to do it perfectly."

Clint's face relaxed considerably. "Wonderful. If it's all the same to you, I'll just keep my feet on the ground," he called out in his lazy tenor that was just a *tad* nasally, as he gave Sonja a respectful nod. He swaggered his way over to a picnic table, sat on its top, and folded his long legs under himself in one smooth motion.

Is Clint Davenport scared? The thought gave me a childish thrill of pleasure. Finally, something I could best him at.

Sonja narrowed her eyes but otherwise ignored his comment. "I'd like each of you to pick a telephone pole; there should be about six of you to a pole. Fern, you'll need to pick a pole with someone who's as close to your size as possible," she said, lifting her chin in his direction.

Fern pressed his lips flat and looked around. The only person who was even close in height was Clint, but Fern still outweighed him by at least fifty pounds. "I guess I'll have to sit this one out," he said quietly, as though it was a problem he was used to.

The resigned look on his face made my heart hurt.

"Hold on a second." Taking a deep breath, I arranged my face into a pleasant expression and walked over to Clint.

His eyes pivoted towards me the moment I started moving in his direction; as though he'd been expecting me to approach.

God, he's cocky.

I willed my cheeks not to color under his intense gaze, which skimmed over me with bemused curiosity.

Time seemed to slow down as the dirt crunched under my feet loudly and the breeze ruffled the hem of my tank top.

When I came to a stop in front of him, he swung a lazy, almost goofy grin at me. "Howdy," he said in a not-unfriendly tone.

His voice like warm whiskey coating my insides. I took a deep breath. "Hey, Clint—" My voice broke and I paused, trying to remember what I wanted to say to him.

Fern, you want to help Fern, my subconscious prodded.

I forced a smile on my face. "Fern isn't going to be able to climb if you don't partner him. Do you think you could reconsider…please?"

Although his lazy grin stayed in place, his eyes jerked to the top of the telephone pole, confirming my suspicion: Clint was afraid of heights. I'd seen that look many times at my climbing gym.

"You wouldn't have to climb yourself," I said quickly. "You just have to put on a harness and make sure he doesn't fall. It's easy. The pulley does most of the work," I said, hoping that if I kept talking, eventually he'd say yes.

He returned his gaze to me and narrowed his eyes.

I couldn't tell if he was studying me or contemplating my request, but I held his gaze, struggling to keep my breath even. Despite working with him for two years, he still made me nervous.

An unbidden memory forced its way into my consciousness. Narrowed eyes, hot coffee, me wearing ill-fitting interview attire. I colored instantly.

Jiminy Cricket.

I pulled at the front of my white tank top, which felt far more revealing than it had when I'd left the cabin. "All you have to do is catch him if he falls. You would stay on the ground the whole time." I raised my palms out towards him as though trying to calm him down.

He raised a brow while a few thoughtful seconds ticked away. "Okay. I'll do it." But his usual bravado had been replaced by a resolved seriousness.

I'd seen behind his façade of cool confidence, and I liked it. Clint was human after all.

It also made me feel special, like Clint had *let* me in, just a tiny bit.

One barrier down.

How many more stood in the way of getting all my interview questions answered?

"Thanks, Clint." My voice must have been warmer than I'd thought, because he did a double-take. The smile that always played on his lips finally showed up as diamonds in his eyes.

"So, Badass has a soft side after all?" he said, using the nickname he'd given me the year before when I'd landed Devon a guest spot on national television; a tactic that was above and beyond my job description, but well in line with the role of a marketing manager.

Or director! God, my subconscious could be so bossy.

In the past, he'd always said it like a bro comment, but today it was a playful tease.

A warm, fudgy feeling took up residence in my gut and I scowled at how much I liked it.

It was one thing to find Clint physically attractive (who didn't?), but a very different thing to have dopey, school-girl feelings for him.

As though in answer, he gave me a lazy nod and I pictured him wearing a Stetson, fingers hooked in the loops of his jeans, a stalk of wheat jutting from his thick, full lips.

Where the hell do I get this stuff?

I gave him a quick nod and headed back to Fern, painfully aware of Clint just two steps behind and one to the side. I felt his every move like there was a cable connecting us.

Chapter 2: Swagger

~Clint~

Damn. Crap. Damn, I thought, as I walked behind Erin, my eyes glued to the mesmerizing swing of her hips.

She'd changed in the years that I'd known her, the softness of girlhood melting away into a stronger femininity—both mentally and physically—that I found incredibly sexy. For a brief second, I pictured her powerful thighs clasped around my waist like a vise and felt a dangerous throb in my cargo shorts.

Although originally my mental cursing had been for the climbing exercise I'd agreed to, it continued because of the salacious thoughts I was having about Erin. Thoughts I'd been having more frequently in the last couple of weeks, as my promotion meant we saw each other almost daily.

Not seeing each other, man, working together.

Although I'd known the promotion meant more time spent together marketing the show, I hadn't anticipated how pleasant I would find this new requirement. How much I'd enjoy staring into Erin's velvety eyes that were so dark, sometimes they flashed black when she was annoyed at me.

And she seemed annoyed at me frequently. Sometimes I annoyed her just to see the fire in her eyes and the heat in her cheeks. So much passion in such a petite person. It was—dare I say—adorable.

Adorable? When was the last time I'd found anything *adorable?*

After a moment of wondering at my uncharacteristically whimsical thought, my mind turned back to Erin, as it had been doing with increased frequency.

It was hard not to think about someone when you interacted with them (almost) every day.

And there was just so much to admire.

In addition to her fiery eyes, I also liked her hair. Specifically, I fantasized about unwinding her braids and feeling the weight of them in my hands, and then loosening them to see what her long hair must look like cascading against the pecan-colored canvas of her back.

Her voice mesmerized me, too. It was simultaneously invigorating, mysterious, and relaxing like Handel's *Water Garden.*

But even as I admired her, I remained wary.

Something was changing between us, or maybe it was only changing inside me. Perhaps it was because our interactions didn't feel completely professional. Unlike the rest of my colleagues, Erin and I didn't just talk about news, she asked me personal questions like, "Tell me about growing up in Boston," and "What drew you to studying Chinese in college?" It was like we were just chit-chatting, shooting the breeze, getting to know each other.

It was…disarming.

I'd found it so much easier admiring her from afar. As the (lowly) substitute host of *WUA,* our paths had rarely crossed. Not that I hadn't been aware of her, because I had. Whenever she was near, I *knew* it. I *felt* it. Like I was a heat-seeking missile capable of reading only a single energy signature and it was hers.

Maybe once a month we'd bump into each other in the communal kitchen and trade a jab. Like the time I commented on the (alarming) number of almonds she put into her cup of (full fat) Greek yogurt.

"They. Are. Just. Almonds," she seethed, although she might as well have said, "Could you be any more of an asshat?"

Her scowl had scored her face so deeply—the lines on her usually unmarked forehead, cavernous—that I wished I could've rewound my words and listened to my delivery.

See, that's the beauty of working in radio. Most of the time I could fix my words. Rewinding, reviewing, re-recording until I get the inflection *just* right. And I rerecorded a lot. It was the only way to ensure my baseline sarcasm—which I'll admit is an acquired taste— never went too far for the millions of Americans who listened to me every morning.

But in person, in real-time, I couldn't do that.

And by the look I often elicited on Erin's face, I frequently said the wrong thing.

Like the time I asked her when she was going to start wearing Fern's letterman jacket after seeing them in the kitchen together five days in a row.

She'd rolled her eyes and walked away without answering.

No wonder she was constantly annoyed with me. If I wasn't being an asshat, then I was reverting to schoolyard teasing. We were more like frenemies than friends.

However, now that I was *the* host and had the pleasure of Erin's attention Monday thru Friday, the ache in my body—the one that had her name written all over it—had spread from my gut to my loins to my head.

Perhaps it was even in danger of spreading to that icy region known as my heart.

All these thoughts passed through my mind in the space of a few seconds, and when my attention returned to Erin's swaying hips walking in front of me, *beckoning* to me, I sighed and shook my head.

I'm a goner. A dangerously enjoyable stirring in my pants reminded me to get my thoughts under control.

Erin glanced back at me, her eyes narrowed in question, before quickly turning forward, keeping her pace swift, clearly not wanting me to walk beside her.

But how I *longed* to walk beside her, to match our steps, maybe even hold her hand.

Hold her hand? I broke out my imaginary cat-o-nine-tails and flogged myself a few times.

The truth was, Erin had infected me, and I wanted to do the same to her. I wanted her to obsess about me the way I did about her. I wanted to hear my name on her lips over and over again; during a run, over coffee, at a museum, eating dinner, in the shower, folding laundry, in bed, hell, anywhere.

Mother Teresa. I shook my head as images of me and Erin flashed through my mind, causing points of pain and pleasure to pulse all over my body.

I wanted her so completely, it hurt.

Give it up, man. She's not for you. The voice of Discipline—which had gotten me through years of military service—spoke up. It had had enough of my wallowing.

And when Discipline spoke, I listened.

I slid into place the partition in my brain that shuts the chatter off. I was good at focusing, something I'd learned as a student and honed as a pilot. Call it my superpower. You don't become the host of America's most popular radio show in fewer than ten years without it.

Unfortunately, Erin Hung had a way of scattering my focus, but as long as I—

Bam! I collided into her luscious backend.

I'd been so caught up in my thoughts, I didn't notice that she'd stopped.

"HEY!" Erin rolled over like a startled pill-bug; fingers still wrapped around her shoelaces which she'd apparently been tying.

"Oh, shit. Sorry, Erin." I offered her my hand, feeling like an ass.

Her eyes flitted to my hand and she took it with a scowl. As I lifted her up, she glanced at my fly, making me wonder if she'd felt my chubber during our collision.

Then she met my eyes. Her brow knit together, questioning.

My face burned like it was on fire. "I'm so sorry, Erin."

Idiot.

After a few moments of heart-pounding embarrassment, she bent down to finish her task.

I tried to look away, but my eyes were drawn to her spectacular backside as she tied her shoes with her knees locked, bending only at the waist.

Why didn't she hunch down like a normal person, instead of looking like some rubbery-jointed acrobat hoisting her unignorable ass in the air?

Feeling oddly protective, I side-stepped to block said view from anyone else.

I glanced around, but the only person looking our way was Fern, who narrowed his eyes and gave me a look like a bucket of cold water to my face.

I sucked in a breath. *Erin's boyfriend.*

An ugly tendril of jealousy ignited in my chest, infusing my blood with its acrid smoke.

The two of them were disgustingly inseparable at the office. Ever since he'd started at WUA eight months, two weeks, and seven days ago…but who's counting? And they were *always* laughing. I'm not sure when I started to find laughter annoying, but I'm pretty sure it began eight months, two weeks, and seven days ago.

Erin stood and gave me an expectant look. "Let's do this." She tugged on the floaty piece of tissue paper masquerading as a tank top and cocked her head towards Fern.

Harriet Tubman...nipples.

As if the neon pink of her sports bra wasn't enough of a distraction.

I was finding it really hard to keep my cool.

"Are you coming?" Erin called.

Apparently, the command "to walk" hadn't make it to my feet. "Yup, on my way," I said.

Fern's face broke into a beatific smile as we approached.

God, they were nauseatingly adorable.

I had noticed.

I noticed everything about Erin: new hairstyle, new outfit, new lipstick—on the rare days that she wore lipstick, and boy, did I love those days. Her soft, full lips gave her a permapout that was even more pronounced with lipstick. She had this berry-colored gloss that I particularly loved. When she wore it, it looked like she'd just stuffed a bunch of boysenberries in her mouth and forgotten to wash off their juices. The sweet, warm color contrasted beautifully with the ebony of her hair and the pale gold of her skin.

When we got to the base of the pole, Fern extended his hand. "Thanks for doing this, Clint," he said, disarming me with a nervous look. "Erin is hellbent on getting me up this pole."

I shook his hand and considered if I'd misread the cold bucket look earlier. "No problem, Fern. Happy to help out."

He grinned, reminding me that I had no beef with Fern. If I was being honest, I even liked the guy, he was kind of impossible not to like. He reminded me of Cary Grant, all pretty manners and perfect blazers.

In our very casual office, Fern was the only man who could be counted on to wear a jacket to work—sport coat with leather patches at the elbows—no matter what the temperature was outside. Personally, I never wore anything more formal than a polo shirt, and I was the top of the food chain. Even today Fern looked formal, opting for pants when almost everyone else was in shorts and a windbreaker that he managed to wear with authority, like an FBI agent.

"We all set here?" Sonja asked our group.

An uncertain, "Yes," resounded from the six of us gathered around the telephone pole, although Erin's voice was decidedly more chipper than the rest.

"Great. Darius will be by in a second with your harnesses." Sonja jerked her thumb towards one of the other instructors.

A mild breeze kicked up and Erin shuddered, wrapping her arms around the tissue paper top covering her torso.

"Take this," Fern said, his tone brooking no disagreement, as he unzipped and shrugged off his windbreaker, holding it out to her.

Erin gave him a look that was both chagrined and grateful and put it on. The nylon fabric hung like a circus tent, grazing her mid-calf. She laughed, a warm giggle that made my heart pang, wishing it had been for my benefit alone.

She took off the jacket and handed it back to Fern. "Thanks, but it's just too big. I won't be able to do anything with it on." When he tried to push it back to her, she said, "I'll be fine as soon as I start climbing."

Without even consciously making the decision, I pulled off my top layer, tensing as the mountain air seeped in a bit more. It was cool but manageable. "Here. This might fit better."

Erin eyed my thermal like it was something dangerous. "No, I couldn't."

I frowned. "Come on. I've got another long-sleeve shirt on," I said, pointing to my torso. "I'm fine."

She hesitated.

"Please," I urged, but without the pleading I felt in my heart since we *were* surrounded by four other people. I *really* wanted her to take my shirt. It was like a baton I needed to pass to her so we could take the next step. To where, I wasn't sure, I just knew I wanted to move forward with her.

She cocked her head for a moment, surprise and uncertainty mingling on her face.

"Take it, Erin," Fern urged—

—But she'd already started reaching for my shirt.

I exhaled a breath I didn't know I'd been holding as she took it from my hands.

"Thanks, Clint," she said through lowered lashes, causing my heart to pick up speed.

She pulled the cranberry-colored shirt over her head and rolled up the sleeves.

Damn. My mouth started to water.

The rolled-up arms hung loosely like bells at her side while her breasts filled out the chest in a very inviting way; the subtle waffle pattern bowing outward, Escher-like. My shirt grazed her mid-thigh, like she was wearing a mini dress, showing off her strong, beautiful legs in a very enticing way. The fact that she was wrapped up in *my* shirt made the view even sweeter.

A bit of color rose in her cheeks. "Thanks, Clint. It's very…cozy." She drew the "z" out just a bit, the trill of the letter tickling my ear.

For a moment, it felt like we were in a privacy bubble. Everyone around us seemed to drop away.

A strand of her hair came loose from her elaborate braid and the breeze blew it across her face.

"You're welcome," I said in a low voice, taking a half-step closer, my hand lifting to move the strand out of her face before I'd even realized I'd moved.

Someone cleared his throat, piercing our bubble.

Suddenly aware of my action, I jerked my hand out of mid-air and ran it through my hair.

The corners of Erin's mouth dipped down but she said nothing.

I really needed to stop fixating on her, especially with her boyfriend within jabbing distance.

I took a half-step back, and then another, because Fern's arms were *long*.

Darius appeared with a handful of rope climbing harnesses. "Any of you climbers?"

Erin nodded. "I do Class 5 routes regularly."

Darius's eyes widened. "Great. Why don't you help people put on the harnesses while I get the ropes ready," he said, handing her a collection of brightly colored nylon belts with loops hanging off every possible angle. "I'll double-check them when you're done."

She took the belts and began handing them out, sizing people up with an expert eye.

Her confidence only raised her in my esteem.

"So, what do I do?" I asked as she handed me a belt.

Pursing her lips, she said, "Why don't you and Fern go last, so you can see how it's done." She glanced at the three other *WUA* employees who'd chosen our pole. "Any of you have previous climbing experience?"

"I've climbed a few times," said Kelly Cole, *WUA*'s International Editor, a statuesque woman in her late thirties with close-cropped curls and a voice almost as deep as mine. She'd once been a war journalist, and carried herself with the self-possession of someone who'd seen the worst and lived to talk about it.

"Great," Erin said. "You know how to put on your harness?"

Kelly nodded and took the belt from Erin's hand.

"Everyone, watch Kelly and me as we put on our belts, then we can help you with yours," Erin said in a commanding voice.

I watched as Erin shimmied into the leg loops, buckled them, and then cinched the straps tight around her waist and thighs. When she turned to look at Kelly, the orange straps outlined her ass like a frame. I had to fight to tear my gaze off the majestic sight, grateful I'd stepped away from Fern earlier.

Being around Erin turned me into a hormone-riddled boy.

"It's important to double-back on the waist," Erin said to the group as she pointed at Kelly's belt. "May I?" she asked Kelly, who nodded.

She took the end of the other woman's belt and threaded it through the waist loop one more time, pulling it secure. Then she checked the other straps before nodding. "There. Now her harness won't go anywhere."

"How's it going?" Sonja asked, approaching our group. She'd been circling among all the telephone poles, checking in with the others.

"Erin's pretty much an expert climber," Fern offered.

Sonja inspected Erin and Kelly's harnesses and lifted her brows. "Looks good." Then she turned her attention to Darius who was bent over, pulling and adjusting some ropes, his biceps popping out of his arms like baseballs. "You almost ready?"

"Ready, Boss." Darius stood up straight, his posture impeccable, eyes averted from Sonja's direct gaze.

I guessed that Darius probably had military training, too. I'd tried my best to lose the bearing the military had beaten into me. Slouching had become my own declaration of independence.

Sonja gave Darius a tiny nod and then walked off.

Darius's shoulders relaxed. He gestured to Erin and Kelly. "So, you two are going first?"

They nodded.

"Mind if I check your straps?" He pulled on the straps encircling Erin's thighs and waist, turning her around and inspecting her a bit more closely than I thought was necessary.

The hair on the back of my neck stood on end. I glanced at Fern whose gaze was fixed on the top of the telephone pole rather than on his girlfriend.

Then Darius gave Kelly the same inspection.

Okay, maybe it really was necessary. My heart slowed a bit.

Erin and Darius spoke in a sort of rock-climbing shorthand as they threaded ropes here and there, all of it happening too fast for me to follow.

It was a turn-on watching Erin in her element. Before today, I'd only known "Office Erin" but she clearly had an outdoorsy, athletic side. Which, unfortunately, only made her even more attractive to me.

Finally, Darius turned back towards the group, waving everyone into a huddle. "This challenge looks intimidating because it's a straight vertical that doesn't look like it's supported by anything. However, climbing this pole is no different than climbing a ladder. Any sense of difficulty is up here." He pointed to his head. "Watch how easy it is."

He turned towards the pole then gripped and stood on the alternating metal rods jutting out of either side like Frankenstein's bolts. He climbed halfway up in seconds, then dropped back down to the ground noiselessly.

I had to admit, he made it look easy.

Darius rubbed his hands together and squinted as he looked at the very top. "Although climbing the log is easy, the second part's a bit tougher and will definitely test your balance. The goal is to stand up straight on the top of the log, which is large enough in diameter to accommodate size-nine women's shoes." He glanced around at the men's feet. "Guys, your feet will definitely hang over the edge a few inches." He gave a meaningful eyebrow raise to Fern, who shrugged like he wasn't surprised. "However, remember that if you fall off the log, we're down here to catch you, so there's no reason not to try standing up."

He took a moment to look each of us in the eye as though reinforcing this point. "Then, once you're at the top, there's still one more part to this challenge." He pointed up in the air to some black bars, the kind aerial circus performers use, that were suspended a few feet in front of the log. "Do you see the trapeze bar?"

I hadn't noticed it before, and my stomach flip-flopped as I anticipated Darius's next words.

"If you want to, the third part of the challenge is to jump for that bar."

A collective intake of breath told me that I wasn't the only person surprised by this twist.

Suddenly, the first two parts of the challenge looked like child's play.

Darius put a hand on Erin's shoulder.

My chest tightened. The assumed familiarity bothered me. I glanced at Fern to see if he was feeling the same, but his face was stitched in concentration.

"Since Erin is an experienced climber, she'll demonstrate. Pay careful attention to the call and response we use as I'll expect all of you to do the same."

Erin nodded, stepping up to the base of the telephone pole and directing her gaze upwards.

Darius pointed at Kelly, who was staring at Erin's back with laser focus. "When you're in Kelly's position, your attention needs to be one-thousand percent on your partner. You can't be distracted." He faced Kelly. "Are you ready?"

Kelly nodded.

"I'll prompt your responses," Darius said. "Whenever you're ready, Erin."

She bent her knees, shaking her arms out at her sides and wiggling her fingers for a few seconds. Then she called out, "On belay?" in a strong voice; her gaze focused on her goal: the top of the log.

Everyone at the other telephone poles had stopped what he or she was doing to watch. Erin would be demonstrating for everyone.

"The belay is this device," Darius said, pointing to a piece of metal attached to Kelly's harness. "It helps to hold Erin's weight. By asking 'On belay?', the climber is checking to see if the person holding their rope, called a belayer, is ready. Kelly, you say, 'Belay on'."

"Belay on," Kelly said authoritatively, her hands on the ropes, knees bent, eyes boring holes into Erin's back.

"Climbing," Erin said, but didn't make a move.

"This is Erin indicating that she's ready to go. The belayer says, 'Climb on'," Darius explained.

"Climb on," Kelly answered immediately.

Erin began climbing as though Kelly's words had been a starting gun, and Kelly responded by pulling on the rope in time with Erin's progress, taking up the slack Erin was creating as she ascended.

Erin scampered up the pole, her body clearly familiar with the mechanics of climbing. The ascent seemed like little more than a warm-up for her.

Once at the top she slowed a bit, getting her feet onto the top of the log. Her flexibility helped as she made that same locked-knee waist-bend I'd admired earlier. Once on top, she slowly rose to standing, putting her hands over her head with nary a wobble. The whole performance couldn't have taken more than ninety seconds.

"Nice," Darius yelled as he started to clap.

After a second, UPR's stunned masses joined in, clearly impressed by Erin's athletic demonstration. She'd made it look extremely easy.

"Damn," Fern said, shaking his head, his baseball mitt-sized hands making a resounding clap.

"You must see this every day," I commented as I clapped.

Fern shook his head. "No. I've never seen her climb before. I know she's been doing it for a few years, but this is the first time I've witnessed it."

That's odd. Fern seemed athletic and like he'd be a supportive boyfriend. So why hadn't he been climbing with Erin?

Perhaps all isn't well in paradise.

I was intrigued and—to be perfectly honest—a little bit happy at the realization.

Darius cupped his hands together and called to Erin, "Are you going to jump?"

"Yes," Erin replied evenly, her body devoid of movement as she balanced on the pole, her aviator-shaded eyes trained on the aerial bar.

The bar was just far enough away, that she was going to have to really launch herself at it to compensate for the length of her arms. Fern, on the other hand, would barely have to move to reach the aerial bar from the top of the log.

I tensed as Erin bent her knees, her hands swinging at her side for additional momentum.

"Spotter ready?" Erin called out; her eyes still trained on her goal.

"Say 'Ready'," Darius directed.

"Ready," Kelly called out.

"Jumping," Erin said, but didn't move.

"Jump away," Darius said.

"Jump away," Kelly yelled.

Erin gave a final swing of her arms, bent her knees a little lower, and jumped, launching herself powerfully at the black bar. She grabbed it easily, swinging in the air overhead.

This time the applause broke out immediately, a general hooting and hollering of admiration filling the air.

That's my girl! I thought, full of pride for Erin and not bothering to chastise myself this time.

After all, I couldn't help my feelings, right? All I could do was *not* act on them.

Once the swing had stopped moving, Erin called out, "Falling."

"Fall away," Darius said.

"Fall away," Kelly parroted, her face more relaxed now, while her hands maintained their tensed readiness on the rope.

Erin let go of the bar and hung suspended in the air as Kelly leaned back, counterbalancing her perfectly. As Kelly let the rope out— lowering Erin in the process—Erin struck a few famous flying postures. First, the closed-fist, one-arm-forward pose of Superman, then Peter Pan's swan dive, and finally something magical looking, her hands fanning out over her head as she batted her eyelashes.

"Tinkerbell?" I called out as her pointed toe touched the ground.

"No, Glinda, The Good Witch of the North."

I laughed because once she said it, I couldn't unsee it. I could almost imagine us as Munchkins, crowding around her.

Fern got to Erin first and gave her a clap on the shoulder.

She beamed up at him as she unhooked her harness and switched places with Kelly.

After everyone showered Erin with praise, Darius checked her and Kelly's equipment again, and then turned to Kelly. "Ready?"

She swallowed hard and nodded, looking up at the telephone pole. After a moment, she said, "On belay?" with just the tiniest hesitation in her voice.

"Belay on," Erin answered.

"Climbing."

"Climb on."

Kelly was graceful, but nowhere near as fast as Erin, getting winded the last third of the climb. The second part of the challenge provided an even starker contrast with Erin, as Kelly experimented with kneeling and then sitting on the log, finally getting to her feet by leaning against the tension of the harness awkwardly—which looked like a big mistake in my opinion—before shakily standing all the way up. The pole wobbled under her feet.

"Are you going to jump?" Darius called, the tone of his voice making it clear that it was fine if she didn't.

"I'm not sure yet," she said, her voice quavering as she studied the black bar with intense concentration. "It's farther away than I thought."

"You can do it, Kelly. You got this," Erin shouted. "There's no risk. I'm holding you tight."

Kelly gave a tiny nod. She put her hands on the waist of her harness, as though making sure it was still there.

"Just bend your knees, swing your arms, and jump," Darius said, his voice, liquid calm.

Kelly licked her lips and began swinging her arms.

As though anticipating that Kelly had forgotten the audio cues, Erin said, "Jump away, Kelly. I got you."

Kelly didn't give any indication that she'd heard, but then launched herself towards the swing in a graceless dive that would've been a belly flop in a pool. But her long fingers made contact with the bar and she clutched at it tightly.

She made it.

"Yes," Erin said, the word sizzling as it came out of her mouth, her lips turning up in a broad smile.

"Kelly, don't forget to call out the cues to your belayer. Say 'falling' before you let go," Darius instructed.

"Oh, right. Okay. Falling," Kelly said, her voice no longer quavering.

"Fall away," Erin replied.

Kelly released the bar and floated down to the ground, courtesy of Erin's expert belaying. Despite the slow grace of her descent, I could see that she was trembling. Probably not from fear; more likely an after-effect of the adrenaline pumping through her body.

I knew that sensation all too well.

Even though I hadn't been in a cockpit in almost a decade, I remembered the adrenaline surges and their afterburn. The trembling that started within your bones and reverberated out the tips of your fingers. I started shaking out my arms the way I would have had I been in Kelly's place, like a kind of empathetic physical response.

Erin must have noticed Kelly's trembling too, because as soon as the other woman was on the ground, she rushed over and hugged her.

Kelly clung to Erin as if she were a life preserver.

"You did great. Way to push yourself," Erin said quietly, the words meant just for Kelly.

Kelly nodded, wiping at the corner of her eyes, clearly overcome.

Darius clapped loudly. "Way to go, Kelly. I can see that was a real challenge for you."

Kelly nodded, still unable to form sentences.

"Who's next?" Darius asked.

The other four members of our group stood silent.

"Don't look at me," I said, holding my hands up in surrender. "I'm just here to belay Fern."

A loud sigh came from the man to my left. "I'll go."

Harry Hinkley was a fit, fifty-something who was the finance guy for *WUA*. He had a full head of hair that was as white as snow, and almost constantly muttered to himself under his breath. His climbing partner, Maryam Nazarian, was in her mid-forties and worked in fund-raising.

Harry and Maryam didn't seem as psychologically challenged by the exercise as Kelly, but more physically challenged. Harry got his rump on the pole but never managed to stand, whereas Maryam was able to stand, but missed the aerial swing when she jumped for it.

Then it was our turn.

Darius asked quietly, "How much do you weigh?" so that just Fern and I could hear.

"Two-sixty, two-seventy," Fern said, twisting his open palm from side to side in approximation.

"And you?" Darius directed to me.

"One-ninety-eight," I answered automatically. "After breakfast." I was usually about two-oh-three after lunch and two-oh-nine after dinner, but I figured that wasn't relevant at the moment.

Darius raised his brows. "With that kind of weight disparity, we'll need to anchor you to the ground, just in case."

A bit of testosterone-laced pride swelled in my chest (never a good sign). "I can handle it. His weight will be offset by the pulley and everything, right?"

Darius nodded as though he'd heard this before. "I'm sure you can. It's just a precaution. Safety first." His tone brooked no argument.

My hackles stayed up.

I was not the type of person to back away from a challenge. It was a holdover from my days in the Navy.

Strike that.

I'd been like that my whole life.

After a second, I gave Darius a nod, but the familiar flame of competition increased my body temperature significantly. Usually, I pounded the competitive flame out on long, pre-dawn trail runs, but even though I'd done five miles that morning, the embers of my competitive nature were always lingering, just waiting for the slightest fanning to spark them.

"I need to check your harness," Darius said, waiting for me to nod before pulling on the ends of my belt.

Harriet Beecher Stowe, I thought as the nylon straps clamped down around my pelvis.

I looked down at my shorts and cursed again.

Let's just say that the climbing harness *cups* men in a very different way than it does women.

When Harry had been climbing, I hadn't noticed the way the straps all contrived to push one's package front and center like a codpiece. Then again, the thick, black denim of Harry's shorts offered more resistance to the harness than the thin fabric of my cargo shorts.

I didn't even want to hazard a look in Fern's direction. No telling what kind of heat the big guy was packing.

Darius gave me some pointers on how to handle the rope as Fern got into position. "I'm going to clip you to the anchor now," he said as he attached a rope leading from my harness to a ring secured in a slab of concrete just behind where I was standing.

I exhaled a breath to steady myself, my heart speeding up even though I wasn't the person about to climb the forty-foot-tall pole.

"On belay?" Fern called.

"Belay on," I answered, the ritualized words calming, reminding me of my preflight checks.

When risking one's life, these types of routines are imperative.

"Climbing."

"Climb on."

It took a second for Fern to figure out the spacing of the metal bars. He was either overreaching or underreaching since the climb was designed for average-height humans. However, once he found his rhythm, he scaled the pole quickly.

"It's tiny," he shouted, disbelief in his voice as he stared at the surface area he was supposed to stand on.

"Focus on getting your heels in place. Think of it like a diving board, it's okay if your toes flop off the edge," Darius said, adding a thumbs-up.

Fern didn't answer, instead working on hauling his huge body into place.

I took up the slack, adjusting for Fern's motions, pulling in and feeding out a few inches, moment-to-moment. Keeping my eyes on Fern, my throat tightened when I felt Erin enter my space like a disturbance in the Force.

She shouted, "You can do it, Fern!" and the force of her breath breezed across the skin on my neck sending a zipper of want up my spine.

I gritted my teeth to refocus on my mission. *Fern*.

Despite his size, he was lithe and graceful. Clearly a natural athlete. The telephone pole wobbled a bit as he got into position, but not like it had with Kelly. He wasn't nervous, he was just finding his balance.

"Yes!" Erin cried out as Fern got both feet in place and raised his torso to standing, keeping his knees bent in a deep squat. "You got this."

A hush fell over the clearing. Everyone was watching Fern now.

A full minute passed as he inched upward. He was moving so slow, it almost looked like the pole had decided to sprout upwards.

Finally, he came to his full height, and a smile broke out on his face. The larger group applauded, murmurs of disbelief filling the air.

"Nice." The word escaped my mouth unbidden. I felt Erin turn my way, but I managed to keep my eyes skyward despite the urge to return her gaze.

"You jumping?" Darius called.

"Of course," Fern answered, holding his arms towards the aerial swing, which hung less than a foot beyond his fingertips. "It's not much of a jump."

Everyone laughed.

Fern would do a little hop, grab the bar, and then I'd lower him down like a graceful hippopotamus. No problem.

Then several things happened at once.

Fern slipped off the top of the log and I started rising into the air as warm arms closed around my waist.

"Lean back. I got you," Erin half-shouted, her lips grazing my earlobe as she pulled me back toward the ground.

A fiery shiver shot up my spine.

"You okay?" Darius called up to Fern, who was dangling around the top of the log, his face bright red.

"Yeah. I just lost my focus. I'm fine." Before the words were even out of his mouth, he'd begun pulling himself back onto the log.

"Take in the slack," Erin's words were softer this time, her nearness causing my heart to speed up.

I pulled on the rope.

"That's it," she whispered, her warm breath tickling my ear. "The first time I spotted someone heavier than me, the same thing happened. I'll hold onto you just in case." The soothing concern in her voice like a caress.

I swallowed hard, my sense of pride, concern for Fern's safety, and desire for Erin all warring in my head, making me incoherent.

And I was *never* incoherent.

So I focused on her words like they were the landing system on an aircraft carrier, guiding me home to safety.

"Jumping," Fern called, the words slicing into my muddled brain.

"Jump on." Erin whispered so quietly the words were almost all air.

A soft chill radiated out along my back. "Jump on," I said, barely able to keep my voice even. The feeling of Erin's body—clinging to me—threw my body into disarray.

Focus! I took a deep breath and slid the mental barrier into place that would allow me to compartmentalize and focus on Fern, ignoring Erin.

Fern swung his arms a couple of times—no longer taking the short distance for granted—and jumped, catching the bar. Only, this time I was ready. The line remained tight as Fern swung back and forth.

"Falling."

"Fall on," I said, my self-control firm, just a tiny sliver of my brain thinking about how right it felt to have Erin wrapped around me.

Fern released his hold on the bar. This time, I didn't bob in the slightest. Of course, my and Erin's combined weight was now greater than his.

I belayed Fern down, not as gracefully as Erin had lowered Kelly, but I did a reasonable job.

When Fern hit the ground, the group exhaled and gave him a round of applause.

"Good job," Erin whispered into my ear one last time before releasing her grip on my waist and uncurling herself from my body.

Then—just as suddenly as she'd appeared—she was gone, walking over to Fern and clapping him on the back again. Her smile, only for him.

I felt a sense of loss at her departure, as though she'd taken a part of me with her.

I tried to shake the feeling, but as I glanced at Erin and Fern talking and laughing, it only grew stronger.

Abraham Lincoln!

Chapter 3: Dessert

~Erin~

"Aren't you hungry?" Fern said, elbowing me gently.

I poked at the cold pasta on my plate and glanced around the fluorescent-bright eating hall.

The space looked like a high school cafeteria with rectangular, industrial-strength tables and long benches.

Although I didn't want to admit it, I couldn't concentrate on my food because I'd been spending most of dinner watching Clint out of the corner of my eye. He was sitting two tables away, his head bent over his food as he listened to Yolanda. She appeared to be doing all of the talking, gesturing animatedly, with Clint only giving the occasional nod to show that he was listening.

In truth, I'd been distracted all day, unable to stop thinking about Clint and the pole challenge.

Without even trying, I could vividly recall the sensation of my arms circled around him, the wiry musculature of his back pressed against my chest, the taut ripple of his abs under my forearms. Although I'd been the one doing the saving, grabbing him had darn near knocked the wind out of me. After wrapping myself around him, I couldn't catch my breath and had resorted to whispering in his ear. Although part of me *had* enjoyed watching the skin on his neck break out in goosebumps. Had he'd liked it, too?

And even though I'd spent the rest of the afternoon sitting through hours of team-building exercises, writing seven pages on my personal and professional five-year plan, and taking a hot steamy shower in the communal bathroom, the empty ache in my belly hadn't diminished— an emptiness in my gut that had opened up the moment I let go of Clint.

I'd even put his thermal back on after my shower, justifying it to myself by saying I'd need to wash the shirt before I gave it back to him anyway, so I might as well use it. But in reality, I liked the spicy-minty scent lingering there.

And, okay, I just wanted to feel like a bit of Clint was enveloping me.

"Your dinner's getting cold. You said you love veggie lasagna." Fern nudged me again.

"Ow." I rubbed my rib which he'd hit in just the wrong way.

"Sorry," Fern said immediately.

I must have been kind of loud because Clint's head jerked towards me, our eyes locking.

Uncertain what to do, I smiled weakly.

His expressionless eyes scanned me before turning back to Yolanda.

Jerk. The childish reaction reminded me of when I was seven years old and my first crush, Jordan Tsukamoto, had just pulled my ponytail on the playground.

"Hey, Fern. Why do little boys pick on girls when they like them?" I stuck a bit of lasagna in my mouth and grimaced at the texture of the cold, floppy noodle. I chewed and swallowed, quickly chasing the nasty feeling away with a swallow of water.

He paused. "Not *every* boy does that," he started slowly, like a car getting into first gear. "Just the ones who haven't been taught how to demonstrate their feelings in a positive way." He sighed, and I could tell that I was going to get a good piece of Fern-wisdom.

Even though he was younger than me, Fern was someone you'd call an "old soul" and he regularly dropped golden nuggets that were surprising and profound. He was kind of like Chewbacca and Yoda mashed together, but with less hair.

After a second, he began, "My mom was very explicit about being kind to people I like, male or female. 'If you want someone to know how you feel, show it. Don't go sending mixed messages,' she would say."

I giggled at Fern's impression of his mom, Lorena. Although she'd lived in L.A. most of her life, sometimes her grammar spoke to her early childhood in Mexico.

He continued, "My mom says that it's our society's tolerance of violence that leads to things like little boys picking on girls they like. She always hated the expression 'Boys will be boys.' Whenever someone said it, she'd reply, 'Not if you teach them differently'."

I cocked my head. "Like how she raised you."

He smiled and shrugged, too humble to take the compliment. "If adults didn't tolerate the behavior, boys would find other—more constructive—ways to demonstrate their feelings. I saw my mom redirect my classmates whenever she volunteered at school. The kids loved her because she was the only mom who would really *play*. She'd join our games, whatever we were doing." He got a twinkle in his eye and added, "You should see her play handball. She's faster than you'd think."

I laughed. My father was such a typical macho male asshole, that it was refreshing to hear Fern's perspective. I think that's part of why we became such good friends. He filled a male void in my life that opened up when I left home and my father ignored me because he could no longer control me.

Fern continued, "Because all the kids liked my mom, they listened to her when she gave them advice. I can tell you for a fact that there was no passive-aggressive bullying happening on our playground whenever she was around. She'd teach the kids other ways of expressing themselves."

"Like what?"

He smirked. "She was really into greeting cards. She'd pull out all the arts and crafts supplies and tell us to make cards for a friend and express what was in our heart."

"Awwwwww…" I said, certain that I had heart eyes at that moment.

If I ever became a mom, Lorena was my #momgoals. She'd raised Fern as a single parent and done an amazing job.

My stomach rumbled.

Fern gave me an exasperated look. "Go on, eat. How many times did you climb that pole today?"

I shrugged. "Nine. I planned to do it a tenth time, but I think this elevation is doing a number on my breathing," I said, gesturing to my chest.

After our lunch break, I'd asked Darius if it was okay to use the apparatus. Fern had belayed me so I could feed my climbing habit. I'd welcomed the burn in my arms and legs as I pushed myself to go faster each time, hoping it would drive out thoughts of Clint, but it hadn't.

"You must be starving. Eat," he demanded, which was kind of a funny juxtaposition compared to his usual mild-mannered ways.

I smiled, so grateful for his presence in my life. Even though we'd met less than a year ago, he'd quickly become one of my best friends, and sometimes I wondered what I'd done to deserve him. Not only was he a brilliant graphic designer, but having him at work made my days fly by. Although to the outside world we might have seemed an odd couple, we just clicked.

"Okay, Bossypants, I'll eat." I shoveled the cold, creamy noodles into my mouth. The bottom layer was just warm enough to remind me how much I loved the salty, cheesy goodness of this packaged pasta. What wasn't to like? The tiny matchsticks of zucchini and carrot that made up the "vegetable" component added a nice bit of crunch to the dish. "I don't know why, but I really love this lasagna."

He smirked. "You can buy a five-pound tray of it for like seven-ninety-nine in the freezer section of any grocery store."

I shushed him. "I don't want to know. I prefer to eat my frozen lasagna on special occasions only," I said with a wink.

He laughed, that deep Fern laugh that reverberated off the walls.

I giggled in response and finished my food, but I was still hungry. "I'm going to get seconds." I glanced towards the food tables where someone was in the process of putting down a pie. "Hey! They just brought out dessert. Maybe I'll check that out first."

"I'm in," Fern said as he stood.

***

~Clint~

I watched out of the corner of my eye as Erin and Fern headed over to the dessert table. Her long floral dress billowed behind her as she walked, my cranberry thermal thrown over it.

I liked her in my shirt. If I squinted a bit, I could almost imagine that it was my arms draped around her.

She's with him, dummy. I scowled as my conscience reminded me of the futility of my daydreaming.

The thing was, something felt off about the two of them, although I couldn't figure out what. I'd only ever seen them together at work, but they seemed to be maintaining their professional distance even at the retreat, never even giving each other the occasional affectionate touch or lusty look of a couple in love. And I would know, since I'd been studying them intently the last few days. I wasn't sure why they were acting distant. Our company didn't have an anti-fraternizing policy. Half the reporters in the newsroom were romantically involved with each other at any given moment.

I had to admit that seeing Erin in my shirt flinted a glimmer of satisfaction in me. Even if she was only wearing it out of necessity, it still made me proud, like she was wearing my varsity jacket instead of Fern's.

"Idiot," I murmured.

"Excuse me?" Yolanda said, her patrician face taking on an even sterner expression than usual.

"Sorry. I was talking to myself. I'm an idiot," I recovered, turning my body fully towards Yolanda, but keeping one eye trained on Erin.

Yolanda narrowed her eyes. "That may be, but what does *that* have to do with the special series we've been talking about. The one on homelessness among high school and college students?"

I tried to recall the conversation I'd only half-listened to. "Look, I think we can all agree that it's a very important topic, however, I believe my China idea is better suited to the series format."

Yolanda pursed her lips but didn't say anything, making me wonder if I'd recovered adequately.

After a moment, she said, "I told you, we don't have the budget for that."

I ripped my gaze away from Erin—who was examining the dessert table with an enthusiasm that made me want to laugh—and turned my attention fully to Yolanda.

"Look, Yo," I said, laughing inwardly when she bristled. She hated it when I called her that. "Funding is just a speed bump. We should pick the topic first and find the funding after. The homeless issue is too big and long-term to cover in a one- or two-week-long series. That topic is better suited to regular check-ins, perhaps once a week over a one- or two-year period so we can see how it's changing. That's something better handled by our domestic desk. But a series on China can be like a snapshot in time. A postcard of China right now. That's the sort of topic that's better suited to a short, intense format like we've been discussing."

Yolanda's brow went up as though considering my words.

I took a deep breath. I'd been pushing the idea of going abroad since before I was named host. I let the idea sink in for a moment before going in for the kill. "No one in public radio has taken a show abroad. It's new and fresh. It'll stand out."

Yolanda's mouth twitched from side to side and then back again. I'd seen that expression when she was gauging people's opinions, as though each side of her mouth was a scale weighing the options. Finally, she sighed. "You're right," her tone, aggrieved.

"Ha." I slapped my hand on the table. "I think that's the first time you've ever said that to me, Yo."

She growled. "Don't get used to it." She swept a lock of grayish-blond hair behind her ear and rose gracefully. "I'll speak to Alex," she said, referring to our executive producer. "Let's talk about it when we get back into the office next week." Then she stalked off without a look backwards, her gaze already focused on Alex.

I shook my head. She gave new meaning to the term workaholic.

Now that I was free of Yolanda's grip, my eyes sought out Erin. She was still at the dessert table. I stood, my feet in motion before I'd even decided to get up.

Although I'd admired her from afar for as long as I'd known her, I was finding it impossible to stay away from her in this retreat environment, without the sterile office walls to remind me that ours was a professional relationship only.

Shoving my hands into the pockets of my cargo pants, I walked up to Erin, leaving a foot of space between us. I was so aware of her presence, the air between us crackled.

I surveyed the dessert table to keep from staring at her. Pumpkin pie, cheesecake, brownies, coconut cream pie, chocolate cake, the table was covered with enough dessert to last me two lifetimes. Then again, I wasn't much of a sweets guy. Food was fuel and I simply didn't expend enough calories to indulge in sugar anymore.

Erin seemed to have other plans though, as she placed a small wedge of pumpkin pie next to a similarly-sized slice of coconut cream and then added a couple of round cookies covered in powdered sugar.

"You're going to eat all that?" I blurted.

Erin frowned. "If it's good, yes." She narrowed her eyes a bit and added, "I might even come back for seconds."

My eyes widened. I couldn't imagine being so indulgent. If I ate that much sugar every day, I'd gain a pound in—I stopped to calculate the calories—eight days. If I ate that way every day for a year, I'd gain forty-five pounds. I wouldn't fit into my shirts, or my pants, I'd need new belts—

I kept going on this train of thought, not even noticing when Erin walked away, although Fern lingered, a confused look on his face.

"Are you going to get anything?" Fern asked, his own plate holding a large brownie and a mound of strawberries.

"What? No," I replied, sounding harsh even to my ears. I wiggled my fingers, still secure in my pockets, and relaxed a bit.

Cocking his head, Fern asked, "If you aren't getting dessert, why did you walk over here?"

I started. Apparently, Fern was very observant. "I…uh…just wanted to see what they had," but the lie sounded lame even to me.

Fern glanced at Erin, standing in line for coffee, and then back to me. After a moment, he said, "Why don't you just talk to her…" his tone almost conspiratorial.

I pursed my lips, twice-surprised. First, why was he encouraging me to talk to his girlfriend? Secondly, was I that easy to see through?

I hadn't had much interaction with Fern at work; there was no reason for a show host to work with a graphic designer directly. Around the office, his size and presence had made him seem like he was in his thirties, but now that we were standing face-to-face, it was clear that Fern was not just younger than me, but *much* younger. His face was the baby-smooth surface of someone in his twenties. Late twenties I assumed, given his emotional maturity.

I cleared my throat to give me time to think because it felt like we were speaking in code. I thought carefully about how to ask the right question. I didn't want to give too much away in case I was misinterpreting him. Finally, I decided on, "And that would be okay with you?"

Fern's lips twitched and his eyes grew knowing. He nodded. "We're just friends. I think I'm like a kid brother to her," he said, rubbing the barely-there scruff of his chin.

I inhaled deeply, my chest feeling somehow lighter.

"Why don't you go talk to her?" he repeated, nodding towards the table set with the coffee service. "You kinda came off like a dick just now."

I frowned. "A dick?"

He gave me a look that told me he thought I was an idiot. "No one likes having their food choices or portion sizes commented on. It's kind of a well-known social norm." He rolled his shoulders back good-naturedly. "I'll consider my enlightening you of this fact as my good deed for the day."

Dang it. I glanced over at Erin again. "Thanks," I said with a chin lift.

Fern returned the gesture, his eyes flicking and head bobbing to Erin again, urging me on.

Clearing my throat, I walked quickly over to the coffee table, grabbed a mug, and ambled up to Erin.

She glanced backwards at the line of people behind her and then shrugged. "What can I do for you, *Clint*." She said my name fast and forcefully, like it tasted bad.

63

"Sorry I was a dick back there," I started, quietly, so only Erin could hear. "I didn't mean to offend you."

Her eyebrow lifted, but she kept her eyes averted.

Switching on my hosting personality, I added, "I was hoping I could buy you a cup of coffee to make up for it." I held up the mug as I forced a smile onto my face.

She rolled her eyes. "The coffee's free, *Clint*." Again, she said my name with a strong fricative "c" and a dismissive "nt," just like my sister had when she was pissed at me.

I lowered my voice and leaned in a bit. "Please," I pleaded. "*Please* let me get you a cup of coffee. I feel like a jerk and I want to make it up to you."

She turned to look at me as the line moved forward. She was next. She pressed her lips into a line. "Fine," she said, waving me forward and then sliding next to me.

Success. I put the coffee mug under the carafe's spigot. "How do you take it?"

"Black," she answered.

"No cream or sugar?"

She lifted her plate of desserts. "What do you call this?" her tone, sarcastic.

I nodded. "I deserved that."

Her face softened and I poured her coffee. Then I gestured towards some tables in the back. "Can we sit together?"

She glanced at the mug in my hand. "Aren't you having any?"

I glanced at my watch. "Nah. My circadian rhythms are all wonky right now. Better not chance it or I'll be up all night. Shall we?"

She nodded; her face curious.

I cupped her elbow with my free hand and guided her away from the masses to an empty table at the far end of the hall, grateful that she didn't resist my lead. "Is this okay?" I asked, putting down her coffee.

Erin glanced around.

We were in the emptiest part of the cafeteria. Out of earshot of everyone else. The dining hall was half empty since the nightly campfire and marshmallow roast had already started. Those who were still in the dining hall were congregating around the coffee and dessert tables.

She shrugged. "I guess."

I pulled out a chair for her and then sat after scooting her in.

"What's up?" She gave me a suspicious look. "If it's about work, can't it wait until Monday?" She took a small bite of pumpkin pie, closing her eyes for a moment as though analyzing the flavors before swallowing. When she swallowed, I traced the movement of the food down her throat as her smooth skin stretched and contracted invitingly.

I sucked in a breath. Man, did I want to watch her do that again.

Instead, she picked up her coffee mug, blew on it carefully, and gave me an expectant look.

Teddy Roosevelt. Watching her blow on the coffee was even better than watching her eat pie. I could stare at her beautiful, pouty lips all day long—eating, speaking, blowing…

I swallowed hard, trying to curb my body's physical reaction when I noticed that she was still waiting for me to explain.

I cleared my throat. "I wanted to thank you for helping me with the pole climb." Thinking about how I'd started flying off the ground when Fern fell sent my heart racing again.

She waved a hand in the air, taking a sip of coffee. "You're welcome. Is that what this coffee date is all about?" her tone sounded more playful as she took another sip.

Date? "Would you *like* a coffee date?" I asked, without thinking.

She cocked her head.

God, I was fumbling like a kid in braces. I'd interviewed world leaders, captains of industry, Nobel laureates, but I couldn't seem to think clearly around Erin Hung.

And it felt glorious.

I hadn't felt this way in a long time.

She furrowed her brow, looking around the cafeteria before leaning in conspiratorially.

"Are *you*—

—asking *me*—

—out?"

She said the sentence slowly, as though piecing together bits of a puzzle, ending it with a pronounced tone of disbelief.

I put my elbows on the table and steepled my fingers. *Is* that what I wanted? The words had come out of my mouth without any thought.

When I couldn't answer my own question, I changed the subject. "My shirt looks good on you."

She blushed and then glanced down, running her hand along her thermal-clad forearm. "It's really warm. I'll wash it before I give it back to you. Okay?"

"That's okay, you don't have to wash it," I said, wanting more than anything to have a shirt with her scent so I could sleep with it. "Keep it for the retreat. Just give it back to me on Monday."

She smiled gratefully. "It's been so hot in L.A. that I didn't pack right for the mountains. This muumuu is way too thin for the nights here." She gestured to her dress.

"It's pretty. What kind of flower is that?" I pointed to the bloom on her dress that was simultaneously strong and graceful, just like her.

She glanced down. "Heliconia," she said, wistfully. "It's funny, when I lived in Hawai'i I never wore muumuus, but now that I'm on the Mainland, I can't seem to get enough of them." She took another sip of coffee. "I guess they remind me of home."

"I can relate. I'm from Boston, and I never ate clam chowder when I lived there, but whenever I see it on a menu, I have to order it."

She gave me a small, encouraging smile and I added, "And I'm not even sure I actually like it, but it just feels like something I'm supposed to do. Like I'm showing my hometown spirit by ordering it."

"That's it exactly," she laughed, a genuine smile lighting up her face. Warm honey oozed through my veins.

I wanted to make her laugh all the time.

She took a bite of coconut cream pie and made a face. "Yuck. That is *not* what coconut should taste like." She washed it down with a quick sip of coffee, and glanced at the empty place on the table in front of me. "So, no dessert, no coffee."

I shrugged. "Coffee is something I drink when I need a pick-me-up, and dessert isn't something I eat." I paused for a moment trying to recall the last time I'd had dessert. When it came to me, I thought, *Was that really the last time?* No way I wanted to share that specific memory, so I said, "Only at birthday parties."

She frowned. "Why?"

Maybe this was a simple question for some people, but for me, it was loaded. Though, I could answer from a practical standpoint easily enough. I knew the exact day, month, and year I'd given up desserts.

However, it wasn't a story I shared. In fact, I could only remember telling it to a few other people and all of them had been family.

But I *wanted* to tell Erin.

I leaned back in my chair. "Off the record?"

Her eyes widened and then she leaned back like she was bracing herself. "Okay."

"I don't want to see this showing up in my press kit," I added.

She traced a cross over her heart, her eyes widening in anticipation.

I sighed, part of me not believing I was actually telling this story. "Pilots have strict height and weight limitations," I started, clasping my hands together on the table. "It's necessary to ensure that we can comfortably fit into a cockpit, reach all the controls, et cetera; but it's also a safety issue. When I was tapped for flight school, I kept going over my limit. Not a lot, but enough that I was told if I didn't get it under control, I'd be cut from the program. So, I gave up desserts. Cold turkey." I said, opening my palms up. "Except for the occasional bite of birthday cake," I added.

She shrugged. "But you aren't a pilot anymore."

"It's a healthy habit. Why change it?" I said simply, even though there was more to it than that. I wasn't quite ready to reveal *all* my secrets.

Her shoulders relaxed and she gave me a pitiful look. But at least I could see she was no longer annoyed with me.

I considered that a win.

"Pumpkin pie is one of my favorite things in the world," she said.

I pursed my lips, unsure if there was any food I'd praise that highly. "I guess I'm more of an 'eat to live' kind of person."

She pushed her plate away and held her mug with two hands.

She'd finished her pumpkin pie, left the coconut cream pie, and taken a bite out of one of the cookies.

"You aren't going to finish that?"

"The coconut cream pie is horrible and the cookies were only *meh*. Not worth the calories." She took a sip of coffee. "Not that I'm worried about it. I climbed the telephone pole nine times today—ten if you count the group exercise—a little pumpkin pie is no big deal, but nothing passes these lips," she said, pointing to her mouth (as if I needed another reason to fantasize about her rosebud pout), "unless I actually enjoy it, and the cookies aren't as good as my cousin's."

My ears perked up. I wanted to learn more about her life. Plus, her comment made me hope she might understand my own food issues. "So, your cousin's cookies are your benchmark?"

Her eyes brightened. "Yes! My cousin, Angela, makes snowball cookies, a.k.a. Mexican wedding cookies. That's what these are called," she said, making a face at the discarded powdered sugar balls on her plate. "She makes them every Christmas to give as presents and mails them out all over the country. When I lived in Honolulu, it was like receiving a bit of winter in the mail. Now that I live here, I help her make them."

A wistful look crossed her face, like she was remembering happy times in the kitchen with her cousin. I could just imagine her face dotted with patches of powdered sugar. The moment passed and she gave the cookies a look of disdain. "I had hoped these would be as good as hers, but I don't know what I was thinking. Hers are the best. She'll be glad to hear it, too." She smiled to herself as if it was a private joke.

It was the first morsel she'd shared about herself, and I loved seeing her private side. There was a softness to her face when she talked about her family that I'd never seen and I found it beguiling. Far from satisfying me, this crumb of information was an amuse-bouche, whetting my appetite and making me hungry for more. "Do you have a lot of family in L.A.?"

She shrugged. "A handful. I'm closest to Angela and her mom, Lillian. Auntie Lillian is my dad's older sister and my favorite aunt. There are a few other, more distant cousins scattered around L.A., but I only see them at family get-togethers. All my immediate family is still in the islands." She paused, her eyes darting away as though she'd said too much.

"Go on," I urged. "I like hearing about your family."

She gave me an uncertain look, moving her head from side-to-side in consideration. After a few seconds, I saw the moment she decided to open up to me. There was a light in her eyes and her shoulders relaxed, like we'd crossed an emotional threshold of some kind.

She traced the rim of her coffee mug as she said, "I actually moved to L.A. *because* of Angela. She inspired me to explore life away from 'the rock'," she said, putting the word in air quotes, "and let me stay at her house when I first moved."

I frowned. "The rock?"

"Yeah, you know, like Alcatraz. Hawai'i can feel like a prison if you can't find a way to make a living there. It's a beautiful prison, which makes it hard to leave." The corners of her mouth lifted sadly, making me think she still missed her hometown. "Thank god for Angela. She gave me a job, a place to live, her car to use. I don't know what I would've done without her." She sighed wistfully.

The look on her face made my heart tighten. "What's the smile for?"

She frowned as though annoyed that she'd been caught. But I was not going to be deterred. Erin was finally opening up to me and I wanted to keep the momentum going. "You had a dreamy smile on your face," I added, thinking I'd like to know how to bring that smile back whenever I wanted.

"Did I? Sorry. I guess I'm just happy because my cousin's back in L.A. right now. She and her family live most of the year in New Zealand, but they came back a couple of weeks ago and it's been nice having her around. I guess the cookies made me miss her."

I felt a pang of jealousy at the affection in her voice, and then felt stupid about it.

Why was I getting so worked up by Erin?

Why was I *letting* myself get so worked up by her?

That wasn't *me*. That wasn't *my* life. I had too much going on to allow a romantic attraction even an inch of soil in which to flourish, and yet I couldn't seem to pull away.

In fact, I didn't want to move anywhere except *closer* to Erin.

She finished her coffee and raised a brow as though wondering why we were still sitting together. "Thanks for the coffee. I guess I'm going to head towards the campfire."

My throat tightened in disappointment—

—but she didn't move.

That hesitation was just the encouragement I needed. I reached out as though to stop her.

Chapter 4: Lost

~Erin~

My eyes flicked to his hand and I waited, secretly hoping that he'd reach out for me; touch my hand, touch my arm, touch me anywhere. The awareness of him had my skin on high alert, tingling with anticipation.

Damn chemical attraction. I could no longer deny it. There was definitely *something* there.

I felt like I'd been waiting for this moment for the last two years, and yet, I wasn't sure why. It wasn't like he'd ever encouraged me. If anything, he'd always been aloof and standoffish.

But today, everything had seemed to change.

Several times throughout dinner I'd caught him watching me, only to look away whenever I made eye contact. When I wasn't looking his way, I felt his gaze like a warm heat, branding me. When he told me why he didn't eat dessert—the most personal thing he'd ever revealed to me—I liked the feeling that he was opening up, perhaps a little too much. It had made my heart feel all warm and fuzzy.

I glanced at his hand again and wondered if I should reach out to him, if he wanted me to touch him as much as I wanted it.

Not likely. The errant thought reminded me of who he was and who I was, and I could have kicked myself.

I must be misreading him.

My eyes traveled over his face, taking in the pinched skin around his eyes and the grim set of his jaw.

He looked trapped, haunted, concerned.

Hardly like a man having lustful thoughts.

More like a man conflicted.

I stutter-breathed and his eyes met mine, questioning. Then they darted behind me, reminding me of where we were.

He pulled his hand back and I was surprised at how disappointed I was at the loss of his anticipated touch. My body still ached from earlier that day when I'd released him after anchoring him; an ache the shape and size of his torso.

I pushed my chair back and stood. He rose simultaneously.

Was he mirroring me? I couldn't tell if he was trying to get closer to me or farther away.

My eyes were drawn to his hands as he shoved them into his pockets, making me wonder if the habit had something to do with his story about giving up dessert.

His spine was curved in the familiar "s" I always saw around the office when his flight deck swagger moved him through the halls in a distinctive swerving amble. But there was one important distinction. In the office, his eyes were usually fixed on the forgettable diamond pattern of the commercial carpeting—his brain somewhere far away, contemplating whatever it was he thought about. However, right now, his chocolate-brown eyes were fixed on me.

My face heated, caught off-guard by the intensity of his gaze, and the sadness lurking there as well. I sensed I was seeing a side of him few saw, and it tugged at my heart, as though he'd just jettisoned a guy line connecting our most fickle of organs.

An unbidden squeak escaped my throat and my face grew warmer.

I resisted the urge to fan myself, but in reality, I couldn't have moved if I'd wanted to. My limbs were frozen in place as though locked by the tractor beam of his eyes.

The seconds passed—

—or was it minutes?

It could have been hours.

I was completely unaware of anything except for his eyes, which I now saw were not strictly one color. The deep chocolate was flecked with ebony and encircled by a ring of caramel.

The sterile cafeteria and the background noise of our coworkers had completely fallen away, and it was just the two of us.

He licked his lips and I gasped at my body's response, a sort of hollow clench that burned in my solar plexus.

Finally, he broke the silence.

"Would you like to go for a walk?" his voice a gravelly whisper, as though the words had fought to get out.

"Yes," I said quickly. Perhaps *too* quickly.

His eyes flicked to the exit closest to us, which also happened to be the one farthest away from everyone else. "We should be discreet."

My heart started to pound and I nodded.

"I'll head for that door," he lifted his chin. "Why don't you bus your tray to the collection area and then meet me? I'll wait for you right outside."

"Okay," I answered quietly, my mouth suddenly dry.

A smile halfway between surprise and jubilation erupted on his face. I'd never seen him smile like that in all the time we'd known each other.

I'd be lying if I said I didn't love it.

He cleared his throat, a suddenly self-conscious look replacing his smile. "I'm going." He angled his body towards the exit and started walking, never breaking eye contact with me, until he walked out the door, his hands shoved deep in his pockets, his lazy fighter pilot swagger on full display.

Damn, was he hot.

I'm not sure how long I stood there staring at the door, thinking—

I'm going on an evening stroll with Clint.

The words sounded surreal in my head.

Clint Davenport, the man who'd never paid more than vague attention to me for two years had asked me to walk with him.

What for the love of Jiminy Cricket is going on?

I suddenly remembered that I was holding my food tray, and quickly bussed it to the kitchen. I walked back towards the exit Clint had used as quickly as I could while feigning casual disinterest.

I took a breath as my fingers pushed down on the cold metal bar, which felt like a decision with its solid resistance, as though I was about to embark on a momentous journey and just needed to push through this moment to get there. With some effort, the door swung open into the dim orange of a bug light.

I glanced around, blinking.

Clint was nowhere to be seen

"Clint?" I called into the darkness.

A large palm pressed into my lower back, a touch like a brand.

"I'm here," he said, practically in my ear, his hot breath blanketing the skin of my neck.

A shiver ran through my torso and it wasn't because of the cold. Clint must have felt my reaction because his hand was still on my back, and I thought I heard him suck in a breath.

"Are you ready?" He asked so quietly that for a second, it seemed he was talking to himself.

Ready? For what? But honestly, it didn't matter. At that moment, I was ready for anything. "Yes," I said on an exhale.

He pressed me forward, we began walking, and it felt like the start of something.

Of what? I couldn't tell you, just *something*.

Funny how a thing as simple as walking can take on so much more meaning.

I could just make out the voices of our coworkers gathered around the campfire.

Now that we were actually moving, my chest loosened and I took a deep breath of the crisp night air. I'd never been in an evergreen forest before the retreat, and the scent was not what I'd expected. I would've thought the collective smell of millions of pine trees would remind me of disinfectant, but instead, there was a creamy sweetness in the air. "It smells so good here."

He took a deep breath and I saw the faint silhouette of a shrug.

Although my eyes had adjusted to the darkness, there was nothing but moonlight illuminating us. Clint's large form was more of a suggestion than a solid shape.

"The air's a lot cleaner up here," he said.

"No, I smell something else, something sweet." Just then, a gentle breeze picked up and I closed my eyes, inhaling the cool, butterscotch kisses of the alpine wind. "*Mmm*, butterscotch," I said quietly.

He chuckled a bit. "You think the air smells like butterscotch?"

"Tastes like, would probably be the more appropriate sense, but taste and smell are so closely related, I'll let it slide," I said, teasingly, surprised by my own boldness.

He groaned quietly as we walked along a path laden with pine needles, outlined by large white rocks that glowed in the moonlight. "That sounds…delicious…" he said huskily.

His voice sent a dull ache echoing through my gut, unlike anything I'd ever felt before. Goosebumps raced along my neck, making me shrug my shoulders at the ticklish sensation. I was grateful that the darkness of our surroundings meant Clint couldn't see the effect he was having on me.

I took another deep breath and noticed that our coworkers' voices were growing fainter, while the sounds of the forest around us grew louder. The moonlight was bright enough that the white stones marking our path visibly glowed, and in the distance, I could still see the dim orange porch lights of the retreat center's cabins. Satisfied that we could find our way back, I allowed myself to be lulled by the beauty around me.

It had been a long time since I'd walked in a forest, and the ones I'd hiked in Hawai'i were not exactly "evening stroll" material.

Hawaiian rainforest trails—if you could call them that—were not much more than a suggestion, frequently crossing areas so lush with life it was impossible to see a delineated path. On the other end of the spectrum were the hikes that were so treacherous they required full sunlight. For instance, the trails along the ridges of the Ko'olau Range could become so narrow, that one wrong step could send a hiker into a ravine too steep and deep for rescue. For these two reasons, my forest experience had been limited to the full light of day. There was something slightly dangerous about a nighttime walk through a forest that added to my anticipation.

We didn't talk much at first, or if we did, it was about mundane things like work and the food at the retreat. But it wasn't the conversation that I remember most.

It was the feeling.

The feeling of walking side-by-side with this man that I'd admired for so long. Because the truth was, Clint was pretty incredible. I mean, why wouldn't I admire him? He was crazy-smart, ambitious—but about things that I valued—and he made stuff happen. Not only that, but he was hotter than a summer's day at the beach. And the confidence that usually rankled? Well, now it was a big turn-on, although if I'd been perfectly honest it probably always had been— which is *why* it had rankled.

There was no denying it, Clint *affected* me.

As we walked in the growing blackness of our surroundings, our arms bumped against each other, every collision creating a sparking sensation in my hand that grew with intensity as the minutes passed. Twice during the collisions, Clint's fingers brushed across the back of my hand, creating a static shock which turned into a tingling that gathered at the inside of my wrist like an erotic itch that needed to be scratched. Every casual touch had me catching my breath and counting to ten to keep myself from combusting, or tackling him to discharge all of the energy that was building inside.

It was exciting, and overwhelming, and confusing.

Finally, I spoke to take my mind off whatever it was that was building between us. I pointed to the brightest point in the sky and asked, "What's that?"

We'd just entered a clearing that was brighter than the area we'd been walking through.

"Venus," he said with an authority that I felt deep in my gut.

This man's brain was going to be the end of me.

"And if you turn a bit that way," he said, putting his hands on my shoulders and turning me to the right, "you might be able to see Jupiter."

Jupi-wa?

His hands on my shoulders—their gentle pressure—had driven all sense from my mind.

He must've taken my silence for confusion because he leaned in, his chin hovering over my shoulder as he pointed upwards.

"Do you see it?" he said, his voice a velvety whisper that had me holding my breath.

I was so tense, my shoulders must have been up to my ears. It was like I was a turtle trying to close in on itself, pull all my bits into my hard shell where he couldn't affect me.

But is that what I really want?

My brain was so muddled. I was too busy being in the moment to be able to think about the moment.

"The cloud cover is coming in; this is your last chance. It's right there," he said, leaning in so close I could imagine what the scruff of his chin would feel like against my neck. It made me shiver.

"Are you cold?"

My face heated. "No, I was just, uh, shaking my head. I can't see Jupiter," I said on an exhale.

He laughed. "You're a horrible liar."

I figured it was dark enough that he couldn't see me blushing, but I wasn't taking any chances, so I started walking again. His quick footsteps playing catchup brought a smile to my face.

"So, how long have you been climbing?" he asked, and I was grateful for the distraction.

"Almost four years…" I said, trailing off. He remained silent as though wanting to know more. Finally, I continued, "I come from a family of surfers, but when I moved to L.A. the water was just…well, let's just say I'm a little spoiled when it comes to beaches. Plus, I was living in the Hollywood area at the time, so the beaches weren't exactly at my doorstep. Back then, I was working at a bookstore and one of the regulars was a climber. She invited me to try it out and I fell in love with it."

"What do you like about it?"

"Huh. No one's ever asked me that." I paused for a moment and then added, "It makes me feel strong, like I can do anything. I love the feeling of approaching a new wall or boulder and knowing that I'm going to conquer it. Plus," I said, shrugging, even though he couldn't see it, "I love that I can do it anytime. With surfing, you're always waiting for the swell, and then you have to find which break has the best waves. It can be time-consuming. But I can climb anytime, like today when I did the telephone pole. I guess what I'm saying is that it's an easy addiction to feed."

After a thoughtful moment, he said, "That makes sense."

I got the feeling that Clint—whether or not he meant to—was always weighing other people's words, and I wanted him to find mine worthy.

It was a little disconcerting.

I redirected. "Do you miss flying?"

I heard him suck in a breath and I wondered if his face was pained or wistful.

"Yeah, of course. It's an incredible feeling." After a pause, he added, "But a lot of the things I miss about being a pilot I've been able to find with *WUA*."

My curiosity was piqued. "Really? Like what?"

"The pressure to excel and the exhilaration that comes with it. That was a huge part of being a pilot. You always have to be prepared and be your best, just like with hosting. If I don't get things right *on* the air, there are consequences, just like when I was *in* the air."

"Dork," I said on a laugh, his attempt at humor immediately putting me at ease.

He chuckled quietly. "Sorry, I couldn't resist. But it's true. If I make a mistake on the air, millions of people here it and you know that someone—more than one person, likely—will call me out. And when I'm interviewing the leader of a foreign nation, I have to make sure not to look like an asshole. I'm representing my country as well as the show. But, I enjoy that kind of pressure. Kind of like how you enjoy the challenge of a boulder." He said the last sentence conspiratorially, like I was an equal.

A giant grin exploded on my face and I was so grateful he couldn't see it. "What else is similar?"

He blew a breath out. "Well, the teamwork. Being a pilot means being a part of a family. Also, believe it or not, I like the rigidity of my schedule. I find it calming."

"You *are* a weirdo," I said, unable to understand how anyone could love a rigid schedule.

He laughed. "Yeah, I've heard that before."

We continued ambling aimlessly, sometimes talking, sometimes not. But the truth was, I didn't want the walk to end. There was something freeing about the dark forest, like the outer world didn't exist or matter. Here it was just the two of us and the trees. We could laugh, we could let our guards down.

Here we could be equals.

It was exhilarating.

I was walking on air.

Eventually, it grew late enough that I could no longer ignore how cold it was getting and I wrapped my arms around my torso. Now that my attention was no longer in fantasy mode, I noticed that our surroundings had grown much darker. Looking up, I saw that a thick layer of clouds had moved in and Venus was no longer visible.

My ears became hypersensitive as my eyes adjusted to the denser darkness of this part of the forest. Every pine needle cracked underfoot with loud splinters. The sound of my clothes rustling with an audible *shush*, the cricket song dominating the environment like a thirty-foot waterfall.

Between the visual deprivation of our surroundings, the electricity thronging between us, and the anxiety of wondering if I was imagining said electricity, I felt like my skin was turned inside out.

"It's so quiet, but so loud," I said over the crickets.

Clint humphed. "Well put."

For someone who made his living speaking, Clint was unusually terse, which only served to set me more on edge.

Every single nerve stood at attention.

Just then, a sharp sound pierced the air—four loud hoots that sounded almost like barks.

"What's that?" I cried out, head whipping around, my eyes trying to find the source of the noise. But I couldn't see a single thing.

Hot breath tickled my ear. "I think it was an owl. Maybe a California Spotted."

A what? My surprise returned me to my body to find that I was wrapped up in Clint's arms, his sinewy torso pressed flushed against mine, the curves of our thighs touching.

"Oh, my—" the words were barely out before I felt his hot breath on my face.

My head swam and I held on tighter.

"Erin?" he whispered.

"Uh-huh?" I answered, unsure if I was capable of saying anything else as long as I was pressed against him like this.

"Can I," he swallowed hard, "kiss you?"

"Uh-huh," I said again, but this time there was no quizzical lift to my words. Before I knew it, his mouth touched mine as softly as a butterfly lands on a flower.

I melted into the gentle warmth of his kiss, the fear I'd felt seconds ago, gone.

When he pulled away, my heart ached at the loss. Before I could question what had happened, his lips pressed against mine again, this time with a bit more pressure, the kiss full of question and wonder.

When the kiss broke, I gasped, wishing I could see his face, wondering what he was thinking, hoping that—

And then he kissed me again—

And this time, there was no uncertainty.

Clint pulled me tight against him, crushing his chest to mine, kissing me with a naked hunger that left me breathless and senseless. Exploring my mouth as though I was some long-lost land he'd been yearning to discover.

It was thrilling.

I wound my hands through his wavy, chestnut hair which felt like cool silk against my fingers, and he moaned into my mouth, the sound reverberating straight to my belly, warming me from the inside out.

I was no longer cold.

I wasn't even sure what cold was anymore.

My whole world tunneled down to the warmth and pressure of Clint's lips and arms. He smelled like mint and cedar, a clean, strapping scent that suited him perfectly.

His tongue swept into my mouth, his lips tender but urgent. I'd never been kissed like this before, forcing me to re-categorize all previous experiences I'd had as simply practice.

This was the real thing. *This* was kissing.

I felt so open, so vulnerable, so wanted.

I grew soft in his arms and he supported me fully, his biceps and forearms closing ranks around my torso, the feeling of his hard, sinewy body lighting me up.

I felt delicious pressure on my back as his hand traveled lower, pressing against the small of my back, his erection growing hard against my belly.

"Oh, Clint," I moaned, a bit of my brain turning back on.

"Erin, honey, baby…"

"Clint," I said, firmer this time.

"Erin, you're so—"

Clint! His name finally pushed its way into my consciousness and I froze. *Oh god, I'm kissing Clint.* Breaking away, I pushed at his chest. "What are we doing?" I asked, breathlessly.

And even though I knew there were a million reasons we shouldn't be kissing, I couldn't think of a single one.

He released me like he'd been scalded. "I thought you wanted to."

I turned away from him, cursing myself for getting carried away by the moment, unable to believe I'd just made such a stupid mistake. While he wasn't my boss, he might as well have been. Kissing Clint was a serious professional misstep, and I needed to get away from him and regroup. But as I made to head back to the dining hall, I came to an abrupt stop.

The darkness around us was total.

There were no porch lights.

There were no glowing path markers.

There was just the void surrounding us.

I had no idea which way to go. "Where are we?" I asked, fear welling up so quickly that I forgot the mental self-flagellation I'd just been giving myself.

I heard, rather than saw, Clint turning around.

He muttered something that sounded a lot like "Abraham Lincoln", the sound of crunching pine needles telling me he was turning this way and that. Finally, the crunching stopped and he let out a breath. "I don't know."

I closed my eyes—which was totally unnecessary and yet, it still felt like the right thing to do—and listened hard. But the only sound was the omnipresent chorus of crickets. "Can you hear anything?"

Silence, and then, "I only got crickets, you?" he said, from somewhere to my left.

"Me, too." I sighed. "Please tell me you have your phone."

"What's the point? No wi-fi, no reception. Mine's dead at the bottom of my bag. You?"

I exhaled heavily. "Same." Instinctively, I stuck out my left hand and reached around, trying to catch the smooth jersey of his shirt and feeling sweet relief—like a cool drink on a warm summer day—when I found it. I pulled his hand into mine, all concerns about overstepping forced out by growing dread. "Mind if we hold hands?" I swallowed hard past the lump in my throat, the thought of becoming separated making my skin prickle with fear.

"Not at all," he said, lacing our fingers together, clasping his other hand over mine, probably sensing my unease.

My pulse slowed a bit. "I think we're lost." The bitter taste of bile filled my mouth.

"Yup, I'd say that's about right," a bit of his radio host swagger inflecting his words.

"You could sound a little less blasé," I hissed.

He pulled me closer, relief flooding my body as he wrapped his arm around my shoulder. "Sorry. Sarcasm calms me. I used to be a total dick when I was in the cockpit."

"We're in the middle of nowhere and it's pitch-black. Aren't you worried?" My voice reached into the squeak register.

He clucked. "Really, it's more like an ombré of grays than pitch-black."

Anger welled up in my core and I elbowed him in the ribs, satisfaction filling me when he humphed and then gasped for air. But he didn't complain. *Maybe this is his way of calming me down.* It took a second, but I *was* a little calmer. His sarcasm definitely made him seem in control. "Okay, Mr. Ombré of Grays. You aren't worried?"

He took a long, dramatic breath. "On a scale of one to ten, one being 'not at all' and ten being 'oh shit, a bear is going to eat us', I'm about a four." He gave my shoulder a reassuring squeeze. "Look, the good news is, we can't be far from camp. We didn't walk that long, and since we're close to human civilization, the likelihood of any large animals being in the area is highly unlikely." His voice was a calming tenor that seemed to massage the edge of my nerves. "Besides, it could be worse," he said, conspiratorially.

"Really? How?"

"You could be stuck in the woods with Harry Hinkley."

I laughed louder than I would have thought possible given the situation. But once that subsided, the reality of our situation set in again. I wasn't as convinced as he was that there were no large animals; after all, the area was named Big Bear. But I didn't want to dwell on that. "I don't think we should just stand here."

After a beat, he said, "Agreed, but we shouldn't wander, either. We need to act strategically."

I took a few deep breaths and gathered my thoughts. "Why don't we shuffle our feet until we run into that border of rocks that edges the path. At least then we'll know if we're still *on* the path."

"Good idea. Once we find it, we'll follow it for twenty minutes in one direction. If we don't start seeing the cabins, we'll turn around and walk back. At least we have a fifty-fifty shot."

"Assuming the path doesn't diverge anywhere."

He trilled the air with his lips in a sound of disappointment. "Okay, thirty-seventy shot. Thanks, Ms. Probability."

I smiled, grateful we had a plan and that I was with someone so calm. "Okay. Let's move to our right."

We shuffled right, his arms still around my shoulder like we were in a potato sack race. Since the path was only about five feet wide, it didn't take long for us to knock into some large rocks.

"Found something." I pivoted my foot to the side and tried to determine if the rock was part of the path markers, quickly feeling another similarly sized rock and then another with the outside edge of my shoe. They seemed to be spaced equally apart. "Do you feel them? I think it's the border."

"Agreed. Do you have a preference if we walk right or left?" he asked.

I looked left and right and was about to answer when I got distracted by the complete void of blackness. I held my free hand two inches from my face and wiggled my fingers. I couldn't see a single thing.

My heart started fluttering, fast and turbulent like the wings of a hummingbird, making me feel dizzy. Even though I knew logically that I hadn't moved, without the visual confirmation that I was standing still it felt like I was listing to my left. I widened my stance, shook my head, and focused on thinking about the solid ground I knew was beneath my feet, even though I couldn't see it. I squeezed Clint's hand to further orient myself.

"Hey? Are you okay?" He pivoted so he was directly in front of me, placing steadying hands on my shoulders.

I nodded, and then remembered he couldn't see it. "Yeah. I'm just a little overwhelmed by the dark."

He must have moved closer because when he spoke, I could feel his breath on my face. "We are going to be fine," he said calmly, his voice pitched lower than usual. "You have to keep your head on. I use sarcasm to diffuse discomfort. Do you have something you find comforting?"

I swallowed hard and said the first thing that came to mind. "I sing."

"Fantastic. That's good. Why don't we sing a song together? Pick one."

I thought for a moment. "Do you know "Do-Re-Mi" from *The Sound of Music*?" A tiny part of my brain couldn't believe that I was having this conversation. I was lost in the forest with one of the most famous voices on American radio, about to sing a Rodgers and Hammerstein song. It was almost inconceivable.

"I think I could follow along. You start."

"*Doe a deer...*" I started singing uncertainly, as though I was giving our location away to the enemy with every note. But then I noticed how the cricket song was beginning to recede and it made me feel better.

I sang a bit louder, the happy rhythm of the notes giving me confidence, bright daylight images of Maria Von Trapp starting to flicker through my brain.

Then I sang louder still and Clint joined in, occasionally humming because he wasn't sure of the words.

"Feel better?" he asked, in between notes.

"Yes," I said, and continued to sing, the familiar, happy words soothing me in a surprising way.

"Great. Let's sing and walk. I'm going to take your hand again and we'll start going to the left, okay?" he said, never losing the rhythm of the song. "Hold your other hand out and sweep it in front and to the side of you so we don't walk into any trees. Let's start slow, I'll keep my foot against the rock path. *Me a name…*" he began to sing again without missing a beat.

I followed his lead and moved my legs, which felt heavier. But after a few feet, a bit of my confidence returned, and by the time we'd sung the song four times, Clint knew all the words, and our combined voices had beaten back the sound of the crickets completely. We walked, swung our arms, and sang the song about a dozen more times when Clint suddenly stopped.

"The path's ended," he said. "There aren't any more rocks."

My heart tightened. "How long have we been walking?"

He lifted our wrists, the faint green glow of his watch hands telling us we'd walked for almost twenty minutes. Clint sighed. "Do you want to turn around?"

"No, not yet." I couldn't say why, but something was tickling the edge of my subconscious. "Let's shuffle to the other side of the path and feel for the rocks there."

"Okay, keep sweeping your hand around."

We inched our way in the opposite direction, but still, there was no path. "Clint. Let's walk forward, slowly, with our hands out." I had a familiar feeling.

"Okay," he said, his tone, liquid trust.

I appreciated that he didn't question my hunch.

We took tentative steps, practically tiptoeing our way forward, when my toe hit something solid and smooth. I moved my foot left and right along a straight line, lifting it up and placing it down.

A step.

"Clint, I think we found a cabin," I said, allowing myself to feel excited.

When Clint mentioned the path ended, some part of me had remembered how the path had ended just before my own cabin. "There's a concrete step here."

By the way he was pulling my arm, I could tell he was searching for it, too. I felt his foot next to mine. "Sweet baby Moses, you are a genius." After a pause, he said, "Found the handrail."

I reached forward and sighed with relief as my hand clasped the cold aluminum. "Let's go inside." If this cabin was like all the rest, it wouldn't have a lock.

We stepped onto another concrete step, then another before transitioning to two wooden steps. Finally, we were on the tiny front deck that all of the cabins had.

I took a deep breath and felt the adrenaline leaking out of my body. I was going to sleep like a rock tonight.

The screen door creaked and I could easily "see" the cabin's layout in my mind. Two front doors—a screened one followed by a wooden one—and then we'd be inside the one-room space.

"This way." Clint pulled me so I was directly behind him.

I felt the screen door against my forearm just as the wood door started to creak open.

Suddenly, a dim orange light went on, nearly blinding me. Clint must have found the switch for the front porch.

Tears perked in my eyes. Light had never looked so good before.

Clint released my hand and a second later, the glow of the cabin's single lamp came on, bathing the room in buttery light.

I walked into the small space, closed the door behind me, and let out a loud exhale, overwhelmed with relief that flooded my limbs with exhaustion.

Clint turned to me and smiled, a mixture of regret and uncertainty as he gave my shoulder a friendly squeeze and then let go.

The gesture had a strange finality to it.

It reminded me of earlier that day and the emptiness I'd felt when I had let go of him during the pole challenge.

But now wasn't the time to contemplate that. We might no longer be lost in the woods, but we still weren't back in the safety of the main campsite.

I surveyed the room. It was furnished just like the one I was staying in, which probably meant—

I rushed to the nightstand wedged between the unused twin beds; their mattresses bare except for a single rolled-up blanket on each. As I yanked open the nightstand drawer, an excited breath escaped my throat. I found an orange flashlight, just like the one in my cabin. I switched it on but nothing happened. Unscrewing the back of the flashlight, I cursed when I saw the white corrosion on the batteries. I checked the second nightstand and found the same thing.

"Looks like we're at the very edge of the grounds," Clint said.

I walked over to the front door where Clint was studying a map nailed to the back of it. I'd forgotten about the map. I'd glanced at the one in my cabin the first day I arrived, but I didn't need it once I became oriented to the retreat site.

I looked at the laminated map where a cabin with the number "83" was circled in permanent marker. It was at the outer edge of the illustration.

"What cabin are you in?" I asked, feeling a bit of anxiety at the dawning realization that we might be spending the night together in cabin eighty-three.

"Eleven," Clint said. "You?"

"Thirty-seven. If there are two of us to every cabin—"

Clint cleared his throat. "There are about a dozen of us with our own cabins."

I blinked. "What?"

He shrugged. "The hosts. The senior producers."

I rolled my eyes, too tired to truly be incensed…but still, "Of course you do. Anyway, still, we can't be using more than fifty cabins. I'm assuming it's the ones closest to the center of camp." I sighed as I studied the map, noting how the cabins got farther and farther apart as the numbers climbed. "There's no way we'll find our way back tonight, will we?"

He clucked his tongue. "Not without a flashlight. Besides, who knows if this drawing is to scale. The way it's drawn it looks like my cabin is equidistant between the dining hall and the ropes course, and that's not accurate."

I sighed, cursing inaccurate maps and corroded batteries before flopping onto a bed, the rusty springs squeaking in protest.

See what happens when you do stupid things like walking into the woods with a coworker. How could I have been so dumb?

I'd always been a good girl, a rule follower, and there I was, not even breaking a rule—although there was definitely something forbidden about the situation—and I wasn't even going to get away with it. I was going to have to do the "Walk of Shame" with Clint tomorrow, and I hadn't even earned it.

The unfairness of it all left a bitter taste in my mouth.

Clint crossed the room, sitting gracefully on the other mattress, the springs of his bed making nary a sound. "Look. At least we aren't stuck in the woods anymore. We have shelter, we have blankets. I'd say our situation has improved about a thousand percent from ten minutes ago, and good on you for trusting your instincts when I was ready to turn back."

I pursed my lips and sighed. "I guess you're right," although I was still annoyed. I should have stayed with Fern at the campfire. I could practically hear my mother's voice, *"Bad things happen to bad girls, Erin."*

My mother had been born and raised in a small town in Colorado before moving to Honolulu for college, and—except for the occasional vacation to California or trip home to visit her parents—had never left the islands. She was a small-town girl with small-town values and she would have been mortified at this situation.

I cringed.

"Are you cold?" Clint asked. He reached out and then pulled back when I leaned away from him.

I started to shake my head, but then I realized that I was in fact cold. But I was also tired.

Sooooo tired.

I yawned, covering my mouth with my fist. "I *am* cold…and tired, too."

He nodded. "You're crashing from the adrenaline. Let's get to sleep." He glanced at his watch. "It's not even ten o'clock yet. If we go to sleep now, we'll be up early enough to get back to our cabins without anyone noticing."

I frowned, wondering if it was important to him that nobody saw us together. I bit back the question; there was something more urgent at hand.

He must have noticed my discomfort, because he asked, "What's wrong?"

After a moment's hesitation, I relented. "I have to pee."

A relieved look crossed his face. "Me, too. Let's go." He stood and opened the door, pausing when I didn't follow. "You coming?"

I crossed my arms over my chest. "I'm not peeing in front of you."

He rolled his eyes. "Okay. I'll be right back."

He was gone for a few minutes when I heard a sound like running water and then he reappeared in the door frame, his body filling the space.

Why was he so darn beautiful?

"There's a spigot on the right side of the cabin, exactly where the one on my cabin is located. The water is potable. Want me to show you?"

I nodded and followed him outside. The silver glimmer of the spigot was highlighted by the porch light. I glanced around the clearing in front of the cabin, and saw the path back to the campsite clearly illuminated about ten feet away, the rocks edging it visible on either side. It no longer seemed scary now that there was light. "You can go inside, I'm fine."

He nodded and closed the door.

I walked over to where the path sloped downward, pulled up my muumuu, and then did my business. Sweet relief. I washed my hands and took a few gulps of water, certain that I'd never tasted water that sweet.

Fatigue overcame me. My body felt boneless and I wanted nothing more than to wrap myself in my blanket and forget the stress of the evening. I hadn't realized just how frightened I'd been in the forest. But now that I was safe, I could acknowledge just how scary it had been.

When I re-entered the cabin and lifted my eyes towards the mattress, I froze in place as I took in the bare skin of Clint's broad, muscular back.

My jaw dropped.

He must not have heard me enter because the next thing I knew, he was undoing his belt buckle. His cargo pants fell to the floor, revealing navy-blue boxers with a white check pattern. He bent down to pick up his pants and the thin cotton stretched taut around his runner's thighs.

Oh god.

I must have unwittingly made a sound, because he turned, a cocky smile tugging at the side of his mouth. "Like what you see?"

Instead of answering his smug question, I straightened my back and held up a hand to shield my eyes while walking over to my bed. I kicked off my shoes and picked up my blanket, wrapping it around myself as Clint cleared his throat.

"Yes?" I answered, keeping my face averted.

"These are summer blankets. I think we should..."

I wasn't used to him sounding uncertain. My curiosity piqued, I turned around, keeping my eyes squarely on his face and raised a brow. "You think what?"

At least he had the grace to look embarrassed.

After a second, he said, "I think we should sleep together to stay warm. It was in the thirties last night. These blankets aren't going to be sufficient. They aren't as insulating as the sleeping bags back at our cabins."

There was no way in hell I was going to sleep in the same bed with Clint Davenport.

What if people came looking for us? What if they found us? What would they think of us, cuddled up in bed together, Clint in nothing but his boxers?

I shivered at the thought.

"No thanks. I'll take my chances." Then I remembered that I'd be warmer with my hair down, so I sat up, undid my braids, and ran my fingers through my hair. I gave my scalp a quick massage—not as good as a proper brushing with my koa wood comb and a few drops of castor oil—before replaiting everything into a loose three-strand I could sleep on.

When I looked up, Clint was watching me with hawkish attention.

He cleared his throat. "Suit yourself." He pulled his long-sleeve shirt back on. "Let me know if you change your mind. I'll be the guy who's trying to sleep but is actually freezing." He gave me a disarming smile and then turned away from me, wrapping his blanket around him before lying on the bare mattress.

After a few moments, he said, "Good night, Erin," in a quiet voice. "I had a nice evening with you, despite getting lost in the woods."

I hesitated, but then said, "Me, too." It *had* been a nice evening…until the kiss; or maybe because of it.

My head felt heavy with confusion and exhaustion. Maybe everything would be clearer in the morning. All I knew was that the fear and anxiety of getting lost had killed whatever good vibes the kiss had created.

I reached up and clicked off the lamp.

Darkness fell and I was asleep within moments.

Clint—on the other hand—was not so lucky.

Chapter 5: Survival

~Clint~

At first, I had difficulty sleeping because I was sharing a room with Erin. I hadn't slept in the same room with a woman in about a decade, so to say I was distracted was an understatement. You know what they say, "out of sight, out of mind"? Yeah, well, this was the opposite.

My body tingled but I wasn't sure why. Unease? Desire? Hope? Probably all of the above.

Whatever it was, it wasn't helping me sleep.

Mother Teresa. I cupped my hands to my forehead and replayed the night's events, paying particular attention to the moment when we kissed. Playing and replaying the scene in super slow motion, my body betraying my ability to compartmentalize or deny what I'd felt between us.

I hadn't planned on kissing Erin tonight. Hell, I hadn't even planned on going on a walk with her. But I couldn't *unfeel* the softness of her lips, I couldn't *unremember* the way my body had reacted, and I couldn't *unravel* the feelings that had been developing for her ever since the first day we had met.

I'd watched from afar as she'd blossomed from a quiet, young woman who'd just left home for the first time, into the smart, strong woman that she was now. Today was just one more day of an attraction that had been building for years.

How could I retreat from that?

And yet, I knew I had to.

I didn't want her to be collateral damage.

There were things about me that Erin didn't know; things I couldn't burden her with. She deserved more than the life I could give her, full of baggage that she'd never choose.

But now that we'd kissed, I wanted more.

"Teddy Roosevelt," I muttered and Erin moaned quietly in response.

My body liked the sound of that.

The second reason I couldn't sleep was because I was off my usual routine.

Hosting a national news show while based in California meant that I was used to being in bed by eight, asleep by eight-thirty so I could wake at midnight and hit the trails. After my run, I'd shower, power my first meal—a four-egg omelet on low-carb days, oatmeal with almonds on high-carb days—and then mosey into the newsroom for a two-a.m. editorial meeting.

Upon arrival, I'd be greeted by a room of two-dozen reporters made up mostly of overnight staff who'd been in the office since eight p.m. the night before, monitoring the newswire. After agreeing on what international and domestic news stories we would cover that day, I'd head to my office.

For two intense hours, I'd concentrate on refamiliarizing myself with any prerecorded stories that would be airing that day. These were stories that had a longer shelf life than the day's news and might've been recorded days or weeks earlier. I'd write my intros and outros for each segment that would hopefully string my four-hour show together from beginning to end elegantly and cohesively (on a good day). At some point, I'd eat my second breakfast of the day, maybe plain yogurt with berries or a green apple with a dab of almond butter.

Yup, I was a party animal.

Then at five a.m. Pacific, I'd slide into the hosting chair, slip on my *WUA* branded headphones, and greet millions of listeners with the show's signature tag line, "Wake Up, America!", hoping I didn't sound like a total cheeseball.

But I couldn't change the tag line. Listeners had been hearing it for decades. It was part of the show's shtick and the burden of all of *WUA*'s hosts.

You see, I wasn't the only host, I was just the "senior host." The East Coast host went on the air at five a.m. Eastern. I was considered the show's lead host because I greeted the East Coast at eight a.m. their time and was on the air through most of the West Coast's morning commute. So, the largest percentage of *WUA*'s audience heard my mellifluous tenor every day.

Morning and evening "drive time shows" were the most prestigious in radio, because of their high listenership, and *WUA* was one of the most respected and most listened to radio programs in the country. The show had been on the air for over two decades, making its hosts household names in a long string of household names.

At nine a.m. Pacific, I'd sign-off for the day and then head to my office for a two-hour nap, followed by meetings and interviews to create content for future shows.

At two p.m. I was out the door.

This week-long retreat was doing a number on my circadian rhythms, which were already messed up after years of being on *WUA*'s overnight shift.

It had taken me months to get used to my schedule when I'd been hired as part of the *WUA* overnight crew, clocking in at eight p.m. every night and leaving at five in the morning. The transition from that schedule to my new one had been a welcome change.

No one appreciated sunlight like a person who's worked the overnight shift.

So there I was, lying stock-still, eyes wide, staring at the ceiling, feeling uncomfortably wide awake. I'd stared at the ceiling so long I was starting to make out the pattern of the woodgrain. The cricket song had died down as the night matured, the only sound now was Erin's gentle breathing in the other bed.

And man, did I envy her sleep. In my next life, I wanted to be a cat—a big cat, of course, a lion or a tiger; top of the food chain—but a cat nonetheless, just so I could catch up on the sleep I lost in this lifetime. Between flying night missions in the military and working overnight at *WUA*, I had a lot of sleep coming to me.

Another challenge to my sleep was that I was a back sleeper. As the night air grew cooler, I had to huddle in the fetal position to retain my body heat. It helped a little, but not enough. Although the screened windows were covered by wood shutters, they served more to keep animals and light out and did very little to insulate against the cold.

For the first time in my life, I wished I had a little more body fat.

Then, somewhere around three in the morning, a new noise caught my ear; a mild chattering sound. At first, it seemed the wind was knocking at the shutters, but then realized the sound was coming from Erin. She must be getting cold too.

I was wide-awake, and very, very cold.

"Are you awake?" I whispered.

"Uh-huh," she said, her chattering louder.

"I'm cold and it sounds like you are as well. Are you ready to share body heat?" I asked, mostly keeping the hope out of my voice.

I heard a loud sigh.

"Fine, but not under the same blanket."

I rolled my eyes. I'd gotten over any Puritanical body issues in the military. I'd spoon a billy goat if it meant I'd get a good night's sleep. "No problem," I said, although there was a part of me that was disappointed. But right now, that part was too cold to protest. I stood, walked to her bed, and spooned her with my blanket swaddled around me.

"Is it okay if I put my arm over you?"

"Yes. *Please.*" She was chattering loudly now.

I wrapped an arm around her waist and took a deep breath. She smelled of something paradoxically floral and rich. I couldn't place it, and I would've spent more time trying to figure out the scent, however, now that my arm was around her, I felt her shivering. "Give me your hand."

"Whuh? No. Gotta seep," she slurred, without any real energy to her words.

My skin prickled with fear and I reached under her blanket and felt for her hand. She didn't protest.

Her skin was icy.

I grasped her wrist. Her pulse was weak.

Slurred speech, shivering, low energy, cold extremities; she was displaying the warning signs of hypothermia.

I unwound both our blankets, sat her upright, and lifted off the thermal she was wearing until it hung around her neck like a heavy muff.

"Whatareyou…whatareyou…" she couldn't finish her thought.

Confusion. Another symptom. My heart rate spiked.

I moved faster—too focused to be scared—whipping off my own shirt and wrapping it around her head like a makeshift turban. Then I reached down to lift up her dress, but its long skirt was twisted around and between her legs.

"Erin?"

She didn't answer.

"Shit, fuck, shit." I sat up, gripped the neckline of her dress, and tore the fabric down the middle, far enough so I could lay my bare chest against her back.

She was still silent.

I threw the blankets back over our bodies, tucking them in as best I could, and then pulled her against me, wrapping my arms around the outside of her arms and pulling them back towards her chest to retain her body heat. I nuzzled my scruffy chin into the side of her neck, trying to get as much of our skin touching as possible. Then I did the same with our legs.

She was still shivering.

I hugged her tight. "Come on, Erin. Say something." When she didn't answer, I cursed again.

I had one move left, but she wasn't going to like it.

But I didn't have any choice—if she went into hypothermic shock, she could die.

With my left hand, I rubbed the broad expanse of skin between her neck and breasts, generating heat with the friction. Then I used my other hand to do the same on her stomach, rubbing her like I was trying to start a fire on her skin. As I rubbed, I kept repeating, "Erin, can you hear me?"

After ten minutes, she stopped shivering, and my body was toasty with all the effort. Ten more minutes, and her hands were no longer icy.

Sweat beaded across my hairline, but when she said my name, it was all worth it.

"Clint?" she called, all breathy confusion. "What's on my head?"

I laughed, surprised, but grateful for her words. Her speech was clear and strong.

I exhaled, suddenly realizing how tense I'd been. Her hypothermia had scared me far more than being lost in the woods.

Finally remembering her question, I answered, "It's my shirt. Humans lose a lot of body heat through our heads. You were starting to get hypothermia."

"I what?"

She still hadn't mentioned the fact that my hands were on her chest and we were spooning skin to skin. I needed to explain quickly. "You were developing hypothermia. I had to warm you up fast. That's why I'm holding you this way. I didn't want you to lose consciousness."

Fuck. If she had lost consciousness out here in the woods…

I shook the thought away and pulled her tighter, fighting back the urge to lay a kiss on her shoulder.

"You're okay. Everything's fine," I murmured, probably more for me than for her.

I heard a light snore. She'd fallen asleep.

I touched her nose. It was toasty.

"Sweet baby Moses," I muttered, my forehead falling against her head, exhaustion overcoming me.

For now, I would sleep. Tomorrow, there would be hell to pay.

Chapter 6: What Now?

~Erin~

The next morning, I awoke slowly, the way you do from one of those rare slumbers where it's like you're waking from a dreamworld where one has slept on a cloud. Everything felt hazy, but in a translucent, foggy way and not a hungover, throbbing sort of way. I felt cozy and coddled, like a baby wrapped in swaddling.

It was delicious. I couldn't remember my bed ever feeling this nice.

After a few moments of lying blissfully still in the land of the half-asleep, I became aware of being thirsty and decided to get up, but found I couldn't move my limbs. Was I burrito-rolled in my blanket? I tried opening my eyes, but rectangular lines of piercing white against black forced me to squint. Once my eyes adjusted and the lines came into focus, I realized they weren't lines but bright sunlight trying to force itself into the cracks of shuttered windows.

Shutters? I don't have shutters.

Then I remembered where I was.

I'm still on the retreat.

I yawned and tried lifting my arms to stretch then I realized that I wasn't being held in place by a blanket but by a set of arms.

I screamed and a hand clapped over my mouth.

"Relax, it's just me," a man's voice said soothingly. His breath on the shell of my ear sent a warm thrill through my body when recognition dawned. It was the voice that accompanied me every morning on my commute.

But why was I in bed with that voice?

Then I *really* woke up and the memories of the previous night flooded my brain.

Darkness. Fear. Relief. Cold. Clint's voice urgent and then soothing.

Although I was no longer confused, my heart continued racing as Clint unwound his arms from my body and I bit back the urge to ask him to stay.

The bed groaned as Clint got up and I lifted the thin cotton blanket to my throat and turned to face him.

His palms were out, his face laced with concern, his bare chest annoyingly distracting. "How are you feeling?" he asked as he pulled his blanket over his shoulders and sat on the other bed.

It took a second for me to stop thinking about how beautifully sculpted his lean chest was, all those peaks and valleys that I wanted to explore.

Then I remembered myself and glanced at my watch. It was six-thirty. Breakfast started at seven. If I hurried, I might be able to get back to my cabin without anyone seeing me. I could tell my roommate that I'd gone out for an early hike if she asked.

A tiny corner of my brain heard Clint begging me to let him explain, but I was too focused on getting out of the cabin as quickly as possible to respond to him.

What's on my head? I reached up and pulled what must have been Clint's shirt, only it had been wrapped around my skull like a turban. I threw it on the bed.

I needed distance from him so I could think clearly and figure out how to pick up the pieces after our kiss last night.

Spying my shoes, I swiveled my legs over the side. I felt cold air on my back and the sleeves of my dress began sliding down my arms. "What happened to my dress?" I hissed as I grabbed at the sleeves, yanked them up, tucking them into my bra straps to hold my dress up.

He actually looked annoyed for a second, which pissed me off even more. "That's what I've been trying to tell you. Haven't you heard a word I said?"

Even though he was shirtless, my angry confusion made it easy to ignore the firm ridges of muscle that delineated his chest and abs.

Well, almost easy.

Focus. You need to get back to camp.

I felt a weight around my neck and pulled it off. It was the thermal he'd lent me yesterday. At least it was intact. I got an idea and tied the ripped edges of my dress's neckline behind my neck like a halter. Then I shrugged on the thermal which was long enough to cover the tear in my dress. I untied the laces of my sneakers and started putting them on.

"Erin, wait. Let's talk for a second." He leaned forward, so close that he could touch me if he just extended his arm.

I held out my hand to stop him.

If he touched me, there was no telling what I'd do.

I wasn't sure if I wanted to slap him or jump him.

Or maybe both.

"Clint, I just want to get back to camp before anyone sees us. Clearly, nothing happened. I mean, it's not like you roofied me or anything, right?"

I watched him considering my words like he might argue, but then he stood up and threw the blanket off and my brain went blank again.

His chest was like Kryptonite mixed with chloroform, making me feel faint and boneless. I pushed my palms into the mattress to steady myself.

He leaned past me to grab the shirt I'd had on my head, close enough so I could smell him.

I had to fight not to close my eyes and inhale deeper like a total creeper.

He stepped away and shrugged on his shirt. "Okay. You're right. We should go. I can explain on the way."

His words caused me to snap back to attention. "No. No. No." I shook my head. "*I'm* walking back alone. Give me a ten-minute head start. We'll talk later," I said quickly, walking to the door without a backward glance.

Clint's fingers encircled my wrist, pulling me back. "Hold on a second."

His touch was hot, sparking my temper fueled by embarrassment and something else I couldn't name. *How had I gotten into this situation?* The only thing I could do to keep it from getting worse was to make sure we weren't caught by our coworkers.

I shook his hand loose. "I *said* we'll talk later."

And then I bolted.

I didn't hesitate as I walked through the cabin door, the screen banging shut behind me. When my feet hit the dirt, I jogged for a few hundred feet. Hot tears of confusion pricked my eyes as the cold mountain air slapped my cheeks. But I was too worked up to be bothered by the cold.

Embarrassment, confusion, and *something else* fed my internal combustion.

I felt hot as I put distance between us.

Stupid, dumb, idiotic.

Although my youth had been filled with "do first, think later" acts, I hadn't done anything this thoughtless in years, and the old habit of negative self-talk roared back with a vengeance.

I walked faster, palming at the hot tears that turned instantly cool as they leaked out of my eyes.

I'd worked hard the last four years to build myself up. Leaving Honolulu—the only place I'd ever lived—at twenty-eight had been a big step. People always thought of Hawai'i as paradise, as though nothing ever went wrong there, but it wasn't true.

Yes, it was beautiful, but people were still people.

I probably never would've left at all if it hadn't been for my cousin, Angela, and her wedding in New Zealand.

Four Years Earlier
Waiheke Island, New Zealand

I'd never attended such a glittering event. Even before the wedding started, I knew it would be an experience that was going to live on in my memory forever. It wasn't just the spectacular vineyard setting, high on a hill overlooking a white sand beach, nor was it the starched linens and sparkling place settings. It wasn't even the delicious food and wine provided by the restaurant and vineyard Angela and her new husband owned.

What made this event unforgettable were the guests.

I'd never been around so many sophisticated and interesting people.

How was I supposed to make conversation with these elegant urbanites and not come off like some country mouse?

The pre-wedding cocktail reception had been a breeze since I'd been able to hang out with family. But dinner was a whole other story. Angela had placed me at a table with a bunch of her friends. There was nowhere to hide here.

At one point, I remember sitting in my dining chair, looking around the table at the other nine people seated with me, at a complete loss for what to say. To steady my nerves, I ran my hands over my thighs, caressing the black silk charmeuse slip-dress Angela had lent me, its liquid softness a welcome distraction. I'd never worn anything so beautiful and was grateful that Angela had helped me at least look like I belonged—even if I didn't feel like it.

I prayed for the bread course to start so I could have something to do with my mouth.

At one point I glanced up and saw Angela weaving in between the tables with her new husband, glowing with an inner light. I was one of the few people who knew that she was already pregnant, and that news, combined with being newlywed and in love, had made her positively radioactive with happiness.

I allowed myself to wallow in the (never productive and always bad-mood-inducing) wonderings about whether marriage or motherhood were in my future. However, I quickly stopped that because I had more important things to think about than my love life. I needed to think about my life-life, full stop.

The second reason I didn't want to waste time thinking about my love life was because of how entirely inexperienced I was on the subject. I'd been on less than a dozen dates in my entire life and my sex life was, well, it was nonexistent.

A memory of a hot, humid day in the rainforest flashed through my mind and I shivered. My first experience with sex had not been pleasant.

It had been seven years earlier, so I don't remember exactly what I'd been expecting, but it had probably been something romantic like orchestra music or fireworks. I'd been naïve like that. Of course, when you're having sex deep in the Hawaiian rainforest, it's kind of hard to hope for either, literally or figuratively.

No, what I remembered most were two things.

The first was the sound of Roy Nunes's labored breathing beneath me. I might have been a virgin, but I was no dummy. I wasn't going to be the one lying on the iron red mud of the rainforest.

The second was the mosquitoes. Honestly, I'd been so distracted by the incessant buzzing and biting, that I barely remembered anything else. Instead of using my hands to explore Roy's rock-hard chest, sculpted from hours of surfing, I'd needed them to swat at the insects threatening to turn me into a living pin cushion.

Romantic it was not.

However, I'd accomplished my (admittedly questionable) goal of "losing" my virginity. Not that it was something I'd wanted to get *rid* of; it's just that I was super curious about what was on the *other side*. After all, I'd been about to turn twenty and I was the only one of my friends who still hadn't experienced sex, and (damn it!) I wanted to know what all the hoopla was about.

Roy was a nice guy and had seemed like a good choice for my first time. We met in our astronomy class at U.H. and dated for a few months. Since I didn't want to be a notch on some guy's bedpost, when I found out Roy was a virgin too, I'd made it my mission to bed him.

So after our class together ended, I invited him to go hiking, and brought a condom, along with all of my (somewhat misguided) determination.

And I'd "succeeded."

However, the whole experience had been so disappointing—sweat in my eyes, mosquito bites all over my body, red mud smeared all over my clothes—that I never signed up for round two.

I wasn't like my cousin, who seemed to fall in love easily and frequently. I'd never met anyone who'd made me feel like taking a chance and seeing if it could be better. My mom had always said I was just like her when it came to love. That one day I would find someone, and that would be it; game over. That's how my mom had felt about my dad. Of course, considering how well they've turned out, I wasn't sure if those were exactly #relationshipgoals.

And although Honolulu might feel like a city, in many ways it was a small town.

Our house was located in the hills above Honolulu, tucked between the verdant green Koʻolau Mountains (a.k.a. "Country") and the bustling, tourist-heaven of downtown (a.k.a. "Town"). And everybody knew—or was related to—everybody.

By the time I was twenty-seven, most of my friends had either left for the Mainland or already had kids. And as much as I loved where I was from, I'd had enough.

Been there. Done that.

I wanted more.

Especially now.

Because at that moment, I was sitting at a table of the most interesting, accomplished, worldly *single* people I'd ever been exposed to.

I'd just watched Angela get married to Soren Lund, one of the most dashing—a word that seemed invented for him—men I'd ever met…I mean, seriously, I didn't think guys like him even existed. He was like an office-appropriate version of Thor. And not only was Angela incandescent with love, but she was also a successful children's book author, pregnant with her first child, and she was *thirty-two*.

Remembering Angela's age made my heart burst with hope. Despite what my friends back home might think, I started to believe that maybe I wasn't too old to live the life of my dreams.

That was the moment that I decided to leave Honolulu.

But where should I go?

I looked around the table hoping to absorb by osmosis these people's secrets for success. Angela had sat me at the "singles" table with a number of her friends from business school, as well as a couple of Soren's siblings. There was Celina, Soren's sister who was co-CEO of Lund Enterprises along with Soren; Filip, Soren's brother who was CFO of Lund Enterprises; Hahana, a local New Zealander who was vice president of her family's hospitality company; Dalia, Angela's best friend from business school who worked in finance and renewable energy; Marco, Angela's friend from Italy who worked for a big consulting firm in London; and Therese, Angela's roommate from college who was on the partner-track for a big law firm in L.A. Rounding out the table had been me and my twin brother, Patrick, a professional surfer.

If I'd been uneasy before the wedding, my table-mates only added to my insecurities. It wasn't that everyone wasn't lovely, kind, and solicitous, it was just that they were so damn successful and cosmopolitan. From the way they spoke, to their clothes, to their careers, I was a country bumpkin next to them. I'd never been so conscious of my brother's propensity for slipping into Pidgin. Thankfully, it seemed like he'd noticed that "Wassup brah'" was not going to be an appropriate—or even understood—greeting with this audience and had adjusted accordingly. I probably shouldn't have even been worried about Patrick; as someone who traveled all over the world and sat in on business meetings with the huge corporations who sponsored him, he was probably adept at adjusting to his environment.

Me? Not so much.

Whenever the question of my work rolled around, I'd blush when I answered, "I'm a receptionist at a doctor's office." Not that there was anything wrong with my job. Being asked about it by this group of people made me aware that it just wasn't something I was passionate about.

There just wasn't a lot of opportunity on the islands unless you wanted to work in tourism, or start your own business, but I didn't want to do either. And although I'd received my bachelor's in psychology, becoming a therapist had not appealed to me, either.

I didn't know what to do with myself, I just knew I wanted to make a change.

During a break in the meal, Filip and Hahana stood up and disappeared, leaving the chair next to me free. Dalia slid into the spot, all smokey eyes and sleek black hair. We'd met a few times before in Los Angeles and I'd never gotten over being intimidated by her. Consequently, our previous conversations had never moved beyond politely superficial.

She raised a perfectly manicured eyebrow and leveled a finger at me, a cascade of bangles on her wrist jingling. "Tell me about yourself, Erin."

The hair at the base of my skull tingled—with fear or anticipation, I wasn't sure. "What do you want to know?" I gave a little shrug, trying to seem nonchalant.

"Truthfully?" Dalia asked, her brow inching higher.

I swallowed past a lump in my throat and nodded.

She lowered her voice. "I want to know why you've been sitting here so quiet looking like the kid whose favorite stuffed bunny was just eaten by the family dog."

My stomach knotted.

"You're at a wedding for God's sake. A damn good one too, and believe me, I've been to enough to know the difference." She raised her bangled arm out towards the stunning beauty surrounding us. "We're on a friggin' beachside vineyard in New Zealand. What could be better than this?" She paused and leaned forward. "So my question is this: why so glum, chum?"

Her gaze was intense and I shifted in my seat.

Am I that transparent?

I shrugged. "Nothi—"

She held up a hand but her gaze softened. "Erin, I've never seen you look so miserable. I want to help." It was the soft voice I'd sometimes heard her use with Angela.

Apparently, I *was* that transparent.

I swallowed hard. "I'm just not happy with my life—"

"So change it," she said absolutely, like I'd just told her I didn't like my outfit. "How old are you? Twenty-five? Twenty-six?"

"Twenty-seven," I said meekly.

She held up her arms, bangles jangling. "There you go. You're young. I had no idea who I was at twenty-seven. Hell, I'm thirty-five now and I still don't have it all figured out. Truthfully, I'm not sure if anyone really does." She got a faraway look, but then returned her intense eyes towards me. "The point is, you've got plenty of time to figure it out, kiddo. There's nothing that can't be fixed at your age." She leaned back. "Hopefully there's nothing that can't be fixed at mine, either," she said with a little laugh. Then she gave her head a little shake like that wasn't her point.

I sat up straighter. Although I'd been having similar thoughts, the validation from this sleek, successful creature reassured me. "Thank you," I said, a bit of excitement creeping into my voice.

"You're welcome." She sat back and crossed her arms. "Soooooo…what are you going to do?"

The lump returned to my throat. I didn't know, but there was one thing I was certain of. "I'm going to move off the island."

"Great. Where are you going?"

I shook my head. "I have no idea."

Dalia smiled "Why don't you come to L.A.?"

My ears perked up. My trips to L.A. had been limited to spring breaks visiting Angela and going to Disneyland. I wouldn't say I knew the place well, but then again, it was the place I knew best outside of the islands.

Why not? But where would I stay?

Dalia seemed to read my mind. "Why don't you stay at Angela's place? It's going to be empty for at least a year. Angela's having her baby here and she's said that she doesn't want to take the baby on an airplane until she's at least a year old. She'd probably love to have you house-sit."

When God closes a door, somewhere he opens a window.

"What did you say?"

I blushed. Apparently, I'd vocalized my thought. "It's a quote from *The Sound of Music*. You know, with Julie Andrews? It's one of my favorite movies."

Dalia lifted her chin as though assessing me again.

Maybe she wasn't impressed by my pop culture reference, but her suggestion felt like synchronicity. Just a moment ago, I'd closed the door on Honolulu, and she'd opened a window to L.A.

***

By the time I arrived back at the main campground, it seemed I'd reverted back to the me I'd been at the wedding: all uncertain and shy. My past wasn't far enough away from me that it didn't still exert a powerful pull.

A few people from the fundraising department and a couple of journalists were heading towards the cafeteria for breakfast, and although a couple of them waved at me, no one gave me a look that read "I know what you've been doing in the woods with Clint Davenport."

Seriously, I must have the guiltiest conscience ever.

Then I looked down at my clothes, trying to see myself through other people's eyes and I realized there wasn't anything about my appearance that told the story of what I'd been through last night.

I sighed, a bit of my anxiety leaving me.

But not all of it.

I headed to my cabin and continued my mental flagellation. *What the hell was I thinking? It would have looked extremely unprofessional if we'd been caught together and the worst part was, I would have been suspected of something that I didn't even do! I would have suffered all of the repercussions without even getting to enjoy the crime.*

I didn't even want to think about what my mother would have said. She probably would've told me I deserved whatever I got.

When I arrived at my cabin, my roommate wasn't there. I exhaled; there would be no questions for now.

I grabbed my brush and relaxed into the ritual of braiding my hair.

When I was done, I pulled off my destroyed muumuu and took a few moments to study it.

*How did he...*I gripped the untorn edge of the dress and tried to rip it, but the thick banding of cotton at the hem made it impossible for me to tear.

I couldn't believe he'd ripped it halfway down the back without me noticing; further proof that he'd had a good reason.

I shivered, suddenly curious to hear the whole story from Clint's lips.

Throwing on a new tank top, I realized there hadn't been a single moment this morning when I'd been scared by the fact that I was lying in bed with Clint, my clothes torn.

Embarrassed, annoyed, turned on…I'd felt all of those things, but not *scared*.

In fact, part of me wished I hadn't jumped up so quickly, so that I could have enjoyed feeling his skin against mine. As it was, I'd bolted so fast, I couldn't even recall being consciously aware of his touch.

I took off my shoes, slid on a pair of clean leggings, then retied them.

And now that I had some mental distance from the situation, and some physical distance from Clint's fighter-pilot charisma, I was becoming very curious about what had happened.

I remembered being cold. So cold that there was a part of me that had wanted to take Clint up on his offer of sleeping together. But my strict upbringing had rebelled at the thought.

Although my family had been in the Hawaiian Islands for six generations, we were ethnically Chinese. My father's generation had been the first to marry outside of that ethnicity.

Although my grandparents might wear aloha prints and play the 'ukulele, the food at the table was usually Chinese and the

sanctimonious feelings about sex were *definitely* Chinese.

So, although part of me had really wanted to cuddle up with him, I hadn't been able to get over myself. And I'd missed out on the perfect opportunity because last night I'd actually had a reason to feel his arms around me. The funny thing was, he *had* held me, I just couldn't remember it.

I closed my eyes and tried to recall. After a few moments, I conjured a memory—or was it a fantasy?—of his muscular forearms pressing against me and a feeling of warmth and safety.

If I'd been more like my cousin, I would've taken advantage of the opportunity. I was handed the chance to have Clint Davenport cradle me skin-to-skin without any expectations, and I passed it up.

What an idiot I was.

Jiminy Cricket! My face was so hot, I was probably all red and splotchy.

I grabbed my water bottle and drained it in one go.

My heart gave a grateful pang that it was Clint I'd gotten lost with last night, but I didn't have long to ponder that before there was a knock at the door.

My heart leapt and I rushed the few steps to open it.

It was Fern.

My heart fell. Part of me was disappointed it wasn't Clint.

"Good morning," Fern said with his typical upbeat attitude.

"Good morning," I said, suddenly noticing how hungry I was. "Let's eat. I'm starving."

Once we were seated, our plates heaped with steaming scrambled eggs, bacon, toast, and hash browns, Fern looked around to make sure no one was listening and leaned forward.

I didn't need to be psychic to guess what he was going to ask.

I grabbed my coffee mug and blew on its surface to give me something to do.

"So…what happened last night?" he asked, his voice quiet, the clanking of utensils and clattering of plastic trays muffling it further.

What happened indeed. I shrugged.

If last night had happened with someone from outside of work, I would've told Fern. Actually, if it had been anyone but Clint, I would have spilled my guts. It was a good story, kind of funny even.

But because it was Clint, I couldn't say a word.

Hosts on radio shows were like gods walking among mortals. They were literally the only famous person in a room full of not-famous people. It made for a strange office dynamic.

"We went for a walk. Nothing happened." Well, at least nothing that Fern was curious about had happened, that part was true.

"I waited by the fire until midnight, but you never came back."

I cleared my throat. "Oh, well…we got lost in the dark. It took us a while to find our way back."

He gave me a look that was half-suspicion and half-disappointment, like I'd hurt his feelings by not trusting him with the truth.

Part of me felt bad. Fern was one of my best friends. But he was still a coworker, and I didn't want anyone at work to know I'd spent the night with Clint. There'd be no closing Pandora's Box if *that* news ever got out, and my reputation at work was too important to risk ruining it over an accidental sleepover where nothing even happened.

"If nothing happened, why is Clint staring at you with puppy dog eyes?" Fern asked, his tone, knowing.

Damn it! Fern was too observant for his own good.

Chapter 7: Flying High

~Clint~

After Erin walked out of cabin #83—correction, make that *bolted*—I spent a few minutes straightening up, erasing all evidence of our night together.

Our night together.

Good thing I didn't have a fragile ego or I might've been knocked down a few pegs. Granted, I'd been out of the dating game for a long time, but I didn't think I was as rusty at it as Erin's reaction to my cuddle suggestion, well, suggested. I got the sense that she considered it "wrong", which was kind of adorable in a way.

Adorable? That woman had really gotten under my skin.

I needed to clear my mind.

I studied the map on the back of the cabin door and plotted out a nice, long run. I needed a good ten miles to pound out the last nine hours—and the confusing blend of emotions they'd brought with them—but I didn't have time for that. Though if I took a circuitous route back to the main campground, I might be able to get in a solid five miles with enough elevation changes to make up for the shorter distance.

Before I left, I picked up the blue thermal I'd wrapped around Erin's head and held it up to my nose. I inhaled deeply, trying to place the rich floral scent I'd started associating with her. I knew she was from Hawai'i, and the fragrance definitely reminded me of the islands, but it wasn't like I was a flower guy. But this scent seemed familiar. It took a few moments, but finally, it came to me.

Gardenia.

Complex, rich, and sweet, it suited her perfectly.

I took the arms of the shirt and tied them around my waist so my sweat wouldn't mask her scent. Then I banged out the cabin door and took off, eating up the dirt trails with my legs as my mind devoured the memory of Erin.

I hammered out mile after mile, weaving through the pine trees, hurdling the occasional large rock. Despite the beautiful landscape, I barely registered my surroundings. Even though I'd tried to shake it off, again and again, my mind returned to Erin and the feeling of her lips during our kiss and the shape of her body as I'd held her through the night. She was soft and firm in all the right places and her body had notched into mine like a key into a lock.

I groaned.

Instead of helping me forget Erin, the run seemed to be locking her in deeper, as though etching her into my cells like a tattoo needle with each pounding step.

I'd forgotten how good it felt to have a woman in my arms, the simple pleasure of sleeping with someone I desired, and the way it permeated even my unconscious awareness.

Having lived so many years when sleep was my most precious commodity—first as a pilot and then on the overnight shift at *WUA*—I was a student of sleep. And I could tell that my body wasn't as rested as it should've been given the four hours of sleep I managed to get. (And believe me, I could do a lot on four hours).

Instead, there was an edge to everything, like a wire with Erin's essence on it had worked its way under my skin and kept poking me, from the inside out. It was almost irritating, except it wasn't. I had the irrational desire to scratch, but I shut down that impulse with the iron force of my will. I might be crazy about Erin but I wasn't about to harbor any strange hallucinations.

It had taken me years to master my body, and I wasn't going to allow something as fleeting as physical attraction undo the habits that had achieved so much for me. My self-mastery had kept my almost-forty-year-old body as lean as a twenty-year-old. It was how I'd become the host of a major radio show in ten years, a feat that usually took fifteen or more—nineteen if you added in journalism school. It was how I'd ended up…alone—

I shut down that line of thought almost before it entered my mind and did a mental check-in of my body to distract myself. *Feet, good. Ankles, good. Knees, fine. Calves, burning. Thighs, tired. Upper body, good.* My legs were fatiguing earlier than usual, the telltale burn of lactic acid letting me know I was going to need more rest. I needed to take one of my famous twenty-minute naps later. My naps were famous in the office because they were so precise, you could set a timer by them.

Suddenly I realized I'd come upon a landmark stand of trees that had been on the map. I'd almost missed them. The trees forked the trail and I took the path that would lead me back to camp.

It wasn't like me to miss visual markers. I definitely needed more sleep.

Sleep was fuel as much as food was to me. My days in the military had trained me to rest when my body required it, but not to indulge. In fact, the military had burned all taste for excess right out of me: excess sleep, excess calories, excess attachment. I was a machine who only had time and energy to focus on three things: work, peak physical conditioning, and...

Even if I had the mental bandwidth to think about my third responsibility, I wasn't going to. Because if I did, I'd have to admit that I was enjoying the break from it, and that wouldn't bode well with my delicate emotional state.

Delicate emotional state? I barely recognized myself and I'd only spent one night with Erin.

One night physically, but you've been thinking about her for years, my inner voice chimed in sounding downright sarcastic.

I couldn't let myself indulge in thoughts of Erin. I knew my limits, and I only had the bandwidth to do three things well, and what was the point of doing anything if you weren't going to do it well? Three wasn't a random number. I knew my limits because I'd been trying for years to become a better photographer, even going so far as to carry a heavy Nikon SLR with me everywhere. However, my images had not gotten any better because I simply didn't have the time, energy, and mental space to dedicate to it. I knew that if I ever got the time to "attack" photography, the way I did the other three areas of my life, I would master it.

Maybe in another year some space would open up in my life, once I'd settled into my role as lead host. Just because I had the position didn't mean I could rest. Now that I had the job, I needed to do it well. Only then would I be satisfied.

Maybe then I could think about cultivating a relationship with a woman.

Erin, you numbnut. Cultivate a relationship with Erin.

When had my inner voice become so bossy?

As I jogged into camp, I slowed my pace, leaning against the porch of my cabin as I caught my breath. Without thinking, I pulled the shirt from around my waist and started using it to mop at my dripping forehead when I smelled it; gardenia.

A throb in my pants let me know that while my run had allowed me to mentally check off the "exercise" box in my mind, it had done nothing to take my mind off Erin.

"Teddy Roosevelt," I muttered.

As if to torture me further, at that moment, I saw Erin walking to the cafeteria with Fern, giving the other man a wide smile as they chatted. She looked like a ninja princess, her hair in the elaborate braids that ringed her head like a crown, her strong, sleek legs clad in black leggings topped by a black hoodie.

Damn it. Even though I *now* knew they weren't a couple, it didn't stop a hot lance of jealousy from stabbing me in the gut.

She should be walking with me.

I shook my head at the errant thought. *Et tu, Cerebrum?*

The world was conspiring against me. I hadn't anticipated that becoming *WUA*'s host would come with such a compelling distraction. Then again, it wasn't exactly a surprise, either. Erin had worked closely with the previous host. Maybe I'd simply chosen to overlook this obvious fact; a lie I'd told myself so that I didn't have to contemplate that Erin had been distracting me ever since she started working at *WUA*.

I frowned. Lying to myself was not a habit of mine. It was one of those bad traits of lesser mortals that I'd left behind in flight school, or at least I thought I had.

A bell from the cafeteria sounded—the breakfast food would be cleaned up in fifteen minutes.

"Benjamin Franklin." I was behind schedule, and I *hated* being behind schedule.

I jogged up my cabin stairs and hurried to the showers.

Eight minutes later I was in the cafeteria—dressed in a clean pair of running shorts and two fresh, long-sleeve shirts—and had loaded up a plate with eggs, some lean-looking sausage, and a banana. I also poured myself a cup of coffee, which I definitely needed today, and saw Yolanda waving me over to her table.

I *barely* managed not to roll my eyes as I really didn't want to talk about work now. However, I hadn't gotten this far in life without a healthy appreciation of authority, and although Yolanda wasn't my boss, she was my superior. I checked my attitude and joined her.

"Where have you been?" she said, looking at her watch. "I've been waiting for an hour." Her tone made it clear that she expected me to work through every meal, as we had the last couple of days. Although she hadn't specifically asked me to do this, we'd established a pattern.

"Sorry, Yo," I said, my inner imp jumping for joy when she flinched.

I sensed she tolerated the nickname because I was a motivated worker and I made her look good. My predecessor, Devon, had been on autopilot her last couple of years, making it clear she was ready to move on to something bigger. She hadn't even bothered attending editorial meetings the last six months she was the lead host, while I'd been at every single one since joining the show.

Yolanda gave me a tight smile. "I know I'm asking you to go above and beyond by working through our meals. But your promotion was unexpected and we can't lose a second establishing you." She stared at me stoically. "Stations and listeners hate host changes, especially when it means losing a long-time one. Even if listeners didn't particularly like the person, there's something about the familiarity that creates its own inertia. Fortunately," she paused dramatically, "you have a leg up since you were the substitute host." Her face twitched as though trying to decide if she was going to tell me something. "I fought for you to get the spot because you are capable, a hard worker, and our audience's familiarity with you will make the transition easier. Some of the powers above me wanted to do a nationwide search and get the biggest name possible. Others were miffed that someone without a journalism degree would even be offered the position."

I swallowed hard, surprised by this news.

One of my superpowers was a Teflon-coated ego. It was part of why I'd felt comfortable leaving the armed forces to start over as a production assistant on *WUA* alongside people ten years my junior. Sure, I hadn't known anything about journalism or radio, but why would that stop me from making it onto the airwaves? At least, that's what I'd thought. This same confidence had blinded me to the possibility that I wasn't the top choice to replace Devon.

Fortunately, I had an excellent poker face.

"Ah, I see you thought you were the obvious candidate," Yolanda said, lifting a perfectly manicured brow.

Okay, not so excellent poker face.

I tried to relax my features, but felt nothing to relax.

"You have a tell. The left side of your jaw tightened for just a moment," she said, by way of explanation.

Although I'd always admired Yolanda, she'd just risen a few more notches in my esteem. I'd known she was smart and hardworking, but now I had to add strategic, diplomatic, and cunning to her list of admirable traits.

"Tell me, Yo—*landa*," I said, my tone conciliatory. "What would you like to discuss?"

She nodded approvingly and started talking about things like visits to top markets, the editorial calendar, and a range of other things.

I did my best to listen while eating, but my seat had a perfect view of Erin, which made doing both activities difficult. Instead of listening with the rapt attention I would've normally given a superior, my gaze was drawn to Erin's graceful fingers wrapping around her coffee mug as she pursed her lips, blowing on the steaming beverage just before wrapping her lips over the rim of the—

"Clint!"

My attention snapped back to Yolanda's steely gaze.

"I've never seen you like this before," she said in consternation.

Her words reminded me of my earlier assessment that I didn't have the bandwidth for Erin.

"You're usually the one person at our editorial meetings that I can count on. Don't make me regret fighting for you."

Yolanda would've made a great drill sergeant.

I was just about to promise to do better when the next activity was announced. "I'm sorry, Yo—*landa*. I promise I'll do better at lunch."

She lifted her chin. "I'm going to hold you to that."

Just as I was about to stand, Darius's amplified sounded over a megaphone. "Stay exactly where you are. The last person you spoke with is going to be your teammate for the next event."

I sighed. *Partnered with Yolanda? This retreat just gets better and better.*

Yolanda seemed to have a similar thought because she was looking at me like I was a sweaty pair of socks.

"We're going to be doing a course called 'The Odyssey'. Follow me outside," Darius said, waving the group towards the exits.

Yolanda swept a loose tendril of gray-blond hair behind her ear and huffed. "I can't wait until this week is over."

"I agree," however, that wasn't completely true. While I would enjoy getting back to my routine, I *was* enjoying seeing Erin outside of the office.

We filed out of the cafeteria along with the rest of the herd, a loud cacophony of conversations filling the air. Yolanda took advantage of the time we spent walking to continue our conversation from breakfast.

After ten minutes, we arrived in front of a contraption that looked like a treehouse-cum-spiderweb.

I felt unsteady taking it all in.

The Odyssey was made up of such a dizzying array of beams, cables, and ropes, that it was hard to see what was going on. There were long wooden beams suspended by ropes, ropes crossed into "X" shapes, rope ladders suspended parallel to the ground. No wonder they called it a "ropes course." It looked like a variety of fun-house bridges all designed to challenge one's balance and coordination.

"Oh, God," Yolanda said.

I felt a sudden camaraderie with Yolanda. "Don't like heights?"

She snickered. "No. No fear of heights. Fear of wasting my time is more like it. What am I supposed to learn from something like this?" She waved her hands around trying to encompass the vastness of The Odyssey. "I did that stupid log thing yesterday, what more does Alex want from me?" she said, referring to *WUA*'s executive producer. "If we're going to win a Peabody, I need to…oh wait, there's Alex. I'm going to go talk to her." Yolanda marched away without another word.

I watched her go, half-amused as I imagined the hell she'd raise with Alex, when I noticed where Erin and Fern were standing. I sidled in their direction, keeping enough distance so I wouldn't be noticed.

"You will be going through The Odyssey in teams of two," Sonja said loudly, immediately silencing the crowd with her authoritative tone. "As I said yesterday, the goal is to try the activity, not to be perfect at it. Progress is success. I know some of you sat out yesterday's activity. I'd like to encourage you to push yourself further today."

I sighed. I'd thought I'd left the days of pushing myself at the behest of someone else behind.

"Erin and I are going to go through the course together to demonstrate for you what it looks like," Sonja said as Erin approached her and took a proffered harness. Once they were outfitted, Sonja continued. "Unlike yesterday's log challenge where the teamwork was more indirect, today you'll be working *very* closely with your partner."

Sonja then took the stairs up to a small platform and clipped her harness onto a cable. "This is called the X-cross," she said, pointing to where two ropes were crisscrossed parallel to the ground at foot level and an identical pair over her head. "This is really just a warm-up to get you comfortable with walking on ropes at a low level. As you see, we're just a few feet above the ground, so there's really no danger here."

Sonja and Erin each grabbed an overhead rope and stepped out onto their individual foot ropes, walking diagonally towards the other side and then taking turns crossing where the ropes intersected at the "x". They proceeded across the element quickly, clipping out of that cable and then onto the next one for the second challenge.

"This next element is called Bridge Builder," Sonja said, referring to a series of eight-foot-long wooden beams suspended parallel to the ground and parallel to each other, like a bridge that had lost a number of its planks. "This one requires a bit of teamwork. You and your partner will need to slide this piece of wood," she indicated a plank about two-feet wide, "across the beams, to bridge the gaps, so that you can walk across it. The plank's not as long as the expanse you have to cross, so you'll have to stop in the middle and move it again."

Sonja and Erin demonstrated. When they finished that obstacle, they clipped off the safety line, climbed a ladder up to the next level, clipped onto a new safety line, and demonstrated a couple of more elements. They then climbed to the third level and I felt my throat constrict and my breathing become short.

Yes, I know, ironic that a former pilot should have a fear of heights. Even more ironic, my fear had nothing to do with my years as a pilot.

Cass—

I stopped myself before I could go down that rabbit hole. Self-indulgence wasn't something I tolerated, especially not when Erin was skittering across a tightrope some twenty-five feet in the air.

I watched Sonja and Erin lean their torsos towards each other, their hands on the other woman's shoulders, forming an inverted V-shape as they shuffled across the ropes that were growing apart. Their bodies leaned farther and farther out.

My throat tightened with each of their steps.

When they made it across to the next platform, I felt my breath ease up a little bit.

Only one element to go.

On the final obstacle, they locked arms around each other's waists and lunged across large squares of wood that were placed just a tiny bit farther away from each other than necessary. I sipped tiny breaths each time they lunge-jumped forward to the next square. Their crossing seemed to drag on and I exhaled with visceral relief once they reached the safety of the final platform.

My chest expanded like a balloon and it suddenly dawned on me that I'd never experienced acrophobia for somebody other than myself. Unable—or perhaps unwilling—to plumb what that meant, I took another deep breath and studied the course instead, impressed by its logic.

The first level required no physical skill and no touching and was designed to give confidence and lull one into advancing. The second level required more skill and a bit of touching, setting you up for the final level which required almost zero skill again but lots of physical teamwork—in addition to the fact that it was two-and-a-half-stories high. It was a brilliant design to ease people out of their physical, emotional, and mental comfort zones.

"Once you're done with the sixth element, you get to grab onto this zip-line and cruise over to the amphitheater where one of my team members will brief you on the next activity." Sonja clipped Erin in and sent her off on the zip-line.

Erin let out a yelp of delight as she sailed away.

The sound made me smile. If anyone had been paying attention, I must have looked like a loved-up dope.

"I'll stay up here to make sure everyone is clipped into the zip-line properly," Sonja continued. "Darius and the rest of my team will be stationed at the beginning of each element to make sure everyone is following the safety protocols. Let's get started."

Some of the more eager among our group began moving to the first element where Darius and Fern were handing out harnesses, the gentle babble of conversation once again filling the air.

Harry Hinkley was walking past me when he stopped and turned. "You going to give it a try today, Clint?" Harry asked in his lazy drawl.

I gave the barest hint of a nod. "Maybe," which was a total lie because until that moment I'd been a firm "no."

"Come on. It's fun, and it's good to challenge yourself," Harry said, a bit of hesitation in his voice, like he wanted to ask me a question. Then he turned his head as though deciding on a different course. "I would've thought you'd be an adrenaline junkie, what with your background and all."

"Thanks, Harry, but I've had a few lifetimes of adrenaline." I dropped my voice lower at the end of the sentence, making it clear the conversation was over.

Harry shrugged and then moved on to the line of people waiting for a harness.

I turned to the skies and muttered, "Marie Curie." Harry Hinkley had just called me out. *Me.* Clint Davenport, Rhodes Scholar, former fighter pilot, and semi-professional snooker player.

I stood up to my full six-feet-one-inch height, shoved my hands in my pocket, and straightened my ruffled feathers.

Just then, Erin came jogging over, a radiant smile brightening her face.

My heart started beating faster and before I knew what I was doing, I'd walked over to where she and Fern were standing.

The smile disappeared from her face.

"Hey, Clint," Fern said, his gaze studiously neutral.

Erin's eyes lowered to the ground, reminding me less of the Erin I'd come to know and more like the Erin she'd been when she'd first joined *WUA*.

Is that the effect I have on her? My heart seemed to pulse with disappointment.

"Hi, Fern." I shoved my hands even deeper into my pockets. "Hi, Erin," I said more quietly, suddenly nervous.

What was it about Erin that made me feel like the gangly, pimply teenager I'd once been?

After a beat, Erin looked up. When her long black lashes finally revealed her almost-black eyes, she nearly knocked the breath out of me

"Clint," she said, her voice robotic as it hit the percussive "c" and ended with a dismissive "t."

A chill rolled down my back. She might as well have said, "Fuck off." It would've had the same effect.

Darius joined us. "Are you and Clint partnering up again?" he asked, looking at Fern.

"What? Oh, no. Erin and I were going to partner," Fern said, running a hand through his thick brown waves.

Darius frowned at Fern. "I don't—"

"I was supposed to partner with Yolanda, but she disappeared. I'm fine sitting this exercise out," I said, not wanting to encroach on Erin's plans.

Darius turned to me and I could tell that he was about to give me the "You really need to challenge yourself to get the most out of these exercises" talk when Erin suddenly spoke up. "Darius, you're closer in size to Fern than Clint is. If you partner Fern, I'll partner up with Clint."

I sucked in a breath.

The idea of going up on the course was suddenly substantially less frightening and even mildly appealing. Somehow, I just knew that I wouldn't feel the anxiety I'd felt before, if I was up there with Erin, but I didn't know why.

There would be time to unpack that mystery later.

"Sure. Yeah. If Erin will be my teammate, I'll give it a shot," I said, surprised as the words tumbled from my mouth.

I could feel all eyes on me, a mixture of surprise and curiosity mingled there.

Darius broke out in a wide smile and clapped me on the back. "That's the spirit. Get to the back of the line and Fern will bring you some harnesses when we have a moment."

Oh, bloody hell! The hardnesses…no wait, harnesses. My running shorts were made of an even thinner material than the shorts I'd worn yesterday. "Abraham Lincoln," I muttered under my breath.

"Excuse me?" Erin asked.

Heat ran into my face and soared out the ends of my ears in an uncharacteristic show of embarrassment. My famous-people blasphemy was not something I wanted to share. It was my own personal quirk. "The harnesses. They take some getting used to."

She nodded as though she'd heard that before. "Yeah, they hug your privates in all sorts of weird ways, but it's all in the name of safety." She frowned as she studied his shorts.

Is she checking me out?

She shrugged. "At least you have good legs."

She looked like she was about to smile, but the moment passed as she turned to the sound of her name.

"Here you go," Fern said, handing her two harnesses, before rejoining Darius at the front of the line.

"Thanks," Erin said, inspecting them before handing me one.

But I barely noticed the mess of nylon and metal in my hand because I was too caught up on her last sentence.

Did she just compliment me? But that couldn't be…I must have misunderstood her comment. Maybe she meant I had good legs in that they were strong enough to handle a harness…but that didn't make sense. No, she *must* have been complimenting me.

A seed of hope sprouted in my chest, like a hot little diamond, beautiful but barbed, its many facets dispersing any clear thinking I hoped to accomplish.

I cleared my throat, needing to say something but also realizing that the setting was not exactly private. I stepped into the leg loops to give the people in front of us some time to move forward.

"Look, about…earlier," I said, instead of "this morning" which would have been clearer but also less discreet.

She glanced around.

We were the last people in line so there was no one behind us. The couple in front of us were about five feet away.

She stepped into her harness, pulling it up her legs and buckling the waist, although her motions seemed slower than the previous day.

Was she stalling too?

In a quiet voice, she said, "Not now. I know you did what you *had* to do; you'll just have to fill me in on the specifics later."

"Later tonight?" I asked, unable to keep the hope from my words as I adjusted the straps around my thighs.

She frowned, her eyes darting to the people in front of us who were now at least ten feet away. She started to tighten the buckles around her thighs and my eyes followed, wishing I could reach out and finish tightening her straps.

Damn, she's sexy. The thought flitted into my mind, unbeckoned, followed quickly by—

Whoa. Perv alert! When did I get so pervy?

She waited a few beats—completely unaware of my inner struggle—and then said, "I think it's best if we don't draw attention to ourselves. Fern is already suspicious, and I would really prefer not to have any rumors about—"

"We'll be discreet, I promise. Please," I implored, doubling back my harness belt. It wasn't like me to beg, and yet...I didn't care.

She froze, but after a beat, she said, "Let's just do the course, okay?"

My throat tightened.

I'd completely forgotten about The Odyssey.

Being around Erin made everything else drop away.

I laughed inwardly. I'd managed to forget I was about to climb a twenty-five-foot-tall structure designed to provoke my fears. You would've thought that putting on the harness—which was hugging my running-short-clad pelvis in all the wrong ways—would have reminded me, but no.

Erin's presence had meant that the only thing I could think about was...Erin.

I resisted the urge to adjust the front of the harness; touching anywhere near my cock, with Erin around, was a recipe for a hard-on. I could only imagine the show I was putting on. My ass probably looked like a ballet dancer with the way the sheer material of my shorts was now plastered to me. I refused to look down for confirmation, it was better not to know.

"Right, the course," I said, taking a deep breath.

On the one hand, I was happy for any excuse to be close to Erin, but on the other hand...*what the hell have I agreed to?*

As though reading my thoughts, Erin laid a hand on my forearm, sending a tingling heat racing up my neck. "It's going to be fine. Just take deep breaths, focus on the element we're working on, and pay attention to me," she said evenly, her tone designed to soothe. "I take it your," she cleared her throat, choosing her next words carefully, "*difficulty* with heights...it's not a lifelong thing, right? I don't see how one could be a pilot and be acrophobic."

"Actually, there are plenty of pilots who have a fear of heights," I replied, happy to move the topic away from my specific fear to the more general fear I'd seen in some of my Navy peers.

Her eyes widened and she looked like she was going to ask me a follow-up question when her eyes dropped to my harness. Her cheeks pinked as she stared just a beat too long.

Ballet dancer for sure.

She cleared her throat. "Want me to check your harness?"

Hell yeah! I gave myself a mental fist-bump as I struggled to keep my tone neutral. "Sure. Thanks."

"Excuse my touch," she mumbled, not meeting my eyes.

"Go right ahead," I said.

There was literally nothing she could do to me that I wouldn't welcome.

Nothing.

She stepped directly in front of me, her eyes trained on my waistband. She lifted her hands in the air and wiggled her fingers as if trying to decide on the best way to touch me. Her eyes flitted to mine with a regretful look in them.

She was absolutely adorable.

I struggled to keep my face neutral. My lips quivered with their desire to break out into a smile. "Don't worry about me," I said, giving my traitorous lips something to do. "Do *whatever* you have to do to make me safe." That made my inner imp gleeful and my skin tingle with anticipation.

"I, um," she cleared her throat. "I need to find the top of your pelvis bones."

Her voice wobbled on the word "pelvis" and I don't think I'd ever heard anything quite as delightful.

I lowered my voice. "Do your worst," I dared.

She ignored my tone and simply nodded, gingerly pulling at the front of my harness, investigating the edge where my waist met the belt.

Oh yeah. Even though she touched me with clinical aloofness, I welcomed it.

Her thumbs pressed gently on my iliac crest and my gut panged.

"Your harness needs to be above this bone," she said. She removed her hands and a hole of want opened up in their place.

She grabbed the sides of my harness and lifted it. "Hold it here," she said, authoritatively.

I like the sound of that. In Control Erin was even more of a turn-on than Sweetly Embarrassed Erin.

I did as she said.

She undid and then redid my waist strap, jostling me as she cinched it tight. "There. That's better." She seemed very comfortable now. In her element. "Now your thigh loops," she said, and then knelt down, all business.

Harriet Beecher Stowe and all that is Abraham Lincoln! My eyes were riveted on Erin's head directly in front of my cock.

Blood surged downward and I bit the inside of my cheek to keep from getting an erection.

I hazarded a downward glance. *Teddy Roosevelt.* It was even worse than I had imagined, the straps of the harness were practically encircling my cock, outlining the soft flesh with the hard edges of the unforgiving webbing material. At least the webbing was keeping me somewhat restrained, and my shorts were the same black as the harness, so it all blended together.

Kind of.

She wiggled her fingers again, keeping her eyes trained on the buckle of my right thigh, which was three inches to the right of my package. She moved tentatively, managing to tighten the strap down without brushing against my penis, even though the back of her hand came within a half-inch.

I was left half-grateful and half-wanting by that half-inch.

When she finished, we exhaled simultaneously, although I sensed it was for different reasons.

She moved to my left leg and without hesitation, tightened the strap, the back of her hand just grazing my shaft. "Oh, shit," she said, abruptly standing as she covered her mouth with her hand.

I hunched over, feeling like the wind had been knocked out of me, but in a good way.

"Are you…okay?" she asked, leaning over and putting a hand on my shoulder.

I closed my eyes and nodded. "Yeah. Gimme a sec," I said through tight lips, my body a mosh pit of desire and electricity. My cock, *throbbing*.

I was going to have blue balls, no question.

I sucked in deep breaths of cool air, and thought about a recent story I'd covered about flesh-eating bacteria. Oh yeah, nothing like a little *necrotizing fasciitis* to kill an erection.

"I'm sorry, Clint," she moaned quietly.

I shook my head. "Nothing to be sorry about." And it was true. The sensation of Erin's hand brushing against my penis had been fantastic.

Only the setting was problematic.

However, I knew that she thought I was in some sort of pain, and wanted to allay her concern. "Really. It didn't hurt," I said, a bit quieter. "I just…" I trailed off and then added, "Need a second."

I heard Erin inhale quickly as she stood, removing her hand from my shoulder, perhaps understanding my words.

I called on all of my training and will power to bring my rebelling body to heel.

After a couple of minutes passed, Erin said, "It's almost our turn." Her voice, neutral.

I nodded, took a few more breaths, and then straightened up, my body back under control.

We walked slowly, catching up to the back of the line.

I glanced up at The Odyssey for a moment before turning back to Erin.

Although the sight of dozens of my coworkers walking, climbing, and jumping on an adult jungle gym should have amused me, I had no interest in watching. I was completely absorbed by Erin's presence, not even noticing when the occasional person fell off an element and shrieked until the safety cable caught him or her.

Erin's face took on the look of intelligent curiosity that I'd often seen at the office. "Can I ask you a personal question?"

I *hated* personal questions, but I didn't want to push Erin away so I nodded.

"How can a pilot have a fear of heights?" she asked.

Relief swept through me. "Well," I paused, gathering my thoughts. "The pilots I knew in the Navy, their acrophobia didn't manifest in the cockpit. It would show up when they were doing something else; parachuting was a big trigger." She nodded for me to continue. "It turns out, most pilots' fear of heights only shows up when they aren't in control."

"When they fly, they feel in control, so the fear doesn't manifest?" She summarized.

I smiled. It was so easy to talk to Erin.

It made me realize then that I never conversed like this with anyone. All of my time at work was spent in focused conversation, I never "chatted", and although I was gifted at putting world leaders, titans of industry, and other newsworthy individuals at ease during my interviews, those were always calculated conversations based on what I knew of those people's backgrounds, interests, and recent activities. I never let my guard down and just talked free form the way I did with Erin.

It made me feel lighter.

"That's it exactly."

She smirked. "No wonder you have an issue with the ropes course. You are *definitely* a control freak," she said, with a teasing smile.

I mock-glared at her. "Hey. I resemble that comment," secretly grateful that she had assumed this explanation applied to my acrophobia specifically.

A loud chuckle escaped her lips, and she clapped her hand over her mouth. "Oh god. Sorry."

"Sorry for what?"

But before she could answer, we were interrupted.

"Hey, you two," Darius called out, waving us forward and checking our harnesses now that we were on-deck to climb. Once the couple in front of us had completed the first obstacle, he clipped us onto the safety cable. "Climb on," he said, then added, "and have fun."

I was about to say something snarky when Erin said, "We will," with such earnest enthusiasm, it shut me down.

Fern was right, I could be a dick.

The realization didn't sit well with me.

Erin took my hand and squeezed it, sending warmth flooding through my torso. "Ready?" she asked, giving me an encouraging look that reminded me of the way my mom and dad had looked at me before every Little League game.

We'd be the penultimate pair to begin The Odyssey, Darius and Fern would follow behind.

I nodded. "Ready," and it was true—with Erin holding my hand, I was ready for anything.

She let go of my hand and said, "This one is really easy. Just grab the rope overhead and walk across your foot rope. We'll cross in the middle where they intersect, one at a time like Sonja and I did."

I did as she said and, needing a distraction, picked up the thread of our earlier conversation. "Why did you apologize earlier?" I asked, as I put my foot out onto the low rope and felt it bob under my weight.

My acrophobia didn't appear, probably because I was only a few feet from the ground. I turned my attention to Erin, who'd already taken three steps along the rope, looking as comfortable as if she was walking on the ground.

"Oh, that. Habit, I guess. My mom hates my laugh. She says it's un-ladylike and that I sound like a hyena."

I heard the sadness in her voice and noticed that if I sped up, we would meet at the point where the two ropes intersected. I ached to be close to her and used my long legs to their full advantage, drawing even with her in two steps.

She raised a brow, glancing across as the distance between us shortened—eight feet, six feet, four feet. "You're cruising."

Her praise was spring rain on the dry, dead soil of my heart. I smiled. "I'm motivated."

She cocked her head, her brows a question. She seemed about to open her mouth when she shook her head and kept moving towards the intersection.

I would have paid money to know what she was thinking—big money. I focused on keeping up with her instead, wanting to be close to her.

About a foot from the intersection, we stopped simultaneously. Our ropes were so close now, mere inches separated us. If we took a step forward at the same time we'd be embracing, which would look strange since everyone else who'd done the element had simply taken turns crossing the intersection.

I looked forward and behind. The closest people were Fern and Darius, and they were at least ten feet away. I took a deep breath, and said, "Well, *I* love your laugh. I'd like to hear it more often, actually."

She inhaled quickly, looking around to see if anyone heard. Swallowing hard, her throat moved with the effort.

I suddenly remembered how it felt having my chin tucked into the side of her neck, and wondered if I'd ever get to feel that again.

Erin's eyes darted along the diagonal rope and she made to step forward, as though trying to escape me.

I mirrored her.

"Clint," she said, the single word saying "what the hell are you doing?" and "why are you being annoying?" but in a quiet tone that made it clear she wasn't really bothered.

My lips puckered into an impish smirk.

She really brought out such a strange, playful side of me.

Lowering my voice, I said, "I just want to be close to you." Goosebumps broke out on my arms at my own audacity.

A look of genuine confusion lit her eyes. "We *work* together," she said, her lips barely moving.

But I noticed that she wasn't looking around to see who was watching. Instead, her eyes were fixed on me, pupils dilated, her chest, heaving.

I decided to take a chance and inched closer. Our shoulders brushed together.

She sucked in a heated breath.

My eyes darted to her chest as her nipples puckered, sending a throb straight to my cock.

Blue balls for sure.

We stared into each other's eyes, our torsos just barely touching, heat reverberating in the space between us.

The hair on the back of my neck stood up, mirroring a similar movement in my pants.

"Clint, everyone is around," her tone almost begging, but she didn't pull away.

I had an idea.

I feigned a wobble and reached one arm around her, pulling her flush against my chest, giving myself a mental high-five for my brilliance. "Aahh," I yelped, for good measure, hoping it sounded believable.

I'd never been a good actor.

"I see you're going for the simultaneous cross," Darius said, cupping his hands to yell at us. "I think you have it. Clint, try not to bobble, your weight will throw Erin off-balance."

Erin's eyes narrowed, but he could sense a smile lurking. "He thinks we're trying to be fancy by crossing the intersection at the same time."

"Do I get to keep my arm around you if we try that?" my tone was more than a little suggestive.

She cocked her chin. "You are unbelievable."

My inner imp did a jump for joy. "That wasn't a no."

She shook her head and smiled. After a weighty exhale that seemed more exasperated than annoyed, she said, "We need to shuffle a bit so we're exactly over the place where the ropes cross." The authority in her voice sent a zip of electricity up my spine.

"Yes, ma'am." I kept my voice playful as I followed her direction, never removing the one hand I had around her, even though it made balancing much harder.

"Clint, put both hands overhead," Darius called.

I pretended not to hear him, focusing instead on Erin's body pressed against mine, the dancing light in her intelligent eyes, and the sweet smell of gardenias.

Once at the crossover point, Erin said, "Now we need to turn one-hundred-and-eighty degrees at the exact same time. Clockwise, okay?"

"Yup, I got it."

"You should really let go of me to do this," Erin said without any conviction.

"Not a chance."

She smirked. "Okay, on the count of three. One, two, three."

Erin pivoted while twisting her arms overhead. I barely did anything, hanging onto Erin as her momentum carried us both, switching from my right arm to my left overhead, and then rewrapping my newly freed arm around her waist, pulling her tighter than necessary.

I was tempted to wrap a leg around her too, but thought that might be pushing my luck.

It was over in a moment, but it felt like we'd crossed some threshold.

I flexed and opened my fingers on her back and noticed when goosebumps erupted up her arms.

"You..." she swallowed hard.

I loved watching her throat move. I wanted to lick—

"You should really let go of me. There's no reason for you to be holding me anymore." Her voice had a breathy quality to it, and I was certain that she was as affected by me as I was by her.

My inner imp gave me the thumbs-up.

Erin looked forward and back. "Clint. *Please*. People are watching."

I pulled her tighter and she gasped. "Promise you'll meet me tonight."

"Clint," she pleaded.

"Promise," I said, in my most commanding tone.

She sighed. "Okay. I promise."

I released her, returning both arms overhead before turning towards Darius and shouting, "I did it. I can't believe I did it," and hoped I wasn't overdoing the enthusiasm.

Darius pumped his arm in the air.

Erin rolled her eyes, but couldn't stop the twitch in her lips.

The rest of The Odyssey seemed to roll under me like the miles I pounded out every morning, effortlessly. With Erin by my side, it was easy. The anxiety I'd felt for her safety was gone because I had some sense of control. Not only was I not afraid, but I was enjoying myself.

It was fun working with Erin to solve the problems the course presented, and I really liked all of the public touching we got to do. The touching was even more exciting because it felt like we were getting away with something. To outside eyes, they were just the gestures required to complete the challenges. However, I could tell by the way Erin's breath would hitch, or her cheeks flush, that her heart was probably beating as quickly as mine, and it wasn't from the physical exertion.

She asked me some questions about the night before, about why I'd torn her dress. But I was relieved to find that her tone was curious, not accusatory. In the end, I sensed nothing but gratitude, which was a huge relief.

By the time we got to the final element, I was a bit disappointed that the course was ending. I couldn't remember the last time I'd had this much fun with a woman.

"This is the one element where you actually *need* to wrap your arm around me," Erin said in the teasing tone she'd been using ever since the second element.

I clapped my hands together. "Sign me up."

She shook her head. "*Who* are you?"

I arched a brow. "I'm not sure, but I like him," I said, as much to myself as to her.

She turned back towards the challenge. "This one is more awkward than it looks because the squares will swing a bit as we jump onto them. We need to land lightly and synchronize our timing."

"Got it. We are synchronized cats. Can I wrap my arm around you now?"

She laughed. "Yes."

We wrapped one arm around each other's waist and raised the other arm overhead, grabbing the overhead rope.

I'd forgotten how rewarding a team of two could be.

Together, we could take on the world.

"One, two, three," Erin said as we lunged forward to the suspended square piece of wood just a few inches too far for a normal step.

We made it, pulling each other tighter for balance.

I looked down and noticed the height for the first time since we'd started.

I waited for a flash of anxiety, fear, nerves...but nothing happened. I smiled. "That was easy. Let's do the next one."

We crossed the element in record time as exhilarated laughter bubbled between us, starting as a giggle and ending with loud guffaws. Once we reached the far platform, I threw my arms around her, pulling her in for a hug as we continued to laugh, tears leaking from Erin's twinkling eyes.

I could have stood there all day. Holding Erin in my arms soothed something inside of me that I had never thought would heal.

"Nice job, you two. That was real teamwork," Sonja said, her voice suddenly reminding us that we weren't alone on that little platform twenty-five feet in the air.

Erin froze and I dropped my arms like we'd been caught by the school principal.

"Thanks, Sonja," I said. "It was all Erin. She was the admiral; I was the seaman."

That last sentence sounded dirtier than I'd meant it. *Maybe not the best choice of words.*

Fortunately, neither of them appeared to notice.

Sonja nodded, giving Erin an approving look. "You're a natural. If you ever want a job here, let me know."

Erin's eyebrows bounced. "Thanks. I'm having a lot of fun."

"Spoken like a ropes instructor. Some people call it a challenge; we call it play," Sonja said.

Erin nodded.

"You ready for the zip line, Clint?" Sonja asked.

Truthfully, I would have stayed on that platform forever if it meant keeping a giggling Erin close, but she'd promised to meet me later, so I'd have to be patient. "Yeah."

Sonja clipped me into the safety cable and I whizzed down the line, wondering at the empty feeling that overcame me as the distance between me and Erin grew.

When I arrived at the end of the line, another instructor unclipped me and I waited for Erin to appear. The next person to arrive was Fern.

"I take it you aren't happy to see me," he said dryly.

"Mother Teresa," I cursed, under my breath, annoyed at how transparent I was.

"We might as well go. Erin and Sonja were deep in conversation when I got on the zipline," he added.

I nodded, but of course, I couldn't help but glance back as we walked away.

Erin was nowhere to be seen.

Chapter 8: Cabin #83 Revisited

~Erin~

I watched from the platform as Clint zipped down the cable, his tawny hair ruffled

the speed.

I wonder what his hair would feel like between my—

"Could you imagine working here?" Sonja said, breaking into my reverie.

"What? Oh. Working here?" I glanced around at The Odyssey apparatus, which had been so much fun, I could have happily done it all over again.

It was hard to believe that what Sonja and Darius did was actually considered work. I was used to paying to climb, not the other way around.

Sonja nodded. "I'm always looking for new people." She turned back in the direction of the final element. "Look, here come Darius and Fern."

I turned and watched as the two men traversed the final obstacle easily, their long strides allowing them to simply step from square to square.

"No fair," I said, and was greeted by Fern's laughing gaze.

In two more long strides, Fern and Darius were on the platform.

"What can I say? We're just two tall dudes," Fern said as he high-fived Darius.

"That's got to be a record," Darius said.

Sonja trilled her lips. "Like Erin said, it wasn't much of a challenge for you two."

"You zip-lining?" Fern asked, turning to me.

I shook my head. "Go ahead. I want to talk to Sonja for a bit. Tell Clint not to wait for me." A pang of guilt accompanied my words, but I needed a moment to myself. Being around Clint was fun, overwhelming, and addictive. I needed some space so I could think clearly.

Fern nodded as Darius clipped him into the line.

Sonja and I spent the next couple of hours talking about the life of a ropes instructor and going over The Odyssey course with an eye towards facilitation.

By the time I left her—and started walking to the cafeteria for lunch—it felt like a whole new world had opened up. A path that I didn't even know existed had suddenly been illuminated.

It was exciting.

Then again, I enjoyed my work at *WUA*. Could it be more challenging? Yes.

But I loved public radio just as much as I loved climbing.

It was my love for listening to public radio that had led me to volunteering during pledge drives, which ultimately led me to apply for a job. When I'd gone in for my interview at *WUA*, I'd been dumbstruck hearing the voices from my car radio echoing down the hallways. Putting faces to names and laughing when they looked nothing like what I'd expected.

Except for Clint. He'd looked *exactly* like I'd imagined. Hot and cocky.

Then I remembered my promise to meet Clint later, and my excitement took on a nervous flavor.

I couldn't deny the attraction between us, but where was it leading? What did Clint want? Was he proposing a retreat fling, or something else? And what did I want from him? What did I want in general?

It was the last two questions that bothered me the most. I'd been so focused on changing my life's trajectory that I'd back-burnered my love life. I'd dated a little bit when I'd been working at my cousin Angela's bookstore, but between throwing myself into work and feeding my climbing habit, there hadn't been time for dating. And I turned down the few guys from the gym who'd asked me out. I didn't want to have to find a new place to climb if things didn't work out. Of course, the truth was, I would have probably broken that rule if any of the men had been compelling enough.

Compelling like Clint.

My attraction to him was allowing me to easily ignore my discomfort over the fact that we worked together.

But what did I want from him? I didn't feel like I knew him well enough to answer that.

Even though we'd worked together for years, all I *really* knew about him was what his resume said. I didn't know anything about his personal life. He didn't wear a wedding ring, and I'd never heard him mention a wife, but what did that mean?

Maybe he was divorced.

I frowned, not because he might be divorced, but because I didn't even know this most basic fact about a man whom I'd woken up with, his limbs intimately wrapped around mine.

The thought of how warm and safe I'd felt in his arms took my breath away.

I *wanted* Clint, that much was clear. What wasn't clear was *what* I wanted from him.

Despite my cavalier attitude towards my first time (aka: "losing my virginity")—an experience I'd wished I could change a million times—I wasn't one for casual intimacy, no matter how tempting the attraction. I just wasn't raised that way.

Then again, I'd *never* been as attracted to anyone as Clint. The Odyssey course had been one long game of foreplay, and it had been the most fun and intimate time I'd ever shared with—

Anyone.

Every time our bodies came into contact, my skin erupted in shivers.

Every time he gazed at me with his heated caramel eyes, my breath faltered.

Every time he said my name, my heart beat a little faster.

Every. Damn. Time.

And then, when he'd hugged me at the end of the course, I'd been strangely disappointed, because a kiss—like the one we'd shared the night before, when Clint's mouth had introduced me to a minty, windswept world where my thoughts became mist—would have been so much better.

Who would have thought that a ropes course could be so tantalizing and flirtatious?

Jiminy Cricket.

I stumbled over a small rock in my path, the moment bringing me back to my body.

I took a deep breath.

Removing myself from Clint's testosterone-laced orbit, had reminded me of all the things I didn't know about Clint or about my future. A lot needed to happen before anything could *happen* between us.

Satisfied that I'd puzzled all of that out, I entered the cafeteria.

My eyes were drawn to Clint immediately. He was seated with a direct view of the front door, but he didn't look at me. Instead, his face was a mask of concentration as he spoke to Yolanda.

A barb of disappointment lodged itself in my gut, but I ignored it. He had a job to do. His every moment couldn't be spent on me.

Walking through the tables, my attention was half on finding Fern and half on Clint and Yolanda. The two of them were a matched set of intensity. I wasn't sure I could ever feel their level of passion for their jobs. While I enjoyed doing marketing for public radio, it was definitely a vocation, not an avocation, something I hadn't really thought about until Sonja had opened my eyes to other possibilities.

Motion out of the corner of my eye caught my attention; Fern was waving from a table near the desserts. I made some charade-like hand gestures indicating I would join him after grabbing food.

I got in line and put together a perky salad, grabbed a huge slice of corn bread and a bowl of strawberries and whipped cream before walking over to Fern.

"Where have you been? You missed the last activity," he asked as I sat down.

"Hmmm? Oh yeah. Sonja told me. A trust walk and journaling exercise. How did it go?" I tried to keep my focus on Fern despite the incessant urge to glance over at Clint.

He shrugged. "It was fine. What kept you?"

I told him about my conversation with Sonja. "The only downside is, it would be a pay cut. Ropes instructors aren't exactly raking in the dough."

"Money isn't everything," he said with his trademark maturity.

"True, but I have a mortgage and a dog. Big Bear is nice, but I don't know about *moving* up here." I waved my hand in the air, forking at an unruly piece of kale. "It's just a lot to think about. I'm not making any quick decisions."

I had just taken a bite when Alex da Silva, *WUA*'s executive producer, approached our table. "Erin, Fern," she said in her curt, business-like manner.

Although Alex was shorter than both of us, she carried herself with the authority of a former war correspondent, which she had been at one time. She had on at least six chunky silver rings and her hair was cut short on the sides and stood up on top in a sort of faux-hawk. She was a rock star in public radio with a Peabody, an Emmy, and a Grammy to her name.

"Erin, could I borrow you for a second?" Alex said, more of a command than a request.

I chewed as I glanced at Fern and then at my full tray of food. After three passes on The Odyssey, I was famished.

"You can bring your food," she said.

"Go ahead," Fern offered.

I swallowed. "Okay." Then I picked up my tray and followed Alex to an empty table in the corner.

Alex immediately launched into what was on her mind. "Yolanda's been talking my ear off this entire retreat. She can't get out of work mode, but I guess I understand. She feels responsible for facilitating a smooth host transition, and she feels like this retreat is standing in her way."

I nodded as I took another bite of salad.

"The thing is, a lot of the success of this transition actually rests with you."

I swallowed a bit too soon, a ticklish piece of kale in my throat causing me to cough. I doubled over, hacking.

Alex stood and smacked me on the back, dislodging the kale, which I spit into my napkin, eyes watering.

"You okay?" she asked.

I nodded and dabbed at my eyes; my throat still raspy. "I don't—" I coughed again, bending over with the effort. After a bit more hacking and tearing, Alex shoved a cold glass of water into my hand and I took a few small sips.

The tickle in my throat subsided.

It took a minute for my vision to clear and to regain control of my voice. My cheeks heated with embarrassment. "Thanks for the water."

"Clint brought it over," she explained.

Clint? I couldn't help it; I glanced to where he'd been sitting earlier and watched as his eyes held mine for a second before turning back to his conversation with Yolanda.

I turned back to Alex, who said, "Take your time. Have another sip of water. That was quite a coughing fit."

I lifted the glass to my lips.

Once I was firmly in control of my voice, I returned to our conversation. "How am I responsible for the transition?"

She leaned forward, resting her elbows on the table as she held two fingers in the air. "There are two parts to a host transition, the on-air and the off-air. As our marketing coordinator, you are responsible for the off-air side. Last time we went through a transition this big, we had a marketing director in place. Talking to Yolanda reminded me that you've never been through a host transition, which is why I wanted to talk to you. It's important that we get our stations everything they need to communicate the host change to their listeners. We'll need you to put together a comprehensive press packet on Clint that the stations can use on their websites and we can put on ours."

This bit of information didn't concern me as I'd anticipated this need and had already started working on it. Pride welled within me at this validation of my instincts.

But I held my tongue.

She continued, "I'll need you to work with Clint on recording audio teasers for all the stations, and I want you to reach out to the Top Ten markets and see if they have any events coming up that could use a host presence."

That would be easy enough. I'd done teasers with Devon and occasionally helped coordinate events for her, although not on this scale. It would be more responsibility, but it sounded fun.

I continued to listen silently, sensing an opportunity.

Alex finished. "It's going to require a lot more from you. You might even want to think about changing your hours so you can have more overlap with Clint. You should probably spend three to five hours a week with him for the next four to eight weeks. Depending on how long it takes for you to get everything done." She licked her lips, folding her hands together and resting them on the table.

"That sounds like a lot more work…"

She nodded. "I agree, which is why I wanted to find out how you felt about being promoted to Marketing Manager."

An electric thrill raced up my spine. "Promoted?"

"You've done excellent work the last two years, and this increase in responsibility would certainly warrant it. I might even need you to manage another one or two employees, perhaps someone who can help with the website and copy-writing or maybe a PR consultant."

A promotion. This was exactly what I'd been wanting. A new challenge, a raise, and the opportunity to do more events sounded particularly intriguing. Maybe I could find my way to my avocation at *WUA* after all.

The new title would be a bonus. Marketing Coordinator sounded like a title for a twenty-something. Marketing Manager was definitely more how I saw myself.

"Of course, if you don't want the promotion, you can stay in your current capacity and I'll hire someone above you." Alex waited a beat, and then stood. "You don't have to answer me now. Think about it. We can discuss it in the office next week. Enjoy the rest of your lunch," she said, before walking away, not waiting for an answer.

Accept the promotion or have a manager. *Or quit and become a ropes course facilitator.*

I picked up my tray and walked back to Fern.

"What was that about?" he asked as I sat down.

"She offered me a promotion," I said, taking another bite of salad and making sure the kale wasn't too big this time.

His eyes lit up. "That's great."

I nodded, my brain racing.

At that moment, Sonja announced that there would be an afternoon break followed by dinner and an improv exercise in front of the campfire.

A whoop of cheers went up.

Sonja smirked. "I won't take that personally. We know all the togetherness gets intense. This is your mid-point break. The final two days will be nonstop." She made a gesture towards the door. "The pool will be open during the break and staff will be at The Odyssey if anyone wants to try it again."

The *WUA* staff scattered like cockroaches.

It seemed like everyone needed a little personal space.

I noticed Clint's retreating back, his head ducked to listen to whatever Yolanda was saying as they headed out of the cafeteria together. I couldn't deny that I was disappointed that he didn't turn to catch my eye, and that bothered me.

Sonja approached, splaying her hands on the table as she leaned forward. "If you're up to it, I was thinking you could help us facilitate the improv exercise tonight."

I flushed. It was nice to feel wanted, and today I was getting it from multiple sides.

I'd have to remember this feeling for those days when my self-esteem took a beating.

"Okay," I said. "What do I have to do?"

Sonja smiled. "I can fill you in at dinner. I'll look for you then," she said before walking away.

"I'm going to the heated pool. Want to come?" Fern asked.

I looked down at my half-eaten lunch and shook my head. "No thanks," I said, stifling a yawn. I hadn't slept well in cabin #83. "I'm going to finish eating and then take a nap or go for a walk."

I had a lot on my mind, some alone time would be good.

"Okay. See you at the campfire."

It was one of the endearing things about my relationship with Fern. We were each other's go-to person for anything work-related. This was the first time I'd ever felt inconvenienced by our unspoken agreement. And the reason why? Well, let's just say that it started with a capital C.

"Sounds good," I said, trying to keep my voice light. "I'll see you then."

Finishing lunch gave me a bit of energy, and I wanted to continue the silent mulling I'd done during my solitary meal, by going on a walk. So I went back to my cabin, threw a book and a water bottle into a backpack, and headed off into the woods.

After fifteen minutes of walking, I realized that I was headed in the direction of cabin #83 and a spark of happiness made me curious to see it again. Maybe I'd unconsciously been heading there all along.

A sense of purpose made me walk faster and after another ten minutes, cabin #83 came into view along with its neighboring cabins which had been hidden last night. Although the location was further from the cafeteria, this area looked just the same as the cabin I was staying in. The path was well-maintained, the paint on the cabin was unchipped, the screens were intact. It was funny how remote and isolated I'd felt the night before when I couldn't see.

I unlatched the external shutters and opened them up so the afternoon light could filter in, and then walked up the stairs, banging through the two doors, leaving the wood one open for ventilation. My eyes traveled over the space, surprised to find that it looked like we'd never been there. Not that there was much for Clint to do to tidy up, but it was sweet that he'd taken the time to do it just the same.

I laid down on the bed we'd shared last night, trying to see if I could catch the minty-cedary smell of Clint, but—maybe because I was surrounded by a pine forest—I couldn't pick out anything distinctly Clint-like.

I sighed, disappointed that there wasn't more evidence that we'd been there.

Tucking the blanket under my head like a pillow, I got out my book and read.

"Errrrr-innnnnnn."

I inhaled a deep stutter breath as a voice called me back to consciousness. I ran my hand over my face, feeling a trickle of saliva at the corner of my mouth.

I must have fallen asleep, I thought groggily as I ran my hand over my braids.

"Errrrr-innnnnnn," the voice repeated, but I was awake enough to recognize how softly it was saying my name.

My brain cleared a bit more and then suddenly my back went rigid because I knew that voice.

I rolled over to face the door and saw Clint sitting on the opposite bed, a heathered blue shirt clinging to his chest with sweat, his hair also damp.

I sat up and wiped at the other side of my mouth, saying a small prayer of gratitude when I didn't find saliva.

"I guess I fell asleep," I said, still bleary-eyed.

"Yeah, I was pretty tired too," he said, shaking his Adonis curly hair out of his eyes.

I'd never seen his hair so curly; his sweaty run must have activated it. *What would it feel like to run my fingers through that gorgeous hair?*

My heart beat faster.

He continued, completely unaware of my wayward thoughts. "I took a twenty-minute nap before my run." Then he leaned back across the narrow twin bed, his eyes guarded but hopeful.

"Yolanda finally let you go, huh?" I asked, not sure if I was able to keep the twinge of jealousy I felt out of my voice.

His lips twitched and he arched a brow. "She's kinda my boss."

I immediately felt foolish. I wasn't jealous of Yolanda per se, what I was jealous of was the time Yolanda got to spend with Clint. She had the "right" to spend time with him...I didn't. "Of course. Forget I said that."

Then I remembered that Alex had just given me a reason to spend more time with him. That would be a nice side benefit of the promotion.

He nudged my foot with his. "I think it's cute that you care."

Blood rushed into my face and my heart beat loud in my ears. I didn't even have time to process what that might mean when he asked—

"What are you reading?" his eyes flicked to the book laying open on the bed.

I turned to the book, grateful for the distraction from his heaving, sweaty chest. "My cousin gave it to me. It's one of her favorites. It's beautiful, but tragic," I explained, handing him the hardback.

"What happened to the dust jacket?" he asked, running his hand over the red linen cover.

"I hate dust jackets."

"But the book will get damaged without it."

I shrugged. "It's not a collector's item."

He shrugged like it didn't matter, but I got the feeling he thought a book without a dust jacket was blasphemy. I filed it away under the mental heading labeled "Clint Davenport – Personal Information."

He flipped open the cover and read the title page. "*The House of Mirth* by Edith Wharton. 'To my favorite cuz. A beautiful cautionary tale. Don't be a Lily. Love, A.'" He looked up from the book. "Is that the cousin you keep telling me about?"

"Yes. Angela." I watched as he turned to the first page and read a bit.

"It's a period book?"

I nodded. "It's set in New York in the late 1800s. Angela said that it's fun to read about how different New York was back then, but I've never been, so I can only imagine."

"You've never been?"

I blushed, only this time it wasn't because of Clint, but because of my own insecurities. "I've never been outside of Hawai'i and California, except for New Zealand for my cousin's wedding."

His eyes widened, and I could almost feel him judging me, reminding me of the vast chasm of experience between this beautiful, worldly man and me.

Then I remembered all the good vibes I'd been getting that day, not just from Clint, but from Sonja and Alex. I sat up straighter, refusing to feel ashamed for who I was. It wasn't that I didn't want to travel, I'd just never had the opportunity. *Anyway, California is a big place—*

He shrugged. "New York is loud and there are tall buildings. Boston and Manhattan are pretty close to each other. Closer than Los Angeles and San Francisco," he said, using his fingers like two points on a map and bringing them closer together.

I relaxed as he talked. His words soothed my initial embarrassment; perhaps he hadn't been judging me after all.

He closed the book and rested it on his lap. "When I was a teenager, my friends and I would take the train into Manhattan. It felt like a grand adventure," he said, his eyes twinkling with the memory. "But it was also pretty rough. I can't believe our parents let us go unsupervised. There's this one part of the city, called Times Square. My friends and I thought it would be a laugh to check it out. Back then, it was a lot grittier than we were expecting. The only people who went there were looking to score drugs. It's been cleaned up a lot though."

"Well, the part of the book I'm reading is all country homes and bridge parties—"

"Kill me now," he deadpanned.

I frowned. "Not a fan of fiction?"

He shook his head. "I read biographies and histories almost exclusively. Maybe the occasional social science book, but zero fiction."

"Zero?"

He shrugged. "It's a waste of time," he said, with the authority I so often heard him use on his show.

I arched a brow. "Full stop?"

"Full stop," he said, his jaw tensing.

"That's awfully judgmental of you, *Clint*."

He winced. "Look, I'm sure they're fun—"

"Fiction isn't just fun, *Clint*," I said, feeling my temperature rise, but not in a pleasant way. "You can explore ideas and learn vicariously through the characters, especially if you identify with them. Good fiction can be as truthful as non-fiction, you just don't know *whose* truth it is."

He arched a brow and rolled his jaw as though he was considering my words. "You're telling me that this book," he said, holding up the hardback as though it was a rotten egg, "will actually *teach* you something?"

It was clear by his tone that he'd never considered this possibility.

I leaned forward. "Actually, maybe *you* should read this book. I think you could probably learn more from it than me."

He sighed. "Look, I didn't come here to fight."

I narrowed my eyes. "Why *did* you come here?"

"To see you, of course. I mean," he ran his hands through his hair, making my fingers itch with the desire to do the same. "I didn't plan on it," he said with an exhale, studying his hands for a moment. "After all, I didn't know you were here, but when I started running, I found myself heading this way, and then when I saw the shutters open," his voice softened as he met my gaze. "I figured you were inside."

I was still annoyed by his wholesale dismissal of fiction and, if I was being completely honest, the fact that he'd ignored me at lunch. Except he hadn't really—

"Did you bring me the water at lunch?" I asked.

He nodded. "I heard you coughing, and Alex was just *sitting* there," he said, his tone biting. "So I jumped up and handed you my water."

"But you were three tables away."

He shrugged, only this time it wasn't annoying, it was sweet and endearing. "You needed help…"

If my heart could have fanned itself like a Southern belle about to swoon, it would have. I licked my lips. "Why didn't you stick around?"

He sighed heavily. "Yolanda expects me to work through meals with her. She's riding me hard on this host transition; wants us to come out of the gate with some spectacular content so that no one will miss Devon."

I thought about what Alex said at lunch and glanced at my watch. "It's almost time for dinner."

"I need to grab a shower," he said. "And then I have to work through dinner with Yolanda, but we can meet after—"

"Actually, I can't." I stood, grabbed my book and bag, and straightened the bed before heading outside, waiting for Clint to catch up before I started walking.

There was a little part of me that wanted to keep going; to put distance between us. It was impossible to think clearly when I was near him.

"But you promised," he said, his tone tinged with dismay. He then walked around to the shutters and closed them, which further softened my heart.

At this rate, I was going to be a puddle soon.

Keep your distance.

Then he was right next to me, the air between us vibrating like it had all morning long; tempting, exciting, erotic; and I couldn't seem to remember why I should stay away. Intellectually, I *knew* there were valid reasons, and yet, being around Clint made it impossible to think of what they were.

I stuffed my book into my backpack and slung it over my shoulder.

"Let me carry that for you," Clint said, reaching for the bag.

Damn it. That was it. I was a puddle.

Then I remembered what he'd said about fiction, and a bit of annoyance returned.

Clint's strange combination of jerk-face and chivalrous was confusing.

I pulled the bag higher on my shoulder. "That's all right. I wouldn't want you to have to carry a dirty *novel*."

The light in his eyes went out. "Okay, I can see that I hurt your feelings. What can I do to make it right?" He held out his hand, his gaze trained on my bag.

I arched a brow and gripped my bag tighter. *Let the punishment fit the crime.* "You can read it."

His eyes widened, but he recovered quickly, his Adam's apple bobbing as he swallowed hard.

His pride must taste pretty bad right about now.

He took a deep breath. "Okay." He opened and closed his fingers, signaling for me to hand him my bag.

His acquiescence surprised me, in a good way. So I handed him my backpack and decided to make his punishment easier for him. "I bet you could find an audio version of it, so you could listen while you run."

His eyes lit up. "Hey, that's a great idea. I could probably read three times more books a year. Thanks."

We started walking back in silence, but close enough that our arms occasionally brushed against each other. I felt every accidental touch flutter through me, leaving me flustered and wanting.

"You never said why you can't meet me tonight," he said, his tone once again dismayed. He put his hand on my shoulder and turned me to face him.

I sucked in a breath.

Although sunset was still two hours away, the sun had already dipped behind the surrounding mountains, casting a warm glow on Clint's hair, setting off his bronze curls. His eyes looked about two shades darker than normal, as though he was scared of what my answer might be. Then there was his voice. In the two years I'd known him, I'd never heard him speak this way, as though he actually cared what the answer was. As though he had something to lose. I'd heard him debate and cajole his way through conversations, his voice a lash, but I'd never heard him beg before, his voice like a silk handkerchief. Just like I'd never seen him as lighthearted as he'd been on The Odyssey.

Perhaps the driven, opinionated, occasionally jerk-face Clint Davenport I knew was just a sliver of the whole man. What if there was even more to his playful, chivalrous side than I'd seen so far?

A spark of hope erupted in my chest.

He seemed to be working hard trying to be honest about his feelings, so I met him halfway. "I *want* to see you tonight, it's just that something's come up."

His face relaxed. "You *want* to see me." The light returned to his eyes, a small smile dancing on his lips.

I warmed when I realized that it was my words, my presence that did this to him; that seemed to bring out a lighter, happier version of himself.

"So why can't you?" he asked, evenly.

"You're not the only one who has to work on this trip," I started, and proceeded to tell him about my afternoon with Sonja as we strolled back to camp.

As we talked, he kept turning towards me, watching me intensely, as though trying to understand every possible nuance of my words.

I'd be lying if I said I didn't enjoy his attention.

"Do you like the idea of working with Sonja, here, at this retreat?" he asked, once I'd finished.

I nodded, taking a moment to notice just how excited the idea made me feel. "It's funny, but when she first brought it up, it just sort of intrigued me. But as I've been talking about it with you, I find the idea is growing on me. Being a ropes instructor is definitely more interesting than what I'm doing right now," I said, thinking about the rote press releases, daily e-newsletter, social media, and website updating that took up most of my day.

Although our office was intellectually interesting, my job no longer was. I'd clearly outgrown it. I loved my coworkers, most of whom were off-the-charts smart and great conversationalists. Another perk was the shelves upon shelves of free books, sent to the editors and reporters, and then put on a bookshelf near the kitchen once they weren't needed anymore. My library collection had grown considerably. However, I couldn't deny that the work itself had grown tedious.

Perhaps the promotion Alex had dangled in front of me would change things.

He gave me a wan smile. "That's great. I'm happy for you." His words and tone seemed at odds.

"Didn't you think The Odyssey was fun? It seemed like you were having a good time."

He pursed his lips. "I was having fun because I was with *you*. That's what made it enjoyable for me. If you hadn't offered to be my partner, I would have found some way out of it."

"Really?" I blinked quickly at the admission, his words confirming something I'd only dared to suspect.

I'd offered to be his partner because I'd sensed his fear and thought I might be able to help him get through it. I'd also done it because I was indebted to him for keeping me calm—and alive—the night we'd been lost. It was my way of paying him back. However, despite the kiss and the flirty fun we'd had on The Odyssey, this was the first time that I really allowed myself to consider the fact that Clint Davenport *liked* me. *Like*-liked me. Not like, like a friend, but *liked*—

"You're surprised," he said, a bit of wonder in his voice as he studied my face. His eyes lit up as though he'd had a realization. "You know," he stopped and looked down at his hands as he rubbed his palms together. "The last twenty hours have been the most amazing and the most terrible in my entire life."

My heart leaped and then fell so rapidly, I felt a little dizzy.

He continued, "Erin, I've noticed you ever since the day you walked into the office. I remember you were wearing a very serious black pantsuit. You looked like a secret agent. But your hair." He paused, twirling his hands over his head. "Your hair was in this bun sort of thing and there was this tropical-looking flower holding it all together. I thought the flower-suit combination was very…surprising."

I colored. I remembered that day with perfect clarity.

It had been the day I'd come in for an interview with Yolanda and Alex. I'd bought the suit the week before at some discount retailer. It was more formal than anything I'd ever worn before and had cost more than anything else I owned. When the time had come to do my hair, I didn't know how to professionalize my waist-length locks. So I'd twisted it up on top of my head and clipped it with the only thing strong enough to hold the weight of my hair: a plastic plumeria I'd bought at an ABC Store in Honolulu.

But I was surprised that he remembered that moment. We hadn't met that day, although I'd seen him walk through a hallway, talking to another reporter.

He continued, "Since then, I've been avoiding you. It hasn't been hard since I was working on the overnight shift. Then when Fern joined your team, you two seemed like such a great couple, I had no reason to pay attention to you."

I started. "You thought Fern and I were a couple?"

He nodded.

"You know he's seven years younger than me, right? He's barely out of college."

The look on his face made it clear he hadn't known. "Oh. No, I didn't know. He seems so much more mature. I thought he was late twenties at least." He paused a moment as though processing that new information. "Anyway, he told me that you two weren't together."

"You two talked about me?" I pointed to my chest. "About us?" I waved my hand in the space between us.

The word "us" felt foreign on my lips—I'd never had the need to use it romantically—but no other word seemed appropriate.

However fledgling, Clint and I were venturing into the realm of "us".

It made my pulse quicken.

That moment, in those alpine woods, was the most romantic thing that had ever happened to me. I wanted to sear it into my memory, hoping I could recall every beautiful detail of it.

Clint glanced ahead. "We'll be in view of the campsite soon. There's so much I want to tell you, but I don't want to fit it into these tiny slivers of time we have together." He ran a hand through his hair, rubbing his scalp as though for inspiration. He stopped and took my hands.

The moment felt reverent. If we'd crossed one threshold on The Odyssey, we were crossing another now.

A gentle breeze whispered past my ears, the pine needles rustling with the wind.

"Are you free this Saturday? Will you have dinner with me? We can talk about everything then," he said, again with the silk handkerchief voice.

My mouth dropped open.

Clint Davenport just asked me out.

One of America's most widely heard voices wants to have dinner with me.

A swirl of confusing thoughts and emotions erupted inside me. *What would mom say? What would Alex say? But we have to work together. What about my promotion? And what about the fact that I didn't even like you that much twenty-four hours ago?*

All of these thoughts planted themselves firmly on the "no" side of the scale.

And yet the word that bubbled its way up through the doubting masses was "yes."

"You will? Swell," he said, a boyish grin taking over his face.

"Swell?" I said on a laugh.

He shrugged. "It started as an affectation, and now I just like the word."

I shook my head. Clint Davenport was turning out to be a very surprising man.

Chapter 9: Improv

~Clint~

I was beginning to surprise myself.

In the last twenty-four hours, I'd gone from a confirmed bachelor—who had a serious but benign crush on a co-worker—to a man with a date. I couldn't even remember the last time I'd been on a date. It must have been before I started working at *WUA*, because it was impossible to date with the hours I'd been keeping the last decade.

And now I was not only going out on a date, but going out with *Erin*, the woman I'd admired from afar for two years.

I found myself smiling like an idiot all through dinner. Yolanda kept looking at me like I was crazy.

"Are you listening to a word I'm saying?" she said, pushing a lock of hair impatiently behind her ear.

"Yes, you want to create some new desks, one for sustainability and one for poverty in America," I said blithely.

She scowled, like she was annoyed I'd gotten it right. "Those aren't exactly upbeat topics. Why do you sound happy?"

I checked my face and tried to get the sides of my mouth to point downward, but I just couldn't seem to do it. I didn't remember ever feeling this excited before about anything except flying. It was like Erin had unlocked an unknown reserve of hope and good cheer I hadn't known existed.

"I'm just in a good mood," I said, still unable to straighten out my face.

She narrowed her eyes, but before she could say anything, I said, "I think those are good topics, but what about my idea to go to China for a couple of weeks?"

She sighed. "I like the idea but we have to find funding before we can commit to it." She crossed her arms over her chest. "China would be an expensive series to produce, not to mention logistically challenging. Maybe we should do a domestic special first? What about something from Detroit? That city is facing some hard times."

"Or Silicon Valley?" I offered, knowing I was poking the bull.

Yolanda pretended to throw up, which was a hilarious look on her patrician face. "I'm so tired of Silicon Valley. I want to do something *newsworthy*," she said, with an ambitious gleam in her eye.

At that moment, a loud voice cut through the air. "Please everyone, come to the campfire. We'll be doing some team-building exercises out there," Sonja called with her megaphone. There was mild grumbling, to which Sonja answered, "Remember, you had a long free afternoon. This will be fun."

I practically jumped out of my seat. Campfire time meant Erin.

"I think I like you better when you're in L.A. The mountain air seems to make you unusually energetic," Yolanda said with a wry arch of her brow.

"I love you too, Yo," I said with a wink.

"Save it for the listeners, Davenport."

I knew I was being an idiot, but I had never felt so good; it was like the first flower of spring had a baby with the first day of summer break.

I tried to slow my gait so we could walk out together, but Yolanda shooed me forward like an annoying puppy.

When I got outside, I walked to the front row of benches closest to the campfire and sat down, not even noticing as I sat next to Fern.

"Heeeeeey, Clint. Fancy seeing you here," Fern said, in a voice that made it clear he wasn't at all surprised.

Apparently, I was giving off *eau-de*-bust-my-balls.

"Fern," I said with a lift of my chin. Then I remembered that Fern had likely just eaten with Erin and I rolled my shoulders back in what I hoped was a casual gesture. "So, how was dinner?"

"Erin. Ate. With. Sonja," he said meaningfully.

Abraham Lincoln. I was being too transparent so I switched gears. "How do you like working at *WUA*?" I asked, glancing around quickly, but not seeing Erin anywhere.

Fern arched a brow, but after a moment he said, "I like it a lot. Even though I was working the last few years, it was at the university I attended, so in some ways, this feels like my first real job."

It was hard to believe that Fern was only twenty-five. With his height, his deep bass voice, and his serious-beyond-his-years eyes, he had the gravitas of a man ten years his senior.

I couldn't shake the feeling that I was talking to a peer. "What were you doing at the university?"

He licked his lips. "While I was a student, I worked for the basketball coach. That switched to full-time once I graduated. He was trying to convince me to go into sports management, maybe get my MBA."

"But you don't want that," I guessed.

He shook his head. "No. I don't."

After a few moments of silence, I asked, "So what *do* you want to do?"

Fern looked down at his feet, and suddenly he looked like a man of twenty-five, uncertainty coating his features. "I want to be a priest." His usually strong voice was a fraction of its normal self.

I'd heard a lot of things in my life, but I'd never met anyone who wanted to be a priest, which seemed strange. *Is it that rare?* I was genuinely intrigued. "Catholic? Protestant? Luther—"

"Episcopalian," he said. He got a thoughtful look. "Funny, you're only the second person I've ever told."

I felt a strange pride at that. "Let me guess…Erin was the first."

He nodded. "She's like the older sister I never had. I'm an only child, and I guess Erin misses her brother."

My ears perked up. "Erin has a brother?"

Fern *tsked.* "A *twin* brother."

I inhaled swiftly, feeling like I'd just been sucker-punched.

Erin's a twin.

I was just about to wonder at how little I knew about her when she appeared along with Sonja, Darius, and two other camp facilitators named Lily and Jayden.

Sonja stood in the middle of the dirt area that was playing the part of a stage and raised her hands to the crowd, her face in intermittent darkness with the campfire behind her. "Hello everyone, and welcome to our evening of improv. Since we gave you the afternoon off, we expect you to all be well-rested for this activity." After a dramatic pause, she continued. "These exercises can be surprisingly profound and I want to encourage you to think about how you could incorporate them into your office culture when you get back to L.A. Don't just leave what you learned up here in the mountains."

She rubbed her hands together and pointed to Erin and Darius, whose features were also half-lit by the orange flames. "This game is called 'Yes, And'. It's a great way to improve your listening skills. There is no negation here, you can only accept what the other team member says. We'll demonstrate it for you. Whenever you're ready," Sonja said to Erin and Darius as she stepped back into the dark.

They took center stage. Erin glanced around at the audience and pressed her lips together. She shook her arms out and turned to focus on Darius's face.

My hands gripped the edge of the bench and I leaned forward.

"Erin, guess what? I just found an asteroid from outer space," Darius said.

"*Yes, and,*" she stressed the two words. "I saw something streak across the sky last night. Maybe that was it. Do you have it with you?"

Darius mimed pulling something really heavy out of his pocket. "Yes, and it's dense. Here, feel it," he said, miming handing it to Erin.

Erin's hands fell almost to the ground, and the crowd laughed. "Yes, and wow, it *is* heavy. And it's really hot too. Oh, ah, oh, ah," she said, juggling the imaginary rock from hand to hand.

I looked around at the faces of our coworkers; everyone was fully engaged in Erin's performance. She was clearly in her element, all traces of her earlier nerves, gone.

She threw the 'asteroid' back to Darius and he began tossing the hot rock from side to side. They went like this, back and forth for a while, the laughter in the audience growing as Erin and Darius's reaction to the hot rock became more and more animated.

My chest swelled with pride.

Darius prepared to throw the asteroid again, this time squatting low and swinging his arms in the air as he flung the imaginary rock skyward.

Erin shielded her eyes with her hand. "Yes, and do you see it?"

Darius copied her gesture. "Yes, and I think it's that tiny glowing dot."

"Yes, and it's growing larger; it looks like it's coming back down."

"Yes, and you better stand back," Darius said, motioning for her to back up as he retreated a few steps.

"Yes, and is it making that whistling sound?" Erin said, alarmed.

I could practically hear the whistling; I was so engaged in their scene.

"Yes, and, here it comes!" Darius said, pointing.

Darius and Erin's eyes seemed to track the same object in the sky and Erin jumped when her eyes hit the ground. She walked towards the spot she was staring at and peered downward. "Look at the size of that hole!"

The audience erupted in laughter.

"And...scene," Sonja said, the audience clapping as she returned to center stage. "Thanks, you two, great job," she said to Erin and Darius. She turned back to the audience. "'Yes, And' seems like a simple game, but it does a lot of important things for a team. It forces people to listen, rather than thinking about how they are going to react. It allows a team experience what a safe environment—where there are no mistakes, but only ways to move forward—feels like. These are things that benefit any workplace.

"Now, I'd like you to partner up with someone. In the beginning, use the words 'Yes, and' to keep you on track, but you don't need to use them every time as long as you remember not to negate what your partner says. Please begin."

The buzz of conversation erupted, filling the night air.

Two things happened almost simultaneously that brought me a strange mix of relief and satisfaction. One, Fern turned to speak to the person on his other side while Erin made a beeline in our direction. As she approached, I had the sudden realization that I'd been missing her; being near her, talking to her, watching the small changes in facial expressions you can only see up close.

I hadn't missed anyone in a long time.

When she got to where we were sitting, she glanced at Fern's back, and then back to me. "Hi," she said, looking up through lowered lashes.

My mouth felt suddenly dry. "Hi," I answered, once again feeling like a teenager. The only thing missing was drawing circles in the dirt with my toe. *Harriet Beecher Stowe, get ahold of yourself, man.* After a beat, I said, "You did well with Darius. Have you done improv before?"

A look of pleased relief suffused her face. "Nope, first time. But it was fun. I had no idea where it was heading."

"You and Darius didn't talk it over?"

She shook her head. "No. It was completely spontaneous." She cocked her head. "You want to give it a try?"

I'd never been a spontaneous person; spontaneity was the enemy of discipline.

My hesitation must have shown because Erin said, "Don't over-think it. Just talk."

I rolled my head from side to side, trying to loosen up like I did before my daily run. Then I jerked my head to a spot a few feet away that would give us some distance from the other improv teams forming around us.

I shook out my arms and then nodded. "Okay. Hit me."

She put her hands on her hips and gave me a once-over. "Nice tie," she said, pointing at my chest.

I looked down at my shirt. "But I'm not—"

Erin raised her brows, silencing me.

"Oh, right. Hold on a sec." I did a mental backpedal. "Yes. And. Thanks…Erin," I said. The next words out of my mouth surprised me. "You like it? I picked it up at a strip-club on Sunset."

Her eyes went wide. "Yes, and really? Which strip-club?"

Why did I have to say strip-club?

I tried to concentrate, but my mind was a complete blank.

So instead of thinking, I just said the first thing that came to mind. "Yes, and, I got it at the one with the sign of the giant chicken holding a cast iron skillet in its hand, or wing, you know the one."

She chuckled, her eyes dancing.

My heart clenched at the happy look on her face knowing that I'd put it there. Was there a better feeling in the world than making someone you cared about happy?

Then she said, "Yes, and, you mean the strip-club that's famous for its chicken and waffles? Didn't you eat four waffles there one time?"

I couldn't help but laugh. I hadn't eaten a waffle since before flight school, and I couldn't even fathom eating four, although my mouth watered at the thought. "Yes, and you should come with me some time. I think you'd be impressed by the food and the artistry of the dancing."

Her eyes narrowed and I could tell that this scenario was challenging her ability to say "yes, and", but she recovered quickly and said, "Yes, and I heard that you've been known to get up and demonstrate some pole-dancing. Isn't there a move named after you?"

A pleasant tingle radiated through my limbs. I don't know why, but the banter was turning me on, even as it was venturing into the absurd. "Yes, and it's called the Davenport Double." Because I could guess what the next thing out of her mouth was going to be, I beat her to the punch. "Why don't I demonstrate it for you? You can follow along."

Erin's face lit up, a combination of surprise and glee. "I can't wait. What do I do?"

What have I gotten myself into? I couldn't even begin to imagine what kind of strip-club worthy move I could make up on the spot. There wasn't even anything resembling a pole around.

What sexy move could I do that would still be office-appropriate?

And then inspiration hit. *I can do anything.*

I put one hand on my hip and Erin mirrored me. Then I put my other hand on my other hip, and she followed. Then—perhaps because of the chicken reference I'd made earlier—I started flapping my arms and poking my head forward and back. Erin mimicked me all the while. After a few moments of this chicken dance, we both erupted in laughter.

As we laughed, I studied Erin's face, noticing how one of her eyes was just a little larger than the other, but when she smiled the difference disappeared. She also had dimples on both cheeks, but they weren't the typical dimples that looked like holes, more like high slits where the cheekbone meets the eyes. She also had the best laugh I'd ever heard; a musical sound that was deep and full that I wanted to listen to forever.

I glanced around, wondering if anyone else was appreciating Erin's laugh, but it looked like everyone was engaged in their own version of the exercise. It was surprising how private our interaction felt at that moment, even though we were surrounded by seventy other people. I took advantage of that, and while Erin was still laughing, I held out my hand and pulled her into a dance frame. "This is the second part of the Davenport Double. The chicken dance is part one."

Erin rested her left hand on my shoulder, sending ripples of pleasure along my neck. "I see. This must be the part that earns you the big tips. I can't imagine the chicken dance is very popular with the customers."

I frowned. "You'd be surprised. There are a lot of people with poultry fetishes."

She tossed her head with another deep laugh and I had to resist leaning in and tasting her neck.

I took a deep breath and engaged long-dormant memories of cotillion lessons. I spun us away from the group into the fuller darkness ten feet away.

Fred Astaire would have been proud.

I heard Erin take a double-breath, but it was too dark to read her expression.

We danced slowly in a sort of loose box step.

After a few minutes of pleasant silence, she cleared her throat. "We aren't playing the game anymore, are we?"

I shrugged. "I don't know. Call it a trust exercise, call it improv, call it dancing. I don't care what we call it as long as I get to hold you."

She sighed and relaxed into my embrace.

I pulled her closer, my body humming at the contact.

She wrapped both arms around my neck and laid her head on my chest.

"We are still on for dinner Saturday, right?" I asked quietly. "And remember, the only answer you are allowed to give me right now is 'yes, and'."

I felt her smile into my chest.

"Yes, and," she said, breathily.

We continued to sway in the dark to a song we both seemed to hear, and I was certain that I'd never felt more satisfied in my entire life; not the first time I sat in a cockpit, nor the first time I sat at the microphone as *WUA*'s lead host. There was something about holding Erin in my arms that put me at ease, soothed an itch that I didn't know could be scratched. My mind didn't race, I wasn't plotting the next step in my life.

I was just *being*.

Swaying in the dark with her for a few stolen moments, the crackling of the campfire and the dim cricket-song our only accompaniment, was going to be burned into my memory forever.

But it wasn't going to be enough. I wanted more.

A lot more.

Darius's voice sailed over us. "Great job, everyone. Now we're going to show you the next improv technique. Please take a seat."

"I have to go," she said, quietly, not lifting her head from my chest.

"All right," I replied, as we continued to sway.

Erin laugh-sighed. "You have to let go of me."

"Oh, right." I took one final second to appreciate this moment before releasing her.

There was a moment's hesitation, and then the soft sweetness of Erin brushing her lips against mine. "Thank you for the dance," she whispered, and then she was gone.

Chapter 10: Next Steps

~Erin~

The next thirty-six hours were a confusing mix of longing for time to slow down—so Clint and I could find a moment to spend together—and hoping that the time would pass quickly so we could just get to Saturday night, damn it!

But every time I looked for Clint, he was talking to Yolanda, a serious look on his face. The two of them appeared to be constantly engaged in a debate to the death. He'd even taken to carrying around a notebook, jotting furiously in it during their conversations.

Meanwhile, Sonja was keeping me busy. She took every opportunity to show me what I could expect if I were to join their team. For the duration of the retreat, I took part in facilitating every exercise

Truthfully? I was loving it.

When the time came to leave, I hoped Clint and I would be on the same motor-coach back to L.A. Although I don't know why, since I still wasn't comfortable with our coworkers seeing us together. And I knew there was no way I could act casual if I was sitting next to him. Just his physical proximity did strange things to my body.

It didn't matter anyway. I was stuck in a conversation with Sonja as I watched Clint and Yolanda board the first bus. As the vehicle pulled away, I realized we'd forgotten to exchange phone numbers and my heart deflated.

"It's been great having you here, Erin. You infuse a fun energy into our group. I think you'd be a perfect fit," Sonja said.

I appreciated her praise, but half my attention was on the brake lights of the large, gray bus pulling out of the parking lot.

A part of my heart had left with it.

All I could manage was a half-hearted, "Thanks, Sonja."

"You ready?" Fern's deep bass boomed, followed by his heavy hand on my shoulder.

I stutter-sighed as Clint's coach disappeared behind a stand of pine trees. I lifted my chin to Sonja before I followed Fern onto the second coach. We headed to the very back of the bus where the two of us could spread out on the plush bench-seat that could have sat four.

As the bus filled up, most people chose to sit alone. It seemed like everyone needed a break from all the togetherness.

"Want to talk?" Fern whispered.

Exhausted, I shook my head.

I grabbed an eye mask from my bag and pulled it low.

"Sweet dreams," Fern said.

I could only hope.

***

The next morning, I took a long, hot shower and then jumped into my car and drove thirty minutes southwest to my cousin Angela's tidy Spanish bungalow tucked into one of Hollywood's leafy green canyons.

Although it wasn't even noon, the thermometer on my car already read eighty-eight and climbing.

I knocked on the solid wood door, decorated with huge, hand-wrought nails, and was welcomed with a small whining sound from the other side of the door. "It's okay, Atti, I'm here sweetie. Mama's here," I cooed, through the wood.

"Aunty Aw-win's here," a small voice called through the door.

I laughed. The combination of my dog and my niece—who was technically my first cousin once removed, but who's keeping track?—was cuteness overload.

"Coming, coming," I heard Angela call.

The loud thwacks of deadbolts being thrown sounded and then the door slid open easily, despite its size.

"Erin, honey, it's so good to see you, come in," Angela called, her pregnant belly covered by a vintage apron printed with drawings of herbs and their scientific names.

"Aunty Aw-win, pick me up!" KJ demanded, her blue-black curls bouncing, her cherubic face, imperious, hands fisting open and closed.

"Hi, KJ," I said, depositing a kiss on the child's head. Then I scooped up the four-year-old in one arm and my Shiba Inu, Atticus, in the other and walked into the coolness of the entryway, the tile floors a welcome relief to the sweltering September sidewalk.

It always amazed me that September was the hottest month of the year in Los Angeles, even though it was the month when Fall would begin.

"Are you hungry?" Angela asked, as she passed through the living room into the kitchen, which was covered in colorful tiles that fit her sunny personality perfectly.

I sat at the kitchen table, which was tucked into a nook overlooking an outside patio with a burbling fountain; the tinkling of the water making me feel even cooler.

Atticus gave me a single lick on the cheek—a huge display of affection for my usually aloof ball of fur—and then settled into the seat cushion as KJ snuggled into my chest, staring at Atticus with giant, dark eyes.

"I could eat." I was always happy to eat anything my cousin made.

I studied Angela, who had that pregnant glow everyone always talked about, as she returned to the kitchen counter and continued rolling out some pie crust. "What are you making?"

"Chicken pot pie. I know it's too hot for it, but I had a craving, and we had leftover chicken from dinner," she said, her eyes never leaving her work.

My mouth watered.

"Why didn't you become a chef?"

She shrugged. "I don't know if I'd like it. I enjoy cooking for my loved ones, but *having* to cook?" She paused and blew at a lock of mahogany hair that had fallen in her face. "I think that might take all the fun out of it." She wiped her hands on her apron and tucked the wayward lock back up into her messy bun. "Besides, literature is my first love."

She'd written multiple children's books and owned a children's bookstore called Jabberwocky. It was located in a cool part of L.A.— Melrose. When I'd worked there it had been a crash course in living in the melting pot that was Los Angeles.

I'd found working there fascinating.

Not only did I find a new love for Ethiopian and Indian food, but I was exposed to every ethnicity and nationality possible. And not just ethnic diversity, but diversity across every category: political, sexual orientation, religious. A Hasidic Jewish community located in the area had been my first exposure to that sect.

Melrose couldn't have been more different than Honolulu and I loved it. In some ways, it felt like home because my face fit in just as much as everyone else's.

Just like me, Angela was *hapa*, however, her mix was different. My dad and her mom were siblings, and that's where we got our Asian blood. But whereas my mom was Caucasian, Angela's dad was Latin. When we were together, people would mention the resemblance, but I didn't see it.

"I miss this house," I said, remembering how decadent it had been to have a three-bedroom home with a garden and garage all to myself the first year I'd lived in L.A.

"You're always welcome to stay here when it's empty," she answered, referring to the nine months of the year when her family usually lived in New Zealand. "Of course, that won't be for a while." She rested a hand on her belly.

"I'm excited you're having the baby here this time. I can't wait to help out with him or her. I wish I'd gotten to help with this little one when she'd been born." I gave KJ a jiggle. The little darling had been born in New Zealand and I hadn't met her until she was a year old, when Angela brought her to L.A. for a visit.

She gave me a tired smile. "I'm glad, too. It will be nice to have so much family around." She paused and gave me a serious look. "Newborns are exhausting, which is why we'll be staying here until I feel rested enough to travel back to New Zealand."

I glanced out towards the patio. "Where's Soren?"

Angela was about to open her mouth when her lips curled up in a tired smile. "Speak of the devil."

"The devil? Did my lovely wife just call me the devil?" Soren asked, depositing a quick kiss on Erin's cheek before heading over to his wife. His sun-kissed blond hair fell into his face as he wrapped an arm around Angela from behind, nuzzling a kiss into her neck. He gave her belly a loving rub. "How's our baby?" he said quietly.

"Our baby is doing great, although *I'm* a bit tired," she answered, setting down the rolling pin to wipe her forehead with the back of her hand. "I forgot how hot September could be."

"I offered to put air conditioning in but you said—"

"It would ruin the integrity of the architecture. I remember," she huffed. "Screw the architecture. We need A.C."

"I'll get right on that." Soren leaned down and half-whispered, "In the meantime, what do you need? Do you want me to finish the pie or take our kiddo outside?" in his posh British-sounding accent, a look of loving concern on his face.

I sighed. Watching the two of them was like tuning in to my favorite television show. I'd never seen a better-matched couple.

#RelationshipGoals

Angela gave him a grateful look. "Please finish lunch. My feet are tired. KJ seems happy with Erin. I just need to sit for a bit."

He took the rolling pin out of his wife's hands and gave her a little push. "Go sit in the living room and put your feet up. I'll bring you something to drink and get the pie in the oven. Then I'll call someone about installing A.C."

"Thank you, *mi amor*," Angela said, jerking her head in my direction.

I picked up KJ and followed my cousin towards the living room where we sat in front of the dormant fireplace in a grouping of four leather club chairs arranged around a shared ottoman.

She sighed happily as she lifted her feet onto the ottoman.

"Everything felt great until the last trimester started," she said, rubbing at her calves. "Now I just want to sleep and have my legs rubbed, and I have almost two months left." She exhaled loudly.

Atticus had followed us, jumping up into his own club chair. KJ squirmed out of my arms and pulled herself up to sit with him. Angela's eyes tracked her daughter.

"Thank goodness for Atti. KJ is so happy having him around."

I suddenly felt guilty taking him home. "Do you want me to leave him?"

She shook her head. "No, I wouldn't want to deprive you. Besides, KJ's grandmothers are close by and happy to help. I just need to tell them I need it. I only began feeling really pregnant the last couple of weeks."

Soren approached with a champagne flute and handed it to my cousin. "Sparkling water with a twist of lime."

She took a grateful sip. "Oh, that's perfect. Can you bring a pitcher of it, please? I'm so thirsty."

"Of course. Erin, would you like some too, or something else?" he asked, his deep-blue eyes trained on me.

I nodded. "Sure, I'll have the same."

Angela drained her glass, which Soren refilled when he returned with a flute for me.

My cousin finished her third glass and set her flute down. "Okay, I feel settled now. Sorry, it takes so long these days. I've never felt so earthbound. The gravity of being this pregnant is intense." She made an effort to smile, her eyes widening as she studied me. "So how was your retreat?"

I'd been waiting for just this moment. I was dying to talk to someone about Clint. "I'm so glad you asked," I gushed, unleashing a torrent of words as I told her about everything that had passed with Clint, as well as the job offer from Sonja and the potential promotion at *WUA*.

By the end of the story, Angela was leaning as far forward in her club chair as her belly would allow, looking re-energized. "Wow, a new love interest and a possible career change in the same week. You've been busy. And you're supposed to see him tonight?"

"That was the plan, but we never exchanged phone numbers."

"I'm sure he'll figure something out. He sounds like a resourceful man." Her face turned serious. "But what's wrong? You look wary."

I shrugged, fiddling with the welting of the chair. "Everything was easy up on the retreat, but what if it doesn't translate well to the office? I just know Mom would think dating someone from work was a big mistake."

She shrugged. "I understand. Not dating at work is normally a good rule, but sometimes your feelings for a person mean that the normal rules don't apply." She arched a brow, reminding me that she had personal experience with this. "I wouldn't recommend casually dating someone at work, but it sounds like you and Clint have a real connection. Besides, you aren't the sort of person to enter into something haphazardly, and Mr. Fighter Pilot sounds like the cautious type as well."

"But it feels intense, and the truth is, I barely know him," I said, voicing my greatest concern.

Her brows formed a deep V. "Isn't that what dating is for?"

And just like that, my apprehension dissipated.

I was getting ahead of myself.

Angela was right. Clint and I just needed to date and get to know each other, while keeping things professional at work.

It sounded so easy.

What could go wrong?

***

Two delicious helpings of chicken pot pie later, I loaded up Atticus and drove home. I had just pulled up to the entrance of my secure, underground parking garage when my phone rang. I pulled my cell from my bag with one hand and grabbed the device to open the gate with the other, all while keeping my foot on the break.

Atticus must have sensed the tension of the situation because a low growl rumbled in his throat.

My phone's screen showed a six-two-six area code that I didn't recognize. "Hello?"

"Erin? It's Clint."

How was his voice even sexier on the phone?

My heart sped up. "Clint? Hi!"

Just then, lights flashed in my rear-view mirror and a car behind me honked. Atticus barked.

"Is now a good time?"

"Um…" I fumbled my parking remote, clicked it, and the iron gate began sliding open. "No, it's fine," I said as Atticus growled, his paws on the passenger seat shoulders, glaring at the car behind us.

"Great. I just wanted to solidify our plans for tonight."

"Tonight?" I didn't mean it to come out as a question, but I was using most of my brain to hold the phone to my ear, put my car in gear, navigate the downward slope of the driveway, and hold Atticus to the seat so he didn't tumble forward.

It was not easy.

"Is tonight not good?"

"No. I mean yes," I said, my voice higher than normal as the car slid down into the subterranean parking lot. I turned the corner towards my space in the rear. "What I mean is that no, it's good." *Does that even make sense?* Now *I* was confused.

I pulled into my spot and put my car in park, a rush of relief flooding through me as I turned it off. "Clint?"

There was no answer.

I glanced at my cell.

There was no signal.

"Damn it!"

"Atti, move!" I grabbed my bag and water bottle and jumped out of the car. "Come here, Atti," I said, turning back to the driver's seat where my Shiba now sat patiently, having jumped over the center console. "*Atti,*" I warned. "Come here!"

Atticus didn't move.

I sighed. *Damn Shiba.*

Shiba Inus are notoriously opinionated; often described as the "cats of the dog world." If a Shiba didn't want to do something, he or she didn't, and at thirty pounds of pure muscle, Atticus was *just* strong enough that I couldn't force him.

I raced around to the trunk of the car, grabbed Atticus's leash and bed, and returned to the driver's side, clipping the leash to his collar.

Atticus leaped out of the car in a graceful arc worthy of a show jumper and then pranced alongside as I directed us to the elevator.

I sighed at Atticus's slow pace as I stared at my phone, waiting for a signal to appear.

"Come *on*, Atticus," I cajoled.

He stopped cold, his proud head held high, his fluffy sickle tail curled tight. He refused to make eye contact.

"Really? You're choosing to have an attitude at *this* moment?"

Atticus continued to stare straight ahead, not deigning to look at me.

I closed my eyes, took a deep breath, and rolled my shoulders back, trying to ignore the feeling that a ticking clock was counting down the seconds since Clint's dropped call. "I'm sorry, Atticus," I said calmly.

He moved his head a fraction of an inch towards me, indicating that he was listening. *I will hear your apology, Human.*

"I shouldn't have yelled at you. Now, will you please get in the elevator?"

Atticus turned and glared at me for a few seconds before he started prancing towards the elevator, setting our pace again, his posture as imperious as ever.

I sighed. My fur baby could be a handful.

When the elevator slid open, I hit the button for the sixth floor and watched as my phone continued to have no reception. When the elevator dinged for our floor, we exited and still, no signal.

"Why?" I asked as I studied the screen of my phone like I could will it to work.

By the time I got to my door, I had an epiphany and switched the phone to airplane mode and then on, and sighed with relief as three bars lit up my screen along with the words, "two missed calls."

I dialed Clint's number as I unlocked my door and pushed into the foyer/dining room of my condo, placing my keys on a brass hook decorated with a painting of a wave. I unclipped Atticus from his leash and placed it on the same hook.

Clint picked up after one ring. "Erin?"

He sounded happy I'd called.

I smiled as I wiped at my forehead, grateful that the A.C. in my condo was going. "Hi, Clint. Sorry. I was entering my parking garage when you called and the signal dropped."

He sighed, and I thought I heard a bit of relief in the sound, which made my insides go gooey. "I just wanted to confirm dinner tonight. I thought I'd come by around five?"

I glanced at my watch; it was a little after three-thirty. My heart leapt. "Five sounds great."

"Great," he echoed. "You live near Old Town, right?"

I paused, unable to decide if I was thrilled or freaked that he'd found out where I lived. "How did you know?"

"I asked Fern when I couldn't find you yesterday. He would only tell me the general location, but he gave me your number."

I flushed with pleasure at his foresight, my scalp tingling. "I'll text you the address."

"Sounds good." He paused, and then, "I thought we could walk around before dinner. There's a great dim sum place near you."

"Lunasia?" I asked, my mouth watering.

"That's the one."

"I love that place."

"Great," he said again, his voice brighter. "I'll see you soon. Goodbye."

"Bye," I said, my voice revoltingly dreamy.

I've got it bad.

I ended the call and realized I was still standing in the entryway of my condo, one hand leaning on the key hook.

Atticus was staring at me from his perch on the sofa, his beautiful face full of judgment. *You pathetic human female.*

I rolled my eyes. "Hey, Atti. You want to go for a walk?"

Atticus tilted his head down. *Fine. I will allow myself to be seen with you in public.* He then gracefully leaped to the ground and sauntered over to the door where he stared with his face straight ahead as I clipped on his leash.

I shook my head. "You have the biggest attitude, Atti."

He lifted his chin. *Thank you for noticing.*

I grabbed a pair of rubberized sock booties from a basket in the entryway and sat on the floor, wiggling them onto his feet.

He refused to meet my gaze. *This is humiliating, Human.*

"It's hot outside. I don't want you to burn your feet. I'm not going to be able to give you a walk again until late."

He didn't fight, but I knew he hated the booties. Whenever he wore them, he walked like he had chewing gum stuck to his paws.

Once we returned from our walk, I took another shower. Although it would cool off once the sun went down, it had been in the low nineties all afternoon. After my shower, I plaited my still-wet hair into a crown braid and then picked out a floaty red summer dress. The neck of the dress was just wide enough that it sometimes slipped off my shoulder, requiring a strapless bra. When I put on my bra, I hunched my shoulders forward trying to create more cleavage.

I'd gone down a full cup size since taking up climbing and sometimes I missed being a little curvier.

Oh well.

Once I was dressed, I added some dangling gold chain-mail earrings for sparkle and swiped a bit of lip balm across my lips. I pressed my lips together and studied my reflection, smiling when I realized I was more excited than nervous.

At that moment, the buzzer for the security door downstairs squealed. I ran over to the intercom. "Who is it?"

"It's me, Clint. Clint Davenport."

As if there'd be another Clint at my door, I mused. That was actually kind of cute. "I'll be right down." I threw on some sandals and added some water to Atticus's bowl. "Be good."

He lifted a brow from his sofa perch. *Whatever, Human.*

I grabbed my keys and handbag and headed out the door. As my elevator descended, my heart sped up in inverse proportion, my mouth growing dry with anticipation. When I exited, I immediately saw Clint standing beyond the glass and metal security door, his tall, lean frame bent in his usual lackadaisical way, as though the entire world was on Clint Davenport Time instead of Greenwich Mean.

When I got to the door, I stopped, took a breath, and then pushed it open, feeling like I was crossing a figurative as well as a literal threshold. I'd done that so many times lately, it was starting to feel routine.

There was no gray area tonight; this was a real date. Things in the office would never be quite the same.

My stomach felt uneasy.

Clint turned, his lips twitching up into a smile that his eyes echoed. My cheeks warmed.

"Hi," he said softly, his radio tenor reverberating through my body as his gaze wandered over my form.

"Hi," I said, surprised at how shy I felt under his penetrating stare.

"You. Look," he paused, as though searching for the right word. "Dazzling," he said, with the percussive trill of a cymbal.

Pleasure swept over me. I took in his crisp linen shirt and broken-in denim, which somehow looked formal on him. "You look pretty good yourself."

He smiled again and then lifted his chin. "It's a might hot. Are you okay going for a walk?"

I lifted a brow. "I'm from Hawai'i, remember?"

"Good point. Great then. Should we walk towards the park? Or maybe we should grab a drink on Colorado," he said, referring to the busy shopping street a few blocks away.

"How about boba," I said, craving the cool, sweet, creamy concoction.

He seemed to wince at the word "boba" but then said okay.

"Too much sugar for you?" I guessed.

"I'm more of an unsweetened iced tea kind of guy."

"I know just the place. It's a tea bar. You can get unsweetened, organic iced tea if you want."

He nodded and then held out his hand.

My heart skipped as I laced my fingers with his.

He closed his hand, his eyes crinkling up at the corners. "Lead the way."

We started walking north towards Colorado Boulevard, a high-traffic main street filled with shops and restaurants, settling into a comfortable meander conducive to conversation. Part of me was in utter disbelief that I was holding Clint's hand, walking around in public. Odds were slim we'd see anyone from work as it had never happened to be yet. However, the fact that it was even a possibility filled me with a bit of nervous excitement; the thrill of the forbidden.

We spoke about everything and nothing, from recent movies—Clint listened as I tried to explain the last Harry Potter movie, but there was just too much he didn't know—to books—I listened as Clint praised the interdisciplinary brilliance of *Guns, Germs, and Steel*—to office politics—we both agreed that Yolanda needed to chill the eff out.

When we arrived at the tea shop, Clint read the front window. "Heavenly Tea," he said, reading the English words. Then he added, "*Zhòng shén zhī chá.* Tea of the gods," pointing at the Chinese characters below the name.

My jaw dropped. "You can *really* speak Chinese." His bio mentioned that he'd studied it in college, but I'd studied Spanish for two years and could barely order off a menu at my local Mexican restaurant.

"I can read it and I'm conversational in Mandarin, but this shop is Taiwanese. I won't be able to speak with them," he said, holding the door open and waving me in.

I was impressed. Although my grandmother spoke Cantonese, my father knew only a few phrases. I'd often wished I'd learned Chinese, but if I'd studied it in school, it would've been Mandarin, the official language of China. Part of me had rebelled at the idea of learning a form of Chinese and then not being able to converse with my grandmother because it wasn't her dialect.

"Why did you choose to learn Chinese?"

"East Asian politics was my major in undergrad and I enjoyed it so much, I minored in Mandarin. I spent a year teaching English in Beijing between undergrad and flight school," he said all this offhand, as though he was talking about someone else.

For all his swagger, Clint didn't seem to like to talk about himself. I hadn't thought a person could be humble and cocky at the same time. It was an interesting insight into a complicated and private person.

We got our drinks and then headed back outside, me enjoying my winter melon milk tea with boba, and Clint drinking unsweetened iced oolong.

"Mmmmm. This is really good. You should try it." I rolled my eyes with exaggerated bliss and had to admit that part of me liked egging him on.

His eyes narrowed in playful warning, a look that sent a ping of electricity through me.

Yummy.

And I wasn't thinking about the drink.

"I told you. I don't do sugar," he said, sipping on his tea as though not even tasting it.

"That's not true. You said that you eat birthday cake."

"You remember."

I nodded. "So what's your poison of choice?" I asked.

He raised a brow. "Devil's food cake," he said with a pause that made me sense that he could probably taste it right now. Then he added, "With a *thick* layer of chocolate frosting, and I mean thick. At least half-an-inch."

"Wow. You don't mess around."

He shrugged. "Go big or go home. I eat one giant slice with an ice-cold glass of milk." He closed his eyes, and I could practically see him savoring it.

"Do you want a moment alone with your cake fantasy?" I asked, a huge smile on my face.

It was fun watching Clint lost in such a sensual memory. He wasn't his usual, in-control self.

He took a few more moments, his mouth curved in delight, and then opened his eyes. "Wow. I should do that more often. That was almost as good as actually eating it."

I shook my head. "You are a strange man."

He winked and started walking again, turning south on a side street. The manicured green of a large park came into view.

"And that's it? That's your entire sugar intake for the whole year? No pumpkin pie for Thanksgiving or cookies for Christmas or…what *do* you celebrate?" I asked, remembering my promise to myself to get to know him better.

"I celebrate Christmas, although it's more of a seasonal tradition than a religious one for me, and no, I don't eat Thanksgiving pie or Christmas cookies. I told you, birthday cake only. And by only, I mean *only*."

He was leaving something out, but I didn't know what. "Well, I feel sorry for you. My cousin, Angela, makes the best Christmas cookies in the entire world. Her friends have asked her to sell them, they're that good."

"Ah yes. The snowball cookies. Well, maybe I'll make an exception for one of *her* cookies," he said, his eyes glancing at my lips.

My face warmed. "Really? You would?"

"Sure. For you, I'd happily eat one of the world's best Christmas cookies."

I don't know why, but for some reason, this made me extremely happy.

He smiled big and it reached his eyes, and I had the urge to kiss him. But instead, I wrapped my lips around the boba straw and took a sip.

"How about we sit in the park?" he asked.

"Great."

We sat at a shaded picnic table next to a playground full of children.

I sat, facing the playground, but when Clint went to sit, his eyes took in the children and he paused; turning the other way, giving the playground his back.

I frowned. "You don't like kids?"

His eyebrows knit together. "What? Me? No. I love kids." It seemed like he might say more but he didn't.

"Then why did you turn your back on the playground?"

"Did I?" When I gave him a look that said, "Yeah, you did," he shrugged. "I guess I just prefer the visual quiet of the park."

I could tell he was being less than honest and it reminded me of all the things I didn't know about him. "Are you married?" I asked, a hint of suspicion coloring my tone.

"What? No." Then after a moment, he asked, "Are you?"

"No," I replied, not knowing why I felt entitled to ask him the question and then offended when he threw it back at me, but there it was.

My first attempt at getting to know him better was a solid fail.

"Okay. Good. I'm glad *that's* settled," he said, his tone lighter. After a moment, he asked, "You really think I'd ask you out on a date if I was married?"

I sighed. It was time to be honest. "No. It's just that I don't know anything about you. I mean, I know what the public knows, your impressive resume, however, there's a lot that's missing."

He rolled his shoulders, his face pensive. "I'm a private person."

"A private person with a public job."

He nodded. "Good point. Actually, it's the only thing I don't like about the job, the feeling that the public has some right to me. I'm not an entertainer, I'm a journalist. The 'celebrity' part of it," he said, making air quotes with his fingers, "I don't like that at all." Then he sighed and crossed his arms. "At least it's radio so most people don't know what I look like," he said, pointing a finger around at the park goers, as though they might be his biggest fans and they didn't know that their hero was right in front of their faces.

One of my responsibilities was going through the emails sent through the "contact us" form on the website. Most of them were fan letters for the host, although a few were complaints about stories heard on the air or opinions about the grammar on the *WUA* website. Oxford commas and excluding the second space after periods were things that some public radio listeners had strong opinions about.

Devon had been on the air so long that the fan letters were mostly from girls and young women, thanking her for being a positive role model. Ever since Clint had taken over, the emails had taken a risqué turn.

Well, risqué for public radio.

I'd been surprised that some of Clint's fans asked him out on dates, and there'd been a massive uptick in requests for autographed photos. We had a photoshoot scheduled for the following week so we'd have new images of him. Now that he was the host, all of our marketing materials needed to be updated.

"So, tell me something about yourself…" I suggested, trying to ease into the getting-to-know-you portion of the evening.

The song from *The King and I* played in my head.

He shrugged. "There's not a lot to tell. I'm a simple guy. I can sleep on a floor. Wear the same clothes every day. I like to read a lot; non-fiction like we discussed, though I'm making an exception for *The House of Mirth*." He winked at me. "I've always wanted to be really good at photography, but I can't seem to get any better. I've been driving the same Subaru Outback for over ten years. That's about it."

I scowled. "You say you're a simple guy, but you aren't that simple. You're a Rhodes Scholar, former TOPGUN pilot, and now *WUA's* host. Clearly, you are very ambitious and a hard worker."

He moved his head from side to side as though he was weighing his thoughts. "Ambitious? I don't know that I'm ambitious. I didn't become a pilot or host because I wanted to impress anyone. Those were just the jobs that interested me, and I did what I had to do to get them. Does that make me ambitious? I don't know. Focused, yes. Absolutely, I'm a very *focused* person, but ambitious? Nah. I just enjoy being on the frontlines of the news and want to do a good job of it. If it's up to me, I'll retire at this job. *Maybe* I'll write a book someday, a biography or a history book. Maybe something about the Kennedys or World War II, but other than that, it's smooth sailing from here on out." Then he gave me a sideways look and said, "So what about you? What deep, dark secrets are you not telling me?"

A shivering tingle broke out on my back as he turned his attention to me. *Do I have any secrets?* I didn't think I did. So why did I feel guilty as charged? "I don't think I have any secrets."

He sat up straighter. "Look, I know we've kind of gone about this backwards. I mean, in some ways it feels like we've known each other for a long time because of work, however, we've never talked about anything *but* work. Then last week we had that—how do I put it?—surprisingly intimate experience of being lost in the woods, and now here we are. So maybe we should just clear a few things up, okay?"

I nodded, but wasn't sure what he meant.

"I like you," he said. "A lot, and I haven't dated anyone in," he pursed his lips, "a long time. I don't know where this is going, but I can't stop thinking about you. I like who I am around you. You make me *feel* things."

My heart clenched at the sweet words, and I was about to reciprocate when he continued, "But we work together. So we should probably talk things out first, or keep things quiet, or…" he shook his head. "I don't know. What do you think?"

I twisted my straw inside my cup, watching the last bit of granulated ice melting in the September heat.

This was exactly what I'd been afraid of—exposing our feelings to the reality of our situation. The retreat had been like a surreal bubble. I wasn't sure if "we" could survive outside of that safe place.

I didn't know what to say, so I chickened out and changed the subject. "Are you hungry? If we go now, we'll beat the dinner rush."

Chapter 11: One Step Forward, Two Steps Back

~Clint~

A mountain of food sat between Erin and me; noodles, dumplings, and vegetables that filled our table, while sesame oil and jasmine tea perfumed the air.

As always, the smell of Chinese food returned me to my time in Beijing, reminding me of the sights and sounds of that huge city that was simultaneously ancient and cutting-edge. While part of me wanted to talk about my experiences there—sensing that Erin would enjoy hearing about them—I was too preoccupied with my dinner companion's mood to bring it up.

Ever since we'd left the park, she'd been virtually silent. Even my attempt at speaking with the server in Chinese—which was a total loss since she spoke Cantonese and I spoke Mandarin—didn't bring a smile to her face. And despite all the food, she hadn't taken a bite. In my limited experience with her, I knew that wasn't a good sign, especially since she'd done most of the ordering.

"This looks amazing," I said with forced enthusiasm.

She gave me a tight smile. "My grandma says that a Chinese table should be so full of food there's no room for flowers."

And still, she didn't pick up any of the tantalizing morsels.

I started putting some things on my plate, hoping she might follow my lead. I took a bite of veggies wrapped in bean curd, marveling at how quiet the restaurant was without the loud clacking of dim sum carts. "The idea of made-to-order dim sum all day long is brilliant. I wonder why more restaurants don't offer it."

She picked up her teacup and blew on it thoughtfully, the only acknowledgment of my words was a small murmur of agreement.

I put down my chopsticks, frustration creeping in. Anger, uncertainty, fear, if she'd just give me an emotion, I could work with that.

But I couldn't work with nothing.

"Erin, what's wrong? You said you wanted to eat, but you aren't eating."

Without meeting my gaze, she lifted her chopsticks, picking up a dumpling, and deposited it on her plate as though it was heavy. She studied it for a few moments and then met my gaze, but her eyes weren't sparkling and playful as they'd been in Big Bear. Instead, they appeared weighted with heavy thoughts.

Maybe my declaration in the park had been too much. It had been a long time since I'd opened up to anyone, and the last time I had, I'd carried significantly less baggage. Maybe it was wrong of me to be willing to saddle Erin with my life. After all, she was so free; it was part of what I liked about her. I didn't want to kill her spark with my obligations.

"Did you know—" she started

"Maybe we should—" I said, simultaneously.

"You go," we said, at the same time.

We laughed and adjusted our napkins, a bit of the tension lifting.

She finally ate a dumpling. "So. Good." Erin shook her head as if unable to believe what she was tasting.

I relaxed, enjoying the vicarious thrill of watching her eat.

After she swallowed, she said, "You know, paper, silk, and cast iron might be China's most useful inventions, but dim sum is its most delicious, in my opinion…and the most fun." She added the last two words like an afterthought. "It's fun tasting a lot of things rather than eating just one dish."

"It's the Chinese version of Spanish *tapas*, or maybe a better analogy is English tea."

She nodded. "Did you eat a lot of it when you were in China?"

I shook my head. "No, the dish that I got into in Beijing was hotpot."

She scrunched her face. "Hotpot? I've *never* had that. What is it?"

My chest loosened at her show of enthusiasm.

Aviva Vaughn

"They bring a literal pot of hot broth to your table. It's electric, like a slow cooker, so that it stays warm," I said, lifting my hands to indicate a bowl about a foot wide. "There are many different broth flavors, and you can adjust the spice level to your preference. Then they bring you an assortment of uncooked vegetables, meats, and noodles and you put them in the broth and cook them. Mutton hotpot was my favorite."

"Sheep?" she said, eyes wide. "I didn't even know Chinese ate sheep. My *Popo*," she said, her word choice letting me know that she was referring to her maternal grandmother, "has never cooked me sheep."

"Well, you said she speaks Cantonese, and dim sum is from the Canton province, so that's probably why you're more familiar with that food. Beijing is in the Hebei province. China's a really big place and the provinces have their own personalities, cultures, and cuisines."

Her face grew thoughtful. "I guess I knew that in *here*," she said, pointing to her head, "but I didn't know it in *here*," pointing to her heart. "Since I've never been to China, to me Chinese culture is my family and our traditions. I never really thought about the fact that I only know a small part of it."

I shrugged. "It's just like here. California, New York, Hawai'i; same country but a totally different vibe."

She nodded. "That makes sense. Thanks for that."

My heart warmed. "You're welcome."

"Tell me about Boston," she said as she began earnestly filling her plate with food, her demeanor noticeably warmer.

I grew more relaxed. We'd overcome our first challenging conversation with minimal casualties. It seemed like a promising start.

I relaxed and told her about the historic home I grew up in, in Arlington, about the dairy farm owned by my uncle that I'd spent summers at, and about my French-Canadian grandmother's fantastic pea soup.

It was funny, but I hadn't thought about my childhood in ages. But once I started talking, I couldn't seem to stop. She was such an enthusiastic listener and she asked such interesting questions.

"I wonder if growing up in a city so central to America's story is part of why you love history so much. I mean, Hawai'i became a part of the U.S. reluctantly and by force, whereas Massachusetts is one of the states where our country was born."

Insightful.

Nothing turned me on more than a big brain. I mean, everything about Erin was sexy, but her brain was still my favorite part of her body.

"I've never thought about it that way, but that makes sense. You can't walk around Boston without feeling like you're walking in the pages of an American history book."

We continued to eat and talk and I grew more impressed by Erin's perceptive observations. Although she hadn't seen a lot of the world, she had a strategic mind that made interesting inferences and connections. She would have made a good journalist, or psychologist, or probably anything that she wanted to do, really.

I found her fascinating.

After almost three hours of conversation and food, I was full, although it seemed like I could have kept on talking forever. But I'd eaten more than I had in years, the leisurely meal reminding me how much I'd enjoyed my time in China; the flavors and overheard snatches of conversation reminding me of a simpler time in my life.

A tiny flicker of pain raced across my chest, but I ignored it. I wasn't going to let anything interfere with my enjoyment of the evening.

I hadn't been this full since my pre-Navy days and—I'm not sure why, perhaps it was a subconscious memory of the days before I'd been so disciplined with my diet—I had a sudden craving for something sweet. "Do you like *jian dui,* or egg tarts?" I asked, referring to a couple of dessert options I'd liked as a student.

"I thought you didn't eat—" She seemed to catch herself. "Never mind. Forget I said anything. Of course, I like them. I love them both."

I signaled a server and placed an order, the server whisking away our teapot for what was probably its fifth refill.

The meal—and all my reminiscing—had strengthened my desire to take *WUA* to China. I was going to double-down on my efforts with Yolanda in the coming week.

Erin patted her mouth with her napkin and gave me a thoughtful look. "Alex offered me a promotion."

"Really? That's great." I wondered what had brought up the change in topic.

"She asked me to start work earlier so that I had more overlap with your schedule. A lot of my new duties will have to do with making sure the host transition is as smooth as possible."

"Really? That *is* great," I said again, but this time I really felt it. The idea of spending more time with Erin had my stomach doing flip-flops.

"Her offer has me thinking…" Erin started, biting her lip.

Ordinarily, I would have found her lip-biting beguiling. Instead, I felt a twinge of unease.

"Maybe we need to back up a bit."

Scratch that. It was more than a twinge.

I cleared my throat, trying not to show how off-balance her statement had made me. I'd thought we'd been making progress. "Back up? How?"

The server returned with a full teapot.

"Well," she started.

Now I don't know about you, but in my experience, most sentences that started with "Well" *don't* go well.

I girded myself.

She continued, "We're going to be seeing each other a lot at work…" she hesitated, and for a second, I thought maybe she was reconsidering. But then, "Maybe it's best if we just focus on our professional relationship and get to know each other better before we rush into anything…" she paused and then popped her shoulders up as she said, "*extra*."

"Extra?" My brows went up. I certainly *felt* extra for Erin, but wasn't sure I liked being categorized *as* extra. It felt superfluous, ancillary, like an addendum, when she felt so necessary to me.

Then again, hadn't I just been thinking that it wasn't fair to saddle Erin with all of *my* extra, so why was I getting my panties in a bunch?

I cleared my throat just as the desserts arrived at the table. Although the sunshine-yellow of the flakey egg tarts and the glossy golden glow of the *jian dui* were beautiful, the idea of eating them no longer held any appeal.

Erin squished a sesame seed-covered *jian dui* between her chopsticks and blew on it. "Aren't you going to have one?" Her eyes flicked to the plate where the other two golf-ball-sized desserts sat.

"I'm suddenly full," I lied, feeling like an idiot.

The date that I'd been so looking forward to, that I'd been fantasizing about for the last forty-eight hours—hell, really for the last two years—was not going as hoped.

Eject, eject! Maybe it would be better to cut the date short than to risk it getting any worse. Besides, it wasn't like we wouldn't be seeing each other on Monday, and the day after that, and the day after that…

I sat up straighter, suddenly realizing that this wasn't a hard pass. She had mentioned that she didn't know me well; maybe she just needed to do some more reconnaissance. That was something I could understand. "Maybe you're right. Maybe we should take a step back."

Even though that's not what I really want.

She gave a small nod, and then bit into her dessert, although she didn't seem to enjoy it the way she had the rest of her food.

I lifted the teapot and refilled Erin's cup before my own, the way my host family had taught me in Beijing. I picked up my cup and blew on the aromatic liquid as much to cool it off as to avoid having to say anything.

"What time do you think I should come in to the office? Alex asked me to spend three to five hours a week with you for the next couple months. She wants to use you to market the show a lot more than she did Devon." She placed her chopsticks onto her plate and then folded her napkin off to the side.

I perked up. She wasn't kidding when she said we'd be spending a lot of time together. The only other person I spent that much time with was Yolanda. Maybe the slow and steady method *would* be better. "I'm on the air from five to nine and I have to leave the office by two, that's a hard out for me." I licked my lips, considering. "You don't have to do it all the time, but you should probably sit in on the editorial meeting once or twice. It's pretty interesting, although it happens at two in the morning. My only free time is from eleven to two, although Yolanda always takes up some of that. Why don't you stop by my office on Monday at one? I warn you though, I might have to cancel if a news story pops up."

She nodded. "Okay. That sounds good. So until further notice, friends?" She stuck out her hand.

A strange mix of longing and hope overcame me, making me feel like an inexperienced teen again. Then again, I *was* kind of an amateur in the love department.

I shook her hand. "Friends."

Chapter 12: An Off Day

~Erin~

Shit! Shit! Shit!

On Monday morning, I stumbled into the office at nine-thirty after oversleeping. It wouldn't have been so bad if I'd been planning to come in at my usual time, which was nine, however, I'd been attempting to get in for the editorial meeting at two.

The morning had not gone as planned.

After waking to my alarm at midnight, I showered and dressed, and then spent an hour attempting to coax Atticus into a walk. When he refused, I fell asleep on the couch, only to wake a little after eight, which sent me into the worst of morning traffic.

I was in such a funky mood; I couldn't even listen to *WUA* on my drive. I was afraid that hearing Clint's voice might send me over the edge.

As I got to my cubicle my phone rang. It was Michel, Alex's assistant.

"Hi, Michel," I said, trying not to sound winded.

"Hey. Erin," he said in the staccato way he always greeted me. "Alex wants to know if you're free for a meeting in the next. couple. of. hours."

"Um, sure, of course. I'll come right over." I hung up and smoothed my hair into place, trying to ensure that whatever rattled feeling I had inside wasn't showing on the outside.

"What's up? Off already?" Fern said from his chair in the cubicle to my left.

I looked down at him, which was something I was only able to do when he sat in his office chair.

For some reason, Fern liked to have his swivel chair real low, his legs sprawling under his desk like he was watching T.V. while splayed on a beanbag.

"Alex wants to meet. Gotta go. Talk later," I said before stashing my leather hobo into my filing cabinet.

I couldn't help being a little nervous. The only other official meeting I'd had with Alex had been my interview, and that hadn't been one-on-one.

Carrying my notebook and coffee mug, I wound my way through the quiet cubicles of the business office—all heads bent in purposeful typing—towards the kitchen, which was located in between the administrative/business side of the *WUA* offices and the creative/journalistic side. The kitchen was like the corpus callosum of the office, facilitating the flow of information between the two areas as people met while pouring coffee, burning microwave popcorn, or grabbing their lunch from the communal fridge.

I grabbed some coffee and then banked around the reporters' cubicles to Alex's corner office.

The general volume on this side of the office was much louder as reporters and editors discussed upcoming story ideas at some of the small conference tables or over cubicle walls. Ideas flew like audio paper airplanes tossed into the ether.

"Go. right. in." Michel said, as he kept his eyes trained on his computer, while his eyebrows still managed to point me to the office.

I knocked on her slightly ajar door, and then entered when she waved me in.

Like all of the perimeter offices in the building, Alex's space was all glass with window coverings only on the walls facing outside. Only one office in the building had interior window shades specially installed for one of the editors who wanted privacy as she pumped breast milk.

"Ah, Erin. Great. Have a seat," Alex said, motioning to the two chairs in front of her desk.

The sun hit my eyes as I sat, bright morning light glinting off the vast acres of glass that covered the skyscrapers. I squinted and held up my hand.

Alex started. "Sorry. I forget how bright it is since I'm not facing it. Let me lower the shades." She turned and fiddled with the blinds, softening the light in the room. "Better?"

"Yes. Much better. Thanks." I settled into a chair and put my notebook and coffee mug on her desk.

She smiled, leaning back into her office chair, a yellow legal pad balanced on one knee. "So, did you think about the promotion?"

Straight to business.

I shifted in my seat. I *had* thought about her offer, although maybe not as much as I should have, since at least half of my brain had been consumed with Clint all weekend.

After we shook hands at the restaurant on Saturday, the date ended with a very platonic—almost frigid?—walk back to my condo. Clint had said goodnight with a tip of his head, his hands shoved into his pockets, with at least three feet of space between us.

I'd spent the better part of Sunday taking Atticus on long walks, trying to puzzle out my feelings. However, I couldn't seem to reconcile the fact that I was disappointed at the way the date had concluded...even though it had been *my* idea for us to "back up."

Part of me was even mad at Clint, which was crazy since he had simply agreed with what I'd suggested.

Be careful what you wish for.

Part of me had wondered if his interest was so superficial that the merest suggestion of difficulty had caused him to back away. It wasn't as though I'd meant the request as a test, I'd been sincere in believing that it would be good for us to get to know each other better.

Of course, a little bit of resistance would have been nice.

If he had just said, "That's a smart plan and all, but let's try anyway," it would have made all the difference in the world.

I had all these thoughts in the second it took to respond to Alex's question. "Yes, I've thought about the promotion and I'd like to accept."

I'd decided this on one of my long walks with Atticus, in between the longer stretches of thinking about Clint. It had been a pretty easy choice when I considered the alternatives. As I saw it, there were four options.

One, I could take the job.

Two, I could stay at *WUA* and have someone hired above me for a job I felt perfectly qualified to do. Why would I agree to that?

Three, I could quit and work for Sonja in Big Bear. But that was a radical life change I wasn't prepared to make, at least not yet.

Four, I could get a job elsewhere, but this made no sense. If Sonja hadn't offered me a position, I wouldn't have considered quitting. I loved public radio and enjoyed my job. I just wanted more…so why would I leave?

And as long as I was staying, I might as well take the promotion. Besides, I was proud that Alex had offered me the opportunity. It was validation that I was doing a good job.

As far as my interest in Sonja's offer, that was going to require a lot more investigation and consideration. I was certainly curious about the opportunity in Big Bear, but that wasn't enough to make a life change.

Alex smiled, swiveling her chair forward as she stuck her hand out. "That's great, Erin. You were my first choice. As I mentioned, you might need to add to your team. I think you'll need someone to help you with the writing, so maybe a junior copywriter?"

I nodded and made a note. "I think a social media specialist would be a good investment."

Her eyes lit up. "That's a great idea. By the way, there are a couple of other things I want to make you aware of. Devon never left Los Angeles in your time here. She'd been on the air a long time already when you joined us. Like Clint, we made a big deal about her promotion to lead host, and for the first five years, she traveled a lot visiting the radio stations in big markets like New York and San Francisco, but then she got tired of it.

"Part of the reason we hired Clint was because he told me he was committed to doing whatever he needed to do to make our clients, the radio stations, happy. He said he'll fly wherever we want if there's a need. I want you to take advantage of having a motivated host and book him everywhere. Start with the stations in the top ten markets. I want him to be seen. I want to remind people of why they pay for our program and why it's a must-have show for their stations."

I took notes, suddenly understanding why I was going to need a team. It sounded like I'd have my hands full with the stations alone, which was an exciting new challenge.

"Another thing," she said, leaning back in her chair again. "Yolanda and Clint have been talking about doing a special series. I know they've been kicking around the idea of taking the show to China, but I'd rather they did something domestic so that it can happen quicker. Whatever it is, I'm going to want you to market the heck out of it, so just a heads up."

China? Funny that Clint hadn't mentioned this on our date. I wondered if anyone in the office knew of his personal relationship with the country.

I took a few more notes, the twin flames of excitement and trepidation rising in my chest. My promotion was going to push me out of my comfort zone, and I welcomed it.

"I'll have H.R. draw up the offer letter for your promotion," then she paused and folded her hands in front of her. "Now, there's something else you should know. Because you're an internal hire, there are some constraints as to how much of a raise we can offer you. I'll do my best, but I just want to let you know in advance that our parent company is kind of a stickler about their compensation structure."

I frowned, a flare of concern igniting in my chest.

"Anyway, we can talk about that once I have the letter. It might take a week or two since it has to come from headquarters in D.C." She stood, making it clear that the conversation was over.

I stood.

"Do you have a meeting with Clint set up yet?" she asked.

"Yes, and I have a list of biographical questions I'll be asking him so I can finish up his press kit. He also has a photoshoot later this week, so we'll have new pics."

She nodded. "Excellent. I knew you were the right person for the job." She sat and rolled back towards the computer keyboard, turning her back to me.

I took the hint and let myself out, walking straight into Michel.

"Soooo…" he said, drawing out the word so that it took a few seconds for him to finish. "Tell. Michel. Everything."

Michel had a way of making everything dramatic, which might have correlated with the fact that he was an aspiring actor.

"Don't act like you don't know."

Michel pursed his lips, a dark lock of hair falling into his eyes. "Just tell me anyway."

"I took the promotion. Why would I let someone get hired over me?"

His eyes flashed as he wound his slender arms over his chest. "You and Maverick will be working closely together then, right? I hate you."

I'd learned that "I hate you" was a compliment from Michel. "Maverick?" I asked, smoothing out the edge of my black vest.

"You know, from *Top Gun*."

"Oh. Right." I feigned looking at my watch. While I usually loved bantering with him, Clint was not a topic I wanted to discuss, especially with someone as prescient as Michel. "I gotta go. Talk to you later, Meesh."

I walked back to my cubicle and threw my notebook on my desk, as I sat in my office chair. I took a long sip of my tepid coffee. "Aaahhh," I sighed, finally feeling the adrenaline of this morning trickle out of my body. I'd barely been in the office half-an-hour and already I was exhausted.

"Can you talk now?" Fern asked, swiveling his chair to face me.

I shook my head, lifting my chin to the four occupied cubicles in front of us. "Lunch later? Grand Central Market? I could go for some carnitas."

He nodded. "It's a date."

***

A few hours later, we were sitting in the historic arcade of Grand Central Market.

The open-air marketplace dated from the early 1900s and used to serve the Victorian mansions that had populated the area. As the city had changed, so had its offerings, and some of the bow-tied, white-aproned cheesemongers and butchers had given way to *taquerias,* bento box vendors, and pizza joints. However, it was always evolving, and recently a few trend-setting food entrepreneurs had set up shop, too.

Despite all the many food options, I only ever ate one thing when I went there: carnitas. My favorite spot was a simple fast-food counter that roasted their pork to perfection.

"The Mexican food here has ruined me for Hawai'i," I said around another bite, wiping a bit of the dripping juices off my cheek.

"There's Mexican food in Hawai'i?" Fern asked, his tray filled with eight carnitas tacos—small round tortillas that looked like sushi bites in his large hands—to my three.

"Yeah, but it's slim pickings and the food isn't like here, or like your mom's," I added, recalling the one time I'd had dinner at Fern's childhood home, where he still resided with his mother.

Fern, or Fernando as his mother called him, was a native of Los Angeles, and had grown up in an area not too far from Downtown called Highland Park. It was just him and his mom, and Fern had said that there was no way he'd let his mom live alone. He'd even chosen to attend a local college, just so he wouldn't have to leave her. Fortunately, there were a lot of schools to pick from. I had never seen a more bonded parent-child unit in my life; it was sweet.

"You are welcome anytime. Mom enjoyed cooking with you. She says you're a fast learner. We'll be doing tamales for Christmas if you want to come over and help make them."

"Yes, please. I'd love to," I said, swallowing another bite of pork taco that I'd dressed with a heavy helping of tomatillo salsa, cilantro, and onion. *Heaven.*

"So…" he said, not so subtly changing the topic. "I've been politely waiting for you to tell me about your date…"

While I knew he would ask, I didn't know what to say, largely because I still didn't know how I felt about it. So I stuck with the facts. "We had a nice dinner, but we decided that we shouldn't get involved since we'll be working so closely together."

He lifted a brow. "That's it?"

Although Fern was a close friend, he was still a coworker and my direct report. So far, I hadn't told him anything about Clint beyond what he had witnessed himself. Maybe it was better that way.

I shrugged. "You know, I just got this promotion, which sounds even more involved than previously explained. Clint and I will be meeting on an almost daily basis, so I don't think it's a good idea to make that any more complicated than it already is. I also need to consider Sonja's offer. The ropes course really called to me, but I need to find out more about it. Right now, I need to focus on *me*, get my life and career established. Romance can come later."

It felt like I was trying to convince myself as well as him.

He gave me a stoic look and nodded. "That's probably for the best," and then turned back to his carnitas.

I was grateful that he agreed, and even more grateful that he didn't push the issue. But when I took the next bite of food, the formerly vibrant flavors tasted bland. I put the rest of my taco down and pushed the plate away.

"Full already?" He said, finishing off his fifth taco.

I nodded, although it wasn't my stomach that was bothering me; it was something else. Because ever since the moment Clint and I had parted ways, a part of me was missing.

Did I make the wrong choice?

Chapter 13: A Secret

~Clint~

I glanced at my clock. It was almost one, which meant that Erin would be walking through the door at any moment. I surveyed my office, which I'd spent all of my naptime minutes straightening. The books that had been strewn across my desk and coffee table were now in their proper place on the bookshelf, as straight as soldiers; reams of old, marked-up scripts had finally been put in the recycle bin; and the olive drab military blanket—a beloved memento of my grandfather— and eye mask I used for naps were folded away in my cabinet.

I glanced at a carafe of water and two glasses that I'd moved three times from the coffee table in front of my couch to my desk and then back to the coffee table.

Although I would've liked to sit on the couch with Erin, I sensed that the desk would make it clear that I was adhering to our agreement of keeping our relationship business-oriented. If we sat at the couch, it seemed inevitable that our knees might touch or our arms might brush against one another.

I shook out my arms at the zip of electricity that coursed through me as I thought about such innocent contact.

I am a sad, pathetic, lonely man.

Standing up from my desk, I walked over to the coffee table and grabbed the carafe and glasses just as Erin knocked on my door.

"Come in," I said, walking back to my desk. I poured some water and pointed to one of the chairs in front of my desk. "Would you like some water? Please sit."

As she walked in, I hurried around to pull out the chair for her, and she took a seat.

"Thanks," she said, with an uncertain smile that she'd been using ever since we left the restaurant Saturday night.

I missed her usually open smile and vowed to try and bring it back as I closed my office door and then took a seat.

Erin opened a folder and pulled out a couple of sheets of paper. "I don't know if you've heard, but I accepted the promotion and Alex has a lot of things she wants us to work on together."

Although I didn't care for the "all business" tone, I was grateful for the news that I'd have an excuse to be around her regularly.

"So, first things first, the press kit. I want to finish it this week and I have a lot of questions for you. You ready?" she asked.

I nodded.

"Tell me about your childhood. Parents, siblings, any hints of the adult you'd turn into?" Her pen hovered above the paper as she waited.

I felt the familiar tension in my chest whenever anyone asked about my personal life, even on such a basic level. I'd always been a private person, and when I started making a name for myself in radio, the desire to carve out a space that was just mine only intensified.

I thought back to the day I'd sat in Alex's office, discussing the offer to make me the new lead host. She'd told me that I'd have to open up if I wanted the job; that listeners didn't just want to hear my voice but to be my friend.

"You know I hate talking about this kind of stuff." I sighed, and then had an idea.

Her face stiffened, but before she could say anything, I continued, "But, I have an idea that would make it a lot easier."

"Shots of tequila?" she deadpanned, the hint of a smile tugging at the corners of her mouth.

I laughed, grateful for the return of her lighter side. "Now *there's* a good idea. But I was thinking of something else. How about I'll answer your questions if you answer some of mine? *Quid pro quo*."

She frowned. "I'm not the one being interviewed."

Holding out my palms, I said, "I'm just offering a suggestion. It's human nature to open up when someone else is doing the same, and you want answers, right?" I hesitated, and then added, "It'll help put me at ease. It's hard for me to talk about this stuff."

I'd filleted my heart and laid it out for public perusal.

Her eyes softened. "Fine. But not a one-to-one ratio. I'll answer one for every five of yours. Okay?"

"Four," I countered.

She narrowed her eyes but I saw the corner of her mouth tug up. "Fine. Now answer the question."

A thrill zipped up my core. "As you know, I grew up in Arlington, Massachusetts just outside of Boston. My father was an airline pilot. My mother was a flight attendant....I know, it sounds ridiculous, right?" I said, in answer to her raised eyebrow. "My father had been in the Air Force before that, and his father had been in the Army, so we have a history of military service. Growing up with a pilot father, I guess it was inevitable that I'd fall in love with planes, and I always had my eyes set on the TOPGUN program because I liked the idea of being on an aircraft carrier."

"Why?"

"They are these huge, self-contained cities on water. When I was a kid, they seemed awesome, larger than life. I wanted to be on one, and I wanted to fly, so TOPGUN it was."

I smoothed out the top of my pants and leaned back. This was a part of my life that I'd walked away from a decade ago, shut the door, and hadn't looked back.

There hadn't been time.

"What's it like?"

"That's a big question." I shook my head. "I'm not sure I can explain what it's like being on an aircraft carrier, it's a singular experience."

"Try," she said, gentle urging in her voice.

I looked off into the distance, trying to put myself back on the U.S.S. Dwight D. Eisenhower. "Well, first of all, it's really loud. It doesn't matter where you are on the ship, you can't get away from the noise the planes make taking off, landing, being moved around the ship from the runway to the mechanic shop below deck."

"The planes don't stay on deck all the time?"

I shook my head. "No. Just the ones that will be flown that day. The Eisenhower, or Ike as we called it, had eighty-five aircraft. There are these huge elevators that move them up and down. The flight schedule gets posted the night before, around dinner time, so you never know if you're flying from day to day. I remember getting butterflies as they'd post the list, wondering if I'd be flying a day or night mission."

I was starting to get into it now, I could almost see the flat gray interior of the aircraft carrier with its low, narrow hallways that twisted and turned endlessly; the tiny bunk and locker that was the entirety of my personal space for months at a time, and the boisterous mess hall which was always the center of socializing.

"The night missions gave me the jitters. There's nothing scarier than landing a jet onto a moving aircraft carrier in the black of night. The runways have almost no light on them—to keep the carrier safe from enemies—and you're landing on a runway that's only five-hundred feet long while going one-hundred-and-fifty miles an hour all while the ship is sailing at about thirty-five miles an hour. It's a tough target even if the water is smooth." I paused and glanced at Erin's open mouth. Clearly, she was getting the idea. I leaned forward. "It's even worse if the water is choppy because the deck can pitch in any direction, the wind is a factor, visibility might be compromised." My heart started beating faster at the memory; I put my hand over it to soothe myself.

"That sounds crazy. How do you even stop when you're going so fast and the runway is so short?"

"The plane has a thing called a tail hook, and when you land, the hook catches a cable and yanks the plane to a stop." I jerked my hand back to illustrate. "Literally, you go from one-fifty to zero in a second." I rubbed at the back of my neck at the memory.

"That must be why you're so confident. I bet nothing makes you nervous after doing that."

Nothing but you. "You're probably right. It takes a lot to frazzle me now."

"Where was your aircraft carrier stationed?" she asked, writing furiously.

"Mostly in the Persian Gulf and the Mediterranean in support of the Gulf War. While I was on the Ike, women were introduced onto aircraft carriers. On that first deployment, fourteen women got pregnant," I said raising my brows. "The Ike earned the nickname *The Love Boat* because of that." I smiled. I hadn't thought about that in a long time.

"It sounds like you enjoyed your time in the military. What made you leave?"

Before panic could overtake me, I remembered our deal. "Hold on a second. I think I've answered about fifteen of your questions. It's time you answered one of mine."

She sighed. "Don't exaggerate. It was really just one question with a few follow-up questions." She pursed her lips, but despite that, her eyes were bright and cheery.

It felt good to tell Erin about my past; it made me feel closer to her. I hoped it was having the same effect on her.

"Okay," she sighed. "One question."

I rubbed my hands together. "Tell me about your family."

She shrugged. "My dad was a pro surfer—"

Something clicked in my head. "Johnny Hung?"

I nodded. "You've heard of him?"

"Of course. He was in that famous surf movie *Christmas on the North Shore*."

She nodded like she'd heard this before. "Yup, that's my dad. My mom's from Colorado, but she's lived in Hawai'i so long, you'd think she'd been born there. She was pre-med before she got pregnant with me and my brother—"

"You're twins, right?" I said, remembering what Fern had told me.

She paused, her eyes widening. "Yes, that's right. He's a professional surfer, too, and we look nothing alike. He got my mom's blond hair and blue eyes and I took after my dad, which is funny because in terms of personality he's way more like my dad; kind of stoic and self-centered, whereas I'm more like my mom." She wrinkled up her nose like she wasn't sure if she liked that fact.

"So, you aren't close?"

She narrowed her eyes. "That's two questions."

"Come on, Erin…" I cajoled.

She shrugged. "We used to be closer. I also have a half-sister from my dad's first marriage, but we didn't grow up together." She paused and picked up her notebook. "Okay, so why did you leave the Navy?"

I dragged my fingers over the surface of my desk. "A family tragedy." My throat tightened and my heart panged.

Even that tiny confession cost me.

How had she'd so effortlessly pulled out of me something that I never told anyone? She hadn't needed to badger or cajole, and it had even felt good to tell her; part of me had *wanted* to tell her.

But I shouldn't feel this good letting her in. This wasn't the way to keep my distance.

I needed to retreat.

Besides, if she knew the whole truth, it might ruin my chances with her forever.

How can I answer this question and not reveal everything?

I was just about to tell a half-truth when Erin said, "I'm sorry. We don't have to go into that if you don't want to. The listeners aren't entitled to everything. I can just write that your priorities shifted, how's that?" She glanced down at her list of questions and made some notes.

Did they ever. "Thanks. That sounds good." The tension in my chest relaxed.

Crisis averted.

She shifted in her seat. "Why don't you ask me another question?"

I saw what she was doing and I was grateful for it. I couldn't remember the last time anyone had taken my feelings into consideration. Most people treated me like a robot, an overachiever who would get the job done, no matter the cost. *Feelings? Clint? Bah!*

It was like she actually cared.

I asked the first thing that came to mind. "What's your favorite movie?"

She screwed up her face. "That's your question?"

I riffed, "Hey, you can tell a lot about someone from their favorite movie."

A hint of a smile drifted across her face and my heart lifted. "I can't pick one—"

"Pick a few." I was surprised to find I really wanted to know, imagining Erin's face, lit-up by a movie screen, her pouty lips sucking in kernel after buttery kernel of popcorn, licking her fingers after each one—

A dull ache in my gut let me know I was entering dangerous territory.

Fortunately, Erin saved me from my fantasy by answering—

"Well, my favorite sci-fi is *Highlander.*"

I raised my brows, intrigued. "Which one?"

She scowled. "There can be only one."

We burst out laughing at her quoting of the movie's most famous line.

"But seriously," she said. "The sequels are so bad; I pretend they don't exist. I stopped watching after the third one."

"Fair enough. Continue."

"My favorite silly comedy is *Happy Gilmore* and my favorite rom-com-slash-Christmas movie is *Love Actually.* My favorite movie of all time is *The Sound of Music.*"

I might have guessed at the last one, given her choice of songs the night we were lost. "You have well-rounded taste in movies."

"I didn't peg you for a movie watcher," she said.

"Not a lot, but yes, I do watch them. But only movies. I don't watch any television. I can't risk investing that much time in fiction," I added.

"What are your favorites?" she asked, pen poised to write.

"*Citizen Kane, Pulp Fiction,* and *Some Like it Hot.*"

She wrote quickly. "Interesting. That's a surprisingly diverse combination, although I've never seen *Citizen Kane.*"

"Now that's a travesty." I got a thought. "You know, a really good friend would help you with that little problem." I gave her what I hoped was a playful smile. "I just happen to own a DVD of it. "

Without looking up from her notebook, she said, "Sure, I'd love to borrow it."

Disappointed, I said, "Okay. I'll bring it for you."

She asked me a few more light questions and before I knew it, my "five-minutes-until-two" alarm went off on my phone.

"Sorry, Erin, I have a hard out at two."

She practically jumped up. "Oh right, sorry. That went fast. I only got through a fourth of my questions. When can we do this again?"

I started powering down my computer. "If this time works for you, you can stop by every day this week. Like I said before, if a story comes up, I might have to cancel," I said, trying to keep the hurt from my voice. I was still smarting from the way she'd deflected my invitation to watch *Citizen Kane* together.

She nodded and smiled, although the smile didn't make it to her eyes. "Got it. See you tomorrow," she said quickly before heading out the door.

I watched her retreat, a sad feeling rising in my chest.

My two-o-clock alarm sounded, reminding me I needed to get on the road immediately. "Teddy Roosevelt," I muttered, grabbing my keys and my leather bomber jacket and heading out the door.

***

An hour later, I was waiting in a ridiculously long queue of idling cars, my ancient Subaru standing out among the sparkling European imports. At least today my time in the car had been augmented with the audiobook of *House of Mirth*. While the book wasn't one I would have chosen, I found myself enjoying the depiction of old New York and the warm, intelligent voice of the narrator, Anna Fields.

Finally, I pulled into the parking lot. A woman with a reflective orange vest waved me forward. I rolled down my window. "Hi, Maria. How are you doing?"

She shrugged. "Oh, you know. It's my turn to play bad mom in the parking lot." Suddenly she lifted her head and shouted to someone in the distance. "You can't park there; you have to stay in your car until I tell you." She shook her head and muttered, "Newbie," under her breath.

I inched forward when two kids came running to the car, their flying hair reminding me of when I was their age. They opened the rear doors and jumped in, breathless as they threw their backpacks into the backseat.

I extended my hand for fist bumps. "Hey, Max. Hey, Mia."

"Hey, Dad," the tweens said in unison.

Chapter 14: A Brilliant Idea

~Erin~

The next morning, I made it out of my condo by one-fifteen in the morning and couldn't believe how magically fast the freeway was, as I made it to work in under twenty minutes. Even though it was hell on my fuel economy, I drove with my windows open, the first hints of cooler fall air a welcome change from the hot weekend. As soon as I pulled off the freeway, I rolled the windows back up. Downtown L.A. was not the sort of place you want to drive with windows down in the middle of the night. Fortunately, the *WUA* office was located on the northwest edge of downtown, near the intersection with Filipino Town. This part of the city was fairly safe, and at this hour, the streets were quiet and empty.

When I used my security card to enter the administrative side of the *WUA* offices, I was brought to a halt by the utter silence that greeted me. Overhead lighting flickered on as the motion detectors sensed my presence, the illumination preceding me by a few feet as I walked to my cubicle. I glanced around at the empty cubes, my mind filling in gestalt apparitions of Fern, Harry Hinkley, and the others filling the chairs where they normally sat.

It was creepy.

I stowed my bag and grabbed my notebook, hurrying over to the programming side of the office, the overhead lighting flickering on just seconds before me. Voices grew as I approached the kitchen. Hearing them, I felt relieved. It was funny how scary being alone could feel when you didn't expect it. You'd think that from living alone, an empty space wouldn't freak me out, but it did. When I got to the kitchen, I took a deep breath and rounded the corner into the sunny yellow room which smelled of burnt popcorn, coffee, and toasting bagels.

"Morning," I said.

A trio of voices said hello—Joe, the overnight engineer, Val, the finance editor, and Zoya, the European news editor. There was a fourth person who I didn't know; he was wearing a smart gray suit and had a youthful twinkle in his eyes despite his patchy white hair and slightly stooped posture.

I held out my hand. "Hi, I'm Erin."

We shook.

"Harold. Harold Greenberg. Nice to meet you."

"Harold has a seat on the New York Stock Exchange. We fly him in quarterly to give us an overview of the financial landscape," Val said, handing Harold a mug of coffee.

"I'm a crystal ball gazer," Harold said merrily.

Val *tsked*. "Don't let him fool you, Erin. He's as smart as they come."

Harold gave Val an adoring smile. "You all treat me like a king. I love coming here. I'd do anything for you."

"Well, it's nice to meet you, Harold," I said, already liking him.

Joe took a bite of his toasted bagel as he pushed his glasses back up his face. "What are you doing in the office at this hour?"

"I thought that observing Clint as he goes about making the show would be helpful."

"Erin is the head of our marketing department," Val explained to Harold. "It's her job to make Clint a household name and keep his fans happy."

"And keep the stations happy," I added.

"Ah," Harold said, understanding coloring his face as he reached into his pocket. "Well, if you ever make it out to New York, look me up. I'd be happy to show you around the stock exchange," he said, handing me his business card.

"Thanks." I took his card and pocketed it, the idea of visiting New York suddenly taking on a more solid shape in my mind. It would be fun to see the streets that Edith Wharton described so eloquently in *House of Mirth*. For a second, I wondered if Clint would ever read the book, but Val quickly brought me back to reality.

"We should get to the war room. It's almost two and Clint likes to start right on the hour," she said.

Even though Yolanda was the senior producer, it was Clint's show.

We banked around the reporter's cubicles, passed Alex's office, and turned left towards a long hallway that housed Val, Zoya, and the other senior editors, and culminating with where Yolanda sat. The long row ended at Clint's corner office. Outside of his space stood a large oval table that accommodated twenty, with people pulling up chairs or stools in the general vicinity once all the table space was taken.

I pulled up a chair in the outer ring, allowing the editors and reporters to take the prime real estate at the table, and opened my notebook on my lap.

Yolanda passed out an agenda, but Clint—sitting at the head of the table—was clearly in charge, radiating confidence and authority. Yolanda took the seat to his left.

I avoided looking directly at Clint, the sting of the previous day's meeting was still fresh.

It bothered me that he was making it harder for me to do my job, playing this game where I had to answer his questions to get mine answered. It was harder to maintain my professional distance when our conversations felt so personal. The meeting had walked the edge of intimate in a confusing and frustrating way. I felt like a mouse being toyed with by a cat.

And then when he summarily dismissed me at five to two without the barest of explanation?

Jerk.

"Are Mae-Lin and Gordon on the line yet?" Clint said to no one in particular, pointing a finger at the black conference call device in the center of the table.

Did he always sound so arrogant?

"I'm here," two voices said through the black box.

"Hey, Mae-Lin. What's happening in Asia?" Clint asked in his lazy swagger, leaning back in the chair with a bored look on his face.

Mae-Lin Wang was *WUA*'s reporter in Asia, while Gordon Smith was stationed in London. They both gave updates about what had happened on their respective continents while America was asleep.

After they spoke, Clint said, "Stories for today's show?" making a few marks on a yellow legal pad, his face still blasé.

The editors took turns speaking, the ones in charge of South America and the Middle East mentioning stories, followed by the lead reporters of various desks that covered issues in the United States ranging from the arts to healthcare to entertainment.

Clint was scratching on his pad with his pencil when an expectant silence fell over the group. He glanced at the agenda and then gave his first smile of the day. "Harold! You're here." He seemed to see the older gentleman for the first time. "Whatcha got for us?"

The room released a collective breath.

The king was happy.

I scowled. Maybe I wasn't the only one who felt like a mouse with Clint around.

"Well, it's been a busy quarter on Wall Street," Harold said with a gleam in his eye.

Clint sat back like he was listening to his favorite uncle.

Harold spoke for about thirty minutes, after which Clint glanced at his watch. "Do we have time for pitches today or should we save that for tomorrow?"

Yolanda was leafing through a multi-page handout, the senior editors mimicking her movement. "It doesn't look like there's anything that won't keep until tomorrow."

"Great," Clint said, slamming his hand down on the table. "Meeting adjourned." He walked over to Harold and threw an arm around his shoulder, walking the older man into his office and shutting the door.

The room was suddenly a flurry of movement and conversation. I dashed over to Val and asked, "What's that?" pointing to the multi-page document everyone had been leafing through a moment ago.

"It's a collection of pitches, both from our own reporters and stringers." When I gave her a confused look, she added, "Freelancers. This document is a list of ideas for future segments. Some of the stories require a fast turnaround and others have a longer lead time."

"Can I have a copy?" I asked.

"Sure. Take mine. It's a living document on our internal server. You could probably access it there, too, but we print it out for the morning editorial meeting," Val said, handing me the sheaf of papers.

"Thanks." I paged through it and was about to return to my cube when I remembered how quiet my side of the office would be for another six hours. "Do you think it's okay if I sit at the conference table? The business side of the building is deserted."

Val nodded. "Go ahead. It's a free use space when there's not an editorial meeting," she said, before heading to her office.

I walked back to the kitchen and grabbed a mug of coffee before returning to the war room. A handful of people still chatted around the table, a pleasant babble of conversation that put me at ease. I inhaled the aroma of the fresh coffee and sighed, soaking in the atmosphere, wondering at how far I'd come.

When I'd first arrived in Los Angeles I commuted from my cousin's home in Hollywood to her bookstore on Melrose where I worked. That was how I'd fallen in love with public radio. One day, when I was flipping the radio dial, I heard the strains of Hawaiian music, which had led into a story about the anniversary of Pearl Harbor. I'd enjoyed the show so much, my car radio stayed tuned to the station day after day. When a membership drive happened a few months later, I volunteered to answer phones since I couldn't afford to make a donation. Six months later, I volunteered again and learned that one of my favorite programs, *WUA,* had an office in Los Angeles. For weeks, I checked their website for job opportunities until finally one appeared that I'd felt qualified for: Marketing Coordinator. The job description had only requested four years of job experience, and I'd had six, even if it hadn't been in marketing.

When I got the job, I couldn't believe that Devon Lopez, the voice that had accompanied me on my commute every morning, was now going to be my coworker. Meeting her had been a thrill and she'd been generous enough with her time that I'd come to think of her as a mentor.

I'd taken it personally when Devon left *WUA* with only the cursory two-week notice. Part of me thought I'd deserved a heads up. On the day I heard the news, I went to her office and closed the door, trying to keep my voice upbeat as I said, "Congratulations."

"Thanks, Erin," she'd said, barely looking up. "I'm just signing my new contract now. You know, you have to jump when an opportunity presents itself." She signed her name to a few pieces of paper and then shoved them into a manila envelope, finally meeting my gaze. "I'm sorry I didn't say anything, but the TV network didn't want to let their audience know that their anchor would be leaving until they had a replacement, which meant I couldn't announce it either until everything was hammered out," she said with a genuine frown.

I felt a little better. "We'll stay in touch, right?"

She winked. "I'd be disappointed if we didn't."

And now I was sitting in the war room, the holy of holies in our office.

It was exhilarating.

I read through the pitch list, surprised and entertained by the diversity of ideas; imagining what the stories might sound like on the airwaves. I considered myself a public radio junkie, and this list was like a drug.

A wisp of an idea came to me. *I wonder if other listeners would feel the same way?*

There were stories from all over the world. From breakthroughs in HIV treatments to the opening of the new Museum of Chinese in America opening in Manhattan. From the latest in the conflicts in Afghanistan to updates on construction happening at Ground Zero. On-going news such as the fight to legalize marijuana to openings of art exhibits. From heavy to light, from serious to silly, the ideas ranged all over the map, literally and figuratively.

About an hour after I'd begun reading, I heard Clint's voice. "Always great seeing you, Harold. I've got to get to work figuring out what I'm going to say on the air. See you next time."

"See you next quarter. And congratulations again." Harold walked out of Clint's office with the same bright smile he'd had when he'd greeted me earlier, his eyes lighting up when he spotted me. "Hello again, young lady."

Color rose in my cheeks. Harold was simply too sweet for words. "Hello, Mr. Greenberg."

He *tsked*, walking over to me. "Harold, please. Mr. Greenberg was my father," he said with a lift of his brows that seemed to indicate there was no longer a Mr. Greenberg.

His words from earlier suddenly ran through my head. *I'd do anything for you.* "Mr. Greenb—I mean, Harold. Do you have some time to talk?"

He shrugged and sat down. "I'm all yours. I'm done here and my car is waiting for me downstairs. I was just going to head back to the hotel for a nap before I catch a plane later. What do you want to talk about?"

Almost five hours later, I was on my fourth cup of coffee and felt like I might jump out of my skin with excitement. After talking to Harold, I left a note on Michel's desk, asking for a meeting with Alex. Once the sun started coming up—and it was no longer dark on my side of the office—I went to my cubicle and fired up my computer, typing away like a woman possessed.

When Fern saw me, he raised a brow. "How long have you been in the office?"

"Since two," I said, not looking away from my computer. "I came in for the editorial meeting. I'm working on an idea."

"Maybe you should slow down on the caffeine, Secretariat," he said, his words sounding slow to my ears.

My phone rang and I almost jumped. It was Michel. "Hi, Meesh."

"Hey, early bird. Alex is free. Right. Now. If you hurry. She has a meeting in twenty."

"I'll be right there." I hit a key that sent the document I was working on to the printer. "Gotta go. I'm meeting with Alex."

Fern's eyes widened. "You're in the big leagues now."

I grabbed my notebook, stopping by the printer on my way to Alex's office. I couldn't believe it was only nine and I'd already done so much. Somehow—in my hyper-caffeinated state—I'd failed to realize that I'd already been in the office almost eight hours.

I entered Alex's office, shut the door, and handed her the printout. "New York," I said, dramatically.

She gave me a quizzical look. "Good morning, Erin. How are you?" she said slowly, her eyes sliding over the document.

I shook my head. "Sorry. I've been here since two. I'm a little wired," I said, suddenly noticing that I was waving my hands in the air a little *too* energetically. I put one hand on my waist to keep it stationary.

She arched a brow. "You think?"

I shook my head. "That's not the point. The point is, I had a great idea." I sat but couldn't seem to keep my right leg from bouncing.

"Shoot."

"You said that you wanted Clint to do a domestic special. What if we take the show to New York? We already have a studio there, so it'll be easy for him to broadcast, and there are a ton of New York-related pitches on the pitch list. See page two of the printout," I said, without taking a breath.

Alex turned to page two. "New York Yankees on track to win the World Series, cost overruns and design disputes on Ground Zero construction, how the High Line and a pedestrian-friendly Broadway are changing public space in the city," I said, listing off the ideas quickly.

"So..." She met my gaze, clearly not convinced, but I could tell I had her attention.

I leaned forward, drumming my fingers on the desk, ready to unleash my secret weapon. "What if the New York Stock Exchange invited Clint to ring their bell?"

Her eyes lit up. "Go on."

"Harold Greenberg was here today and we hit it off. I asked him how the opening and closing bell ringer gets chosen, and he said that he knew the people in charge, and that he was ninety-percent sure he could make it happen." Electricity surged through my limbs, fueled as much by my excitement as by my exhaustion.

The look on Alex's face made it all worthwhile. I could see the wheels turning.

"The stock exchange bell," she said, a thoughtful look on her face.

I leaned in for the kill. "Harold says no one from public radio has ever rung the bell."

Her eyes widened and she rubbed her chin. After a few moments, she nodded her head like she'd made a decision, but when she began to speak, her tone was cautious. "You know, the editorial staff is very territorial…"

I had anticipated this. I'd heard people in the administrative staff throw out story ideas to the reporters only to have them shrugged off. Naturally, the good ideas would appear on the air at a later date with only the barest variation and without any recognition for the person who had originally thought of it.

But I didn't need everyone to know this was my idea as long as Alex knew it and I was compensated accordingly.

Besides, the feeling I was experiencing, of coming up with a new and exciting concept? A concept that might play itself across the airwaves of my beloved public radio and on the most listened to radio program in the U.S.? That was practically payment enough. I couldn't even imagine how incredible it would feel when I actually got to *hear* my idea come to life. *That* would be amazing.

I mentally crossed my fingers and exerted all my energy to keep my voice even and humble. "I leave it up to you to pitch it to Clint and Yolanda. You don't have to say it was my idea." Then I had an epiphany. "But you know what might help? Since Clint really wants to do a special in China, maybe the fund-raising department can find potential donors who Clint could schmooze. I could plan a reception for after the bell ringing. Harold told me there's a conference room at the exchange that's used just for that purpose. Maybe we can leverage this domestic special to make the international one happen."

She sat up straighter. "We could invite all of our current donors, too. I bet there're even people who'd fly in for an event at the stock exchange." She rubbed her hands together and nodded. "This is a great idea, Erin. Really great. Get the ball rolling with Harold, ask him how soon we could get slotted in."

"Already done. When we parted ways, he said he was going to look into it either way just to find out. I think he's as excited about it as we are. He emailed me a couple of hours ago to say that the person who chooses the bell ringer is open to considering Clint, and that the first available spot would be the second week of November," I said, stifling a yawn.

"That gives us two months," she said thoughtfully. "It's quick, but it's doable. I like it. I'm going to go talk to Yolanda about it now. Tell me when you hear from the NYSE about what needs to happen to move forward. Great work, Erin." She gave me an appraising look. "Why don't you go home now? You look like you could use some sleep."

I looked at my watch, it wasn't even ten, but my eyelids felt heavy. If I stayed at the office any longer, I might not be able to drive home safely. "Good idea. Thanks, Alex."

As I drove home, I had the nagging suspicion that I'd forgotten something, but try as I might, I couldn't figure it out.

* * *

After I woke up from a four-hour nap, I ate, and then called my mom. We hadn't spoken since before the retreat; we were overdue for a conversation.

"A promotion? That's wonderful, baby," Mom said, in the light pidgin accent that reminded me of home.

Although Mom wasn't from the islands, she'd lived in them for over forty years and had adopted all the mannerisms of a local—from dress, to language, to food. In some ways, my mom seemed more Hawaiian-Asian than my father, spending a good deal of her free time researching the Hung genealogy. She'd even chosen a Hawaiian name, choosing to go by Alani rather than her birth name, Rachel.

"Thanks, Mom. I'm very excited."

"You aren't going to pursue that uddah' job? The one in the mountains?" A tone of warning in her voice.

I rolled my eyes, grateful Mom couldn't see. I knew it had been a risk telling her about Sonja's offer. "I'm happy where I am," I said, deflecting. However, after this morning, the sentiment was especially true.

"Well, I'm glad someone's happy," she said begrudgingly.

I held my breath. "What's wrong, Mom?"

"Your faddah' and braddah' are off at some surf contest, and I'm all alone."

It was a familiar complaint, but one that had grown louder since I'd moved to the mainland and could no longer keep her company.

"Why don't I come visit you?" Mom said; a statement, not a question.

Visit. Me? But my sense of duty overcame my sense. "Yeah that would be—"

"I can come out tomorrow."

My heart started racing. "Maybe it would be better—"

"No, tomorrow is great. I'll text you with my arrival information. You won't even have to pick me up, I'll get a ride to your place," she said, without taking a breath. "It will be so fun. I'll see you soon. Bye, honey."

Click.

"Fuck."

Chapter 15: Distance

~Clint~

The next day, I was banging away at my computer, taking out my frustrations about Erin on my keyboard.

I'd thought we'd had a nice conversation on Monday, and had been looking forward to another one the day before, but then she never showed. She hadn't even had the courtesy to email me and cancel…or explain.

And she'd looked so cute at the editorial meeting. It had been beyond difficult to concentrate on anything anyone said when she'd been sitting in the vicinity, her bright yellow top like a beacon. Her hair had been in a long, low ponytail, the velvety black of it making my fingers itch.

I was so caught up in my thoughts that I didn't even notice when Yolanda walked into my office.

"Jesus, Clint. What did that keyboard ever do to you?" she asked, sashaying into the room and then closing the door behind her.

Yolanda was like that. She never asked for meetings, she just took them.

I sighed and turned towards her. I wasn't about to tell her the real reason I was pissed off, so instead, I said, "It's nothing. A story isn't shaping up the way I'd hoped. What's up?"

Yolanda put her arms out defensively and said, "Now, hear me out."

I rolled my eyes, leaned back in my chair, and put my feet up on my desk. I picked up a baseball and tossed it from one hand to the other, back and forth. "Hit me," I said, prepared for the worst.

"Alex has a really good idea. She was going through the pitch list and she noticed a number of New York-related stories. Anyway…" She told me about Alex's idea for a New York special, the bell ringing, and the event for donors.

When she was done, she folded her hands over her chest and waited.

I shrugged and tossed the baseball in the air a few times. "That's not a bad idea," I said, trying not to begrudge the source.

"Don't be a spoiled sport. I know we like to pretend that the only good stories are the ones we come up with, but this is inspired." After a pause, she added, "I've known Alex twenty years and I've never heard her come up with its equal. It's genius. Just don't tell her I said that. I wouldn't want it to go to her head."

I shrugged off my annoyance that this idea was coming from above us and said, "So the target date would be November?"

She nodded and stood. "We're just waiting for confirmation from the NYSE on a date. We should schedule a special meeting today to start pulling ideas together. Even if this New York thing doesn't pan out, we can still use the stories in our regular show."

I gave a final nod. "Sounds good."

"Great. One o'clock in the war room. See you then." She closed the door behind her before the word "but" even left my lips.

Mother Teresa.

I threw the baseball in the air a few more times and then pelted it at my couch, a satisfying *whomp* sounding as it hit the upholstered back.

Swiveling back to my computer, I stared blankly at the monitor for a few moments. Then I opened an email and typed into the subject line, "The pleasure of your presence is requested…"

I re-read it, highlighted it, and deleted it. It could be interpreted as passive-aggressive—which was accurate—but beneath me. Or knee-scraping, which was not at all how I wanted it taken.

I was pissed off and I wanted Erin to know, but without sounding pissed off.

I tried again, typing, "Some notice yesterday would have been nice…"

"Pffft," I blew out. *I am a childish idiot.*

But this wasn't news to me, which was why I *never* entered people's email addresses into the address space until I was certain I'd be sending the message. I considered the fact that I deleted fifty-percent of the emails I wrote to be one of my best personality traits.

My mom had always told me, "You can't control how you feel, but you can control how you act."

It was one of my mantras.

Eventually, I typed, "Change to 1 p.m. meeting today." Satisfied, I wrote the rest of the message.

Erin,

I can't meet at one today because Yolanda scheduled an "all-hands-on-deck" meeting,   for a special series we are planning to do from New York. You should come to the

meeting. You might find it interesting. I hope you are okay. I was waiting for you   yesterday.

Clint.

I read the message again before entering Erin's email and hitting the send button; my exercise in self-restraint having burnt out my more caustic emotions.

I went back to work, trying to focus on a conclusion I needed to write for the next day's broadcast. However, instead of quippy or intelligent one-liners that summed up recent shenanigans surrounding the selection of the next Olympics' hosts, my mind kept returning to Erin; her deep, intelligent eyes; her kind, open heart, big enough to have feelings for a jerk like me; and the way she made me feel, light and hopeful.

How could I ever be worthy of her spark, and yet, how could I live without it?

Eventually, I was able to get enough words down to fill the time needed, while the majority of my attention was spent on checking to see if Erin had responded to my email like a druggie waiting to score my next hit.

By the time one o'clock rolled around, I hadn't heard from her *and* I'd forgotten to eat lunch.

When I walked out my door to the war room conference table, I was beyond irritable.

All of the editors and reporters who might have a story to contribute to a New York special were gathered around the table. I stood at the head, glancing around at them, Yolanda to my left, the other fifteen or so assorted faces looking up at me expectantly— except the one I was hoping to see.

I put my hands on my hips. "You know why we're here." I surveyed their faces with my most commanding gaze. "New York is one of America's most historic and vibrant cities. It's home to about six percent of U.S. citizens. We have the chance to set the tone for this new era at Woo-Ah in an exciting way." I paused, satisfied with my little pep talk.

Sitting, I turned my legal pad to a fresh page. "Let's get started."

***

~Erin~

"Really? Harold, you are the best. The. Best. Yes, thanks. You, too. Talk soon." I ended the call, stood up from the desk in my condo, and did a little jig.

The date for the closing bell ringing was set for November twelfth; we had exactly eight weeks to plan everything…and there was a lot to plan.

I called the *WUA* office and asked to be transferred to Alex.

"This is Alex."

"Alex, it's Erin. Harold did it. We're confirmed for the closing bell on November twelfth."

"That's great. I'll tell the editorial staff. They're in an emergency planning meeting right now."

I glanced at the clock on my laptop; it was a little after one.

My meeting with Clint. That's what I'd forgotten the day before…and now for a second time.

I exhaled loudly. In all the excitement/exhaustion of the last thirty-six hours, I'd forgotten to tell him I wouldn't make it for our meetings.

After getting off the phone with my mom the day before, she'd texted, telling me she'd be landing at the airport at two-thirty the following day. I'd immediately called Alex, explained the situation, and asked if I could work from home. Alex had agreed as long as I kept her in the loop on any developments in New York.

"I need to ask you for something. It's kind of outside your purview, but because the series is so soon, we need everyone to do a little extra," Alex said hesitantly.

My curiosity was piqued. I'd never heard Alex speak with uncertainty. "Sure. What is it?"

"I need you to arrange all of the accommodations. Find us a block of rooms at the best price possible. I'll have Michel send you a list of everyone who'll be going."

I was surprised by the request. Then again, this whole thing had been my idea and it wasn't like we had an in-house travel agent. Besides—I rationalized—it might help me negotiate a higher raise. I was going above and beyond and showing myself to be a team player.

"Sure. I'm happy to help. But I can't get on the company server from here. I'll send Michel an email from my personal account. Also, do you have a budget for the reception yet? I want to get started on that today, too."

"I'll be sure to get that to you."

I briefly considered asking about my promotion paperwork, but decided that was a conversation better had in person. I didn't want to seem impatient. There'd be plenty of opportunities to ask about it in the coming week. "Thanks again for being flexible about today. My mom's never been to L.A. so I feel like I really need to pick her up at the airport."

"I get it. We all have moms." After a pause, she added, "But don't expect any time off between now and New York. This was your idea, now you have to help make it happen. But hey, at least you'll get a trip out of it."

I brightened. Although I'd hoped I'd be included in the trip, I hadn't been sure.

My heart soared. "Oh my god, Alex. Thank you. That's amazing."

She exhaled like she was embarrassed. "You deserve it, kid. You better go get your mom. I'll see you in the office tomorrow."

A little over an hour later, I received a text from Mom that she was at the luggage carousel, waiting for her bag. I eased out of the restaurant parking lot a half-mile from LAX and pulled into the long "arrivals" lane. As I weaved in and out of traffic, I prayed that the airport gods would bless me so that I wouldn't have to circle more than once, since it took thirty to sixty minutes to complete the loop. If all went according to plan, my mom would be curbside just as I was pulling up.

My phone rang.

"I'm here at the curb. I'm wearing a blue muumuu," my mom yelled over the loud background noise. "I can't believe how busy this place is."

"I'm one terminal away, Mom. Just stay where you are and wave your hands in the air."

Fifteen minutes later, Mom was in the car and we were speeding away from the airport, headed back to Pasadena.

"It's so good to see you, honey," she said, smoothing a stray lock of silvery blond hair out of her face. "Well, look at that braid. Doesn't your hair look nice like that."

I tensed up. I know that sounds totally irrational, but my mom *never* gave me compliments. When I replayed her sentence in my head, I decided it sounded sincere so I said a simple "thanks" and kept my eyes on the road. It was a little after three, which meant that rush hour would be creeping on as we drove.

"Look at all the cars..." she said breathlessly looking out the window.

I could easily imagine what she was thinking. It hadn't been that long ago that I'd had the same thoughts; the sheer number of cars and people in Los Angeles was mind-boggling. In Honolulu, people liked to complain about traffic, but that was because there just wasn't enough flat, open land to build more roads. In Los Angeles, that wasn't the issue; there were plenty of roads, but there were just *so many* cars.

And the sight of them. It's one thing to intellectually know there are a lot of cars, and another thing to see them in all of their shiny, metallic glory. The view of a full freeway in Los Angeles, especially when passing an interchange like the one we were coming up on—where the ten and the one-ten met just south of Downtown—was an engineering wonder to behold; ribbons of cement tied into a fluid bow of engineered stone set with glittering automobiles like gems on a tennis bracelet.

As if on cue, Mom said, "Would you look at that," her voice full of wonder at the barely-inching-along parking lot of cars that marked afternoon drive-time in Los Angeles.

I snapped on the radio and instantly relaxed as the familiar voices of *The Wrap-Up,* or *tee-woo* as we called it in the office, came on the air. *TWU* was produced by the same company as *WUA* and was located one floor below our offices in the same building. Alex had mentioned that we would be borrowing editorial resources from our sister show for the New York special. Apparently, their executive producer wasn't happy about it, but the CEO of our parent company had insisted. The big-wigs in D.C. had become invested in the events that were beginning to unfold given the high-profile nature of the NYSE bell-ringing and the funder event.

Listening to the day's stories relaxed me, and Mom seemed satisfied to stare out the window. If I'd been paying more attention, I might have recognized her silence for the unhappiness that it was instead of writing it off as the silence of an awed tourist. But the truth was, my guard was up. In the years since leaving my parents' house, I'd become aware of the—unintentional—baggage my mother had saddled me with, with her quick-to-criticize and slow-to-praise ways. I kept waiting for her to say something critical about my appearance or my driving. Instead, she said nothing.

Minute by minute, my defenses seeped away. It had been almost a year since we'd seen each other, during my annual Christmas trip home. Maybe things would be different this visit.

One could only hope.

I glanced at my mom and noticed that she looked tired, the skin around her eyes more lined and crêpey than I remembered.

Guilt washed over me.

"My work is over there," I said, pointing in the direction of the *WUA* offices, trying to infuse this visit with a bit of positive energy.

"Which one?"

"It's that short one right off the freeway."

"I see it." Then she laid a hand on my forearm. "Now, I know that you're busy at work, but I'd really love it if you could take some time off—"

"Sorry, Mom, but that's impossible," I said, shutting her down. "My boss explicitly told me not to take any time off for the next two months."

A few moments of stunned silence passed and guilt began to color my annoyance. "If you'd given me more notice, we could have scheduled your visit for a better time, but you're going to have to look out for yourself while I'm at work," I said, as gently as I could. "I can spend time with you on the weekend. And if you want, you can borrow my car. I can take the metro to work."

"But I thought—"

"If you had asked, I would have told you to come another time, but you seemed so determined," I cut in, not wanting to give her any wiggle room.

She'd already impinged on my independence by showing up. I was not going to let her make me feel bad for trying to do my job well.

I hazarded a quick glance at her, noting that she looked sadder than I'd ever seen. "How long are you staying? One week? Ten days?"

"Well...actually..." she cleared her throat, sounding a bit chagrined. "I bought a one-way ticket."

At that moment, traffic slowed and I came to a complete stop. I turned my full gaze on her. "You what?"

Her eyes got wide. "Erin, I've left your father."

"You what!?"

She smoothed the thin fabric of her dress and looked away. "I was tired of being ignored. I was his cook and his maid, not his wife. Do you know how long it's been since he took me out somewhere, or gave me a card, or even said 'thank you' to me?" She shrugged quickly, as though removing a weight from her shoulders. "He used to like spending time with me, now he treats me like a nuisance. I'm done."

I blinked rapidly when a loud *honk* reminded me that I was still on the road. A large gap had opened up in front of me and I took my foot off the brake. I drove in silence for a few minutes.

Finally, I asked, "What did Dad say when you left?"

I saw her shrug out of the corner of my eye, but she said nothing.

"Mom…" My scalp tingled. I had a feeling I wasn't going to like the answer.

"I didn't tell him anything."

"You didn't leave a note?"

"No," Mom said, sniffing a bit.

"But Mom, he's going to be worried. What's he going to think when he gets back from his trip and you aren't there?"

"I don't know and I don't care," she said, her voice quivering.

I looked over, surprised to see silent tears streaking down my mother's cheek. "Oh, Mom. I'm sorry."

She wiped at her face and shook her head. "I gave up my future for your father." She paused as though she was going to say more, but nothing else came.

We drove the rest of the way in silence, me trying to decide if I should call Dad and wondering what to do about the news that my mom planned to stay indefinitely. When we arrived at my condo, Mom said she was hungry, so I gave her directions to some local restaurants and reminded her that I needed to get back to work.

As soon as Mom walked out the door, I dialed Angela.

"She what?" Angela exclaimed.

"That's what I said," running a hand over my braids.

"Shit."

"No kidding. What do you think I should do?"

"Honestly, I'm kind of curious to see what Uncle Johnny does."

"Angela!"

"What? He's a big boy. He needs to know he can't take her for granted. What's the worst that's going to happen to him? He has to make his own dinner? Buy his own toilet paper?"

"What if he thinks Mom's been kidnapped."

"He can call her on her cell, Erin. Look, I think you should honor your mom's wishes, at least for one or two days. If your dad doesn't call her, that's a sign of a much bigger problem. Besides, you can always get my mom involved. She's probably Aunt Alani's best weapon. You know how your dad worships my mom."

I brightened. She was right. Dad idolized Angela's mom, Lillian, who was like a second mother to him since they'd been latchkey kids growing up. Dad had told me that Lillian had been the person who taught him how to read and helped him with his homework every day, not to mention making dinner for him, their younger sister, Phyllis, and their parents once Lillian was old enough to cook.

I exhaled with relief. "You're right. Okay, I'll give it a couple of days. Do me a favor and don't mention it to your mom yet."

"My lips are sealed. Bye, cuz," Angela said.

Mollified now that I had a plan for how to deal with my parents, I jumped back onto my laptop to continue my work-from-home day.

There were a couple of emails from Alex, requesting that the hotel rooms be close to the mid-town studios where *WUA* had an office, but still accessible to the financial district where the NYSE was located. She also included the contact information of someone in the New York *WUA* office who I could reach out to if I needed guidance. I made a quick call to that person, which further helped narrow my search for hotels, and got to work.

It wasn't until the sun started setting that I realized I was still working and Mom hadn't returned, even though she'd left a few hours ago.

I stood and stretched my arms over my head; the hours of sitting in one position had made my back stiff. At least I had a solid lead for accommodations for the *WUA* staff, although I'd need to run the idea by Alex since it was a little out of the box.

As I powered down my computer, I heard a key in my door and was relieved when Mom walked in, a big smile on her face.

Clearly, she had enjoyed her first day of independence.

"Hey, honey," she said, closing the door behind her, a takeout bag in her hand. "I brought you dinner."

***

The next morning, I took the metro into work, having given my mom a list of places that she could visit and a plan to meet for dinner.

When I walked to my cubicle, I was greeted by a DVD of *Citizen Kane* on my desk and Fern's big smile. "Hey! Where were you yesterday?"

I frowned, shoving the DVD in my bag. It was a show of kindness that reminded me I needed to apologize to Clint. "It's a loooong story, but my mom flew in yesterday."

"From Hawai'i?" He frowned. "Is everything okay?"

"There's some stuff going on with her and my dad."

"I'm sorry. Let me know if I can do anything."

I had an idea. "Maybe you can. Let me think about it a little more and we can talk later. I have a meeting with Alex I need to prep for right now."

An hour later, I was sitting in Alex's office, explaining about the members-only hotel I'd found. "There's an annual one-thousand-dollar membership fee, but when you consider the number of nights we need, we're still saving money over booking a regular hotel."

She studied the simple spreadsheet I put together with the help of my cousin Angela and her MBA.

Angela liked to joke that she got a master's degree in Excel and PowerPoint and I took advantage of it.

Alex looked up at me. "This makes sense. Nice job finding such a great price in that neighborhood."

I beamed. "The facility is bare-bones, but it's clean, well-located, and within our budget."

Our very tight budget.

"Great. Run with it," she said, handing back the spreadsheet.

"There's one other thing," I said as Alex started turning back to face her monitor.

She returned her gaze to me, a look of forced patience. "Yes?"

"I'd like to attend the editorial meeting regularly. A lot of what happens there can help me market the show better. But as you can imagine, the timing is rough. I was thinking that I could make a habit of attending the Monday meeting, as long as I can leave early that day to compensate."

"Sure. That sounds like a good idea," she said, her tone dismissive.

I was just about to leave, but I figured I was on a streak, so I said, "One *final* thing…" I hurried, since she was clearly ready for me to leave. "I was wondering if the paperwork for my promotion came in."

She gave a rueful sigh. "Sorry, Erin. Everything has been so crazy this week, I haven't had a chance to connect with HR in the D.C. office. But I promise I'll do it soon." She raised her brows as though checking to see if I had "one other thing."

Forcing a smile on my face, I checked my disappointment and walked out of her office, almost running into Clint, who was holding some flowers.

"Oh, sorry," I said, grabbing his elbow to steady myself.

Clint cursed something that sounded like "Mother Teresa" but then looked up and met my gaze.

"Erin," he exclaimed, his face rearranging itself from surprised to stony in a second.

I straightened up, trying not to let his reaction affect me—

—but it did.

He looked like he was going to say something to me but then turned to Michel and put the vase—which was really a beer-stein-shaped coffee mug emblazoned with an Ivy League crest—on Michel's desk.

Or at least he tried to, but as soon as he set the mug down, the tall sunflowers began to topple. "These flowers aren't doing well in my office. I thought they might get more light over here."

The mug contained five sunflowers, rubber bands gripping the bunch in three places along three-foot-long stalks, a blue plastic packet stuck in the middle band.

I watched fascinated, amusement filtering in as Clint continued to struggle, trying to defy the laws of physics by getting the sunflowers to stay upright. Every time he tried to remove his hands, the top-heavy flowers started tilting, threatening to topple their puny vase.

Michel raised a brow at me as if to say, "Is this guy for real?" Then he cleared his throat. "Nice flowers."

"Yeah, a fan sent them," Clint said without looking up, his eyes focused on his hands wrapped around the base of the glass.

"Did you cut the stems before you put them in water?" I asked.

Still jostling the would-be vase, Clint replied, "Are you supposed to?"

"Yes. The stems seal themselves, like scabs. You have to re-cut them so that they'll take in water," I said cheekily, allowing a bit of my annoyance to shine through.

Michel nodded. "Preferably at an angle."

Clint stopped and looked at Michel, eyes widening. "At an angle?"

Michel shrugged. "That's how my mom taught me."

Clint narrowed his eyes, which fanned the flames of my annoyance.

Did Clint think a little Floral Care 101 was beneath him?

I decided to jab a little deeper. "Also, the blue packet will do more good for the plants if you put the contents *into* the water," I said, a bit of sarcasm dripping into my words as Clint continued to handle the flowers like they were a dirty diaper. "It's plant food."

Clint paused and gave me an appraising look. "Damn it, Erin, I'm a fighter pilot, not a florist." His face making it clear that he thought his statement was quite clever.

I bristled. *Was that a joke?*

He raised a brow. "Get it? Kirk and McCoy?"

I narrowed my eyes. "Well, a truly well-rounded man could do both," I said, giving him a saccharine smile.

His jaw tensed.

Michel's eyes got round as he looked back and forth between the two of us.

Clint turned to Michel and shoved the coffee mug into the other man's hands. "Can you handle these for me?"

Michel nodded.

Clint took a threatening step towards me, momentarily closing the distance between us—my heart fluttering at the primitive thrill his close proximity inspired—and then just as abruptly he pivoted around me and stomped down the hall to his office. His door slammed behind him.

Alpha male much? I thought, the hair on my neck still buzzing. "What a jerk."

Michel shrugged. "He's not that bad when you get to know him. He's just hard to get to know. I still don't know him very well."

I swiveled to face him. "How long have you worked here?"

"Eight years," he said with a sigh, fingering the petals of the sunflower. "But he's *so* hot." Then he narrowed his gaze. "But you two seem to have an unusual chemistry…" With an arched brow, he said, "I don't think I've ever seen either of you so. Hot. And. Bothered."

I pursed my lips to avoid gasping.

Michel was the last person I wanted gossiping.

"I have no idea what you're talking about. See you later, Meesh."

Walking back to my cubicle, I tried to shake off my anger, but it wasn't easy. I was still annoyed by Clint's stomping off. I knew I owed him a "thank you" for the DVD and an "I'm sorry" for missing our meeting two days in a row, but right now I didn't feel like giving him either.

When I got to my desk, I pulled up a new email, entered his name, and typed, "a few things" in the subject line.

Clint,

Got the DVD. Thanks. Let me know if you can still meet at one today. Your photoshoot is this Friday. Need to discuss wardrobe and work on finishing our interview.

Erin

A few minutes later I got a response.

Roger one o'clock.

I fumed.

By the time one o'clock rolled around, what had started out as being annoyed at Clint had festered into feeling livid. I walked into his office unannounced, as he was typing away on the computer, and closed his door just a bit louder than necessary.

I felt a sense of satisfaction when he tensed at the sound.

He turned, rolling away from his computer to the broad side of his desk and folded his hands together, looking like a high school principal getting ready to discipline a wayward student.

Of course, that thought just sent *all* the wrong messages to my body which promptly broke out into delicious, naughty shivers.

Traitorous body.

It was impossible to be in his presence and ignore all of his…his Clint-ness. That beautiful auburn hair, with just a hint of wave, although I remembered how much curlier it had looked on the retreat after his sweaty runs.

Hmmmm…sweaty runs.

His tan, muscular forearms covered with thick, ropey veins that I wanted to touch.

Touch!

The teensy, smug smirk that always threatened the corner of his mouth.

That mouth!

As usual, I couldn't think clearly in his presence, and I also couldn't promise that I wasn't just a little bit drooling.

He narrowed his beautiful, chocolate brown eyes at me and I thought I sensed amusement.

I bristled.

I needed to harden myself against this man and his many, many charms.

I rolled my shoulders back and attempted my most emotionally distant tone. "Let's get through as much of the interview as we can and then we can talk photoshoot," I said, not waiting for a response. "Why public radio?"

"I believe quality journalism should be free to the public," he said tersely.

"When did you know you wanted to be a host?" I lobbed quickly.

He returned my volley just as fast. "I didn't. It wasn't until I got here that I figured that out. I've always been very curious and I like being able to get my questions answered by the source."

We continued like that, back and forth, our words devoid of emotion and as fast and angry as a John McEnroe versus John McEnroe tennis match. He didn't exercise his right to ask me any questions, which hurt my feelings. But I didn't let myself dwell on that and focused on getting my job done. We finished quickly, and although the answers weren't as fleshed out as I would have liked, they would do. The only question he'd refused to answer was when I asked him his callsign in the Navy and he'd said, "Next question."

"Do you have a sport coat or suit jacket?" I asked, putting my notebook down.

"Yes, one brown tweedy sport coat," he said as I wrinkled my nose, "and two suits: navy and charcoal."

"Bring the suit jackets and your five best dress shirts, one white and the rest solid colors that are bright. Bring as many ties as you can," I said, sensing he didn't have that many. "They'll be shooting you from twelve to one—"

"Don't I get a say in this?" he interrupted.

Without missing a beat I said, "No. You don't. I'm speaking on Alex's authority.

His jaw tensed.

My neck tingled, and it wasn't entirely unpleasant. There was something sexy about the predatory look Clint got when he was frustrated. The way his muscles went rigid, the sparks in his eyes, the ticking in his chiseled jaw.

As usual, Clint's presence was overwhelming my good sense.

I stood, needing to get away from him before I said something stupid. "There will be a make-up artist and a hairstylist. Be prepared to be nicer to them than you were to Michel this morning."

His brow twitched up. "Anything else?"

"Yes. I'll be sitting in on the Monday editorial meetings, and next week we'll need to use our one-o-clock meeting time to record new teasers."

Every radio station loved having the show hosts record audio that promoted the radio program along with the local station. Next week was going to be one endless loop of, "I'm Clint Davenport, host of *Wake-Up America*, letting you know that it's never too early to stay up to date. Tune in to your local public radio station, KXXX at XX.X FM for all the latest."

"Got it," he said, and turned back to his computer.

He was so cold, it made me feel like I must have hallucinated the week of the retreat. But why was I surprised? This was the Clint I'd known for the past two years. Retreat Clint had been the aberration.

I saw myself out, stifling the urge to be conciliatory.

If he wanted a war, a war he would get.

Chapter 16: Trying New Things

~Erin~

Warm lips and furtive hands licked, sucked, and tugged at my body, somehow covering every inch of me at the same time with a neediness that seemed overwhelming and yet not enough.

Was it possible to feel both at the same time?

Even though I couldn't see his face, I knew who this was. Clint's presence held a weight for me that didn't need sight for recognition.

Reaching for him, my hands and arms closed on air.

I tried to kiss him back, but when my lips touched his they seemed to vanish; the wet pressure I was seeking, elusive.

Rough licking at my neck was both annoying and welcoming, and then—

"Wake up, sleeping beauty. I made breakfast. Portuguese sausage, rice, and eggs with *furikake*, just the way you like," my mom's voice called to me through the foggy depths of my dream.

My eyes fluttered open to find Atticus, staring down at me, cocking his head from ten o'clock to two o'clock like he was waiting for me to answer some question he'd just asked. *If you don't want your sausage, can I have it, Human?*

He licked my face again, his scratchy tongue like living Velcro.

"Atti," I sigh-laughed, annoyed that I'd been wakened from my nightly fantasy of Clint.

If I could only have him in my dreams; I wanted to be able to enjoy them fully.

The dreams had been my constant nocturnal companion ever since leaving Big Bear, and I both welcomed and dreaded them. Sometimes they left me fulfilled and happy, reminding me of the clandestine moments we'd shared on the retreat. Other times they left me sad, wondering how long it would take for me to get over him. Of course, it's hard to get over someone you see almost every day.

This particular dream had been more frustrating than others; perhaps a subconscious reflection of our interactions from the past week. It had left me with a nagging ache that seemed to start between my legs, radiate up through my gut, and then ping off my heart like a homing beacon.

I pulled Atticus into a cuddle, wanting to fill the need my unfulfilling dream had left me with.

Atticus tolerated the cuddle for about a minute before wiggling out of my grasp and giving me a stern look. *If you wanted affection, Human, you should have gotten a cat.*

I watched his pert sickle tail as he trotted out of my room. *Maybe I should have adopted a cat.*

"Food's getting cold," Mom called, her voice sailing in from the kitchen.

"On my way," I said, stretching groggily from the air mattress on my floor, having given my mom the bed like a good daughter.

In all my years since graduating from college, I'd never been so grateful for the weekend. The previous week had been the most intense of my life. I'd crammed three weeks of work into one. Between Mom and work, I hadn't gone climbing a single night. Although part of me would've liked sleeping in, the smell of Portuguese sausage was too alluring to ignore, so I got up, threw my braid behind my back, and washed my face.

Then I walked to my second-hand dining table, where Mom had laid out two bowls of eggs and rice, with another plate covered in oblong pieces of sausage on top of a paper towel soaked orange with their oil.

"Thanks, Mom. This looks great." I curled my legs under me as I sat on a dining chair, stretching my nightshirt over my knees. I leaned one arm on the table and barely stifled a yawn as I reached for the coffee cup Mom had put out for me.

Atticus jumped into my lap, sniffing in the direction of the sausage.

I ruffled his head. "Not for you, Atti. I'll feed you in a bit."

He growled. *Ungrateful human. You live to serve me.*

Mom clucked. "You work too hard."

I humphed. "I don't think you've ever said that to me before."

She shrugged. "I had to be hard on you kids growing up so that you wouldn't become lazy and indolent." My mom's Hawaiian accent had softened over the last week. She continued, "But now that you're a productive adult, my work is done." She took a sip of coffee. "By the way, I've been listening to your radio show every day. I really like it. And that Clint Davenport's voice is so hunky."

Hunky? I raised a brow, curious to see if this new version of Mom was the real deal, or just part of her midlife crisis. I put some sausage on my plate and sprinkled on a generous helping of *furikake,* the mixture of sesame seeds and shredded seaweed decorating the top of my eggs and rice. "So have you heard from Dad?"

She shrugged. "He's left me a few voice-mails, but I haven't listened to them."

My fork clattered. "Mom, you have to talk to him."

She sniffed. "No, I don't. I texted him that I was safe and staying with a friend."

"A friend?"

"Yes. He doesn't need to know where I am, and I'm not ready to talk to him yet."

I considered this as I chewed my food. "If you're planning on sticking around, maybe you should talk to Aunty Lillian. Maybe even stay with her for a bit. She's got a big house and she could probably give you some good advice about Dad—"

"You want me to leave already?"

I almost choked on my food.

Swallowing carefully, I answered, "No, Mom, of course not. It's just that my place isn't that big and I thought you might like more space." I chastised myself inwardly for the lie. It was *my* apartment; didn't I have a right to my own bed? *Damn filial piety.*

Atticus laid his head down, flattening his ears as though he was disappointed at Mom's extended stay, too. *Great, another human to deal with.*

We ate quietly, Mom occasionally asked a question about work, and I occasionally asked a question about how she'd spent the last few days. Mostly it was companionable, however, it was hard to shake the feeling that I was a kid back under the strict roof of my parents' home.

Then I remembered our plans for the evening. I'd felt guilty spending almost no time with Mom since her arrival, so I'd planned something special. Since Mom was adamant that Lillian and her family not know about her presence in L.A., it narrowed our social circle. "We have dinner plans tonight."

Her brow lifted. "With whom?" she asked suspiciously.

With whom? My mother had never used the word 'whom' before.

"A friend from work. He lives with his mom and she's an awesome cook. She offered to teach me how to make tamales. I thought we could do it together. It'll be fun," I added.

She got an uncertain look on her face. "I don't know. I was thinking we could watch a movie, or maybe walk around Old Town and have dinner at Lunasia."

"Mom, you've eaten at Lunasia almost every night this week."

Her face fell. "It reminds me of home."

I clenched my teeth. *Jiminy Cricket.* "I didn't mean to hurt your feelings, Mom, I just thought it would be fun to do something different."

She took a sip of coffee and nodded. "I know, baby. I know. It's just—" Her voice cracked as a sob bubbled up in her throat. "I miss your father."

I went and put my arms around her shoulders. "You should check your messages," I said quietly, hugging her tighter as soft sobs racked her body.

She shook her head. "What if he doesn't miss me?"

It was a valid question. Johnny Hung was a mercurial, self-absorbed man who'd spent too many years as a surfing god— worshiped by his adoring fans and the sports media—to be self-aware enough to understand his wife's feelings.

Just then, my phone rang from its charging perch on the kitchen counter. Crossing to pick it up, I read the screen. "It's Dad."

She froze. "I don't want him to know I'm here," she hissed, making it hard to believe she'd just been crying over the man a second earlier.

Her rapid seesaw reminded me of my own feelings towards Clint. "But, Mom—"

"Erin. I'm your mother," she snapped.

I tensed, feeling like a disobedient child. My reaction to that tone of voice was Pavlovian. "Okay. I won't tell him." The call was just about to go to voicemail when I accepted it. "Hey, Dad, what's up?" I asked, trying to sound nonchalant.

"Do you know where your mother is?" he barked.

"Jeez. A hello would be nice."

"Do not play around, Erin. Your mother has been gone for four days and she won't take my calls."

I sighed. *Talk about a rock and a hard place.* I didn't want to lie to Dad, but I also had a promise to keep to Mom. I needed to walk a fine line. "I know where she is, but I promised not to tell you. She's safe though."

"Is she with you?" he pushed.

I tensed. "I can't tell you *anything.*"

He huffed. "I don't know what's gotten into her. She's been acting strange the last few months and then she vanishes," he spat out, sounding more annoyed than upset.

I sighed and sat back down, avoiding my mom's curious gaze. "Strange? How?" I asked, taking a bite of my lukewarm eggs.

"Wanting to go out more, dropping hints about restaurants and movies. Trying to hold my hand."

I rolled my eyes. No wonder Mom took off. Dad made hand-holding sound like a communicable disease. Granted, I'd never seen them hold hands. They'd been long past that stage of their relationship before I was old enough to notice, but still… "That seems strange to you?"

He cursed. "Come on, Erin. We're old married folks. We don't do that stuff anymore."

"Maybe you should try," I deadpanned, surprised at my boldness.

"Listen, young lady. Don't you take that tone—"

Anger flared in me. "I'm thirty-two, *Dad.* You don't pay my rent. You never call. Don't you dare try and tell me what to do."

It felt good to get angry, although I might have been taking a bit of my Clint-induced feelings out on my father. *Oh well, it's not like Dad doesn't deserve it.* "I have to go. I was in the middle of breakfast and you're ruining my appetite. Bye."

"Erin, don't you dare—"

I ended the call.

Damn, that felt good.

I raised my eyes to my mother, expecting a high-five, but instead, she gave me a disapproving glare.

"Erin Mei-Yung Hung," she said with dismay. "I didn't raise you to speak to your father like that."

My mouth dropped open.

There was no winning with these two.

"Now we need to spend the day cleaning your apartment. I can't believe you can live with this much dust."

And, she's back.

By the time we were done, we had washed, ironed, and put away all of my laundry (and I mean EVERY. SINGLE. PIECE.), changed my sheets, dusted all the surfaces, and cleaned the stove-top, microwave, and refrigerator.

I was exhausted and it was only a little after two.

No climbing today either.

"The window treatments need to be wiped down," she said, running her finger along the vertical blinds.

"I'm pooped, Mom," I said, throwing myself onto my microsuede couch, my head sticky with perspiration. "Besides, we need to shower before we go to Fern's, and I need to stop at the store to pick something up. I want to leave by four-fifteen."

"Fern? Your friend is named after a plant?"

I threw my arm over my eyes. "It's short for Fernando."

"Oh. Okay. Well, I'll go shower."

"Okay. If I fall asleep, just wake me up when you get out," I said, my eyelids heavy, hopes of a Clint dream making me chase sleep like a lovesick suitor.

Mom let me rest, waking me with enough time to shower and change.

I awoke refreshed but disappointed since the nap had been dreamless. Perhaps a nap wasn't enough time to let my subconscious do its thing.

Fortunately, the promise of an evening at Fern's place lifted my spirits.

We stopped by a store on our way to the charming craftsman Fern called home, located on a narrow street with a mixture of old, rangy trees and weedy patches with stumps. It was a little after five and the sky was golden, filled with the beautiful, honeyed light of that time just before sunset.

His neighborhood—Highland Park—was one of the older parts of Los Angeles; a hilly suburb developed in the early nineteen-hundreds on the outskirts of Downtown, back when Downtown was truly the center of the city. The homes were small, although recent gentrification had begun changing the size and profile of the homes as well as the residents.

I could easily pick out which houses were inhabited by young hipsters, with their colorful, Feng-shuied front doors, their trendy mid-century-inspired landscaping, and their hybrid cars.

"Welcome," Fern said as he opened the door, his head almost grazing the door frame. "Atti!" he held his arms out to the dog who looked practically fetal in Fern's arms. "Long time no see, boy." He lifted Atticus to his lips for a kiss.

I rolled my eyes. Atticus went gaga for Fern.

When Fern was done welcoming Atticus, he gave me a big hug, which felt strange since we never hugged at work.

Strange, but nice.

"*Hola*, welcome. *Gracias por venir*," Fern's mom, Lorena, said, waving us in, a colorful half-apron tied around her waist.

"Thank you for having us," Mom said, handing Lorena the pineapple and tequila bottle we'd picked up as she kissed the other woman on the cheek. "I'm Alani."

"Lorena. Oh! A *piña*, thank you. And *mmmm*," she said, sniffing the prickly fruit, "it smells sooo good. Maybe we can make pineapple margaritas." She held the two items up.

"Actually, Mrs. Haddad, I was thinking we could do something creative with the pineapple," I said, clapping my hands together.

"What did you have in mind, *mija*?"

"Well, I really enjoyed the *al pastor* that you made for me last time I was here." I turned to Mom and explained, "*Al pastor* are pork tacos with pineapple."

"They are typical to the area of Mexico that I'm from. It's like Mexican shawarma," Lorena said to my mother.

I nodded. "Mrs. Haddad was born in Mexico, but her husband's father, and *her* mother, were of Lebanese descent. *Al pastor* is a fusion of Lebanese and Mexican cuisine."

Fern chuckled. "Was Erin always this into food?" he directed to my mom.

My mom shook her head. "No. I think Los Angeles has brought it out in her."

I nodded. "You have so many more types of food here than we do in Hawai'i, Fern. You would feel seriously deprived." I looked back to Lorena. "Anyway, I liked the pineapple in the tacos so much, I thought it would be fun to try putting it in the tamales, too. Maybe do a pineapple salsa as well. A fusion of my culture and your culture."

Lorena gave me an affectionate smile. "I love that idea."

Fern nodded. "Me, too."

Lorena cranked up the Spanish-language radio station, and the four of us cooked, ate, and drank late into the night, everyone agreeing that the *al pastor* tamales were an inspired idea.

By the end of the evening, Lorena and Mom were doing tequila shots on the couch in front of the brick fireplace, cackling like college roommates.

"Wanna sit outside?" Fern asked.

I laughed. "Yeah. Our moms are being obnoxious." But I felt good that my mom had made a real connection. She looked happier than she'd been all week.

"Do you want anything else to drink?"

"Just some water," I said.

I didn't have my mom's alcohol tolerance, having inherited my father's Asian intolerance. I'd nursed a single margarita all night, and had stopped drinking around nine. It was almost ten, and I was feeling sober enough that I could drive us home soon enough.

"I'll get it for you."

Fern fetched me some water and we sat at a round, metal table perforated with a floral pattern. The matching chairs made a loud scraping sound as we pulled them out. A menagerie of potted succulents surrounded us on the concrete patio, and a fragrant vine with white flowers wound up the wood and metal gazebo.

I pulled my light wrap tight around my shoulders; it was the coldest night we'd had so far in September and my short-sleeve top felt inadequate.

Atticus snuggled into my lap. *Warm me now, Human.*

"Fall is finally coming," I said.

He nodded, a buzzed smile on his lips. "I haven't seen my mom have this much fun in a long time."

I laughed. "Me, either. We should get them together more often."

"If it means that you'll be here, too, then sign me up," he said, his eyes turning from sparkling to dark in a heartbeat.

Shifting in my seat, I tried not to read into his statement. Fern was one of my favorite people and I didn't want to say anything that would jeopardize that.

He cleared his throat. "Is your mom going to be staying for a while?"

I sighed. "I really don't know. But I can't take sleeping on the air mattress much longer. If she decides to stay more than two weeks, I'm going to ask her to move to my aunt's place in the Valley. She's got room and would probably love the company."

"Good idea," he said, his eyes darting to my mouth.

I licked my lips nervously. "Fern—"

"Erin—" he started saying, and then stopped, smoothing out his jeans as he sat back in his chair.

I got the feeling that there was something he needed to say. "You go."

He leaned forward, putting his hands on the table. "It's just that," he paused. "I have so much fun with you, and you're so easy to talk to."

I had to admit that few people in the world understood me as well as Fernando Haddad. He was also one of the kindest and most thoughtful people I knew, and not bad to look at, either, but there was the issue of—

"Can I kiss you?" he asked earnestly, a slightly breathless quality to his question.

"Fern, we're…you're…" there were so many reasons why we shouldn't kiss, I hardly knew where to start. "I love you, but we really shouldn't."

I hadn't been planning to say the words, but once they were out, I recognized the truth of them. I loved Fern and didn't want to imagine my life without him.

His eyes brightened at the word "love" and then flickered out as I finished my sentence. "You're probably right," he said leaning back in the metal chair, his head hanging like Charlie Brown's dejected Christmas tree.

If he had tried to convince me, or pressure me, I wouldn't have done what I did next, but my statement of love had me thinking that maybe I *should* kiss Fern. Sure, there would be complications at work, but we could figure that out. Besides, being with Fern would probably be the easiest thing in the world. He was my best friend...

I grabbed his hand and pulled him towards me and then suddenly, Fern's tender lips were kissing mine, lightly like a question, hesitant and tasting faintly of tequila and lime.

But while I felt warmth and comfort, there was no spark.

Zero. Zilch. *Nada.*

While Clint's kiss had been spectacular, nuclear fusion starlight, Fern's had been warm lips, pressed together for seemingly no apparent reason.

My heart bleeped out a sad homing signal at this realization, wondering where its mate had gone.

After a moment, we returned to our chairs, looked at each other, and laughed.

Atticus looked between the two of us as though trying to decipher the joke.

"It was a nice kiss, really," I offered.

"Don't patronize me. Even I can tell that we have no chemistry." He sighed, smoothing out the front of his jeans. "Oh well, I just like you so much as a person, I thought we should *try*. No harm, no foul?"

I nodded with a big smile. "No harm, no foul."

Chapter 17: Dragon Well

~Erin~

The weeks passed and the stress level at the WUA offices climbed to higher and higher levels of mania as the date for the New York special approached. No one was free from the stress as the short schedule and multiple goals meant that almost the entire office was involved in some way. The special was not just an editorial event but a publicity and fundraising one, too. It was all-hands-on-deck.

For me, it was an endless stream of phone calls and emails, arranging the hotel rooms, managing the guest list, responding to requests from radio stations for Clint's autographed photos and possible appearances, picking food and flowers, and on and on and on.

Of course, the local New York station wanted to take advantage of having Clint in their backyard—my idea—and I figured why stop there? Why not hit the other two big markets in the area—Philadelphia and Boston—especially since Clint was from the Boston area.

"Good thinking, Erin. Make it happen," had become Alex's standard response to my suggestions.

As I enlarged my duties with all of my creative thinking, I had to garner resources wherever possible, enlisting the help of a peer in the D.C. headquarters to assist with the food and flowers, delegating the creation of the invitations to Fern, and handing off the teaser production to Joe in engineering.

Why, you ask?

Because Alex's earlier promise of having more team members, as well as written confirmation of my promotion and raise, still hadn't come through.

If I'd been more experienced, I might have been worried, but I was simply too swamped to do more than feel mild frustration. Part of me also figured that all the work I was doing would help me get a bigger raise (and maybe even a bigger title?) than promised. The idea of being "Director Hung" was still a pipe dream I liked to nurse.

The other thing was that I could see that Alex was buried beneath the same mountain that I was, the behemoth of New York.

The special was less than two weeks away when I found myself running around Chinatown, on a mission.

By now, everyone in the editorial department had agreed that a future special about China was a great goal and that New York could be a stepping stone towards its realization.

I could only imagine how thrilled Clint was about that and I felt a sad pang that I would never know.

He'd looked especially good today in charcoal slacks that had hugged his lean, muscled frame, paired with a white shirt whose sleeves he'd rolled up, exposing the beautiful veins on his forearms that made me want to lick the route they mapped on his body.

Lick his veins?

My obsession with Clint Davenport was truly out of control.

Focus, Erin, focus. I had been wandering around the streets of Chinatown rather aimlessly on my fool's errand, and thinking about Clint didn't help. The tension between us had never eased since our McEnroe-esque afternoon and he rarely met my gaze unless I was speaking to him directly.

While I'd (more or less) gotten to the point where I could no longer remember why we were annoyed with each other, he didn't seem to feel the same way. In fact, the way he avoided looking at me during editorial meetings was positively frigid.

Men.

Never mind that my mother was still in town. Which had me feeling even more animosity towards the other sex, since I thought my father should've flown in by now to try and make things right with her.

But I didn't have time to think about that. I needed to focus.

The fund-raising department had been able to identify at least a dozen New York-based institutions as possible donors for a future special about China, which was why I was on a mission. I'd squeezed two-hundred-and-fifty dollars out of the budget by eliminating one of the ten flower arrangements for the stock exchange reception. My goal? To find an affordable, but meaningful, gift to give to the two-hundred guests who would be attending said event.

Fortunately, Chinatown was practically spitting distance from the *WUA* offices, and I'd driven into work so that I could swing by on my way home.

Ordinarily, I loved visiting Chinatown; it reminded me so much of the one in Honolulu. The sights, sounds, and smells were like coming home. I enjoyed walking past windows filled with live turtles and fish, colorful paper lanterns blowing in the breeze, the omnipresent red and gold of good fortune written on paper scrolls fluttering on the sidewalk displays.

But today I had a purpose, and it was looking less and less likely that I was going to complete it successfully.

I lost track of the number of stores I visited, all of them running together in a nameless flow of sandalwood fans, stone figurines, and silk accessories.

I was just about to enter another shop when my cell phone rang. It was Sonja, the ropes course instructor from Big Bear. I immediately felt guilty because I'd never called her, and answered quickly. "Hi, Sonja. How are you?"

"Erin, I'm great. How have you been? Long time no talk."

I winced. "I'm so sorry I haven't been in touch. A huge project at work has taken over my life."

She chuckled. "No problem. I just wanted to reach out because I have a large group coming up in a couple of weeks and I thought it would be a good opportunity for you to spend the weekend. I'd pay you, of course, you wouldn't be doing it for free. You could see how you liked it. I know it doesn't pay as well as your current job…"

I appreciated her honest approach, especially compared with how Alex had been handling everything. *Maybe I should check it out.* "What weekend?"

"November fourteenth and fifteenth."

I clucked my tongue. "Darn. I'll be on the East Coast for work. For the project I mentioned." That was the weekend I'd scheduled events in Boston and Philadelphia for Clint. I wanted to be there to make sure everything ran smoothly.

But I don't have to be. No one had said I should go to the other cities; it was yet another thing I'd taken on my own initiative.

A tiny seed of defiance was planted.

Still, I stuck to my obligations and said, "I'd love to, but I don't think I can make it."

"I understand. Well, you have my number. Feel free to reach out anytime. Take care, Erin." She sounded disappointed.

It sounded like goodbye.

"Thanks, Sonja," I said, feeling like a door was closing as I ended the call.

When God closes a door…

A car honked and I came back to my body. I was still standing on the sidewalk in front of the store I'd been about to enter.

My current dilemma reasserted itself.

How am I going to find a not-cheesy gift with my tiny budget?

After two hours of searching, I was beginning to lose hope.

I looked at my watch and sighed. It was almost six and I still needed to put the finishing touches on my costume for Alex's Halloween party, which was the following day.

But I was determined.

I straightened my shoulders and entered another store. From the moment I walked in, it felt different than all the others. Like I'd pierced some veil and entered a place apart.

This was not a *typical* gift store.

Yes, there were many of the typical gift store items, however, half of the store was dedicated to loose-leaf tea and its various accoutrements, everything arranged almost reverently. Like I'd stumbled on a museum dedicated to the art of tea.

An infusion of excited energy filled me as I glided over to the huge glass jars filled with various shades of green, brown, and black. It reminded me of the crack seed stores back home, except instead of *li hing mui* plums and tapioca ball cookies, it was just jar upon jar of tea.

"May I help you?" a small woman with a neat salt-and-pepper bob croaked in a voice as fragile as china, her watery, gray-brown eyes peering at me from behind thick, round glasses.

I sighed. While I would have loved to spend time learning all about tea, I was on a mission. *But maybe just a little distraction to clear my mind.* "Hi, I'm Erin."

"Hello, Erin, I am Mrs. Fong. Nice to meet you," she said, her voice like fine-grit sandpaper.

"Nice to meet you, Aunty," I said, out of habit, with a little bow of my head.

Mrs. Fong's eyes widened. "Are you from Hawai'i? Yes, of course. It's such a charming tradition to call your elders 'Aunty'. I quite like it. Now, how may I help you?"

"Well," I hesitated, knowing how ridiculous my request was going to sound. "I'm looking for a gift for two-hundred people and my budget is really small."

Mrs. Fong released a tiny sigh and nodded. "How small?"

"Two-hundred-and-fifty dollars." I winced.

Mrs. Fong clucked. "That *is* a challenge." However, instead of disappointment, her tone sounded excited. She rubbed her pale, veiny hands together and smiled. "I *like* a challenge. Tell me more."

Her tone filled me with hope. "It's for a party," I said, trying to figure out how to explain. "Aunty, do you listen to public radio by any chance?"

"Sustaining member of KPCC for twenty years," she answered, one bony finger lifted in the air.

I grinned. "Then you know who Clint Davenport is?" I hedged.

Mrs. Fong clapped a hand over her chest. "Of course I do. His voice makes me feel young again," she said with a sly raise of her brow.

I giggled "You remind me of my *popo*. So naughty," I *tsked* playfully.

She blinked demurely. "If I can't have fun at this age, when can I?"

I smiled big, my chest feeling lighter than it had in weeks. "Well, I *work* with Clint."

She inhaled sharply and I laughed, vicariously enjoying her reaction. It had been a long time since thinking about Clint had brought me anything but pain. Or maybe pain wasn't the right word, perhaps confusion was more accurate.

"Clint wants to do a special series from China. He lived in Beijing and speaks Mandarin, did you know that?"

Mrs. Fong looked smug. "I knew I liked that boy for a reason."

"We need funders for the special, and we have an upcoming reception that is a good opportunity for this. I thought it would be nice to give people a little gift. But I don't want to give anything junky," I finished with a serious nod.

Her eyes lit up. "I know just the thing. Come with me." She walked to a display of five tea jars right in front of her cash register, each of them was as high as her chest, their clear glass, wavy. "Do you know *LongJing* tea?"

"I'm sorry to say that I don't."

"Well, I'm sure you know all true tea comes from the *Camellia sinensis* plant," she said generously. "And any infusion without it is technically a teasan."

I tried to keep my face from betraying my ignorance as I replied, "I might have heard something like that once."

She smiled beatifically. "*LongJing* is a type of green tea, in fact, it's the king of green teas…or perhaps I should say it's the emperor. It was designated as *Gong Cha*, or Imperial Tea, by Emperor Qian Long in the eighteenth century and was a favorite of Mao Zedong who served it to Richard Nixon during his historic 1972 visit to China. Its English name is Dragon Well."

My eyes widened. Growing up Chinese, tea had always been a part of life but I had never heard it spoken about with such reverence. It was like Mrs. Fong was lifting a veil. *Dragon Well.* "How poetic."

She nodded and raised a finger towards the five jars in front of the register. "I have a range of *LongJing* teas from one-hundred dollars a pound up to three-hundred dollars a pound." She swept her hand over the jars from left to right.

I blanched. "Mrs. Fong, when I said I have two-hundred-and-fifty dollars, I mean *total*."

She smiled. "I understand, dear, but you could buy a pound of the less expensive tea and divide it up into a square of tissue paper and then put it in one of these," she said, grabbing and holding up a fist-size silk pouch with drawstrings from a basket on her counter. "I could sell you two-hundred-twenty-five bags, because you should have a few extra, a pound-and-a-half of the one-hundred-dollar *LongJing,* and some tissue paper for two-hundred-fifty-dollars, tax included."

"Really?" I said, leaning forward excitedly.

"Really," she answered, a conspiratorial smile on her face.

My mind was racing now. Fern could help me assemble the gift bags; maybe I could get a few other people in the office to help. Fern could design a gift tag with some history about the tea and a formal "ask" from fund-raising regarding the China special.

It was a perfect gift.

"That's brilliant, Mrs. Fong. Let's do it!"

Chapter 18: No More Secrets

~Clint~

I was sitting on the back porch of my home—located on a quiet street in the shadow of the California Institute of Technology, or Caltech as it was more commonly known—watching as the twins decorated the back yard for their thirteenth birthday party. Although their birthday was really on the twenty-eighth, they often had Halloween-themed parties given its proximity to their date of birth.

Thirteen. That was a fun year, I thought, remembering my own thirteenth birthday party with a twinge of pain.

Soon enough, the twins' giggling pulled me out of my melancholy mood. Max and Mia were having a blast, blowing up balloons, hanging streamers, and arranging various macabre decor along with two of their closest friends.

"No skulls in the fountain," called the patrician voice of Liz Davenport.

I shook my head. "They can put skulls in the fountain if they want to," I called out.

She *tsked*, shaking her finger at me and yelled back, "You spoil them."

I wasn't about to argue. The twins had had it hard enough in life; if I could give them an indulgent birthday party, so be it.

Besides, the skulls would look cool floating in the fountain.

I kicked back in my seat, enjoying the shade of the pergola. Although the weather was suitably cool-ish—at least by Los Angeles standards—at seventy-five degrees, the sun was still powerful, and since it was only two p.m., the shade was welcome. The party would begin in a few hours, starting with a Severus Snape character, who would lead the guests in potions experiments and defense against the dark arts practice. I'd spent a small fortune on replica Harry Potter wands, complete with a bright fiber optic light at their tip, for the kids' friends.

Not that I knew who Severus Snape or Harry Potter actually were, but I knew what they cost.

Liz's short heels scraped across the brick walkway as she approached. "What time are you heading out?"

I had mentioned Alex's party to her and she'd insisted that I attend. It was good for my career and she could hold down the fort while I was gone. Fortunately, Alex was only five minutes away by car.

"I promise I won't stay longer than an hour-and-a-half. What time do you think you'll put on the movie?" I asked, referring to the DVD copy of *Harry Potter and the Half-Blood Prince* that she had somehow managed to score two months before its official release.

And she scolds me for spoiling them.

"Eight," she said, in her typically cool, clipped manner.

I bristled.

I knew she didn't mean to be cold; she'd always been rather transactional in her interactions, and yet, while I found the trait annoying, I couldn't deny that I was probably guilty of doing the same thing. "I'll go then. They won't even know I'm gone."

As if to confirm this, the twins' laughter filled the air as they raced around the yard.

Liz nodded.

I could practically see the thought bubble, "It's decided then," float up from her perfectly coiffed French twist.

***

~Erin~

"I'm having so much fun," Mom said over the loud strains of Earth, Wind, & Fire's *Do You Remember,* a martini glass in her hand.

We were standing by the dessert table at Alex's Halloween party, under a large tent that had been erected in the backyard of her Spanish contemporary home, as a disco ball cast wide, circling diamonds on every surface. Costumed bodies undulated on the wood dance floor that had been set up for the occasion as the DJ played a mix of the greatest hits from the last four decades.

"Alex and her sig-o are huge fans of Halloween," I explained. "Their parties seem to get more elaborate every year."

Not only was almost every person from the WUA staff present, along with their plus-one, there were also several people from other parts of Alex's life. I estimated that there were at least three-hundred people at the party between the tent and the house.

I took my red beanie off, my Tweedle Dee costume was beginning to feel cumbersome. "I'm going to take the pillow out of my shirt."

Mom was dressed as the Mad Hatter. "But then no one will know who you are?"

"I don't care, Mom. I'm not comfortable. I'm going to go put the pillow in the car," I said, gesturing towards the street. "Besides, it's kind of loud in here. I need a break from the music."

"Party pooper." Mom took another sip of her drink and winked.

I bit my tongue. It was something I'd been doing so much lately it was amazing I had any tongue left.

I eyed my mother, who finished off the cosmopolitan she'd been drinking. I couldn't remember if it had been her second or third drink, but the alcohol helped explain my mother's behavior.

After staying with me her first two weeks, Mom had moved in with my Aunt Lillian. However, after a month there, she'd asked to return—feeling like she'd overstayed her welcome—and for some reason, I'd agreed.

Damn filial piety again.

At least this time around she'd offered to sleep on the air mattress, and I'd agreed.

My filial piety only went so far.

"You know, honey, I could see myself staying in Los Angeles," Mom said dreamily, grabbing a mini cheesecake from the dessert table, and taking a bite as she people-watched. "Look, here comes Lorena and Fern."

Fern's eyes lit up when he spotted us and he pulled his mother in our direction, her March Hare costume rounding out our foursome.

"You look so cute," Lorena said to my mom, the two women greeting each other like the good friends they had become.

The four of us had gotten into the habit of seeing each other once a week, and mom had hinted on more than one occasion that she admired Lorena and Fern's relationship.

I had been annoyed at the implication—after all, I wasn't Fern, and Mom wasn't Lorena. I needed to have a serious talk with my mother, I just didn't have the emotional or mental bandwidth. I was too busy with work. I'd resolved to talk to my mom after I returned from New York.

At least my father knew where his wife was. My aunt had told him after giving him a stern talking to. However, Mom still refused to speak to him. Instead, she'd been spending her time researching physician's assistant and nursing programs in Los Angeles, and talking about going back to school.

I thought that was a great idea as long as Mom found her own place to live. I'd only been on my own for four years. I wasn't ready to give up that freedom yet.

"How you doing, Dee?" Fern asked, a smile on his face.

I pulled the pillow out of my shirt, sighing at how much cooler I felt. "I'm great, Dum, now that I took out this damn pillow."

He nodded. "Good idea," he said, as he pulled the pillow out of his matching yellow shirt. "Yeah, that's better. It's too hot for all that stuffing."

"I'm going to go put mine in the car; want me to take yours?"

He shook his head. "I'll walk with you. It's kind of loud in here."

"Cool," I said, hooking my arm through his. "There's something I wanted to talk to you about."

We headed out of the tent, the temperature immediately dropping fifteen degrees without all those warm bodies. It was dark except for the fairy lights strung up for the party, the sun having set a couple of hours ago.

I inhaled deeply, enjoying the scent of fall permeating the air, although some of my East Coast-born coworkers made fun of me for making such a big deal about fall. They didn't realize that for me, the L.A. seasons felt extreme after growing up in the land of eternal summer. "The leaves smell so good."

Fern hummed his agreement. "What did you want to talk about?"

Our feet crunched on the decomposed granite as we walked down Alex's long driveway, which was doing a great job serving double-duty as an outdoor living room filled with couches, armchairs, and coffee tables brought in especially for the party. As we walked, I took in some of the more elaborate costumes. Although mine and Fern's matching outfits were clearly homemade, several guests were wearing professional-looking costumes.

"Is that Marie Antoinette?" I asked, pointing to a woman with a white wig that had to be at least two feet tall.

Fern nodded. "I think so. Did you talk to the zombie? His left eye oozes and he's got wiggling maggots coming out of his neck."

I stuck my tongue out. "Gross. I'll be sure to avoid him." Remembering myself, I said, "So, I made a last-minute executive decision," I began, before launching into the story about Mrs. Fong and the Dragon Well tea as we walked a couple of blocks down the leafy sidewalks of San Marino, one of Los Angeles's most expensive neighborhoods.

Occasionally, we had to move out of the way as children streamed by trick-or-treating. The foot traffic was not as busy as the area around my condo. San Marino was not the sort of neighborhood that went all-out for Halloween. Alex made up for the whole block.

"That sounds really cool," Fern said. "The gift tags will be a fun project." He scratched his jaw like he was already thinking about possible designs.

"And you'll help me assemble them, right?" I asked as I opened the car and threw the pillows in.

"Of course I will."

I sighed. "I can't wait for this to be over. I feel like my entire future is riding on the success of this event." I closed the car door and leaned against my Toyota. "It was all my idea. What if it fails? What if everything falls apart and Alex fires me?"

Fern was the only person in the office besides Alex who knew that the New York special had been my idea. I'd needed to confide my fears to somebody.

"Hug?" He opened his arms in invitation.

I didn't hesitate to walk into his embrace, relaxing into his brotherly hug.

Somehow our lukewarm kiss had cemented our friendship even more, and the hug reminded me of the days when I'd been closer to my brother. "Thanks, Fern. I couldn't do this without you."

"I'm here for you," he said, rubbing my back.

The sounds of the party floated down to the car, and we separated. "Let's go back. There was a chocolate eclair on the table with my name on it."

"Oh, yum. I didn't even see the desserts," he said.

We were walking back to the party, Fern's arm over my shoulder, my arm around his waist, when a familiar voice called out to me.

"Hey, Erin."

I froze.

The hair on the back of my neck tingled.

I'd know that voice in my sleep.

Clint.

We turned and I pulled away from Fern without thinking, suddenly self-conscious, crossing my arms over my chest.

Clint was wearing his usual attire—chinos, a polo shirt, his leather bomber jacket. The only difference, especially noticeable since the sun had already set, was a pair of aviator glasses pushed up onto his forehead.

Fern took his appearance in stride and held out his hand. "Hi, Clint. Good to see you. You just getting here?"

Clint nodded. "Yeah. I have something going on at my house. I couldn't get away until now."

I tried to find something to say, but my mind was blank. I no longer knew how to act around Clint, especially out of the office. My discomfort was heightened by the fact that the darkness of the evening—and the cool leafiness of our surroundings—was reminding me of another night in the not-so-distant past.

A night that I thought about more often than I wanted to admit.

Fern looked from me to Clint, then back to me, and sucked in a breath. "Alrighty, then," he said, a bit louder than necessary, clapping his mitt-sized hands together. "I'm going to get back to the party. Hey, Erin," he said, rousing me from my memory. "Why don't you tell Clint about the dragon tea idea."

He gave me an encouraging nod and turned back to Clint. "Great seeing you."

And then took off.

I'd never seen him move so fast.

Chicken.

I didn't know where to look, not wanting to meet Clint's eyes as we stood there alone, my memories of our time in Big Bear sending chills cascading down my back.

He stepped towards me and my pulse spiked. He must have sensed my unease because he stopped suddenly. Shoving his hands in his pockets, he glanced down the street in the opposite direction of the party and cleared his throat. "Walk with me?" His voice sounded gentle, like he was asking for a favor.

I licked my lips, considering, but my feet had already chosen for me, moving me towards Clint before I'd consciously decided.

He smiled, the corners of his eyes crinkling up, and we started walking. "So, tell me about the dragon tea. I'm assuming Fern is talking about *LongJing*?"

I fell into step alongside him. The side of my body closest to him warmed. "Yes." I hadn't planned on telling anyone about the tea, thinking it would be a fun surprise. "I, uh," I stalled. "It was supposed to be a secret."

"A *secret*, huh?" he said, as though the word tasted bad in his mouth.

I felt like I was being chastised.

Sure, things had been awkward between us, but had we really gotten this bad?

We walked a couple of blocks in silence.

When I found my voice again, I amended, "A *good* secret."

He humphed. "I'm not sure there is such a thing," his tone, pensive. He threw me a sideways glance, his dark gaze lingering on my face.

I heated, wondering if there was a specific secret he was talking about. I'd lost track of all the ones I'd been keeping—me and Clint, my mom in L.A., the true origin of the New York special.

"So, you and Fern," he said, his voice cracking subtly. "Are you two a couple now?"

"What? No," I said, caught off-guard by his change of topic.

"Tweedle Dee and Tweedle Dum?" he asked, although it sounded more like an accusation.

Is he jealous? "Oh, that. It's just because that's what some of the administrative staff call us; because we work together. It's not a comment on our personal lives," I said, surprised by his reaction. "Besides, we thought it would be funny—"

"Funny?"

"Yeah, because we are so clearly not twins. You know, he's Latin and about three times my size…"

He humphed again, only this time there was a hint of relief to the sound.

"How about you?" I lifted my palm up and down the length of his tall, lean form, taking an extra beat to admire him openly. "Is this a costume?"

"Of course. I'm a fighter pilot," he deadpanned. When I rolled my eyes, he said, "It's all in the glasses," a playful twinkle in his eye.

We shared a laugh, and for a moment, the animosity of the last couple of months seemed to drop away and the tension I'd been carrying around in my chest eased.

It was the first time he'd looked at me that way in weeks, and it made my heart ache with longing. *This* was the Clint I'd been falling for; where had he been hiding?

I stopped abruptly, suddenly angry. "What are you doing?"

He frowned. "I don't understand the question."

"This," I said, pointing to the space between us as I came to a stop. "Why are you being all friendly and jokey right now?"

He gave me a chagrined look, his hands still in his pockets. "Just having fun."

"Well, stop it," I barked, surprised by the sharpness of my tone.

He raised a palm to me. "Whoa, Erin. I'm sorry. I didn't mean to…" he trailed off, turning his hand over, plaintively. "I didn't mean to make you mad."

I was not going to open my heart to this man again. It had been too difficult learning to navigate the office after everything that had transpired between us. I needed to stay strong.

Crossing my arms, I turned in the direction of Alex's house when a hand landed on my shoulder.

"Don't…" he said, his voice so soft, I almost thought I imagined it.

He cursed under his breath.

There it was again. I had to ask. Turning to him, I asked, "Did you just say 'Mother Teresa'?"

He looked like he might deny it, but then his shoulders fell. "Yes," he said, like he'd been caught picking his nose.

I laughed despite myself, suddenly curious. "Why?"

He shrugged, suddenly looking twenty years younger, and scratched at his jaw with his free hand. "I wasn't allowed to curse growing up, so I found a way around it that pissed off my mother even more than cursing. I'd say the names of her favorite historical figures. It started out as a workaround, but I loved how it got under my mother's skin. I still do," he said with a boyish grin.

"Clint Davenport, I had no idea you could be so childish."

He gave me a serious look. "Really? I think you know it a bit too well, actually," he said, stepping closer.

I sucked in a breath, inhaling his mint and cedar scent. "Jiminy Cricket," I whispered, my heart speeding up.

He smiled, his dark eyes searching my own. "Is that your curse word of choice?"

I nodded, suddenly feeling dizzy when he gave me a dazzling smile.

"I like it," he whispered.

"Clint…" I said, breathlessly.

He brushed my cheek with his thumb, his gaze skipping from my eyes to my lips, and back again. "Erin," he said, my name, a plea. "I've *missed* you," the ache in his voice, clear.

"I've missed you, too."

He leaned his head down and suddenly it was like I was living the dream I'd been having every night since that night in the woods. When his lips touched mine, it was like he'd fit a key inside my heart.

I sighed, deepening the kiss, welcoming the exploration of his lips and tongue with hungry sighs and desperate moans. I wound my arms around his shoulders and pulled him closer, shaping myself to his chest as he bent me back, his lengthening desire pressing against my belly.

"Get a room," a voice shouted, causing us to jump apart like we'd been burned.

We laughed and looked around for the heckler, but only saw the backs of trick-or-treating kids with parents walking in either direction.

Clint reached for my hand, which I gave to him happily. And just like that, the pain of the last two months seemed to evaporate.

"I've been like Lily Bart," he said. "Making bad decision after bad decision, even when I thought I was doing it for the right reasons."

I gasped. "You read it?"

He nodded. "Listened," he clarified. "Twice. Your audiobook suggestion was such a great idea. I listened to *Age of Innocence* too, although I liked *House of Mirth* better."

"Me, too," I said, giddy that he'd followed my suggestion.

He cleared his throat. "I see what you mean now, about how you can learn from fiction. Lily Bart was ridiculously proud, and I think I have been, too. She had so many chances to save herself and find true happiness, if she'd just been honest." He exhaled. "I don't want to keep secrets from you, Erin. I want you to know everything."

"I *want* to know everything," I said.

His eyes darted down the street. "Are you sure?"

I nodded. For better or for worse. I couldn't explain it, but my heart had chosen Clint, and all I could do was obey.

"I'm sure," I said, hoping I could handle whatever it was that he seemed to be hiding.

He nodded, but it seemed like it was more for himself than for me. Lacing our fingers together, he started walking again.

I wondered where we were going, but I trusted that all would be revealed shortly.

We barely spoke as we walked. It felt like we were in some sort of in-between moment in time, like we'd just pushed pause on the real world.

Part of me was nervous to un-pause the moment.

Finally, he asked, "Did you watch *Citizen Kane*?"

I sighed. "No, I didn't."

"Why?" His voice was soft and without judgment.

"Because I didn't want to think about you. It was hard enough seeing you at work."

He chuckled. "Tell me about it. But I was the opposite. I didn't want to *stop* thinking about you." He squeezed my hand, sending my heart racing.

I'd lost track of how many blocks we'd walked when he pulled me to a stop.

"Ready?" he asked.

I looked around, wondering where we were. This block of homes looked the same as the ones we'd passed. *What makes this one different?* "Um. I think so."

He pulled me down a brick walkway to the wood and glass door of a beautiful Tudor-style home. Taking his keys out, he unlocked the door.

"This is *your* house?" I asked, taking it all in. There must have been four or five bedrooms inside, at least.

"Surprised?" he asked.

I frowned. "Isn't it a little big for one person?"

He smiled nervously, the porch light casting orange shadows on his face. "We need the space."

I froze. *We?*

As if hearing my unspoken question, he said, "You've come this far," his gaze switching between my eyes as though checking to make sure he saw the same thing in both. He took my hands. "I promise that everything will be clear in a moment. I don't want any more secrets. Please," he said the last word quietly, like a plea.

I had no idea how anything I was going to find inside could possibly work in our favor, but I swallowed hard and nodded, and he swung the arched wooden door open.

The foyer gleamed with highly polished wood floors, a Persian rug in brick reds and navy blues running down its center, a period light fixture twinkling overhead.

"Come in," he said, shrugging off his jacket and putting it in the entryway closet. Closing the closet door, he put a hand to the small of my back as he deposited his keys into a cut crystal bowl sitting on top of a cream-colored entry table with elegantly scrolling legs.

My stomach turned. *Nothing* about this house said "Clint" to me.

At first, the house seemed empty, but as the hallway opened to the living room, I saw a pile of wrapped presents on the coffee table. We continued down the hallway and I glimpsed a kitchen full of pizza boxes. As we neared the back door, I began to hear voices, but it didn't sound like normal people speaking, the voices were loud and hollow.

"Good luck today, Ron. I know you'll be brilliant," said a young woman's voice.

We pushed open the back door and a huge inflatable movie screen came into view.

"Is that?" I asked quietly, not believing my eyes.

He nodded. "It's the newest Harry Potter," he whispered back.

My eyes flicked downwards and I could just make out about twenty teenagers lying on the grass, their gazes fixed on the screen.

My mind was swirling. Instead of getting answers, seeing Clint's house was only giving me more questions.

The sound of heels scraping on brick brought me back to my body, when out of the darkness a perfectly coiffed woman appeared.

She gave me a thin smile and then turned to Clint. "You scared me half to death. What are you doing back so early?" she hissed.

"*Harriet Tubman*, do I have to tell you everything? This is my house," Clint said, rolling his eyes.

The woman narrowed her eyes. "Don't curse!"

Chapter 19: Answers

~Erin~

"Liz Davenport, may I introduce Erin Hung. Erin Hung, Liz Davenport," Clint said quietly, gesturing between me and the other woman.

Liz Davenport? Had I walked into some alternate reality? *He said he wasn't married. Is this his ex? And who are all the teenagers?*

"Ssshhh, you'll disturb the kids. Let's go inside," Liz said, the beautiful woman turning us towards the door we'd just exited, and giving us a shove.

We walked into the kitchen, or at least, I think I walked. Truthfully, that moment was an out-of-body experience. When I turned to face Liz in the light of the kitchen, I did a double-take.

Liz was lovely, gorgeous even, in a very elegant, very refined, very *matronly* way.

I frowned. She seemed a bit *mature* for Clint—

"Erin it's so nice to finally meet you," she said, extending her hand as she gave me a warmer smile than the one she'd given outside. "I've heard so much about you."

"You know…about *me*?"

This was getting stranger and stranger.

She furrowed her brows. "Of course, Clint doesn't tell me everything, but he did tell me about you. I could tell he was acting differently; I am his mother after all—"

"His mother?" I exclaimed, a bit louder than I'd meant to.

Clint's lips twitched in amusement. "Yes. My mother."

I met his gaze and knew that he'd been reading my mind.

Heat flooded my face.

Liz looked from me to Clint and back again. "What? She didn't know I was your mother?" She gave me a warmer smile. "Did you think I was a cougar, dear?"

I laughed. Now that I knew Liz was Clint's mother, the resemblance was obvious. Liz had the same air of insouciant confidence as Clint, complete with lazy smile and slouchy swagger.

"I just…I just didn't know." I shook my head.

Liz arched a brow, and again, it was like looking at a female version of Clint. "Well, I've heard a lot about you. Although I'll admit, it's hard for me to be fond of a woman who's tortured my son as completely as you have."

"Ma…" Clint said, his Boston accent coming out.

"Tortured?" I glanced from Clint to his mom.

Liz narrowed her eyes and studied us both. "Why don't I go check on the twins and their friends? Total darkness and raging hormones aren't a good mix if I remember correctly." She pursed her lips and nodded before showing herself out.

I was about to ask Clint if Liz lived with him when he jerked his head towards the living room. "I want to show you something."

I followed him over to the exposed brick fireplace, its outline accented by dark wood and creamy plaster walls. Flanking each end of the mantel were matching marble vases, and in between were framed pictures of two red-headed children, a boy and a girl. There they were as infants, then as kindergarteners, and so on. I picked up a frame and studied it. "Twins?"

He nodded.

I swallowed hard past the lump in my throat. "*Your* children?"

"Yes," he started, my heart plummeting, "and no."

I frowned.

He sighed. "Technically, Mia and Max are my niece and nephew, but I've raised them since they were three. Their mother was my twin."

I inhaled. "You're a twin?" A sudden discomfort registered in my gut as my subconscious raced ahead, filling in the gaps in his story.

He nodded, pulling me to sit on a couch. "Remember when you asked me why I left the Navy?"

I frowned, trying to recall his exact words. "You said it was a family tragedy." The discomfort in my gut intensified, and suddenly, I didn't want to hear the rest of his story, but for different reasons than before.

Because now I knew just how painful it was going to be for him.

He nodded. "My sister and her husband worked for the World Health Organization in Geneva," he said, in a slow, thoughtful voice I had never heard him use before. "In 1999, there was an outbreak of meningitis in Sudan. Over twenty-thousand cases in five months. My sister's husband, Ian, was sent to the region. Our mom flew out to Geneva to help Cassandra, my sister, with the kids."

He took a deep breath. "While Ian was there, he contracted a rare fungal version of the disease. It took a while to diagnose him; fungal meningitis symptoms can be easily mistaken for something else. At first, they thought he had a stroke. Cassandra flew out to care for him, but it was too late. He suffered serious brain damage." He paused, his eyes watery, shaking his head. "I was stationed in Virginia at the time. The aircraft carrier I was on was being refurbished so I was able to take a leave to see my sister in Geneva before she went to Sudan."

The discomfort in my gut had turned to roiling pain. "She never made it back," I guessed, covering his hand with mine, my heart breaking for him. Although my brother and I were not particularly close these days, we had been inseparable as children. His death would be like losing a limb.

He nodded, wiping at the corner of his eye. "She stayed in Ian's place, said that the work helped her deal with her loss. She wanted to figure out what made the outbreak so bad and help doctors in the area identify fungal meningitis faster. Make sure Ian's death wasn't for nothing. Besides, she wanted to make sure she was disease-free before she was around the kids. However, while she was there, she contracted malaria."

I inhaled quickly.

"I was back in the Persian Gulf by the time she passed. I took an emergency family leave to make arrangements and bring Ian and Cassie's ashes back."

My eyes flicked to the matching marble vases flanking the frames on the mantel.

He nodded sadly. "It was her death that triggered my fear of heights, incidentally. I'd never had an issue with them before that. Although climbing with you seemed to cure me. Maybe it's because you are so skilled, I don't feel the need to be in control."

Puzzle pieces were clicking together so quickly, I was having trouble consciously keeping up. All I knew was that everything he said made sense and that Clint—as a complete picture—was coming into focus.

"When I finished my tour of duty later that year, I returned to the house I grew up in and took on the job of being Max and Mia's dad. My mom and I share guardianship. Of course, when I became a father, I needed to do something less risky than flying fighter jets, and mom wanted to leave the East Coast. Too many memories of Cassie in the old house." He let out a long sigh. "So we sold everything and came to California to start fresh."

My head spun. Clint was a dad and a *twin*.

"I'm so sorry," I said. My heart clenched for his loss and I thought of my brother, Patrick. It had been months since we'd spoken. I'd have to give him a call soon.

Clint gave me a sad smile, studying my face as though trying to figure out what I was thinking.

I wasn't sure what to say so I said the first thing that came to mind. "So that's why you have such a big house." I shook my head. "I'm sorry, that sounded weird. I just didn't understand when we walked up to it."

He nodded. "Max, Mia, and my mom all live here. I've spent the last ten years raising kids with my mother." He rolled his eyes. "If that doesn't get me into heaven, nothing will." He paused, his eyes flicking down uncertainly. "I've been so busy being a dad and trying to get my career where I wanted, that I haven't had a moment for anything else…"

His voice had a breathless quality that made my heart beat faster.

When he lifted his eyes to meet mine, I felt them on me like a physical weight. "The truth is," he continued. "I didn't want anything else. Until…"

I sucked in a breath, his gaze hot on my skin.

He smiled then, but it was a twisted, sardonic thing. "This," he said, waving his arms around the living room. "This is my life. This is my baggage," he said, a bit louder. "I have twin thirteen-year-olds and a difficult mother, and they aren't going anywhere." He gave me a look as though daring me to disagree with how heavy his baggage was.

I had to admit. It was a lot to take in; a lot to take on.

He continued, "It's why I agreed with you about just being friends. I was conflicted on whether it was fair to bring you into this, but I've just been so miserable ever since our dinner at Lunasia…" he paused as though considering and then said, "And then when I saw you and Fern today, dressed as Tweedle Dee and Tweedle Dum." He shook his head. "I just got so pissed."

I'd forgotten that I was still dressed as Tweedle Dee.

I pulled the beanie off, forgetting to undo the clips holding it in place. "Ouch." I rubbed my head.

Clint's lips tugged up as he undid them and placed them in my palm, closing my fingers around them. "When I saw the two of you, I thought that I'd missed my chance. That Fern had won."

"I'm not a prize," I said, in a flash of pique.

"You," he paused, chucking my chin. "*Are*. A. Prize," he said, with so much earnest desire, I faltered.

He continued, "But I didn't mean it like that. I just mean that Fern is a great guy. I'm a big fan, and you two get along so well, I mean, you *look* like a couple."

I didn't bother denying it. Clint wasn't the first person to make the comment.

"Anyway, when Fern walked away tonight and left us alone, it gave me a glimmer of hope, and then when we kissed, I knew I wanted to tell you everything, *needed* to tell you everything," he said, gesturing around him. "Which is why I brought you here; so you can make a fully informed decision before anything more happens between us."

I half-laughed. "Having a family isn't a liability, Clint."

He raised a brow as though he wasn't sure if he could agree. "Yeah, but I'm also not your typical bachelor."

True.

It was hard to take in everything he was saying. In the two years I'd known him there hadn't been a hint of a family life…except… "Are the twins why you have to leave at two o'clock sharp?"

He nodded. "My mom does the morning drop-off and I do the afternoon pick-up, drive them to after-school activities, help with homework; that sort of thing."

It suddenly hit me how dutiful he was. He didn't do things in half-measures; he was a father one-hundred percent. I wondered if this sense of duty would work for or against any possible relationship we might try to have.

My heart hoped it would be for.

"But why are you so secretive about it?" I asked. "Why haven't you brought them to holiday parties or mentioned them in interviews?"

He grimaced. "What do you think the first question would be if someone from work met them?"

I already knew the answer. "Who's your mother," I said quietly.

He nodded. "And if I talked about them in interviews, I'd also have to talk about their mother, and they already know their parents are dead without being reminded about it by everyone. I don't want them to read articles about me and be reminded of their loss. It's just my way of shielding them while I can. And I don't want every interview to sing my praises out of sympathy. God knows I'm not a saint." He paused and squeezed my hand. "*You* certainly know I'm not a saint."

A little laugh escaped my throat and I nodded because his words made sense logically, but it was so much to take in; I didn't know how I *felt* about any of it.

"So, that's everything," he said exhaling and sitting straighter.

This new information threw everything into sharp relief. It was hard to believe that I'd been at a Halloween party an hour ago.

"I need some time to think; to absorb it all."

He exhaled like he was disappointed, but he nodded. "Of course. Take your time."

I stood up and he followed. "I should get back to the party. My mom's there and she's probably wondering where I am."

He narrowed his eyes quizzically. "Your mom?"

I shook my head. "It's a long story. I'll tell you about it on Monday."

We walked towards the front door.

"Or you can tell me as I walk you back to the party. I left my car over there."

We walked back at a leisurely pace, neither of us wanting to part ways. I told him everything that had happened during the weeks we hadn't been speaking, explaining about how my mom's visit was the reason why I'd missed two of our one-o-clock meetings. He seemed relieved.

When we arrived at Alex's house, I turned to him and asked, "You're sure that's everything? No more secrets?"

He took my hand and squeezed it. "Well, I guess there's one more thing."

Please don't let it be something big, I thought.

He fixed me with a somber gaze. "Gordo," he said seriously.

I frowned. "What?"

"My callsign in the navy was Gordo. It means 'fat' in Spanish. Remember how I told you about giving up sweets? Well, I liked my dessert a little too much and the other pilots started teasing me about it and the name stuck." He gave me a sheepish grin. "That's why I don't eat dessert except during birthdays," he said, glancing back in the direction of his house. "Mine and my kids' birthdays, that is, and *that's* why I don't tell anyone my callsign," he said with a wry smile. "Now *that's* everything. I have no more secrets from you."

I smiled. The strange confession of his made me feel warmer, like he was trusting me with something precious. "No wonder you don't tell anyone."

He shrugged and smiled, looking more light-hearted than I'd ever seen him.

My eyes danced to his mouth and I wanted to feel his lips one more time before I left.

I pressed a gentle kiss to his lips and he matched me. The moment was tender and full of promise.

"Your secrets are safe with me," I whispered.

Chapter 20: The Main Event

~Clint~

I gazed out the window and soaked up the vista below, leaning a bit to the right for a better view of the Hudson River a few blocks away. Taking a deep breath, I exhaled slowly, feeling lighter than I had in years.

Life. Was. Good.

The New York *WUA* studios were located on the tenth floor of a stone building located on the border of SoHo and Greenwich Village. I was among the twenty *WUA* staff who were temporarily working out of the New York studios for the week. Fifteen of us were from Los Angeles, including Yolanda, Alex, and Erin. The other five were from the D.C. headquarters; mostly marketing and fund-raising folks who'd come to help Erin with the event later that day.

Erin. Just thinking her name made me happier.

I leaned back in my office chair and threw my baseball in the air a few times, although I didn't throw it as high as usual because this office was a lot smaller than mine, made even smaller by the fact that I was sharing it for the week with its true owner, Kiesha Moore, one of *WUA*'s New York reporters.

It was the third day I had broadcasted from the NYC studios, and all had gone well. It gave me hope that broadcasting from China might be easier than anticipated. Now I just had to smile and ring the closing bell at the stock exchange, and then be my most charming self for the reception that would follow. All of which would be easier knowing that Erin was nearby.

After confessing everything I'd been keeping from her on Halloween, Erin (understandably) asked for some time to process everything.

Honestly, it was all that I could have hoped for.

Despite that, we'd shared heated looks and inside jokes in the last couple of weeks, and that had given me hope that we could move passed everything.

My mom gave me hell when she found out I hadn't told Erin everything. "Running from your feelings? Is that the way I raised you?" she'd chastised rhetorically. "No wonder you've been moping around."

Ever since that night, a barrier around my heart had been dismantled, and Erin and I had been growing closer every day. She'd even told me about the *LongJing* gift idea, which was the cleverest thing I'd ever heard. If I got my dream of broadcasting from China, it was going to be because of her.

It made me wish more than ever that things could work out between us. I could easily imagine the great team we'd make in all aspects of life.

There was a knock at the door.

I turned, an idiotically huge smile breaking out on my face when I saw it was Erin.

Then I noticed that *she* wasn't smiling.

I got up, pulled her into the office, and closed the door behind me. Sitting her down in an office chair, I asked, "What's wrong?"

She shook her head, her eyes watery. She looked up, trying not to cry. "I don't know if it's the stress of today or what, but it just feels like a lot has been piling up."

I shushed her as I smoothed her velvety hair, which was just as soft as I'd imagined. "Start at the beginning."

She took a few deep breaths and started, "You know how my mom's been staying with me?" she asked. "Well, my brother just called and said I was enabling her, and that he was siding with our father. I mean, it's not really a surprise; he's so much like my dad, self-centered. It's why we don't talk that much. And my mom has been hinting that I should sell the condo and we should get a bigger place together, like Fern and his mom." She took another breath. "But I'm not Fern. I mean, he's a fricking saint. *I* don't want to live with my mom." She inhaled quickly. "Oh, god. I didn't mean it like that."

"It's okay. It's not wrong to have your feelings about it."

She smiled and my heart melted.

I wanted her to smile at me like that every day. Like I was the sun…or at least the moon. Like I mattered to her just a fraction of how much she mattered to me.

Because I was a different person now that I'd opened myself up to loving Erin.

Loving Erin.

It was at that moment that I realized the truth. I loved Erin Hung.

A trickle of fear crept down my spine, but it was overwhelmed by the pure feeling of joy that the realization brought.

I love Erin Hung.

And apparently, everyone had noticed the change in me, although not everyone had thought the change was for the better. Alex said she liked it better when I was a "sullen cad" and Yolanda complained about me being distracted again.

Everything would be perfect if Erin would just agree to date me, and do so openly. But we'd agreed to hold all decisions until after New York. There was too much going on.

"It's just that…I was living with my parents until I moved to L.A. and I'm not ready to give up my freedom yet. Besides, my parents need to work their stuff out."

I nodded, caressing her arm.

She gave me a shy smile as goosebumps erupted on her skin.

I glanced at the fixed window next to the door, wondering if I could chance a kiss.

She followed my gaze, and when we both saw that no one was outside the door, she fisted the front of my shirt, kissing me fully.

Theodore Roosevelt, I thought, wondering if Lawrence Selden had felt this way about Lily Bart when they'd stolen kisses around the grand country houses of old New York.

I stood, picked her up, and carried her with me until we were right up against the door, out of sight of the window, ensuring that the door stayed closed.

She moaned into my mouth and my cock stirred. I'd had a chronic set of blue balls ever since Halloween. But I didn't care. I'd gone so long without physical affection, that every glance, every smile, every kiss was like a magnum of Veuve, quenching my fiery thirst like a fire hose of the finest champagne.

She ran her hands through my hair and tugged. *Abe Lincoln*, could there be anything more erotic? Electricity seemed to surge through my scalp and out my limbs as she pulled on my hair, intensifying our kiss, her hips gyrating against my pelvis.

"Erin," I said, for no other reason than it was my favorite word in the English language.

If I could add her to the dictionary I'd write, "Brilliant temptress who intoxicates the mind," as her definition.

My lips found their way to the shell of her ear, which I licked greedily, eliciting hungry moans from Erin. My erection stiffened further.

There was a quick knock at the door, followed by Alex's voice. "The cars will be downstairs in thirty."

We stilled, waiting to see if Alex opened the door or said anything else, and then exhaled with relief when her departing steps became too faint to hear.

"I should," Erin pointed at the door, her breasts still flattened against my chest.

"Mother Teresa, you're hot," I said.

"Jiminy Cricket," she whispered and brushed her lips against mine. She leaned her forehead against mine and we heaved against each other. "I should really go."

"Yeah, you should," I said, raising a wry brow. "If you don't leave now, I'll never be able to walk out of the office when the cars get here."

She bit her lip and smiled. "Is it weird that I'm proud of the effect I have on you? All your fans would be so jealous."

I laughed, wanting to pull her in for another kiss. She was too adorable. "You vixen."

She raised a brow. "I'm going now."

I groaned. "Please do."

She laughed and slipped out the door.

***

"It's my privilege to welcome you tonight to this historic room in this historic location," I said from my position behind the monolithic desk at the front of the Boardroom at the NYSE. I held up the champagne flute Erin had put in my hand when she reminded me that I should say a few words to the reception guests.

If anyone but her had made the request, my gut would have burned with the imposition.

I was a journalist, not a ringmaster.

But for Erin, I'd do anything.

I love her.

The words slipped so effortlessly into my mind that I wondered how long they'd been true.

There was polite applause as the couple hundred people took in the glittering decor and their fellow guests, feeling either entitled or grateful for being included in such rare air.

We were on the top floor of the eight-story neoclassical building that housed the exchange. Gilded plaster arches lined the room like sentries standing guard the full-length of the space, which was crowned at one end by a raised, monolithic desk like a judge's bench, except that it was big enough for a half-dozen people. Mounted above the desk was an ornate clock that used to keep time on the trading floor, and above that was an expansive glass and iron ceiling.

Jay Gatsby would have been quite comfortable hosting one of his infamous parties in the space. I know because I'd listened to the audiobook at Erin's suggestion.

The Boardroom was dominated by a large, oblong conference table that was roughly sixty-feet long and ten-feet wide. The wood table was serving as a glorified buffet with salads, fruits, petite fours, and crudités. Tuxedoed waiters milled around the space passing hors d'oeuvres and glasses of wine and champagne. Down the center of the long table were nine huge flower arrangements made up of crimson peonies and golden chrysanthemums, which I knew Erin had chosen because of the significance of red and gold in Chinese culture.

It was a brilliant touch.

Clearing my throat, I continued, "However, it wouldn't be fair for me to take all of the credit. It's a well-known secret that behind every successful radio host is a huge team of reporters, editors, producers, engineers, and administrative staff that make the magic happen. So, allow me to name names today, and point out some of those people who you might not know." Then I named all of the staff present, minus one. "I've left one name for last, and the reason why is because she's the person responsible for this beautiful event, selecting everything from the food to the flowers, and reminding me that I needed to say a few words just now." I smiled and a chuckle rippled through the crowd.

I'd noticed that Erin had frozen at her location over by the food. No doubt she was nervous that I was calling her out, but I'd asked her permission in advance. She'd given it, although grudgingly.

She looked absolutely stunning, wearing a black and red *cheongsam,* the dress's modest Mandarin collar a stark contrast to the thigh-high slits on either side. I felt every flash of her thighs deep in my gut like a bell being rung. Ever since I saw the dress, I'd fantasized about running my hands up her legs.

I hoped she'd give me the chance.

"Please join me in giving a round of applause for the woman who made this all happen, *WUA*'s marketing maven, Erin Hung," I said, putting my champagne flute and microphone down on the desk so I could join in the applause.

Over the previous two weeks, I'd seen the detail with which Erin had planned everything, choosing the music, the menu, the amazing parting gift, and overseeing the flowers, the invitations, and the guest list. It was like she'd taken on a whole other job in addition to the one she already had. Everything was top notch and I couldn't have been prouder.

I glanced around the room, taking it all in. Of the roughly two-hundred guests in attendance, some were people I had interviewed in my years on the air; a good number of the New York-based celebrities, CEOs, and dignitaries I was acquainted with were there. I'd also spoken to some of the potential donors the fundraising department had lined up. A few of them were native-born Chinese so I'd been able to practice my Mandarin.

Erin took the attention well, placing her hands in prayer position and executing several, polite bows while pivoting around the room. When she met my gaze, she raised an ironic brow, just barely narrowing her eyes at me threateningly.

I smiled bigger and winked.

Once the applause died down, I picked up the microphone for a final time. "One last thing. Yesterday was Veteran's Day, and I considered it auspicious that our event would take place so close to that day." I made eye contact with a couple of the potential donors, knowing how important auspicious dates were in Chinese culture. "I'm a veteran myself, as were my father and grandfather. I'm sure that some of you in the room have also served or have family who've served. So today I'd like to ask you to raise your glasses in gratitude for the women and men who have served this country's armed forces. I thank you. We thank you. Your nation thanks you," I said, lifting my glass in the air and then to my lips, struggling to keep the tears I felt welling up behind my lids from falling.

The room grew silent as everyone took a somber sip, and continued to be subdued as I turned off the microphone, placed it on the large desk, and walked down to join the rest of the party.

I knew my closing remarks were a bit of a downer, but I could also tell that people had been impressed. It had been the right note to end on.

I exhaled a satisfied sigh of relief and took another sip of champagne.

The closing bell ceremony had been easy enough, although it had felt a little awkward to do the ringing when higher pay grades than mine had shown up to stand on the balcony behind me. Although in Los Angeles I was outranked only by Alex, and marginally by Yolanda, today I'd been in the esteemed company of the entire C-suite from D.C. headquarters including the Founder and CEO of UPR himself, William Duke.

Duke was a legend in the public radio world, having started out as a disc jockey in some small town in rural Pennsylvania only to go on to become the founder of one of the largest public radio producers and networks in America. I had never met Duke before the bell-ringing ceremony, and I'd gotten the sense that he would have been only too happy to push me out of the way and ring the closing bell for himself. Instead, he had applauded politely, a tight-lipped smile on his face.

Alex had given me a wide-eyed look that conveyed just what an honor it was that I was ringing the bell while standing in front of all the head honchos from UPR, who had stood and clapped behind me like my own personal chorus line.

My inner imp had loved it.

But now the short-lived bell-ringing ceremony was done, and the reception was in full swing. I straightened my tie to remind myself that I was still on the clock while grabbing another champagne flute from a passing waiter. While I didn't usually drink champagne—hell, I didn't usually drink—tonight I was celebrating.

After an hour of mingling with guests, I was eager to find Erin and congratulate her on how well the reception was going. I circled the conference table looking for her, then spotted her off in a corner, talking to Alex. As I approached, I noticed that the conversation appeared heated. The hair on my neck stood up as I closed the distance.

"Oh, hi, Clint. Enjoying yourself?" Alex said, sliding a smooth smile onto her face when a moment ago she'd appeared stern.

Erin's cheeks were flushed, her eyes narrowed at Alex.

"Hey, you two." I glanced between them, unsure how to proceed. "Everything okay?"

"Everything's great. Right, Erin?" Alex asked.

Erin cleared her throat and rolled her shoulders back, not meeting Alex's or my gaze. Her lips were pursed like she was holding something back.

Just then, William Duke sauntered up, clapping a hand on Alex's back. "Alex, I just wanted to congratulate you personally," he said, shaking her hand forcefully.

Alex grimaced under the pressure. "Thanks, William. That means a lot."

Duke looked around the elegant boardroom, a self-satisfied smile on his face. "These are the kind of events we should be doing. High-class, good social capital. I'm glad you came up with it; ringing the stock exchange bell has been your most inspired idea yet. And the content on the air has been great, too. What luck that the Yankees won the World Series, right? We should take *WUA* on the road more often."

Alex's eyes flitted briefly towards Erin, but before she could say anything, Erin said, "Excuse me," and walked away.

Alex looked relieved.

I wondered again what she and Erin had been talking about.

"Well, I'm glad you approve, William. Taking our show to other cities and countries is a high priority for us. As you've heard, Clint has been particularly interested in going to China," Alex said.

At that moment, waiters began circulating with baskets of colorful silk tapestry bags in vibrant jewel tones. One of them approached our group and handed each of us a silk pouch. "A gift from the show. The pouches contain a rare tea," the waiter said with a slight bow.

Duke read the red gift tag tied around the neck of the bag. "This pouch contains an exclusive green tea called *LongJing*, also known as Dragon Well, which was so prized by Emperor Qian Long, he declared it the official Imperial Tea. Mao Zedong welcomed President Richard Nixon with this tea, and now we gift it to you in anticipation of our forthcoming special series on China. *Ganbei.*"

Duke laughed, clapping Alex on the back again. "You've thought of everything. This is brilliant."

Alex colored.

I narrowed my eyes at her, waiting for her to correct Duke, and when she didn't, I started to get an idea about what she and Erin might have been discussing.

I cleared my throat, not willing to let this misdirection of praise continue. "Actually, the woman who thought of these gifts, who planned this entire event was just standing here a moment ago. Her name is Erin Hung. You should congratulate her yourself."

Alex seemed to be turning an alarming shade of puce.

"Really?" Duke said, glancing around. "Will you tell her for me please, Alex? She deserves a raise." After a second, he added, "And a promotion. What is she, a manager? Let's make her a director."

All the color drained from Alex's face and I wondered what she was hiding.

"Excuse me, you two. I'm going to see if any of the potential donors want to commit to funding the China special now that they've received their gift," Duke said, lobbing the silk pouch in the air like a baseball, and then winking when he caught it.

When Duke was out of earshot, I hissed, "What's going on, Alex?"

She took a deep breath, a bit of the color returning to her face now that Duke was out of earshot. She hissed back, "Nothing that concerns you," and stalked off.

I scanned the room for Erin but didn't see her anywhere. The head of fundraising was walking up to me with some people I'd spoken to earlier, a huge smile on her face. "Clint. I have good news for you. The Lucky Dragon foundation has agreed to become a principal funder of the China Special."

I forced a smile onto my face. "Fantastic. *Xièxiè*," I said, joining my hands in front of my chest and giving a deep bow to the couple.

They returned the bow and started talking about potential story ideas.

I did my best to listen, but in the back of my mind, there was just one thought: Where was Erin?

An hour later, I was finally able to extricate myself from a conversation with one of Silicon Valley's more eccentric CEOs to go in search of Erin, but I couldn't find her anywhere. Finally, I texted her, "Where are you?"

A moment later I got the reply. "At the hotel. Trying to catch the last flight to L.A."

A cold chill ran down my spine.

I looked around, decided I'd done my duty, and texted, "Don't leave. I'm on my way now."

Chapter 21: Innocent Temptress

~Erin~

Twenty minutes after I got the text from Clint telling me to wait, there was a knock on my door. I looked through the peephole, half-surprised to see him standing there. Even though I knew he was coming, I hadn't expected him so soon. He must have run the whole way from the stock exchange. I opened the door.

He was doubled over, his hands resting on his knees. "What," *huh, huh* he panted. "Are," *huh, huh.* "You doing?" *huh, huh.* Still bent over, he walked into my room and leaned against the wall.

"Are you okay? Let me get you some water." I filled a glass from my sink while wiping at my face with a wet hand so he couldn't see that I'd been crying. "Did you run here?"

He took the glass and gulped it down. "Forget about me, what are you doing?"

I resumed packing. "I'm leaving."

He finally straightened up, one hand holding his side like he had a stitch. "Why?" he huffed.

"Please don't shout," I hissed. "I've had enough of being abused today."

Eyes widening, he said, "I'm sorry, I didn't mean to shout. I just don't understand." He'd adopted a soothing voice. He reached for my hand, then pulled me to the polyester rolling chairs grouped around a small table in the corner. "Tell me what's going on."

"I quit," I said quietly.

He shook his head. "I don't understand."

Where to start? I didn't know how to tell a story I only knew half of. Alex had been so evasive, talking in circles, I didn't know what was true anymore. The term *gaslight* popped in my head. "I just didn't know what else to do. Alex left me no other choice, and Sonja is so cool and appreciates me. I was tired of being taken advantage of by Alex so I thought I'd fly home and go to Big Bear."

Clint shook his head like he was having trouble keeping up.

I knew I was rambling and probably not making any sense, but I was so flustered.

"Sonja? Big Bear? You mean the ropes course job?" he asked, piecing it together.

"Yes. Sonja's been so kind and she asked me to come up this weekend. And I'm just so tired of Alex's crap." But even as I said the words, I knew I was making excuses. It had been easier to justify leaving New York when I'd been heading *to* something rather than running *away*.

"I don't understand. What crap? Is this about Alex not recognizing your contributions in front of William Duke, because I took care of that. I told him that you were the one who planned everything. He was very complimentary. We even got two China Special funders, all because of the *LongJing* tea. Everyone loved that."

I perked up. "Really?"

Clint smiled. "Yes, really. The way you had the waiters walk around distributing the tea was genius. And the gift itself was such a thoughtful touch, especially with the background story you included. Duke was beyond impressed. He said you deserved a raise."

I cupped a hand over my mouth, tears pricking. "He did?" My heart soared. I'd always believed Mrs. Fong and I had come up with something special, but to hear people's reactions was even better. Especially Mr. Duke's.

He nodded. "Yes, and Alex's face turned white. That was how I knew something was up. And I owe you big time."

I furrowed my brow, not sure what he meant.

"You were so strategic. Using the party not just to fete my promotion and the New York series, but to drive attention to a future initiative…that was so smart. You really leveraged this event. I never would have thought of that, and now I have you to thank for helping make a dream of mine come true. Thank you," he said, his eyes sparkling.

I double-sighed, the anger Alex had inspired dissipating. "I don't think I've ever received a compliment like that," I said, tears threatening, although this time, they were happy tears. "My parents only seem to notice my failures. Quick to criticize, slow to praise."

He gave me a sad smile and put his hand over mine. "Everything was amazing tonight," he said, running his hand through his hair. "No, it was beyond amazing. It was perfect. *You're* perfect. I'm so lucky to have you in my life."

I sucked in a breath, a mixture of warring emotions churning in my gut. On the one hand, I was grateful for Clint's words. It was exactly what I needed to hear; like gentle rain on the raging fire of my anger. On the other hand, it didn't change the fact that I'd been betrayed by Alex and had no one to blame but myself for being so naive and gullible.

"Thank you. That means a lot, but it wasn't just about the reception." I wanted to tell Clint everything, but remembered Alex's warning: *"You know, the editorial staff is very territorial…"*

If I told Clint, would he feel lied to or worse…would he feel manipulated?

Then I remembered what he'd said about not keeping secrets and I sighed. "It's so much more than that. I've been keeping something from you."

I interlaced our fingers and proceeded to tell him the whole story about how I'd had the idea for the New York Special and how Alex had said not to tell anyone. Then I explained about how Alex had reneged on the promotion, stringing me along for weeks with promises of titles and raises, all while piling more and more work on my plate.

"When Alex stood there in front of Mr. Duke, taking the credit for everything right in front of me—after just telling me straight out that there would be no promotion—I was done. I mean, I've worked my ass off the last two months, and for what?" I finished, my hands trembling with pent-up frustration.

He sighed, caressing my cheek with the pad of his thumb, sending shivers of happiness and desire down my spine.

I craved his touch…especially now.

"Erin…" he said, a shadow darkening his face.

I couldn't tell if he was sad, or disappointed, or was chastising me, but my defenses went up. I felt bad enough as it was. Why did I keep putting myself out there for others: for my mother, for Alex, for Clint, and for what?

So I could be taken advantage of.

I hung my head between my hands and sighed.

I knew I wasn't thinking clearly as all of this ran through my mind, but I was tired—physically tired, emotionally tired, tired of letting people walk all over me, invading my space and taking advantage of my good nature.

I was done.

"Fuck Alex, fuck my mother, fuck my father, fuck, fuck, fuck," I screamed, standing up and pacing around my room.

"That's it, let it all out. *Fuck!*" he said, joining in with a smile.

I gave a startled laugh. "I think I like it better when you say Abe Lincoln."

"Aaaaaaabe Liiiiincoooooln!" he shouted, a smile on his face.

I giggled and the heat of my anger ebbed.

I shook my head and sat on my bed. "I just thought that if Alex didn't want me, I should go somewhere I *am* wanted. Sonja made it clear she wanted me. It seemed like a good idea."

The bed dipped as Clint sat next to me. He ran the back of his fingers over my neck and said, "*I* want you," before dipping his lips to my throat and kissing me softly.

I melted.

It felt good to be *wanted.*

It felt good to be wanted by *Clint.*

I wanted Clint.

I turned and saw my own need and desire reflected in his eyes. I pushed him back onto the bed, hitched up the sides of my *cheongsam,* and straddled his hips.

Clint's eyes widened as I loosened his tie and removed his jacket, throwing them both to the floor. He pulled me down and kissed me softly. "Erin," he said reverently, his hands tentative on my thighs.

I loved the way he said my name; it was like he was greeting me after a long separation. It made me feel seen, valued, cherished. "I *want* you," I whispered, pressing my lips to his.

"I want you…in so many ways," he said, kissing me more fervently, his tongue, teasing. "I want you today, and tomorrow, and all the days after that."

My heart clenched. "Me, too," I said, knowing that we were speaking on so many different levels. I started unbuttoning his shirt and hesitated, remembering that we weren't keeping any more secrets. "I don't have a lot of...*experience*."

He pushed me back so he could see my face, his eyebrows lifting. "Well, I've been in a bit of a drought myself. I haven't been with anyone since leaving the Navy," he said, clasping his hands behind his head. He cocked his head to the side, indicating I should lay down next to him.

I loved how easy it was to talk to him, and curled up next to him, my hand on his chest.

"I want you to be happy. I want this to be good for you. Tell me what you mean when you say you haven't had a lot of experience."

I sighed, my eyes flitting down. "I've only had sex once."

He shrugged. "You've only had sex with one person. So what?"

I shook my head. "Not one person. One time."

He inhaled slightly. "Just...once?"

I nodded, meeting his gaze.

His face softened. "Did you...enjoy it?"

I hesitated. *No secrets.* "No."

He turned onto his side, boring holes into my face with the intensity of his gaze. "Are you sure you're ready?"

"Yes. I'm ready. I *want* this. I've been waiting for you," I said, surprising myself with the truth of my words.

"Waiting for me?" His voice full of wonder.

I nodded. "I didn't know it was *you*," I said, placing my hand over his heart. "But from the moment we met there's been something about this." I gestured to the space between us. "I didn't want to have sex again until I found the right person, and you are that person. I want to do this with *you*."

He smiled, took my hand, and kissed it. "That makes me so happy." Then he got a serious look on his face. "Do you remember how it felt the first time?"

I nodded. It had been uncomfortable; a hot, tearing sensation. "Yes."

He smiled kindly. "It's going to feel that way a few times. At least, that's what I've been told."

I blinked and swallowed. I was glad he'd told me. "I still want to."

He sighed. "I'll do everything to make it as comfortable for you as possible. I want you to enjoy this. You *should* enjoy this."

I exhaled heavily. "Thank you."

"Do you," he hesitated. "Do you have protection?"

I frowned and shook my head.

He grimaced. "Me, neither. But I saw a Duane Reade on the corner. I'll be back in five." He paused. "Since neither of us has been sexually active, do we need to have the sex history talk?"

"It's been over ten years for me."

He smiled. "Me, too. I think that makes us both born-again virgins."

I smirked. "Is that a thing?"

"If it isn't, it should be," he said, with a smile that sparkled in his eyes.

My heart sped up.

"Do you want anything while I'm out?"

"Juice would be nice. Something tart like pineapple or cranberry? No added sugar."

He smiled. "You got it." He leaned down and gave me a deep, passionate kiss that had me trying to claw him back down to the bed. He laughed, unwrapping my arms from his neck. "Five minutes."

"Take my key. It's on the bureau." I pointed at the dresser against the wall.

Clint stood, pocketed the key, and walked to the door. "Think of me," he said, closing the door gently behind him.

He had no idea how easy a request that was.

I took advantage of the moment to unbraid my hair and brush it out in long, thoughtful strokes so that it hung in heavy waves down my back, all the while, thoughts of Clint danced through my head.

I doubt anyone would have faulted me for being nervous and yet, I felt (almost) perfectly at ease. I twisted my hair up into a messy bun and jumped into the shower/tub, wanting to wash the day away. I thought I was being fast, but before I was finished, I heard the click of my door.

"That's a great idea. Do you mind if I join you?" Clint's rounded tenor broke through the sound of the shower, echoing off the walls of the small room.

I was relieved when he waited for my answer.

A thrill of fear and shame—born of growing up in a sexually repressed household—zipped up my back. Then I remembered that I wanted this, I wanted Clint, I wanted to be bold. "Yes," I said, my voice cracking.

"Are you sure?"

If I hadn't been sure before, his checking-in erased any trace of doubt. "Yes," I said, stronger. "Yes, *please*," I added with a playful beg.

"On belay?"

I laughed. "Belay on."

He chuckled and the deep, gravelly sound made my pelvis ache with desire.

I heard the crisp *shush* of Clint removing his dress shirt, followed by a *thunk* as his belt buckle hit the floor, and I wasn't sure what was sexier: the sounds or the anticipation.

The next second, his finger hooked around the edge of the shower curtain.

"Permission to enter?" he asked in a voice straight from a military movie.

I laughed and shook my head. It was amazing how warm and playful he could be. "Uh…" I paused, trying to think of an appropriate response. "Permission granted?" my voice went up at the end.

He clucked and his finger—still the only part of his body that I could see—pointed at me accusingly. "That wasn't very convincing," he said, his tone both playful and serious as he shook his finger at me admonishingly.

I cleared my throat, trying to channel the voice of Christopher Plummer as Captain von Trapp. "Permission granted."

Clint's fingers wiggled like the jazz hands the cheerleaders at my high school used to do, and then he pulled back the curtain slowly, his head popping through the steam. "That's better," he said, maintaining eye contact.

Between the purposeful level of his eyes, the steam, and the warm sheeting of the water, I felt rather relaxed, considering I was standing stark naked in front of a man for the first time.

Still, his eyes didn't wander.

But I was ready to be seen, especially if it meant I could look.

And I *wanted* to look.

"Come in. Really. I want to *see* you," I said with as much courage as I could muster.

"Permission granted," he said softly, stepping into the shower and filling up the space with his tight, muscular form. He reached down and took the soap from my hand. "Whatever you want, Erin. I want you to enjoy this. Mind if I wash myself while you're looking?"

I sucked in a breath and nodded, canting my head upward to keep the water from running in my eyes.

He reached his long arms over my head to get some water on the soap, the musky scent of Clint making me lightheaded.

Then he started lathering his chest.

Holy hell that's sexy. My eyes were saucers as I watched, transfixed, as a rich lather developed in the patch of brown hair on Clint's chest. My fingers tingled.

"You can touch me," he offered.

My eyes flitted to his, my breath catching when I saw the tenderness there.

I bit my lip and raised my hand to his chest, running my fingers softly over and under the curve of his pecs.

He sucked in a breath and released a quiet moan.

Pleasure at his reaction flooded my body, my nipples pebbling into tight buds.

Out of my peripheral vision, I noticed his penis bob, and then—before I could stop myself—the words, "Did I do that?" tumbled out.

"That and so much more," he said, giving me an endearing smile. "My innocent temptress."

I screwed up my face. "Temptress?"

He nodded. "Do you know how irresistible you looked when you were climbing the telephone pole in Big Bear?" He took a slow inhale and shook his head like he was savoring the memory.

I started at the strange turn in topic, unable to look away as he began soaping his arms, the milky bubbles highlighting the broad ridges of his shoulders and biceps. I traced the curves and valleys with the edge of my fingertips, eliciting a tight hiss from Clint.

"That feels *sooo* good," he said.

I continued tracing. "Tell me more."

He took a deep breath. "You had on those tiny shorts, and when you put on that climbing harness," he paused, his penis bobbing again.

It was fascinating to watch the way his body reacted to the memories of me. It was better than any biology class I'd taken in school.

"The way the harness outlined your ass," he released a moan. "It was really hard *not* to fantasize about you. I'm sure Harry Hinkley had a raging hard-on."

I laughed at the thought of mild-mannered Harry Hinkley checking me out. "I seriously doubt that."

Clint cocked a brow. "It's always the quiet ones."

I laughed. It felt so natural to laugh together and yet, I could tell it was special, the chemistry between us.

"And then watching you master that telephone pole so handily? Now *that* was hot. I wanted to *be* that pole," he said meaningfully.

I arched a brow and—feeling brave—ran my hand from the top of his thigh, up his obliques, over his shoulder, and then down the hard angles of his back. He was glorious. "You want me to climb you?" I asked softly, closing the distance between us.

Another inch and we'd be skin-to-soapy-skin.

I couldn't wait.

Clint's eyes grew lidded. "Climb on." He swallowed and I saw his Adam's apple bob.

My inner goddess jumped for joy as I noticed all of these reactions. I *affected* Clint Davenport. That knowledge doubled my confidence instantly. "Kiss on," I crooned.

He lowered his head to mine and placed the most tender of kisses on my lips, still maintaining the distance between our bodies; brushing my lips with a feather touch that almost tickled.

What a tease.

My sex throbbed. I ached to feel more of him, the anticipation of the moment when his penis would graze against the wet skin of my torso was agony.

"Kiss me harder," I ordered.

He hesitated.

"You can touch me," I said, sensing his resistance.

He groaned and reached a slick hand for me, pulling me against him in one swift, slippery motion.

Suddenly the front of my body was engulfed in the heat of his, his erection pushing against the tender swell of my belly. I moaned as his soapy skin slid against mine, creating an almost frustrating slickness. I wanted him hard, pressing down on me, opening me up, making me his. I wanted everything.

"Fuck, Clint," I said, the slippery edges of my consciousness receding as desire took over. "More. I want more."

He pulled me tighter, bending his mouth to my neck where he licked and bit and sucked, all the while moaning into my ear. "Erin," he rasped.

I wasn't sure what was turning me on more—the things he was doing to my body or the sounds he was making—but my legs were becoming weak, my body pulsating with need. "I...want," I said, quietly.

"What do you want, my dear, sweet Erin?" he said, as his stubbled chin abraded the side of my cheek.

"Your fingers..." I said, breathlessly.

"Where?"

"Between my legs..."

He brought his lips to my ear. "On your pussy?"

Oh holy hell. My sex clenched as I nodded. "Yes. There. My pussy." Even as I blushed at the word.

"Say it," he said, his hot breath against my ear. "Say, 'Clint, I want your fingers on my pussy'," he urged, a soapy hand skating circles around my lower back, almost but not quite dipping onto my ass.

I swallowed hard. It was now or never. "Clint, I want your fingers *in* my pussy."

He made a satisfied grunt that stirred something primal in me. "Very good. You *are* a fast learner."

The approval in his voice made my body sing. I was good at this. I was a *temptress*.

Clint opened the shower curtain with one hand, the metal hooks skittling across the shower bar as he threw the bar of soap into the sink. A gust of cooler air entered the shower, causing me to shiver. When he drew the curtain closed, he pulled me tight with one arm as his free hand dipped lower.

The anticipation of his hand on my sex was excruciating. And then suddenly, it was there, his strong, sure fingers gliding across my lips which felt plump against his touch.

"Mmmm. Very nice," he said, his lips seeking mine, kissing me with a tender passion that made me limp with need.

"Oh, god. What are you doing to me?" I cried, disbelief at the feelings and sensations coursing through me, the pure want and need he drew from me.

I knew my body was an amazing thing. I'd pushed it hard in my years as an athlete, and it had given me joy, oh so much joy to climb, run, and surf…but *this*. This! I'd never known I could feel *this*. If I had, I would have sought it out sooner. *This* felt incredible.

"What am I *going* to do to you," he said, his voice playful, and jagged, and *threatening*.

My legs felt weak.

"Yes, yes. Yes, *please*. Do it all. I want it all," I begged wantonly, feeling free to express my every desire in his arms.

He teased me, his fingers pressing gently, massaging my mons, my inner thighs, and the tender crease where the two met, with expert strokes. It felt like the very blood in my veins was following the ebb and flow of his hands, my perspective narrowing to the point on my body that he was touching at any given moment.

He contained a universe within the tip of his finger.

It was explosive.

Intense gratitude flooded me for his skillful hands and his patient manner. Any fear or hesitation had been wiped away and was circling the drain along with the soapy water.

"In me," I begged, "in...my...pussy." Each word a labor; breath and language a secondary thought to the want coiling deep in my body.

He answered by running a finger along my seam, dipping ever so slightly inward.

"Oh, baby, you are so, *so* wet," his voice, awed.

I was so lost in the moment that I almost missed the endearment, and yet the word "baby" still managed to ping off my heart.

His finger dipped backwards again and again, each time pressing infinitesimally deeper between my labia, opening me slowly, with aching purpose and precision.

I ground against his finger, unable to stop myself, my desire for sexual gratification taking over.

He was doing this to me, coaxing my body onward, forcing me to move as if he was a master puppeteer.

"Now, Clint, now. I want your finger inside me *now*," I ordered.

His teasing was driving me out of my mind.

He wrapped his other arm around my waist and then dipped his hand lower, slowly pushing against my entrance. "Breathe, baby. Relax."

I took a deep breath, relaxing the muscles of my back, trying to relax my pelvic floor, sensing that it would all feel better if I was loose.

"That's it," he said, humming his approval.

He wiggled his middle finger at my tightest point and then pushed gently, a mild splitting pressure warming at my entrance.

I breathed and relaxed again and was rewarded by his finger moving deeper. More splitting, more breathing, more pushing. We continued this way slowly until suddenly he stopped and I realized his finger was buried inside me, his hand hot against my mons, the heel of his palm pressing against my clit. He twirled his finger inside, rocking against my clit, and the voice in my head roared, "More!"

"More," I squeaked.

He moved his hand slowly, in and out, in and out, twirling as he went, each pass opening me bit by bit, creating swirling sensations in my pelvis. I moved against his hand, bucking, grinding, the splitting pressure dulling as the promise of pleasure took over and began building within me.

"Mmmm, yes," I sighed, as his mouth found its way to my neck and shoulders, licking, biting, nipping as his hand began to pump. "That's it," I said, my words echoing my body's recognition of the sensation that I craved.

For a second my brain wondered at how familiar this felt, like a cosmic dance that my body knew but my brain had forgotten. My body moved of its own accord and I glided along, riding each sensation as it built and peaked, built and peaked, each peak taking me a little bit higher, hinting at some mysterious destination that was just—

A. Bit. Further. Away.

"Yes, *yes*," I cried.

I was close, so close, and then, he pulled out his hand and rubbed my clit in hard, urgent circles, using my slickness to build up a delicious speed.

"Oh, god. Yes." My orgasm built quickly, so much faster and unexpected than when I touched myself. His hand around my waist, a strong, secure pressure, his mouth on my neck, all prickly sensation, his finger on my nub, pure electricity racing up my core.

"Come for me, baby," he urged.

I wrapped my arms around his neck and leaned against his chest, allowing him to take my weight as I squirmed beneath his hand as he rubbed me higher and higher. And then the pressure built to its final apex and I soared off the edge of my pleasure, my knees buckling, a stream of blasphemous babble pouring from my lips as my thighs and pelvis clenched tightly.

Clint switched back to the gentle probing and pumping, the splitting sensation gone, as I rode wave after wave, my back arching and rippling with each contraction, Clint's finger seeming to elongate my orgasm until I shuddered into his arms for the last time.

He wrapped both arms around me and whispered in my ear, "You are so fucking beautiful."

I sighed, happiness, pride, and contentment encircling me like a physical garment.

He laid me down on the floor of the tub and switched the water so that it was filling the bath. Then he got behind me and placed me between his legs, laying me on his chest.

I could barely keep my eyes open. I'd never felt this spent, this beautiful, this *loved* in my entire life.

It was glorious.

He must have grabbed a bar of soap because I felt his slick, sudsy hands slide down my arms.

The tub filled, the water erasing all boundaries between us, my head snuggled into his chest, his strong thighs pressing against my waist.

I never wanted to be anywhere else.

Chapter 22: Badass-er

~Erin~

"You know, you shouldn't run away because of Alex," Clint said, his lips moving against my scalp as the steam of the hot water wafted up from the tub.

I guided his fingers to my neck and he drew wet, sudsy circles there.

"I wasn't going *just* because of Alex. I like Sonja and what she has to offer," I said, the combined effects of the hot water and my orgasm making me drowsy.

"Okay, but riddle me this: if Alex had given you your promised promotion, would you be going to Big Bear?"

I didn't have to think. "No."

"Do you like your work at Woo-Ah?"

"Yes," I said without hesitation. "Especially what I've been doing since you took over. I've loved weaving editorial and marketing initiatives together. That's been really interesting."

He kissed my head again. "And you are so good at it. You see the overlap that none of us do with your brilliant, creative mind." After a moment, he said, "You know, I understand why Alex did what she did. She's not wrong about the editorial staff. We can be a bit—"

"Stuck up? Conceited? Holier than thou," I offered, suddenly wide awake.

He tweaked my nipple, causing me to gasp and arch my back, which made him moan.

His erection moved against my spine, invitingly.

I arched my back deeper, pressing my ass against the base of his stiff length, a tingling ache circling my clit.

"Careful now," he warned, his voice low.

His delicious warning made my entire body pulse.

I knew that Clint's resonant tenor was one of the things that his fans loved, but hearing it like this...*damn.* "If your fans could hear you now."

"Hey now," he said. "This sweet talk is reserved just for you."

I pulled his hand to my lips and kissed his fingers.

He ran his other hand over the tops of my thighs. "I love your legs. I've fantasized about having them wrapped around my waist ever since the ropes course."

My nipples puckered and he ran his hand over the swell of my breasts.

I sighed, mesmerized by the movement of his hands as they skated over my skin, goosebumps trailing in their wake. "How do you make everything feel so good?"

"You think this feels good? Wait until you have your legs around my waist," he said, raking his fingernails down the inside of my thighs.

My body shivered at his touch, desire coiling itself up again in my gut; my inner temptress asking to come out and play. I turned and faced Clint, kneeling. I eyed his erection with open fascination. "Can I touch?"

"Please do," he said, a sweetly smug look on his face. He handed me the soap. "A little of this will help."

I lathered my hands and then placed one closed fist on the very tip of his throbbing member, pushing slowly down, mimicking the shape of my entrance. I pumped him slowly but firmly, three times in a row.

"Whoa, tiger," he joked. "If you want me to last you need to go a little slower."

"What if I don't want you to last?" I asked, eager to pleasure him the way he had just pleasured me. I wanted to see him come undone because of me; watch his face as he orgasmed, feel his cock pulse in my hand.

His cock.

My sex clenched.

He cocked a brow. "Then just keep doing what you're doing. It's your rodeo, princess," he said with that cool, confident swagger that used to drive me nuts.

Still drove me nuts…only now I could admit that I liked it.

"Princess? I like that. I like baby, too. You can keep them both in rotation."

He smiled. "Duly noted," he said, catching his breath as I pumped him again, a little slower, although just as hard. "And what will you call me?" he said on a guttural exhale.

"Top Gun," I answered.

"Because I was a pilot?"

I shook my head. "Because you're my top gun," I said, pumping his cock.

His cock!

He hissed in a breath. "Ride me," he said. "I don't want to hurt you. If you ride me, you can control everything."

My eyes lit up. "Here?"

He nodded. "The condoms are on the counter."

I popped the drain on the tub and grabbed the condoms, kissing and fondling Clint as the water receded. Once the water was sufficiently low, Clint sheathed himself and I straddled his hips.

"Mmm, nipples," he said, drawing one into his mouth, causing me to suck in a breath.

I moved his hot, veiny cock to my entrance, breathing slow and even as I bobbed on his flared head.

"Slow and steady, baby," he cooed.

"Oh, god," I said, arching my back as he drew my nipple in deeper, laving my breast with his tongue.

I circled my hips, swirling the tip of his erection against my sex, which felt plump and slippery, my desire painting my labia.

"Just go slow. This is all about you," he whispered.

I breathed and eased down slowly. *Oh, fuck.* His cock was a whole lot wider than his finger.

Clint snaked his hand between my legs and began slowly caressing my clit in thick, juicy circles. My inner walls instantly relaxed. "Breathe, baby, breathe."

I listened to his soothing words as I lowered myself, concentrating on the pleasure of my clit and the calming rhythm of his voice. I was slick and he was slipping in easily, the only restraint my hesitation at the foreign feeling of being stretched. But after I'd sunk about halfway down, the stretching transformed into a pleasant fullness.

"Kiss me," I said, sucking his lower lip into my mouth as I mentally prepared to slide down, down, down. "Oh yes," I moaned, as I lowered fully, my ass coming to rest on his pelvis.

Clint released a gravelly moan. "I fucking love you."

I would never have guessed a curse could sound so sweet. I didn't know if it was the endorphins talking, but I felt it as well. "I love you, too," I said, tears pricking in my eyes.

He held my face in his hands and studied my eyes. "I'm serious, Erin. I'm done. This is it. I love you."

I nodded, my throat tight with emotion.

"Me, too," I said, and this time I knew it wasn't the endorphins. "I love you, Clint."

He squinted as he smiled at me, his eyes watery.

At that moment, I knew he was showing me a side to himself that no one else had ever seen.

I felt like my heart might explode.

"Climb on," he quipped.

I laughed, the feeling of it, pure pleasure.

"Climbing," I said, and began to ride him, circling my hips left and right.

"Temptress," he whispered, grabbing my ass and guiding my movements.

I gasped as my clit rubbed against his belly and the rough patch of hair that seemed positioned just for my pleasure.

"That's it, baby, you got this," he said, his pupils blacking out his irises.

He interlaced our fingers and I pushed against his hands, leveraging myself up and off, and then down.

As I worked his cock, pumping him slowly and then quickly, clenching my pelvic floor, causing him to gasp; my own desire coiled inside me again, urging me closer to another release. I sped up, the friction on my clit driving me to the edge.

"Oh, Clint," I said, as he clasped his hands around my waist and I pushed against the tile wall, pumping, fucking, gyrating, the sounds of Clint's pleasure and mine, driving me on until—one, two, three—I moaned, a long, low sound as I flopped against his chest, his hips rolling into me a few more times before his moan joined mine and we convulsed together, the wave of our orgasms rolling through us.

***

A few hours later, Clint ducked out to grab food from a Cuban-Mexican restaurant around the corner, bringing back pork and steak tortas on freshly grilled bread, which we shared. The flavors paired perfectly with the pineapple juice Clint had bought for us earlier.

"Why does this taste so damn good?" I moaned as I took another bite.

"Post-orgasm food has been documented to taste better," he deadpanned.

"Is that from the *New York Times*?"

"*The Wall Street Journal*, actually," he said with an arch of his brow. "Forty-two percent better, to be exact."

I laughed.

With every kiss, every word, every look, my heart was growing in size, the bond between us tightening.

I welcomed it.

As if reading my mind, he said, "I'm a dog, you know," he said, offhand. "In the Chinese zodiac. So I'm *extremely* faithful."

I shook my head and laughed. "My *popo* is going to love you."

"Why?"

"Because you might not be Chinese, but you are damn close."

He laughed. "I can't wait to meet her."

It didn't feel strange to speak this way. Even though this was new, it felt serious; like the groundwork had been laid long ago and now we were just putting the finishing touches on everything.

As if to prove how serious, Clint said, "I want you to come over for dinner next week and meet my kids."

"I'd like that," I said, without a moment's hesitation.

He sighed, relieved. "And this weekend, I have plans with friends and family in Boston. I'd like you to come."

This time, I hesitated. "Will anyone from work be there?"

"No. Why?"

"I don't want anyone at work to know, except for Fern."

"Of course," he said, without a trace of jealousy.

I continued, "We need to be like William and Kate at work," I said, referencing the perennially proper Prince of England and his girlfriend. "No hand-holding, no kissing, no whispering."

He pulled me tight and nibbled on my ear. "At least not in front of anyone. I bet they're downright nasty behind closed doors. You know how the English are…"

I play-elbowed him in the gut. "I'm serious. I don't want people thinking I'm getting special treatment. No making out in your office," I said, thinking of our passionate kiss earlier that day.

I shook my head. It was hard to believe that had been less than twelve hours ago. So much had happened.

"Baby, no one is going to think that. Everyone will be too busy talking about how brilliant you are, especially when they find out that you weren't just responsible for the reception, but for the series idea and the bell ringing, and *everything*. You've carved out a niche for yourself that no one else can fill."

My eyes widened. "You can't tell them."

He nodded. "You're right," he said, leveling a finger at my chest, "*you're* going to tell them."

"Me? How?"

"I'm sure you'll think of something," he said, licking some guacamole off his finger. "Put that big brain to work," he said, his eyes flicking to my forehead as he took the last bite of his torta.

That night, we curled up together naked; kissing and touching and talking until we finally fell asleep a little after midnight.

At four-thirty in the morning, Clint woke me with a kiss on the shoulder and then headed out, on his way to the studio for the five o'clock editorial meeting.

I sighed, rolled over, and began formulating a plan.

***

About eight hours later, I was riding the elevator to the *WUA* studios, fidgeting with my hair. I planned to enter the offices at twelve-thirty. Clint would have just signed off the air and would have a few hours to work on the next day's story ideas before he, Yolanda, and Alex would head out for a fundraiser at the local public radio station that I had planned (of course).

I'd asked Clint to further pad the size of the audience by buying everyone in the office lunch under the excuse of celebrating the success of the NYSE event.

I smoothed out the hem of the well-cut red blazer that I'd purchased earlier that morning at Century 21, and took a deep breath, walking into the rowdy and celebratory atmosphere of the New York war room. Clint was sitting at the head of the table, with Yolanda and Alex flanking him.

He smiled when our eyes met, lifting his chin at me in support.

His faith boosted my confidence and I plastered a smile on my face that I didn't feel inside.

Time to put my plan into action.

"Hi, everyone," I said in a clear voice calculated to cut through the conversation.

I waved for good measure.

"Erin," the group of twenty-odd people said in unison.

I warmed. I didn't know all these people knew my name, but even the reporters from the New York staff seemed to be greeting me.

Yolanda smiled big, stood, and walked over to me. She enveloped me in a hug. "Erin, I just want to congratulate you on an extraordinary event last night," she said, speaking to the entire staff. "Everything was so well thought out. I think it was better planned than my wedding."

A few people chuckled.

"And that gift? How did you ever come up with that?" Yolanda added, shaking her head in disbelief.

There were murmurs of agreement.

Other people began coming up, shaking my hand and asking me questions. Wondering what my next big idea would be. What was I going to plan for the China Special?

Clint gave me a knowing wink.

I blushed. It was clear that Alex hadn't told anyone I quit, which fit my needs perfectly.

"Well, I'm not sure if I'm going to be around for the China Special, actually…" I said, letting out a theatrical sigh as though I was really disappointed, which was the truth.

There were sounds of dismay.

I noticed Alex's jaw tighten.

"But why?" Yolanda asked. "We need you. *Especially* for the China Special."

"Hear, hear," Clint cried, raising his glass of water. "To Erin Hung, Marketing Ninja Extraordinaire."

"Hear, hear," everyone rejoined, including Alex, whose face was decidedly less enthusiastic than the rest.

"Well, it's just that," I said, turning to Alex and giving her a meaningful look. "I don't know if everyone is aware, but the entire idea for the New—"

"What Erin means to say," Alex jumped in, "is that she doesn't know if she'll be in the *marketing* position anymore, because she's been offered a new role: Manager of Special Initiatives for *Wake-Up America*."

I struggled to keep my face neutral and replied, "I thought it was *Director* of Special Initiatives for all Los Angeles-based programming." This would allow me to work for *WUA*'s sister show *The Wrap-Up* and any future shows UPR might produce in L.A.

Alex stiffened. "You're right. I misspoke. *Director* of Special Initiatives," she said smoothly, although it seemed like the word "director" left a bad taste in her mouth. "I just need to confirm with D.C. that it's for *all* Los Angeles programs, but absolutely, director it is." After a moment, she added, "That's what William Duke suggested." Her face conciliatory.

I could live with that.

Clint gave me a thumbs-up.

I released a long sigh.

I'd won at last.

Epilogue: Six Months Later

~Erin~

"I'm going to the restroom. I'll be back in a jiff," Clint said, leaning down to plant a kiss on my head.

I watched as he wove in between the round tables of the restaurant, covered in white tablecloths, the loud buzz of other diners filling the air.

I sighed and smoothed out the silk bodice of my red and gold *cheongsam* as I sat back in the ornately carved, high-back chair, my elaborately braided hair piled high on my head.

The restaurant reminded me a lot of the Chinese restaurants I'd eaten at in Hawai'i, California, and New York, with its pops of red and gold, images of dragons and phoenixes decorating the walls. The only difference was that it wasn't in the United States; it was in China.

I was in China!

I fingered the pearls in my ears—a college graduation gift from my grandmother—as I gazed out the window of the restaurant, to the Huangpu River and the city of Shanghai spread out below. I turned and watched as Clint vanished around the corner, and then gestured to the restaurant manager whom I'd been communicating with for weeks by email.

He nodded at me when I caught his eye.

The *Wake-Up America* China Special had concluded a week ago, to great fanfare. The Chinese people had been charmed by the American fighter pilot who spoke their language and the "pretty woman" who went everywhere with him and looked like she could be one of them.

As Director of Special Initiatives, I had been responsible for creating events and marketing opportunities based on whatever stories the show chose to pursue. However, after proving myself to be a strategic thinker, everyone listened whenever I voiced a story concept to the reporting staff.

Many of my ideas had made their way into the special series, including Clint's ping-pong match with an up-and-coming teenager (the teen creamed Clint, to everyone's delight), Clint's attempts at learning how to cook traditional Chinese food (he cut himself with the cleaver—it was just a surface wound, no stitches), and Clint interviewing people on the street as he went out for his daily runs (he was especially popular with the senior ladies).

My work had made me a rising star within *WUA*'s parent company, and there had even been talk about offering me a position at the UPR headquarters in D.C. However, I'd shut that down right away. I loved Los Angeles and didn't want to be on the East Coast.

One particular reason I wanted to stay in L.A. was because it was close enough to Big Bear to facilitate the occasional high ropes course. Climbing had become even more special now that it was something Clint and I did together, and I'd found that going to Big Bear once every couple of months scratched an itch for me that nothing else did.

At that moment, the restaurant manager interrupted my thoughts by arriving at the table with a large, round platter, covered with a lid. He handed me a lighter.

"*Dòjeh*," I said with a bow of my head, saying "thank you" in my limited Cantonese.

I'd been working on learning Mandarin for the last six months, however, my skills were limited to ordering food and asking for basic directions.

Although Beijing was the capital of China, the city of Shanghai had been chosen as the base camp for the China Special because of the world expo, a six-month-long exhibition that was on track to be the largest and most expensive World's Fair in the history of the event.

I'd made it a point to create enough marketing initiatives so that I'd *have* to be included in the China trip, creating speaking gigs for Clint and organizing a reception with Chinese radio journalists.

Although the special series had only been two weeks long, four audio and IT engineers had flown out three weeks before to ensure that the recording studios would be up to necessary audio and data-streaming standards. The reporting crew followed ten days later with me in tow.

Clint and I made plans to stay in China for two weeks after the special to play tourist, which had raised more than a few eyebrows among the *WUA* staff. Although we hadn't mentioned that we were vacationing together, people managed to piece the information together, finding it an interesting coincidence.

During the last six months, we'd managed to keep our relationship secret from everyone in the office. Except of course for Fern, who knew all. However, we had definitely earned the occasional raised eyebrow with our frequent lunches and indiscreet glances. When certain people found out that both Clint and I were staying in China after the special, some raised eyebrows had turned into knowing looks. Fortunately, no one seemed to care. The *WUA* offices were the kind of place where one was more likely to make waves because of intellectual indiscretions than romantic ones.

Also, I got the feeling that when we finally went public, everyone would be happy for us. In fact, Clint had been trying to convince me to let our relationship out of the closet for the last two months, and I'd been thinking about giving in to his request.

He was just *so cute* when he begged.

I looked over my shoulder to where Clint had disappeared, but didn't see him. I was just about to go looking for him when he reappeared, a big smile on his face.

He kissed my forehead again and sat down. "Sorry. That took longer than expected."

I pursed my lips. "Are we already going there? I didn't think we'd been dating *that* long."

He laughed nervously. "Sorry. That came out wrong." He eyed the silver platter. "Did you order more food? I thought we were done," he said, his eyes flicking to a point just over my shoulder.

I sat up straighter, excited for my surprise. "Close your eyes," I said, waiting for him to comply before tilting back the lid of the platter and lighting the four candles. "Okay, you can open them."

Clint opened his eyes and I whipped off the lid saying, "Happy Birthday, love."

His eyes flashed as he took in the cake on the platter in front of me. "Devil's food?"

I nodded. "With frosting at least half-an-inch thick."

He shook his head. "How did you?"

"It wasn't easy. But it's your fortieth, so I thought we should recognize it, even though we're having the real party back in L.A." Two weeks after we returned from China, there would be a big bash at Clint's house, which I had planned with input from his kids and mother.

"I know what I'm going to wish for," he said, his eyes widening.

"Don't tell me. Then it won't come true."

He blew out the candles. "But I *have* to tell you," he said, glancing over my shoulder again. "Or it definitely won't come true."

I was just about to turn around to see what was behind me, when he grabbed my hand and said, "Erin," his voice commanding.

My eyes snapped to his adoring gaze, a shiver lacing up my spine. "Yes?"

"Erin, from the moment I met you, there was something about you that called to me, and the last six months have been the absolute best of my life." He paused and licked his lips. "You've made so many of my dreams come true; some that I didn't even know I had, and others," he paused, his eyes flicking to the vista of Shanghai below us, "that probably wouldn't have happened without you. And I want to make *your* dreams come true too."

A lump developed in my throat. He had already given me so much. Without him, I probably would have thrown in the towel at *WUA* and ran away to Big Bear. But with him by my side, I'd not only achieved the promotion of my dreams, but I'd become even more comfortable in my own skin.

Operation "Brand New Me" was officially complete.

Clint's watery eyes brought me back to the moment, and I squeezed his hands.

He blinked, love and gratitude reflected in his gaze. "Erin, I don't want to live another year," he said, glancing down at his cake, "or another day, or another moment without knowing that you'll always be by my side."

I broke out in goosebumps.

He reached into his navy-blue suit jacket and pulled out a red leather box. He opened it, displaying a cream-colored South Sea pearl the size and shape of a gumball, set in a wreath of tiny platinum gardenias, each flower set with a small diamond in the middle.

The pearl was the most luminous gem I had ever seen. Tears perked in my eyes.

"Erin Mei-Yung Hung. My wish is that you will do me the great privilege of putting up with me for the rest of my life," he said with a sly smile. "That you will encourage me when things are tough, be there to belay me when I'm in danger of falling, and never stop recommending fiction that will expand my mind."

I covered my mouth.

His face turned serious and he said quietly, "Will you marry me?"

I. Had. No. Words.

I'd been so busy trying to plan a surprise for him that he'd completely turned the tables on me. I was overwhelmed into silence.

"Erin?"

Try as I might, I couldn't seem to find my voice, so I nodded instead.

He smiled, reached for my hand, and then slipped the ring onto my finger.

We stood at the same time and Clint embraced me, kissing me and holding me tightly to him, as happy tears fell from my eyes.

I heard clapping behind me and turned, only to come face to face with my parents and grandparents. I covered my mouth in shock for the second time in less than five minutes. "Popo? Gung-Gung? Mom? Dad?"

They were laughing and clapping, my *popo* reaching up and clasping her small hands around my face. "Your fiancé is a real rascal," she said with a wink.

I nodded. "I knew that, but I don't think I knew just how much."

My mom held up my hand, admiring the ring. "Oh, Clint, it is beautiful. And such a unique design."

"For a unique woman," he answered.

The restaurant manager approached and my *popo* began speaking to him in animated Cantonese, the jade bracelet on her wrist flashing. Within a few minutes, we were seated at a larger table with fresh pots of tea while a server cut the chocolate cake. *Baijiu*, a type of Chinese wine, was also procured, and everyone toasted to a long and healthy life for us.

After an hour of chatting and celebrating, Clint and I were standing at the window, gazing out at the twinkling city below.

I leaned my head onto Clint's chest. "I can't believe how happy I am."

He pulled me tight against him. "Believe it, princess. And it's only going to get better."

I sighed. "You know, I *was* going to let you go public with us at the office when we got back."

He sighed in mock frustration. "*Now* you tell me." After a beat, he added, "Maybe I can still return the ring," and lifted my hand.

I turned around and scowled. "Clint Davenport. You are not getting this ring back."

He chuckled, rubbing his nose against mine. "I fucking love you."

Thank you for reading Erin and Clint's story.
I hope you loved it as much as I do. If you did, please take a moment to
RATE or REVIEW it. Your support means a lot to me.
Wishing you love and romance,
Aviva

If you want to know if Erin's mother and father reconcile, and if
Fern ever becomes a pastor (and finds his own love) then sign-up for
Aviva's newsletter at https://tinyURL.com/followAviva

You will also be notified of new releases and special offers and get to
read the exclusive LOVE ON THE ROPES ***BONUS
CHAPTER***

Sneak Preview:

First Thanksgiving

~Erin~

November 2009
Los Angeles, California

"I hear you make the world's best snowball cookies," Clint said to my cousin Angela, rocking forward on his toes, his hands shoved deep in his pockets in what I now recognized as his "defensive eating" stance.

It was one of the many habits he used to keep his highly regimented eating habits in check.

He was standing next to Angela in the colorfully tiled kitchen of her Spanish-style house, towering over her as she rolled cookies. I was across the kitchen seated in the breakfast nook with Angela's husband Soren, their four-year-old daughter KJ sitting on my lap.

Angela studied Clint as she worked, leaning backwards a bit to counterbalance her pregnant belly. "They are world famous," she quipped without a smile.

Clint's brown eyes twinkled as he inhaled, the aroma of cookies in the oven filling the kitchen. I almost fell out of my seat when he added, "I can't wait to taste one."

I cocked my head, my long, black braid falling over my shoulder. "I thought you didn't eat sweets—"

"Shush," he said, as he shot me a smile. "That's blasphemy."

Subscribe now to read the rest.

SNEAK PREVIEW: Keep reading for a sneak preview of the second book in the **Love in Action** series *Love on the Slopes*, a standalone slow burn, enemies-to-lovers, office romcom featuring Erin's twin brother, Patrick Hung.

Sneak Preview: *Love on the Slopes*

Coming Soon

There are three things you should know about Patrick Hung:

1 – At 32, he's a former World Champion of Surfing who wants to win one more title before he retires

2 – He's a twin who hasn't spoken to his sister in months

3 – He wouldn't know what love looked like if it hit him in the face

Of course, it's pretty hard to win a world title if you aren't anywhere near an ocean. Soul-crushing grief has made Patrick "head for the hills", although mountains are more accurate. He's licking his wounds in a small ski resort in California, teaching skiing during the day and drinking at night. Life's good (yeah right!)

There are three things you should know about Stella Walker:

1 – She works the overnight shift snow grooming, which has given her a healthy disdain for ski instructors

2 – No one knows she's in California

3 – She wouldn't know what love looked like if it hit her in the face

When Patrick Hung comes into her life, she doubles down on hating ski instructors. The man is cocky, loud, and has women throwing themselves at him even though he smells like beer twenty-four-seven. But when he drunkenly confides to her why he's really in Big Bear, she realizes they have a lot more in common than just their employer.

When their pasts catch up to them, will it leave them sitting in front of their fires solo, or will winter's last storm bring the two of them *Love on the Slopes*?

Chapter 1: Realization

Pūpūkea, Hawaiʻi

Let's talk. I miss you, the text read.

Have you ever felt like something was missing only to have the missing thing ram into your heart like an out of control MAC truck and then you hit yourself in the head with your palm and say, "Duh!"

Well I have.

My MAC-truck-Duh moment happened when I read that text, only I didn't realize it right away. Instead, I rubbed at my chest and reread the words a few times, surprised but happy to hear from my sister whom I hadn't spoken to in a long time.

Too long.

"You awake, Hung?" my roommate, Kai, said as he walked by the couch I'd fallen asleep on after the party we'd hosted last night.

Palming my eyes, I peeked up over the back of the couch—like a gopher peeking out of its hole—to check the surf.

After a lifetime spent surfing, and sixteen years on the professional tour, I couldn't *not* check the surf; it was pure muscle memory. I couldn't have even told you if I wanted to surf on that particular day, charging the waves was so ingrained in me that if there was swell, I was on my board.

Unfurling myself from the couch—I can't believe I slept there, it was a veritable petri dish with four guys living in the house and our weekly parties—I stood up and yawned, scratching my (well-honed) ass through the board shorts I'd apparently fallen asleep in.

Opening and closing my mouth, I yelled, "Gross," at the residual beer taste and cottony texture of my mouth. Surf, drink, toke was such a part of my day I could have had a clock with those words instead of hours. Surf would have taken up the hours of six to nine am, because if you really want to become good, you have to be on the waves before anyone else so you don't have to compete for the limited supply.

See, that's the thing nonsurfers don't understand about our sport. You can't just "go surf." No, you have to wait for the gods to align the elements perfectly: storm swell, the right tide, and no wind or a mild offshore. Everything has to be just right in order to produce the reason for my existence: surfable waves.

Then, when that happens, you have to compete with every other kook with a board that shows up that day, since it's only safe to have one surfer per wave. You can spend three hours out in the ocean, and if it's crowded you'll be lucky to get three twenty-second rides.

Which is why I always surf in the morning. Dawn patrol is where it's at if your goal is to catch as many waves as you can in the shortest amount of time. Of course, that's made a lot easier by the fact that I live on the North Shore of Oahu, steps from some of the most famous surf breaks in the entire world.

The North Shore is to surfing like Hollywood is to movies; you don't have to live here to make it in our business, but it sure makes things a lot easier.

"Surf's dead, 'brah," Kai said over the tinkling sound of cereal being poured into a bowl.

Kai's my dawn patrol buddy.

Here's my PSA about that: you should *always* surf with a friend.

I sigh, half-deflated, half-elated, because if there's no surf, I can spend the next three hours doing something else. That is, until it's time to drink, 12pm until I fall asleep or pass out (whichever comes first), or toke, 4pm until "see drink description".

Making my way to the kitchen, I try to decide if I'm hungry, jealous of Kai's twenty-one-year-old metabolism.

He's the youngest of my housemates, and something of my mentee. Although he's always shown a lot of promise, his family didn't have the money that would have allowed him to join the tour at sixteen like I did. Growing up with a dad as a professional surfer, I had an endless supply of gear and opportunities come my way. Whereas Kai had a single mom who worked as a cashier at a grocery store, with three younger children to provide for too.

Needless to say, Kai didn't have an endless supply of gear or opportunities.

I met him six years ago when a sponsor of mine set me up with a volunteer opportunity to teach surfing to disadvantaged Hawaiian youth. Although I wasn't Polynesian by blood, my family had been in the islands for six generations, and it drove me crazy that there were Hawaiian kids who wanted to learn but hadn't had the opportunity. This was the sport of their ancestors, it had been created in these very islands, it was their birthright.

Kai had been one of those kids, and he'd shown so much promise that when he turned eighteen, I offered him a place to live in my house. It was a win-win situation, I hated being alone, and it gave him the advantage of having some of the world's best waves at his disposal.

If Kai Kealoha wanted to become a world champion, then I was going to help make it happen.

"Want some cereal, old-timer?" Kai said, his big white teeth gleaming against his bronzed skin.

Stretching my back I waved his suggestion away. "I can't eat like you groms. I have to start my day slow."

He bristled. "I'm *not* a grom."

Laughing, I said, "It's so easy to get under your skin. You'll always be a grom to me."

"Whatevs, old-timer."

It was my turn to bristle. I grabbed the kettle and started boiling some water for my morning constitutional of hot water with lemon. Then I downed two glasses of water, hoping to wash away the horrible taste in the mouth. "What time did the partying stop last night?"

Kai shrugged. "I went to bed before all of you. Andy took off before I went to sleep, but Hiro was still down here partying. I don't know how you fell asleep on the couch."

Probably a sign of my old age. But I wasn't going to say that thought outloud. Although thirty-two wasn't old, in the world of professional surfing, it was definitely up there.

We'd been celebrating the successful conclusion of a surf contest, well successful for me, Kai, and Hiro. Although none of us had won the contest outright, we'd placed well, adding enough cumulative points to our total for the year that I was within striking distance of the world championship.

Although I'd won the championship twice in my twenties, winning at thirty-two would have been even sweeter since it had been six years since I was last crowned.

"Was Andy okay when he left?" I asked, leaning against the counter.

Kai shrugged. "You know how he is. Temper."

My water boiled and I poured some into a mug, squeezing the juice of a lemon into it. I added enough cold water to make it drinkable and then downed it all in one go.

I was just about to jump in the shower when the house phone rang.

No one *ever* called on the house phone.

I picked it up.

"Is this the residence of Andrew Crane?" a male voice asked with cold efficiency.

The skin on my neck prickled. "Yes."

"May I speak to a relative of Andrew Crane?" the voice asked.

Kai later told me that my face turned white at that moment which was why he whispered to me, "What's wrong?"

I never heard Kai, I was too focused on the caller. "I'm his roommate, Patrick Hung."

There was a pause and I sensed the caller recognized my name. "Mr. Hung, do you have contact information for Andrew Crane's next of kin."

Cold sweat broke out across my brow. "What's happened? Where's Andy."

"I'm sorry, Mr. Hung, but I have to speak to the next of kin."

I felt like I'd been gut punched, but then I told the caller the phone number I knew as well as my own. A number I'd been calling since I was old enough to use a phone, and then I hung up.

"Something happened to Andy," I whispered, to no one, although Kai was standing right there.

"What?" Kai asked, kneeling down.

It was that moment that I realized I was sitting on the floor and the phone was still in my hand.

That was when the Mac-truck-Duh moment hit me, and the only person I wanted to talk to was my sister, Erin.

My *twin* sister.

About the Author

Aviva Vaughn (ah-VEE-vah VON) loves reading, traveling, and eating…preferably all at once. She isn't afraid to try new things, which has made for an interesting—although not always straight forward—life.

She is an avid reader and especially likes books with multifaceted characters who reveal something about that most compelling of all subjects: human nature; no matter what species they are or what planet they are from.

Other Titles from Aviva Vaughn

Novels (all books available at tinyurl.com/AmazonAviva)
    BECKONED
    -Part 1: From London with Love
    -Part 2: From Bath with Love
    -Part 3: From Los Angeles with Love
    -Part 4: From Barcelona with Love
    -Part 5: Adrift in Costa Rica
    -Part 6: Adrift in New Zealand

    Love in Action Series (standalone romcom)
    -Book 1: Love on the Ropes
    -Book 2: Love on the Slopes **COMING SOON**

Short Stories
    -PRESSURE (available in Beckoned, Part 4)
    -Her Haven (available to newsletter subscribers)
    -BECKONED, Part 1, Chapter 2, Angela's POV (available to newsletter subscribers)
    -Knotty Naughty Bits Volume 1: a collection of tangled romantic shorts

Links

Subscribe to Aviva's list **at TinyURL.com/followAviva** to be notified of new releases and special offers—and get her favorite **FOOD | BOOK | TRAVEL tips**.

Love my writing? Consider becoming a patron at Patreon.com/Aviva Vaughn

Hi Reader!

It means so much to me that you are here! It means that you love BECKONED and appreciate how unique it is.

If you want more "behind-the-scenes", VIP access, then consider becoming a "patron" and help me bring more of my creative imaginings to life! There's even an opportunity to name a character in my book. To find out more, click Patreon.com/Aviva Vaughn

XOXO,

Book Club Questions

Hey, Book Clubbers! Aviva here.

I'm a book clubber myself, and I love it when books include built-in questions.

Here are some questions from me to you! Have fun.

1. Early on you see some of Erin's old negative self-talk. Are you aware of your own self-talk? Is it positive or negative? Why do you think that is?

2. Erin benefits from her older cousin Angela's mentoring. Do you have someone who's affected your life like that? Who was it? Have you mentored someone? How did that impact your life?

3. Did you or anyone you know want to "get rid of his/her virginity"? What do you think of that idea?

4. Clint's a very focused, very driven person. Is that a good thing or a bad thing?

5. What did you think of the level of communication during the sex scenes? Was it annoying or inspiring? Why?

If you'd like me to SKYPE, FACETIME, ZOOM, GOOGLE HANGOUT, or whatever else there is, into your book club.

Please send a request to BookClubRequest@AvivaVaughn.com

with the time, time zone, date, city, and expected number of people. Thanks!

Thanks, Gracias, Dojeh, Merci, Toda, Gratzie, Shukraan

My sincerest thanks and gratitude to anyone reading this sentence now. You are the reason this book exists.

Thanks to the universe for allowing me to give this story life.

To my family: thank you for giving me the space to write. I know it's not easy! To my Mummy—always my most opinionated and helpful reader—who helps with my little when I need some time to write, and to my Dude, thanks for putting up with me and my crazy middle-of-the-night ramblings.

To my friends who are like family: thank you for inspiring me, literally and figuratively! Especially to CSAK, my soul sisters!

To the members of my Facebook "Book Club": you "get" me. Thank you for your words of support and encouragement. You keep me motivated! Special thanks to Ophelia, Amanda, and Claire. I love you! And to John, who isn't in the book club, but whose emails always make me smile.

To my friends, colleagues and mentors in the indie publishing world: I'm eternally grateful to be a member of your tribe. It is your shoulders I stand on. I promise to pay it forward to the next generation.

To my editors Tbird London and Rebecca Hodgkins. Thank you for polishing my words and for your wisdom and encouragement.

Wishing you love and romance,